HOUSE OF CRIMSON HEARTS

A STEAMY VAMPIRE FANTASY ROMANCE

KINGDOM OF IMMORTAL LOVERS

BOOK ONE

RUBY ROE

SANGUI CITY

Note for Readers

This book is intended for adult (18+) audiences. It contains explicit lesbian sex scenes, considerable profanity and some violence. For full content warnings, please see author's website: rubyroe.co.uk.

This book is written in British English.

PLAYLIST

Something Beautiful - Jacob Banks
More - Billy Lockett
Can't Get Enough - Kat Leon, NOCTURN
Vampire - Olivia Rodrigo
Girls Girls Girls - FLETCHER
Skin And Bones - Morgan St. Jean
Do It Like A Girl - Morgan St. Jean
Me and the Devil - Soap & Skin
Waking Up - MJ Cole, Freya Ridings
Genesis - Ruelle
Street Spirit (Fade Out) - Rosie Carney
Catch Me Falling - Cold War Kids
From Darkness She Rises - BrunuhVille
Creep - The Four Performance - VINCINT
Make It Home - DEZI
Kleptomaniac - DEZI
Ocean Of Tears - Imanbek, DVBBS
No Rest for the Wicked - Klergy
Until We Go Down - Ruelle
Le Monde - From Talk to Me - Richard Carter
I See Red - Everybody Loves an Outlaw

Play with Fire (feat. Yacht Money) - Sam Tinnesz
Lovely - Lauren Babic, Seraphim
Lose Control - Teddy Swims
How Villains Are Made - Madalen Duke
Aphrodite - Sam Short

To all the girls who wished Damon Salvatore had boobs...

This one is for you.

Once upon a time, a vampire corrupted a hunter...

PROLOGUE

Any secret worth its merit is woven in the depths of midnight. Spoken in whispered promises and hapless lies. The soft, breathy words lost to the stars and buried with the moon, night after night until even the sky can't discern the truth.

That was how it happened...

Two families sat beneath the golden glow of fire lamps, a long thin table between them. St Clairs on one side, Randalls on another. Two families bonded by the hatred born of generations of ancestors. Hostility tattooed in their marrow like cancer. Spread thick and fibrous so that it was all they could breathe and feel and think.

As the night struck twelve, they signed a contract. Bloody prints scarred the scroll: a warning, an omen.

Too late, too late. The witch is coming.

Too late, too late. They made the curse.

That was how it started...

CHAPTER 1

OCTAVIA

There's never enough blood.

A man bleeds rivers of claret over my rug.

It's not enough.

Never enough.

Even if I drink the city dry, it wouldn't be sufficient. I want more. *Need* more. There's an aching desire between my ribs, something missing, something lost. I know what it is, but I don't want to think about it. I had my chance and lost it. Well, I'm done with it... with her.

I knead my temples.

Fuck, I'm tired.

I shift in my seat and the staff boy leaning against the wall flinches. Pathetic. I can't even remember his name-Fred? Frank? Let's go with Frank.

"Clean this up. He stinks like piss and fermented fish," I say, pointing at the bleeding man.

"B-but, Lady Beaumont," the staff boy stutters.

I snap my gaze to his and go still. The kind of still that makes death look like the frenzy of birth. The kind of still-

3

ness that gnaws agitation into a human's bones. The vacant, fathomless void twists in Frank's mind until he trembles. I push further. Every cell in my ancient body freezes as if time never existed.

I must say, it's quite the feat of control not to smile at the way Frank shivers. There are very few things I find amusing anymore, but the fragility of humans is one of them. I wait a beat. Two. Then two more. Just long enough for him to drop his mouth and utter a breathy plea.

I shouldn't play, Xavier tells me it's cruel. But I'm not as cruel as our dear sister Dahlia.

Frank twitches. "I—"

"Do I need to repeat myself?" I say every word as slow as it is sharp, my voice a snap and whisper in the air. Movement filters into my limbs again and his shaking eases.

"N-No. I'll get a donor instead," he says and stumbles his way forward to grab the dying man under the armpits.

It's meant to be our strength—blood. Really, I think it makes us feeble.

"Stop, did I say take him?" I rise from my chair. Frank drops the man on the floor with a thud and a gargled moan and then backs away, confusion rippling his brow. It used to bother me—the way they look at me. The way everyone in this fucking city looks at me. Doesn't matter that there are thousands of turned vampires. I am the only one born this way. The only one they fear and all because I wasn't made like the other vampire lines. That, and perhaps my behaviour over the years, hasn't exactly warmed the city to me.

Born to a mother who abandoned her. A freak with eyes the colour of drying blood. I haunt their nightmares. I've tried to embrace it, revel in it, shy away from it. Even mourned the way they treated me for a few decades. But nothing changes.

Humans shrink away from me, hunters hate me, and vampires... well, they don't fear me, but most pander to and revere me. It's sickening. That's why I like to fuck with everyone, because no one ever looks at me for me.

The man bleeding on my rug is fading fast. I grip him by the throat and haul him to his feet.

"You get one chance. Who were you stealing for?" I snarl. Erin, my chief of security, caught him trying to swipe books and grimoires from one of the market sellers on her way into work.

He gurgles under my grip, and I realise I'm crushing his vocal cords. I loosen my fingers a fraction.

"I don't know. Handler. Wanted a book about dhampirs. Said..." he fades further, his skin growing pale.

I shake the man and his head jerks back and forth until his eyes roll back into focus.

"What did they say?" I ask.

"That... That if we didn't open... open the door... war would come."

"What the fuck are you talking about? What door?"

"The one in the Montague territory. Behind the boundary."

"That's a myth," I snarl.

"Not to the handler and whoever they were working for."

I snarl at the man. I need more. His voice box vibrates against my palm. I glance at Frank whose eyes widen. Useless. All of them.

"P—Pl," he begs.

But I'm done with him. I squeeze my fingers until my nails slice through his skin. Blood pours in delicate ribbons down my knuckles and under my sleeve. My fingers squelch through his muscles and arteries, until I'm clenching his windpipe. I clamp around it and wrench it out, letting his carcass drop to the floor.

"Clean it up," I bark and march out of my office. The minute I open the club door, noise rips through the air. A pounding beat thumps so hard through the walls of the club that my feet vibrate. The Whisper Club is busy tonight. I step to the mezzanine balcony and peer down. Humans, donors, and vampires dance like maggots beneath me. It's the same gyrating slick of bodies day after day. The same fucking music. The same human stink.

My club is dark, lights dimmed to encourage all desires to come out to play. The walls are shades of crusted blood. A ring of booths nestles against the walls the same tainted colour. The bar in the centre of the club is the only speck of brighter light, a glass mirror behind the servers augmenting the sparkle.

Optics filled with every type and flavour of donated blood: eau de fear, fuelled by lust, ravished with panic, hang on the back mirror. We like to serve the most expensive and exclusive blood here. One of my side businesses is the donation and collection of more expertly acquired blood. It's a pricy process because danger powers this city. Do you have any idea how hard it is to terrify a human that lives in a world of vampires? It's expensive and ugly.

The music drops to a slower, more sensual beat. The maggots draw nearer, fangs sink into throats and arms. It's that time of night because half the crowd is naked and there are as many fangs biting as there are cocks driving into pussies and mouths. I sense someone climbing the stairs to my mezzanine. I'm about to fire the security guard when Xavier's mop of thick hair appears.

I sigh.

"Favourite sibling," I say and turn back to the crowd.

He smiles.

"Good evening, Octavia." His voice is low and rich as he leans down to place a kiss on my forehead and joins me, peering over the balcony.

Xavier is unspeakably handsome. His jaw is the kind of chiselled that could make a marble sculpture weep. His chin-length hair is a raven gloss that women pay thousands to achieve. And as for his body... while I'm not one to enjoy the male physique, I can appreciate the way women fawn over the canyons carving through his abs and the muscle-boulders perched over his shoulders. Xavier, though, feigns modesty until he wants a woman. And then the ego appears.

"And what brings you to my territory? Are our siblings trying your patience?" I ask.

His lip quirks. "Must you be a bitch this early in the evening? I've only just arrived, and I haven't even had breakfast."

"Well, dear brother, do help yourself. There's a veritable feast of fucking and sucking below."

His eyes drop to the club floor, his lip curls, the barest hint of fang showing.

"It's beyond me why you entertain our siblings," I say.

"The same reason I entertain you." His lip does that quirk thing again and my patience wanes.

"Put me in the same box as them and I will happily castrate you."

"Tave, darling, why waste your time? My balls will grow back."

I narrow my eyes at him. He only calls me Tave when he comes bearing bad news, he wants something, or I've done something to please him.

I face him. "Perhaps, but at least I'll feel better. Are you going to tell me why you're here? You might be my favourite, but I'm busy... attending to... whatever it is I need to attend to."

He rolls his eyes at me. "You're immortal. We don't do busy. We luxuriate and gloat in the endless excesses of time we have. Besides, you have no friends. Who exactly is it that's taking up your time?"

"I have no need of friends. You have enough for us both."

"You sound bitter."

"Only because I'm having to tolerate your presence, *Xave*."

He swings an arm around my shoulder. "You're so cute when you're pissy. But I'll relent. I have come bearing a message from Mummy."

"Must you call her that?"

"What would you prefer?"

"She-devil, harbinger of death, distributor of pain, Lilith?"

Xavier laughs. "Why, we are feeling dramatic this evening, aren't we?"

"Go fuck yourself, Xavier. Tell me what Mother wants or get out of my club. You're making me hungry."

"She requests your presence at dinner."

"Are the others going?"

He nods. "Alas, I am the errand boy today, delivering the same message to all of them. I'm going to the church next."

The Church of Blood is Sadie's territory. There are five of us, two boys, three girls: me, Xavier, Sadie, Dahlia and Gabriel. Mother collected each of us for a different reason, in a different way. None of our histories are pretty. But what I do know is that no good stories follow Sadie St Clair. Some say Cordelia compelled Sadie to watch as she drained her birth mother dry.

Others say Cordelia found Sadie in the mountains, sat cross-legged in a halo of reddened snow. A wolf's tail in one hand and a gnawed hind leg in the other, crusted claret decorating both her cheeks.

But the story most give begins in the Montague Forest, out past the city's border. Cordelia was hunting after dusk. She stumbled across a pretty little thing laid in the leaf mould, still as death. Not quite human, not quite fae. Neither vampire nor witch, nor demon nor dhampir. Cordelia was perplexed because, despite the motionless creature, there was no mistaking the fact Sadie's heart still beat. Slow, slow, slow. Hair the colour of fresh snow draped over her shoulders.

Beneath Sadie lay a bed of decaying roses. All of them curled and singed at the edges as if the girl had leached the life from them.

Cordelia leaned in, brushed a snowy lock away. Sadie lunged, sinking her teeth into Cordelia's face. She stole a chunk of flesh and swallowed. Cordelia still bears the sweet little scar beneath her eye today.

Sadie snarled, all sharp teeth and growls. So, Cordelia took her and locked her in a cage until she learned to be civilised.

Oh, how Sadie screamed and screamed and screamed. She cried out until her voice bled into the walls and left her mute. If you ever visit Castle St Clair and stay late, some nights you can still hear her haunting howls clawing from the walls long past midnight.

All that is to say, none of us really know how Sadie came to be. Mother refuses to speak of her creation. And Sadie has said not a word in all the centuries I've known her.

"Have fun delivering that message," I say and wave a hand dismissively at the debauchery below. "Help yourself to the good stuff on your way out."

He bends to my hand and places a soft kiss on the back of it. "You always did treat me well."

"Hmm. Be a good boy and fuck off now, won't you?"

That, at least, elicits a broad smile, his white teeth and sharp fangs descending. He inclines his head and vanishes. There's a whip of breeze as he uses vampire speed to race down into the main club.

Movement in the corner of the dance floor below catches my eye. It's not unusual for deals to be made in here. It's a haven for the less legal customs in the city. That's one benefit of this mansion specifically. You pay a drop of blood on entry and the mansion keeps your secrets, hence 'Whisper Club'. Magic's a wonderful thing, blood magic especially, and this house is hungry.

I focus on the couple. They stand strangely, both facing out towards the dancers, their hands unnaturally close for two supposed strangers. Something passes between them, and that's when a spotlight flashes over the pair and I realise who it is. My missing piece. Red, my ever-irritating hunter girl.

Oh, this is simply priceless. Just the thing I need to entertain me. It's been two weeks since I saw her. Since that night that turned us from casual acquaintances to mortal enemies—this time.

I hop over the balcony and jump to the ground a floor below.

Human dancers lean away from me, some face away. Even unaware of my presence, their subconscious thinks I'm a freak. Gooseflesh crawls up their arms, signalling a predator is nearby. Well, they needn't worry. I'm far too preoccupied with the fun I'm about to have to care about them. I skirt around the edge of the dance floor and creep silently up behind Red. The music beat shifts up a gear, the light flickers and I stand right behind her. The urge to lean in and sink my teeth into her neck is overwhelming. I inch forward when something sharp pricks at my gut.

I frown and look down.

What. The. Fuck?

The point of a stake is pricking my gut.

CHAPTER 2

RED

Octavia Beaumont stands at my back, breathing down my neck. *Filthy fucking vampires.*

"I smelt you twenty feet away," I growl as I slip the vial of blood into my trouser pocket. Not quite the truth. I felt her presence more than smelt her, given hunter instincts and all. But I don't want her knowing what skills I do and don't have. The less a vampire knows about you, the better. And I want nothing to do with this vampire in particular. I had the displeasure of meeting her ten days ago, when she stole the last shred of family I had from me.

"And I thought vampires were the ones with heightened senses. Would you mind removing that from my stomach? It tickles," she says.

I hold steady. What I want is to gut her, tear her insides out, and choke her with them because of what she took from me. But unfortunately, this vampire is practically royalty and while there are ample justifications hunters have for staking vamps, I'd have to have acres of them to kill this one.

The point of my stake bites at her skin. A drop of blood oozes down the wood. The scent of it wafts and coils into my nose. My mouth drops, salvia builds under my tongue. Fuck. I shake myself off. Heat flooding my cheeks, pooling between my legs. Fuck, fuck. I've been clean for ten days —ever since my sister, Amelia... Anyway, I came here because I wanted to forget. It was a mistake. The last thing I need is to get hooked on blood even more potent than I was on. This was a mistake. I need to leave before I can't.

"Oh, now that is interesting," Octavia says and wraps her cool fingers around my hand and holds the stake in place. Her touch is electric. A vicious spark, both cool and fiery. It's enough I have to fight a shiver.

Then she steps closer to me, sinking the point deeper into her gut. I gasp. But she's unrelenting. One step closer. Two. Then three. Each movement driving the wood into her belly.

"What the fuck?" I hiss, trying to break away and pull the stake out of her stomach. This isn't a game anymore. I might be a senior hunter, but I couldn't justify killing one of the original three, even if she turned my sister. But I can't pull back. Her grip over my hand is like iron. She's so close that I can smell her perfume, warm spices, like the heart of a winter midnight and something a little deep, a little exotic, like maybe it's not from the city.

"Don't. Get. Any closer. Most vampires this close to me end up dead," I say with as much confidence as I can muster. But she's shaken me. The unexpected violence sending me off course.

She smiles and shunts another inch forward. The stake is in right up to the hilt.

What the fuck is wrong with her?

Blood runs quicker down the wood now. It coats both

our fingers. It makes my teeth ache with need, my tongue throb with the desperate desire to lap it up.

But I won't. Not from her. Never from her.

"If you wanted blood, you merely need to ask. I'm sure we can come to an arrangement. I'm always generous to my little blood sluts," Octavia says, her tongue sliding across her lips.

"Fuck you." I shunt the stake. I know by the wince on her face I caught something serious. Her fingers grip my fist harder, crushing my bones until I have to grit my teeth to prevent myself from moaning. She bears her fangs at me, a low snarl emanating from her throat. She steps back off the stake and then bends my hand up to my face. The stake, along with her blood oozing down it, is millimetres from my mouth. I press my lips shut. I will not drink, I will not drink.

She narrows her eyes at me. "I thought you wanted to drink? Here, I'm offering you the highest honour in the city. Do you know what people would do to get their hands on a drop of my blood?"

I kick out, my foot crunching into her knee. She startles, loses balance as her kneecap pops out of place. Her grip on me loosens enough that I yank the stake out of her hand as she jerks her leg and her knee corrects itself.

I suppress a gag.

There's a dancing platform above me. I squat down and leap up, grabbing the pole to stop myself from flying off the other side of the platform.

"Red?" Amelia shouts from another platform across from me. She's dancing with two guys. My chest spasms. My beautiful baby sister. I can't stand looking at her, the way she represents everything we're meant to hate. The betrayal written in her fangs.

The memory of holding her pudgy hand while we stood in front of Mama's gravestone flashes through my mind.

I am so not ready to talk to her. I shake my head at her. "Not yet," I shout.

Her eyes well up, but I don't have time because I glance behind me and Octavia is crouching, ready to spring up after me.

I leap from platform to platform until I'm a few feet from the balcony. Octavia is on the first platform, leaping to the second.

Cat and fucking mouse. This is not the game I came here to play.

I crouch down and spring up, jumping through the air until I land against the balcony railing. The air bursts from my lungs, making me groan. I give a quick look over my shoulder. She's already on the second platform.

Shit.

I scramble over the railing and out the balcony doors. But there's no easy access to drop to the ground from this balcony.

"For Blood's sake," I growl and crane my neck up. "Roof it is."

I grab the drainpipe and clamber my way up to the roof, hauling myself over the lip and onto a flat area. I sprint across the flat section of the roof and have two choices: clamber across the sloping sections and up the turrets or down.

I peer over the edge. There's another balcony and a porch beneath that. Down it is. Octavia, thankfully, isn't using vampire speed, though I know that just means she's toying with me. But I'll take any advantage I can get.

I clamber over the edge, grab the drain and shimmy down the balcony. Another leap and I smack into the porch roof, but I keep rolling. I stretch for the edge but lose my grip and drop over the edge, collapsing with a thud to the ground.

"Fucking vampires," I growl. But I don't hang about. I haul myself up and run through the market, weaving in and out of the stalls, dodging humans and vampires alike.

"Shit." I say and feverishly glance around the market. I can't see Octavia. My heart thuds in between my ribs like the beat of a drum. I just need to get back to hunter territory.

My skin tingles like she's still following me. I'm a fool if I think my running is enough to dissuade her. I can feel her scratching at my skin like fangs.

I run onto a bridge over the canal. If I can cross and veer down the main road through the Peace Territory back towards the Academy, I'll be in public view the whole time.

I reach the peak of the bridge and halt.

Heat simmers at my back. My shoulders stiffen.

"Fuck," I breathe as a river boat full of drunk humans drifts under the bridge.

"Actually," Octavia says from behind me. "I'd love to."

I blink and my hands are on the bridge handrail, laced tight with a rope cuff.

I'm trapped.

My whole body sets alight. Goosebumps flicker down my arms, down my back. I yank against the rope cuff. But I'm well and truly stuck. Mother fucking vampire speed.

Another boat drifts beneath us, this time two lovers entwined, the boat meandering across the canal.

I wrench around to see her, but I can barely see, even twisting my body to the point of pain. She could kill me from this position. Drain me. Fuck me—that thought should disgust me the most. And my brain is screaming that it's a vile thought, my body, though...

Shit. Shit. Shit.

Traitorous little cunt. I hate Octavia. What I want is to punish her for what she did to my sister. Edge her into oblivion so she never comes again. So why is the thought of me tied here, submitting my pleasure to her, making me wet? I shake my head clear, realising it's just about submission, not her specifically.

Octavia leans into my back, pushing my hips against the railings.

"I can smell how much you want me," she purrs in my ear. "Deny it all you want, but the only person you can lie to is yourself."

She runs her tongue along the underside of my earlobe, sending a bolt of pleasure straight to my clit.

I scream in frustration, yanking my cuffed hands harder. If only I hadn't put my blade away, I could have sliced my way out of these cuffs.

There's another boat, a longer one this time, filled with drinkers and people in various states of undress. It drifts towards us.

Her blood seeps into the back of my shirt.

"Do you want my blood?" she breathes against my neck, her lips skimming my skin and sending sparks of heat and fury down my spine.

"I asked you a question," she says, her breath tickles my skin. I want to yank myself away.

Instead, I lean closer. "Why the hell do you want me to drink your blood? So you can track me? I'm not a fucking idiot. I know the minute I ingest a single drop, you'll be able to find me wherever I am."

She shrugs against my back. "Only for an hour or so."

"An hour too long. Besides, you only love this game of chase because no one else will come near you."

The space between our bodies cools. I've pissed her off.

She moves behind me, then brings two fingers up to my face, her blood dripping off them.

My nostrils flare. Fuck. It smells like ecstasy. Like a thousand nights of bliss, and every secret whispered in the wind. I want it. I need it.

No, no, no. Get a grip, Red.

I wriggle against her, but her grasp on me is like steel.

"You want me," she says. "So take me."

The problem is, I do want her, or at least I want her blood. I'm not an idiot. I know I'm an addict. But I've been clean for two weeks. Which makes what happens next even worse. It makes me weak. I'm going against every ounce of training I've ever had. I made one stupid mistake trying blood—I can barely even remember it anymore—and I've been paying for it ever since.

I lean a little closer to her fingers.

In the boat below, a couple stop fucking to look up at us on the bridge. My skin is electric at the thought of them watching what happens next.

I have to fight the urge to bite her fingers clean off. The scent of her iron-rich blood is overpowering.

"Yes," she says. "Do it. Give in. Succumb to your desire."

I slow my breathing. Inhaling through my mouth instead of my nose to prevent the delicious smell reaching my tastebuds. But it's no use. I'm still leaning closer.

Her body presses into my back, her enormous breasts pushing against my shoulder blades, making my knickers wetter. Excitement pools between my thighs.

I know what happens if I lick that blood and it's nothing good. Nothing I want. I do not want to fuck the woman who turned my sister.

And yet, my lips part. Every breath is laboured as I will myself to stop. My body is tense and alive. The restriction of my hands, the friction of her chest against my back, pushing me into the stone railings.

"Say it," she whispers into my ear. "Say you want it and it's yours."

I close my eyes, the words come tumbling out. "I want it."

She pushes her fingers into my mouth. "That's it, Red. Take it like the good little blood slut you are."

I suck her fingers into my mouth, my tongue rolling over her skin, lapping and sucking her deeper.

My tastebuds explode.

She's the most delicious thing I've ever tasted. I glance up at her, those crimson eyes boring into me. She smiles as she pulls her fingers out, lingering on my lip, and then she sucks them into her own mouth and my pussy clenches.

If I thought my body was alive before, this is like nothing else. Adrenaline fires through my veins, tingles and butterflies race to my extremities. Blood floods to my clit. I gasp at the pulsing need throbbing between my legs. I knew this would happen. Blood makes everyone horny. But Octavia is one of the original three. This need surging around me is like nothing I've ever experienced before.

"You want something else, don't you?" Octavia says.

I lean my forehead against the bridge. The rope chafes, burning the skin around my wrists. "Fuck," I growl. Annoyed with myself for succumbing, knowing where this is going. I grit my teeth. "Yes, I want something else."

"Hmm, and what is it you want, Red? Use your words," she hums against my back.

"You. Octavia. I want to drain the life out of you."

"You're sweet, but why don't you tell me the truth?" She shoves her knee between my thighs, forcing me to spread my feet. She's taller than me, so her thigh meets my crotch.

My pussy is so swollen and wet I whimper at the touch, even though it's through clothing.

She must sense my need because she drives her leg higher, forcing the contact. I moan and fall forward, slipping off the bridge railing. She grips me and pulls me back upright.

"Red," she hisses.

"Fine. For blood's sake, I need to come, okay?" I say. I feel like someone lit a match inside me. Like I want to fuck my way around the Midnight Market. Stab every vampire in the city. Haul the humans from the boat onto the bridge and fuck each and every one.

I'm invincible and vulnerable and hornier than I've ever been. I ache to rip the ropes off and fuck on the bridge cobbles. But I don't want to tell her any of those things because I hate her. I hate what she's done, who she is, but I hate her whole fucking species more than anything. Despite that, with her blood coiling through my veins, I need to fuck her.

"What's your safe word?" she says.

And I'm not sure why the word comes to me, but I decide to use, "Elysium."

Elysium? That's an odd choice, even for me. It's a small village on the outskirts of the city. I used to run patrols there a couple of years ago. Octavia stiffens behind me as if she hates the word.

"Problem?" I say, even though it's tough shit. I'm keeping it, especially if she hates it.

"No problem." She relaxes against me and then grips my chin, pointing my gaze down toward the boat.

"You're going to get your orgasm, but you're going to put on a show for those nosy little humans."

"I will pay you back for this," I spit, but my pussy is already pulsing at the thought of being watched. I've never fucked in public, but even the idea of it is turning me on so much I can feel the arousal in my knickers.

"I do hope so," she says.

I glance down at the boat. It's close enough the beat of their music drifts up to the bridge. It's slow and bassy. At least three of the humans are on blood like me, you can tell by their frenzied expressions. Some are openly fucking on the wooden benches, or leaning against the boat's hull, their cocks and pussies in other people's mouths. The other half of the humans on the boat have ceased what they're doing to watch us, enjoying the voyeur show from the shadowy canal.

Octavia's hand slides from my back to my side and down my torso until she drops over my hip and thigh to one of my blade holsters.

I freeze. Is she going to kill me? Is that what this all was? A ploy to publicly slaughter the Hunter Academy's chief of security. The shame. But she pulls a blade out of the holster and reaches around my front to press it against my crotch.

"What are you—" I start, but she flips the blade sharp side up and presses it to the fabric of my trousers. She slices my crotch in two.

I squeal as the blade catches my underwear, shredding that as well.

"Fuck," I scream. "You could have cut me."

"Then I'd have kissed your pretty hunter pussy better," she says and my body melts, liquid excitement sticking to my bare thighs. I don't care about anything anymore, I just need to fuck and come and fuck again.

She slides her knee between my thighs again, pinning me against the railing. She leans against my back and reaches out, gripping the sides of my trousers and yanking, ripping them apart so my cunt is on display for the entire boat to see.

Then she drives her thigh up until it's pressing against my slick folds.

"Now, put on a show like a good girl," she says into my ear, her words trickling down my neck.

"What do you—" I start.

She shifts her thigh, pulling it back and pushing it forward, moving it over my cunt. Pressure flows over my clit.

"Fuck," I whimper and grip the stone rail tighter so my legs don't give out. The sensation spills out from my clit and into my entire body.

She shunts into me, her body pressing against my back and arse. I try not to think about the fact that the height difference means her pussy is against my arse. She grabs my hips, pulls me back over her thigh and then shoves me forward, dragging my pussy against her smooth leather-clad thigh.

I don't miss the fact that neither of us are touching skin to skin. It's my pussy, her leather-covered thigh. And yet, the electric sensations are consuming.

She must read my mind because she grazes my earlobe with her teeth, sending another exquisite shiver down my spine and says, "Do you want me?"

"Yes." And fuck do I. In this moment, I think I'd be willing to give up being a hunter if it meant I got to press my lips to her cunt.

"Too bad. Now. Use my thigh and fuck yourself till you come for the crowd."

She slaps my arse, shoving me forward again, the grinding motion against my clit sending pulses of pleasure through my legs, right down to my toes.

I rock then. I grip the stone rail and rock on her thigh, grinding against her leg, pushing my soaking cunt over and over her. She moves with me, her hips assisting and riding with me until we're moving to the boat's music. As the pressure builds in my clit, my head rolls back onto her shoulder. It makes my neck exposed, vulnerable.

I'm aware of her fangs dropping, her head leaning towards my neck, her tongue running the length of my carotid, but she doesn't bite. She stays completely in control. Just moving with me, teasing herself as much as she teases me. I grind against her harder, faster. She drives her knee higher until I can't take it anymore and the orgasm erupts and spills over into bliss.

I come just as the boat meets the bridge. The humans cheer as it slips under us, taking them away from sight.

She stares at me. There's a moment where I am utterly blissed out, and I swear a ripple of pain crosses her expression. But it's there and gone quicker than I can read it. Then my hands are released from the rope cuffs and I'm in her arms and she's racing, vampire-fast, over the bridge and into a little market garden. She sits me on her lap, cradling me in her arms, the noise from the market muted by the hedges and shrubs. She holds me a moment, until the high dissipates and I crash back to reality, her blood draining out of my system. And I realise what happened. What she did. What I did.

Sweet fucking Mother of Blood.

I scramble out of her arms and step away until my back hits a tall bush.

"Feisty tonight, aren't you," she says and pushes one of her black locks behind her ear. "Why are you drinking blood? I thought your kind frowned upon that."

By my kind, she means hunters—we are the law in this city. It's our duty to extinguish any misbehaving vampire, or any misbehaving creature for that matter.

She's also dead right. If the Academy knew I was dosing... it would be the end of my career, and the fact she knows is not a comfort. They'd probably give me more grace for having fucked one of the original three vampires than they would for dosing.

Did we fuck? What did just happen? Technically, neither of us touched each other. Thank the gods, that gives me plausible deniability.

"Tell anyone and I'll execute you," I say.

She snorts, laughing so hard her head kicks back. A smile curls over her lips.

"You want me. You hate me. You fuck me." She tut, tut, tuts at me, shaking her head, her tongue click, click, clicking in time with her words. Then she's on all fours, crawling towards me over the cobbles. "What are you going to do, Red? You couldn't kill me after I took your sister. What makes you think you can now?"

My whole body tenses. Fire burns through my expression. This is why I hate her. She took the last person that meant anything to me. It's why I hate them all. The bliss of the orgasm drains out of me, leaving behind rage and fury.

Father left us to work for a vampire noble.

Mother was a donor, drained in a supposed accident. When do vampires ever have accidents?

And then Amelia.

Stolen.

All because of a stupid mistake she made, gatecrashing a vampire noble's party. The idiot. She was always so spontaneous. I remember the first birthday she had after Mum had passed. I'd gotten leave from the Hunter Academy, planned everything, but it chucked it down with rain. Amelia didn't want to stop celebrating so she convinced me to dance in the rain for hours. It was fun at the time, but when we both got sick, and I had to train in order to earn enough for herbs and medications... She never thinks anything through.

She always had a 'live for right now' attitude. Well, I suppose she really will live now and forevermore. Octavia was at that party and took advantage. Drained her, stole her from me and turned her into the thing I hate more than anything.

She reaches my feet and stands up, leaning into my personal space. Vampires are cold, and yet heat pulses between us. The scent of her perfume, deep oud and something spicy wafts into my nose.

"I swear on the bones of the Church of Blood, I will ruin you, Octavia fucking Beaumont."

Her eyes glimmer. Those crimson pupils boring into me. She sucks her bottom lip in, and something inside me twitches, as if the sight of her like this is pleasurable.

"Oh, I hope so, Red. I really hope so..." she lets that linger in the air until her meaning is abundantly clear.

"What is wrong with you? You killed my sister," I snarl.

"Your sister is alive."

"No. She's a fucking drainer like you."

"Yes, she's a superior being now. You hunters are all the same. Just because we feed on your life source, you think us monsters. But you're the hypocrites. You kill us frivolously with flimsy reasoning and yet you're the one indulging in a little backdoor blood. At least we're open about our consumption..."

"You're twisted," I spit.

"And yet, I'm not the one whose heart rate is elevated or pupils are blown. And I'm not the one who's aroused by the smell of my blood... No, if anything, I'd say you're the sick one, darling... Because you want to fuck me again, for real this time. I'd bet the only thought running through your head is what my cold little cunt tastes like."

My teeth grind against each other, but I have no comeback.

Her eyes lower to my crotch, the shredded fabric. "You hate me, you gut me, cut me... and yet, you still want to fuck me. Interesting."

A sick smile peels across her mouth. Two perfectly white, perfectly sharp fangs peeking out from her smile.

Heat floods my face. "What just happened... That was... I would nev—"

"—Really?" She shifts right up to me. Her knee pressing against my swollen cunt. Shock freezes me in place. She leans into my neck, inhales the scent of me. "I beg to differ."

But this time she faces me, her pupils are as wide as mine, and that gives me a smug sense of satisfaction.

I sneer. "Looks like I'm not the only one who wants to fuck," I say.

I hate where this conversation is going. She's wrong. I have zero desire to fuck her. What happened was purely the blood in my system. That was the mistake—allowing myself to taste her.

This is unbridled rage. It has to be. I shift on the spot, the prickly shrub leaves poking my back. Unfortunately, her leather trousers stick to my pussy in a way that implies it's more than rage. What the fuck is wrong with me? Vampires repulse me. I shrug it off. They're designed this way. To be alluring. It's part of their 'charm'. It's not real, and she fucking knows it. She's just saying shit to wind me up. This will go away. Once she's seen Amelia through that first month of the change, she'll grow bored with torturing me. She'll find another human to turn and she'll leave me alone.

Someone meanders through the park, a woman. Two in fact, drunk and wobbling. Octavia speeds across the pebbled path as one of the women takes a tumble. Octavia catches her before her head crunches into a giant rock.

She saved her life.

The woman rights herself, takes one look at Octavia and

screams the kind of night-splitting shriek reserved for murderers and horror shows.

"GET THE FUCK AWAY FROM ME, FREAK!" she screams. The women run, fleeing Octavia's presence.

I'll confess, there is a moment where I feel the injustice of this. I'd heard of Octavia's reputation, the fact the city hates her. I hadn't seen it in action though.

Octavia returns to me, her cheeks aflame. I open my mouth to apologise for their behaviour, but she merely continues as if it never happened.

"What I want to know," she starts again, "is why a hunter like you would sink themselves to the level of dosing. Hmm?"

I open my mouth, genuinely about to justify myself to her. And promptly shut it.

"Goodbye, Octavia. Hope you fall on a stake." I shift to the side, push off the bush and walk off. I shrug my jumper off and tie it around my hips, hiding my shredded trousers. She gets out of the way, sitting herself on the garden bench, draping her arms over the back of it.

She sniffs a laugh out. "Tell the Chief I said thanks for the blood bags."

So that's where Roman and Marcel went. I wondered who the Chief gave them to. My bestie lives in another city, New Imperium, and she had a load of trouble with her old mentor, Roman. I helped her out of a patch of trouble a few months ago. Their princess, Morrigan, banished the culprits, and I offered to bring them to our city to serve as donors until the vamps got bored and drained them dry.

"Tell her yourself. When you tell her about me buying blood... I'm sure that's your plan now, isn't it? To ruin me?"

Octavia raises an eyebrow, she pouts, "Oh, I'm going to ruin you alright. But I'll give you a free pass on the blood this evening. I figure you owe me, though."

I shake my head, the audacity. She's an idiot if she thinks I endure going to the Whisper Club for any reason other than the fact I know what I do stays private.

"How gracious of you. But I don't owe you shit."

"Oh? And what makes you think that?"

And this is how I win. "I only buy inside your club. Your mansion keeps the secret for me. Isn't that why it's called the Whisper Club?"

Her expression narrows. She knows I've won. Her nose twitches like she's suppressing the irritation.

"Then I suppose I'll be seeing you again soon, won't I?" And the way her rouged lips curl around the words makes my heart beat a little faster.

Rage.

I cling to it as I walk out of the garden and back into the Midnight Market.

CHAPTER 3

OCTAVIA

I spend another couple of hours in the club before I have to make my way to Mother's after Xavier's summons. As I head towards the exit, Erin gives me a cheeky salute. "'Night, boss."

I clap her on the back. Erin is my right-hand woman. Bit of a vicious type, all brawn, crushing, squeezing and garrotting. And to give her credit, she is one of the few who isn't afraid of me, though whether that's because there's not enough brain attached to the brawn or the fact she's a hunter, I'm not sure. Regardless, we have an agreement. She serves me till her thirty-fifth birthday and I'll turn her. If she serves me another thirty-five years as a vamp, the rest of her immortality is her own.

I'll head towards the Midnight Market carriage station. I'd normally use the club's station, but I don't have my personal carriage.

I step out of the club into the Midnight Market. It's misty. A chill wind whips through the stalls. Roils of white steam peel off the canals to shroud me in creamy shadows.

Today, the mansion door has exited me into the clothing quarter of the market. I wonder if the club is suggesting I change my attire, or if this is where its whims and fancies took it. It's a gift and a curse, this mansion. The house's moods are one reason I adore it. It's secretive and changes its entrance and exit whenever it deems necessary. Finding the place can be a pain in the ass if you're not au fait with its temperament.

I walk along the canal, past dozens of market stalls, racks of dresses and high collared jackets—the fashion of the moment.

"You shouldn't be here, filthy omen of death," a market seller says and turns his back towards me as I'm passing.

I glance up at him. Gooseflesh flecks down the back of his neck as if my being alive disgusts him. Pathetic human. I have swung through every emotion over the years. I used to drain those who discriminated against me, tore their heads from their necks. But that only made the humans worse. I tried reasoning with them, arguing with them until I realised ignoring it and raising my shields was the only thing I could do.

I meander through a new quarter, this one full of witch grimoires, bottles of herbs and potions that crawl in ways that make me uncomfortable. I divert out of this area past sellers dishing out ordinary stock bottles of blood and then past the more nuanced flavours. Though by the odd hue to the bottles, I can tell they didn't collect it in the authentic way our blood is. Knockoffs, no doubt. That said I'm hungry.

"I'll take an A-positive with essence of love," I say.

The seller rifles through his bottles and plucks the right one. "Here, oh—" he says as his eyes meet mine.

His fingers tremble, the bottle shakes in his hand as he moves a fraction further away.

"Forget it," I say, my heart sinking. I walk away, and at times like this I curse my nature and enhanced hearing.

"Vile, disgusting creature," he says under his breath. But it's no matter, I hear anyway.

I step down into the underground, the sleek red walls of the staircase almost shimmery tonight. The stairs guide me down, down, down. Under the market, under the canals and quaint townhouses toward the carriage platforms. When I reach the bottom, I chuck a silver coin into the ticket barrier hole, and it lets me through.

"Lady Beaumont," gasps an elderly human man. He bows his head at me, backs away and stumbles. I lunge to stop him from falling, but he yelps as my hand brushes his arm and that alerts the station staff.

Gods. Why do I bother helping? The stationmaster appears and frowns at me until his gaze meets mine and then a shiver wracks his body.

The stationmaster reaches down to pick the old man up as I sigh and leave them to it. While the vast majority of citizens fear me, the religious revere me enough to stay away. No doubt this man is one of the faithful. The Church of Blood tends to spit out believers. That *she'll* return. The maker. Our witch goddess, the originator of my dear mother Cordelia.

Mother always tells the story in the same way. Where everyone else has varying shades of commitment to the church, Mother despises it.

Once upon a time, there were two families, the St Clairs and the Randalls. And like any respecting families of nobility, they were at war.

For petty things, Mother says. Over land and property. The economy and legacy. None of it seems to matter now and the details have faded even for her. Nonetheless, a local witch took issue with their dealings. Many of the locals were caught in their war, slaughtered and maimed for no reason other than being in the way. So the witch cursed the heirs, Mother and some woman called Eleanor, to become mortal enemies, never able to kill each other.

While their families died long ago, Cordelia and Eleanor lived on. Hatred seeping into their bones like a disease. Burrowing and festering in their souls for a thousand years. And as for the witch? As penance for her crimes, the witch-gods gave her a choice: become the monster she created or spend eternity in hell. And that is how the three vampire lines came to be: one cursed, one chosen, and me: one born.

The witch-vampire was lost to history, though her line was not. She'd turned enough vampires before vanishing for her line to continue.

A claret-coloured carriage pulls up and I jump in.

"Castle St Clair," I say and knock on the carriage wall.

"Alright, miss," the driver says.

We created these carriage tunnels a thousand years ago, shortly after Mother and I came to be. They're the only way we can travel at the peak of suns up. The horses take a while to train up, though. They don't much like being down here, so they're rotated often and taken good care of, and now the tunnels serve all our kind.

Warmth hits me as soon as I slide into a leather seat. The carriage is a deep rouge, plush. I struck lucky this evening. Sometimes they can be shabby.

The tunnels weave like the veins we draw our meals from under Sangui City, traversing across territory boundaries without a care. The carriages down here are rounder than overground ones. They're designed to look like fattened blood cells.

A couple of hours later, the carriage pulls up to the St Clair station territory. To my disdain, Dahlia, my least favourite sibling, is waiting for me outside the station with a horse.

Three men stroll past, I tense up as one of them catches sight of me.

He baulks, grabs the arm of one of his mates. "It's the freak," he says.

"The omen of death," the other one confirms.

The third man makes the mistake. The words I can handle, the words all my siblings ignore, it's the violence none of us tolerate. The third man picks up a rock and flings it at me.

Dahlia, Mother of Blood, bless her violent soul, flings me the reins and lunges to catch it. She races forward and smashes the same rock over the man's head repeatedly until his face is a bloodied pulp. The man who called me a freak pisses his pants, a dark streak spreading down his trouser leg, and the other man runs as she drops the one she's beaten to the ground.

She strolls back smiling, a dark little glint in her eye.

"Sister," she says. "Shall we?"

"We shall, and thank you," I answer. It's a rare occasion Dahlia and I are on the same side. But as much as we quarrel and bicker and hate on each other, we are still family, and she will not tolerate abuse from an outsider. Our relationship is complicated.

Her black hair is quaffed in a similar style to Xavier's, though hers is shorter than his, and cut in a more aggressive shape. She's smaller than me in height, but more than makes up for it in size and unrestrained rage. She has that muscular build created by throwing punches and crushing bones. Five hundred years ago, when Mother turned her, my favourite thing to do was to watch people underestimate her. She's a wretched little thing, all fangs and fury. She's also Mother's favourite. Make of that what you will.

The woman had brought me up for five centuries before Dahlia came along, and yet, Dahlia is her favourite. Xavier disagrees with me, but I know I'm right.

"You look like shit," she spits.

Ahh, back to hating each other so quickly.

"You could at least attempt civility." I sigh.

She jumps on her horse, leans down and holds the reins of mine to allow me to get on.

"Like you do when you're hungry?" she says.

"I don't think you're one to talk about hanger, Dahlia."

She rolls her eyes at me. "That was seventy-five years ago. Isn't it time you let that go?"

"Let go of the fact you drained and slaughtered my girl-friend because you wanted to fuck her, and she wasn't interested?"

"Please, she was a pathetic human woman. I wouldn't have pity-fucked her if she begged. Besides, she wouldn't have survived turning, let alone the Morose Mourning. I was putting her out of her misery before you killed her trying to turn her. Really, you should be thanking me."

At some point in the first five hundred years, every turned vampire experiences the Morose Mourning period. Usually, after the last living relative who can remember them passes. It's some kind of trigger in their minds. The reality of immortality descends and for a while, they mourn life, living, the fragility of mortality. Of course, I never expe-rienced that. I was born this way and know no different.

Which means it's yet another way I'm different from them.

"It wasn't your choice to make, *Dahlia*," I growl.

"Neither was it yours to burn my cottage down with me in it, but you always seem to forget that."

I shrug. "It seemed a fair recompense. Besides, I left you a window unlocked."

She glares at me, but the conversation is thankfully over. We're silent as our horses trot out of the carriage station and ferry us up the long and winding route through forests and mountains to Mother's castle. The family home looms on the top of the highest peak in the city: Castle St Clair, wrapped in shrouds of clouds and mountain mist, its crenellated turrets a beacon of power gazing upon its inhabitants.

As I gaze up at the highest turret, the moon showers the castle with glistening light; it occurs to me that of course Mother wants her castle at the highest point. That way, she can see everything and everyone she controls beneath her.

"You could at least pretend to be enthused over dinner, for Mother's sake," Dahlia says as we slow the horses to a stop in the circular drive and we dismount.

"Why? The only time Mother summons us to a dinner like this is when she's planning war games, imposing another rule or regulation on us or there's bad news."

"Well, if you played by her rules, perhaps we would need fewer dinners," she snaps.

And there is the truth of it. This is why she's Mother's favourite, because despite all her strength, she doesn't have an original thought or backbone in sight. Instead, she placates our mother by being her lapdog. It's pathetic.

I can't even bring myself to respond. I hand the reins to a stable boy as a butler opens the enormous arched oak doors and we enter. Our feet clack against the cold stone slabs as we make our way through the hallways. The walls are lined with a timeline of art through the ages. Every style from the last thousand years. A handful of the paintings are portraits, some of Cordelia, some of my siblings, two of them all—none of me.

Dahlia catches me looking at the portraits, the many that hang of her and Mother and our other siblings.

"When are you going to get over it? You didn't *actually* kill his daughter."

I ignore her. She wasn't even alive to remember the pain.

When I was a child and Mother was busy taking over the city, she would take me on her work trips. She would meet and greet the city's people. One day I was playing with another little girl while Mother mingled with the city's people.

Two days later, we found the man defacing the first portrait we'd had of us together. Mother, furious, demanded to know the problem.

His daughter had died the same night she'd played with me. We knew so much less about the biology of our kind back then. We didn't have a way to prove that I hadn't given her some disease or illness.

The man returned with his friends, they tried to take me, steal me away to hurt me. Foolish really, they didn't understand what I was, how strong I was.

Mother started it. As is the way of her cruelty, she wouldn't stand for their attack. She sank her fangs into one of the men, draining him where he stood. Being the naive child I was, I joined in. And so, at the end of the slaughter, an eight-year-old stood in the midst of a circle of bodies at her feet. Severed limbs in her hands, blood streaking her dress and cheeks.

Cordelia made sure the dead girl's father lived to tell the tale. Her warning to the city. Only her cruelty twisted the message.

It became a myth.

I became a monster.

And the city never forgave me. Now, I don't allow portraits of myself. Only two artists have tried, both human and so had to have an extensive preparation period to even be comfortable in the same room as me. Both made me look like a monstrous demon. It didn't happen again.

Dahlia leads me to the grand dining room. Mother is already sitting on her elaborate throne at the end. She stands and opens her arms.

We have an uneasy sort of relationship. As her adopted daughter, she's always had some level of power and command over me. Something that, as I matured, didn't sit well. I am one of the original three. By rights, I am her equal. Some years ago, I broke away and carved out my own territory and dominion on the other side of the city.

"Sister," Gabriel says as I squeeze his shoulder and walk past. He's leant back, his long, lithe legs kicked up on the table, a book in each hand as he speed reads across both of them.

I don't think I've ever seen Gabriel without reading material in his hands. The faded red leather of the tomes' covers matches the intense rouge of his suit—something else I don't think I've ever seen him without.

Dahlia takes her seat on one side of Mother. I take the same seat on the opposite side. Xavier is already sitting in the chair to my left.

Xavier leans in, whispers in my ear, "Good evening, Favourite."

I smile and kiss his cheek.

Sadie, it seems, is late as always.

A slew of butlers sweep in, depositing trays of bloodied steaks and goblets of warm blood.

"Honestly, Mother, I don't know why you persist in this charade of dinner. You know we'd all be happier with donors at our feet." Dahlia grimaces as a butler deposits the rawest steak I've seen on her plate. She nudges it away, her lips pinching. Xavier tucks in immediately. Gabriel shoves his plate away but pours himself a goblet of blood-wine and passes the decanter across the table to me, which I gladly take.

I pour a goblet and drink several sips. Then, reluctantly, I pick up my knife and fork and cut the thinnest sliver of steak. I chew and swallow, wishing it were bloodier and warmer.

Cordelia glares at Dahlia. "We will have dinner like a civilised family." Mother is in a sweeping gown this evening, her hair swept into an up-do, the only hint of her age a silver streak running through one side of her parting.

"I'd hardly call us civilised," Xavier says, chewing his steak and picking up his goblet. He takes a huge gulp of blood-wine. "Or did you forget the last dinner we tried?"

My mouth quirks. He's talking about the dinner massacre of six months ago. Things got... out of hand. Mother had arranged for several house donors to attend. One of us, I forget who, though I suspect it was Dahlia, lost control, and so ensued a blood frenzy.

Gabriel is Dahlia's birth twin. Whatever Dahlia does, Gabriel does. The pair of them set each other off, which gave Xavier an excuse to join in. I followed suit and Sadie... well, I'm not sure if she's ever really anything but quietly out of control. It's one of the things I admire about her.

"I still haven't forgiven you, Xavier," Gabriel says, taking his feet off the table.

Xavier trapped Gabriel in one of the donor cages... only without any of the actual donors inside. Poor Gabe had to watch in a frenzied state, starving and desperate, while the rest of us drank our fill. It was a cruel torment.

I laughed for three weeks about it.

Gabriel not so much.

He threw himself against the rails hard enough he cracked his own skull and broke several ribs trying to escape.

"I was in medical for two nights after that dinner," Gabriel whines.

"Er... Gabriel, you asked him to put you in there, something about deprivation-kink," I say.

"I did not," he gasps.

Cordelia's face pinches.

Xavier shrugs, "Asked... didn't ask, same-same."

"Hardly," Gabriel growls.

Dahlia's face twists as she glances at Gabriel, "I've seen you in Octavia's club... it wouldn't be the first time you've been put in a cage willingly. I think you get off on it."

"Traitor." He glares at her.

"Loyal to the house always, brother," Dahlia says.

"Enough." Cordelia cuts the conversation off. "I've brought you here for a *civilised* dinner. I expect nothing less. Now, tell me. How is business for you all? Xavier darling, you start."

He sits up a little straighter. Xavier doesn't have an official title, but if he did, it would be schmoozer. Mother collected Xavier because of his beauty and ability to charm the nobles of the city. In other words, schmooze and corral everyone into Mother's line and rules. Basically, he's the family whip—fucking good at it, too. Though I'd argue that using compulsion is cheating. But he doesn't give a fuck if it gets the job done.

"Lord and Lady Woodley are supportive of your continued efforts to push back the hunter territory, though they request you at least attempt to keep their farming lands intact. The humans on the borders of the St Clair and hunter territory are complaining that there are vampires terrorising the human settlements in the region."

"So noted. I'll see what can be done. Gabriel?" Mother turns to him.

He closes his books and places them on the table. "The

Great Library has acquired an unusual grimoire from out of the city. It's ancient. I negotiated for it personally."

Xavier coughs. Gabriel fires him a nasty sneer, but Mother catches the implication. Gabriel might have negotiated, but Xavier was the one who charmed the grimoire over the line.

"And has this grimoire illuminated anything of note?" Mother asks.

"It's still situated in the library vault. I'll be examining it tomorrow, but it's said to contain script written in the lost witch-vampire's own hand."

Mother stiffens. "Well, I should like to examine that myself. Perhaps you'd care for company tomorrow?"

Gabriel brightens. "I'd be delighted."

"Kiss-ass," I mumble.

"Don't be bitter," Gabriel fires back.

"Only as bitter as your single heart."

"Says the pot to the kettle, honey." Gabriel smirks.

"And how do you expect me to date when Dahlia keeps eating everyone?" I snap.

"Mother of Blood, I was hungry, and she wouldn't have survived turning." Dahlia throws her hands up.

The thing is, Dahlia isn't wrong. My ex probably wouldn't have survived the turning, she was a bit of a wet blanket, and Dahlia likely did do her a favour because I was going to attempt to turn her. But I have no intention of letting Dahlia know that. I just like winding her up.

The doors fly open and crash against the walls, cutting the argument short. Sadie walks in, her expression muted, but she swings her hands in a series of gestures that promptly shut all of us up.

"The only one getting laid around here is Xavier," Sadie signs.

It's a fair point. Even Dahlia can't argue with that.

Xavier leans back in his chair, smug that he won a round he wasn't even part of. Sadie moves around the table in a haunting fashion. Her dress is like a plume of smoke, billowing and drifting around her feet, which seem to glide across the stone floor. Moonbeams stretch from the window to the floor, and as she sweeps through them, I swear she flickers in and out of existence. I shiver. She kisses everyone hello, lingering a moment longer on my head.

Sadie and I are drawn towards each other. I always wanted to connect with her the way I do with Xavier, but she's unpredictable, a little feral, and she holds pieces of herself away from us. She tries, though. With me especially, I think I'm her safe place. Everyone thinks Dahlia is the most savage of the five of us. Something tells me it's really Sadie.

Xavier pulls a chair out next to him for Sadie. Of all of us, he's the peacekeeper. He bends to whisper something in her ear. I strain to listen, if only to ensure he's not whispering the same favoured words to her he does to me. Not that I'm jealous. I hate all my siblings with equal fervour.

"Your brothers and sisters were telling me their business updates. What have you from the church?" Cordelia says.

Sadie sags, a wispy noise emanates from her throat. Her hands dart in front of her lightning quick. I keep up, just about.

"The church is fine. Congregation is swelling. Though I am understaffed, and the Trial of Spirit is too difficult. The failure rate and death rates of potential monks is killing my ability to run enough services."

Cordelia doesn't look even remotely upset about this. She hates the church and only tolerates it because it makes her daughter happy.

But I make a note that I may need to employ a sign tutor again to brush up on my speed. I'm fluent, but Sadie speaks fast, and I do hate not being able to catch everything said.

Gabriel and Dahlia are the worst. They share entire conversations in looks and glances, a shift of a shoulder and a wave of a finger—I think it's a twin thing. Either way, it's infuriating always being on the outside.

They're five hundred years old now. I remember their arrival like yesterday because I was furious Mother could bring yet more children into this family. Wasn't I enough? Wasn't Xavier?

The night they joined us, some human came tearing into Castle St Clair, begging Cordelia to come to his village to deal with a problem house. Of course, that wasn't enough to pique her interest. But then he told her the house contained demon children. Well, she'd had a daughter for five centuries, and a son for two and a half. Why not add to the family?

So, she went with the human to the village and found a locked house. Not just locked but sealed shut magically. Some pissed off witch, I suspect. When she broke through the seal, what she found haunted the village for decades. There were dozens of bodies. All of them dead. Only the twins remained alive, stood in amongst the carcasses, their hands clasped. They were gaunt, caked in dried blood. The worst of it, though, the thing that really convinced Cordelia to take them in, was their answer to her question.

"What happened?" she'd asked.

"They upset us," the twins responded.

And that was the end of it. Xavier and I had new siblings. She kept them human, mind you, then turned them against their will on their twenty-fifth birthday.

"And the club?" Mother asks, bringing me back to the present.

"Fine," I shrug.

"Detailed response as ever," she sighs.

"It's good, Mother, trade is excellent. Why are we here anyway? You clearly have something to tell us," I say.

She presses her lips together before turning to Dahlia. "We'll discuss the army later, darling."

Dahlia, her perfect progeny and head of her most valued resource, the vampire security force, smiles sweetly at her, displaying her razor-sharp fangs as she raises her goblet of blood-wine to her lips.

"I've an announcement," Mother says. "I'm tired."

"You had your Morose Mourning seven hundred years ago. Aren't you a little old to be tired?" Xavier says.

"Actually, there are records of some of the elder vampires having a sort of second mourning period," Gabriel says, his hand sliding to pull his books nearer.

"Is that what this is?" Sadie signs.

"No," Mother answers.

"Then what?" Dahlia asks.

"Come on, Mother, put us out of our misery," Xavier says, leaning forward to pour me and Sadie more blood-wine before passing the jug to Gabriel.

"Octavia, could I borrow the club two nights from now? I appreciate it's last minute, but I'd rather do the announcement there. And... we're inviting the hunters," Cordelia says.

We all go vampire still. No one blinks, no one moves.

It's Sadie that whisper-laughs and signs, "Why the hell would you invite them?"

"Well, that's part of the announcement. Octavia, are you amenable?" Cordelia says.

"Sure, but I can't close the club to humans or non-nobles at such short notice. Whatever you're announcing will be public knowledge."

She nods once. "Fine."

My mind races. What the hell is she doing? Is she going to ambush them? If so, I don't want that in my club, not when it will tarnish my reputation. But I don't have time to work out what she's up to as she continues talking.

"Two nights from now, I'll require you all to be there. It's a 9 p.m. start and I'll reveal everything."

CHAPTER 4

CORDELIA

One Thousand Years Ago

Once upon a time, one thousand years ago, a fairytale was born. Two women, star-crossed lovers, destined to meet. Their fates woven through time and history.

And history is where this fairytale begins.

A chance meeting.

A fluke. A whim. A blessing.

Whatever the reason, one thing is certain, this story ends with fireworks...

"Here, darling, hurry now. As safe as you can be on that ankle, okay? We must have you ready for the next marriage ball," Mama says, handing me a pouch of coins.

I huff at her, annoyed that I'm being made to attend another so soon, given the last one is the cause of my ankle issue.

"When is it?"

"Two nights from now."

"And if I refuse?" I say and pull my skirts up. My swollen ankle has developed a plum sheen. The bulge is spreading up my calf.

"Let's not start our day with an irksome attitude. You're prime age for a proposal, Cordelia. We must ensure the right marriage for you and the family. It's a necessary business. We all have to do our part. We are the St Clairs. You can't just marry anyone."

I grit my teeth. Neither interested in marriage nor doing my part particularly. Mama places a kiss on my forehead and heads back into the house.

"Where's Poppa's cane?" I shout after her.

Mrs Blakemore, our housekeeper, pops her head into the hallway, "In the pot there, miss, just move the dress coats."

I shove the coats out of the way and spot the mahogany-stained cane. I pull it out, instantly relieved to lean on it as I hobble out of the door and towards the carriage. The driver aids me as I stumble up the steps and collapse onto the seat.

Of course, even with the carriage dropping me in the centre of the village, it still takes me twice as long to reach the market area. I slip and fumble on the gravelly floor of the market. A kind gentleman assists me to the other side of the stalls. Finally, I reach the street with the healers. Mama would be annoyed with me if she knew I'd come to the healers rather than the doctors.

But I swear sometimes the doctors don't know what they're talking about. They swindle your money and give you liquids that smell suspiciously like watered down whiskey and fermented herbs. At least the healers mix the brews in front of you, and you know what's going into them.

I hobble past a couple of shops, one filled with stones and crystals, another selling elixirs. But neither are quite right. Then I see a little healer shop nestled in the heart of the row. The sign hanging above the door says 'Healing Hearts' and beneath it in tiny letters it says: in association with the Randalls.

I hesitate before entering. Would Mother throw a fit at me for using a store owned by the Randalls? She does so hate them. I decide that whatever healer is in there just works for them, they've probably never even met a Randall. Besides, Mother would be more furious if I return home unhealed.

I step inside. Despite the four walls around me, the shop is light and breezy. Sun streams in through the glass-fronted window and fills the space with warmth. There's a fire burning. It sits in a metal stove in the hearth, the door ajar, spilling warmth into the shop. Crackles and embers drift up into the chimney like little dust motes.

"May I help you?" a woman says.

I startle as she appears from a door at the back of the shop, and I'm unable to find words to respond. My lips part as I take in her appearance.

Her hair is mousy, falling in thick locks that flow like the shallow waves of warm oceans. Her eyes are the deep blue you only find in secluded lagoons. I'm drawn to them, to her. Unable to look away, to think or breathe, I draw a ragged breath in, gulping for air and words.

"Are you okay, miss?" she says.

"What? Yes." No. It appears I'm not. But I don't want to alert her to the strange thoughts racing through my mind.

To the fact that if she hadn't spoken, I may have continued stepping closer and closer until I'd simply fallen into her eyes and buried myself in her soul. What in Sangui City's name is wrong with me?

"I see, so, then have you come to get assistance for another person?" she says.

"What? No." Oh. I see the mistake I've made. Heat flushes my cheeks. "I apologise. Let me try again. I was umm..."

"The pain? It disturbs the thoughts," she says, pointing to my leg. One of her eyebrows quirks up in a smile. Is she mocking me?

"Right. Yes. That. The pain. That's actually what I'm here about. Do you have some herbs that would ease the swelling, perhaps?"

"Of course," she says.

My eyes fall to her plump lips. There's a light rouge colour on them or something that makes them glisten. Heat rises up my neck so fast I have to adjust my dress collar. What a peculiar reaction I'm having to the shop.

"I'm sorry, I'm feeling a little... umm. Could I trouble you for a chair?" I stutter.

She bustles around the shop, moving jars and herbs and bags of I don't know what, until she's moved everything onto a counter at the back and cleared a chair for me to sit on.

It's placed behind me, and she slides her hand over my arm, helping me lower down. Where her palm meets my bare forearm, a furnace erupts.

I gasp. She glances up at me.

"The pain. My ankle," I splutter.

It is most definitely not my ankle. It's the shock of her touch. I've never experienced a sensation like it. Perhaps it's her healer skills. It's bizarre. I've seen a handful of healers before and none so enigmatic as this. She must be truly powerful. The gods must have bestowed an enormous gift of magic on her.

"Are you... you must be a d—" I stop and lower my voice, knowing it's a dangerous thing to name such a creature.

"A dhampir? Yes," she says.

"Your touch is..."

She smiles, dragging her eyes away from me. "Ah. That's not... I've not drawn upon my power yet. I need blood for that."

"Oh," I say and sit up. Realising that if it wasn't her magic, then I don't want to consider why her skin was so warm, so electric.

Suddenly, I'm uncomfortable, hotter than before and wish to leave. I should just get this over with as fast as possible and get back to the manor. I'm sure she will have further preparations for me to contend with.

"Well, anyway. I have an issue. I fell at the marriage ball last night and my ankle... it's rather bruised and swollen. Could you...?" I say.

"Certainly. I'll need to see the ankle in order to assist."

I nod and draw my dress skirts up to my knee. A strange thought occurs to me. That I'm rather glad I'd bathed last night and took extra care to raze my legs. Preferring them to be smooth rather than the stubbled mess they were before the ball. I shake the thought away. Of course, it matters not what my legs are like. This woman is a healer. She cares nothing for the state of my limbs.

"May I examine your ankle?" she says. Her voice is as soft and warm as her eyes, and I find myself quite unable to concentrate on the substance of her sentences. This is most troubling. I wonder if I'm having some sort of lapse on account of the pain from my ankle. Only the pain isn't actually that bad. It's mostly troublesome to walk. The worst of the throbbing ceased overnight.

I lift my leg off the floor. Her fingertips glide against my skin. I swallow hard and have to look away. Every touch is electric. It must be magic. Every press of her finger pads to my calf, my ankle, my foot is unbearable.

Heat and liquid electricity flows from her hands into my body. It swims up my legs, higher, higher. My breathing quickens, my nostrils flare. I'm overcome with... with... I'm not even sure.

She trails her fingers higher up my calf, toward my knee, palpating and squeezing to assess where the swelling stops. Only, with every contact, the current flowing between us soars, until it's ravaging my thighs.

She touches me again, palpating just above my knee, and I must stop breathing altogether as the tingling sensations slip between my thighs to my core.

To the place I touch when I'm alone.

A bolt surges between my legs, my undergarments grow slick.

This is... I don't know what sorcery this is, but it shouldn't be happening.

I jerk away, my eyes wide. "What are you doing to me?"

She frowns. "Examining your lower leg to know where I need to put the compresses and apply herbs."

"You swear on the witch-gods you're not using magic?"

Her frown deepens. "No, miss, it's against our ways to use magic without your express consent. You'd see me draw my blood before you felt the magic against your skin. Is everything okay?"

I shake my head. "I'm sorry, I've made a mistake. This is... I must go."

I'm up and out of the chair faster than I can reliably move. I wobble. She grabs me, catching me before I can fall.

But of course, that makes another bolt of what I now realise is desire surge inside me.

I snatch my hand away, deeply confused, and take my cane and hobble out of the shop as quickly as I can. I leave the woman whose name I don't even know staring after me, that single furrowed line buried between her perfectly teased brows like a marker in the sand of Lantis Bay.

A marker that tells me I can never marry any of the men at the balls.

A marker that tells me Mama is going to kill me.

CHAPTER 5

RED

Listen, I am fully aware that a hunter dosing on a drainer's blood is... awkward. Hell, it's a fucking nightmare, and I swear I never intended it to happen. Believe me, I hate myself for it. But I also can't stop—such is the peril of being an addict.

And yes, I hate myself for what happened on the bridge with *her*.

But every time I take a dose, even a single drop, I'm stronger, more alert, more powerful. Knowing that is twisting me up inside. Fucking with my mind. We—hunters—hate drainers. What sort of bitter irony is it that their blood is making me a better hunter? The problem is when the blood works its way out of my system, I'm completely screwed. I'm wracked with intense fatigue, tremors, and a hunger that cannot be satiated. If that's anything like the hunger newly turned drainers feel, then it's no wonder so many of them desiccate at the end of our stakes for getting out of control.

But of course, the dealers don't talk about the addictive

properties, no doubt a manipulation on their part. Keep us coming back, jacking up their pockets full of silver coins.

If the Academy found out... well, I could kiss goodbye to my job as head of security. I'd never be allowed to teach at the school again. And look, I will give up. It's just... difficult... and right now, I have it completely under control. I only need a single drop a day, alright fine, a few drops. But I make sure I stay in hunter territory while I take it so that any drainer's blood I've taken won't be stupid enough to track or attack me. Vampires never come to this side of the city. It's not worth the risk. Too many hunters too willing to end them on sight and ask questions later.

So I'm safe.

I have it under control.

I step into the Hunter Academy castle grounds, and I'm greeted by a dozen students practicing in the front courtyard before lights out.

"Don't stay up too late," I call.

"We won't," they shout back. One of the students waves and her opponent seizes the opportunity of her distraction to sweep her legs out from under her. I smile. It reminds me of me and Amelia.

When I first joined the Academy at thirteen, right after Mum died, I used to go home on the weekends. The first thing Amelia would do when I walked through the door was throw pillows at me and pretend to be a monster, squealing when I'd wrestle her to the ground.

Amelia went to live with our mum's best friend, Oriana. And even though Oriana treated her like her own daughter, Amelia still craved the weekends when I'd return. I did too. We clung to each other because we both carried the same loss, the same scars on our heart. I think that's why her becoming a vampire hurts so much.

One of the first years yelps, pulling me back to reality. I

glance over just as they're dropped on their ass. Bless them. The first-year students are always this keen. All of them seeking approval. Fighting to be the best in their squad, the brightest, the one with the most hopeful future.

Maybe that's why I'm dosing. Desperate for a little fun. I spent years being responsible. Staying late at training, doing extra shifts so I could send Oriana coin for Amelia. But Amelia was always reckless, a wild and free child in a way I never was. Like that time she brought home a stray cat. She hid it in the garden shed for a month, called it Scraps because she was feeding it the leftovers from dinner. Oriana lost her shit when she found out, but Amelia had fallen in love with the cat. What was I going to do? I ended up bringing it back to the Academy and looking after it for six years until it died all so she could continue to visit. She never did think anything through.

Well, maybe I'm just embodying my inner Amelia now. I've spent my life being sensible, and for what? To lose my sister to the one fucking thing I tried to protect her from.

My fingers trail over my arm, the red tallies totting up. I've added two more in the last couple of months. There's fifty-eight now. One for each kill. Though some of those tallies are creatures and not vampires. But there aren't enough drainers on my arm to satisfy the rage that pools in my gut for what they've taken from me. *Who they took.*

I make my way through the castle, past the lecture rooms and training halls. Past the student accommodation and into the staff digs. Most of the staff and trainers have other homes. Families they return to so they don't stay in the castle.

My family is dead. Or might as well be.

When Amelia turned two weeks ago, I lost everything. There's no one left now except me. I unlock my door, slide onto my bed and pull the vial out, popping it on my bedside table.

I pick up my sketchbook and a charcoal pencil and I draw. I lose myself in marking the paper, my mind wandering as I smudge lines and use my tiny putty rubber to wipe away highlights. When I'm done, I realise what I've drawn. Who I've drawn. Even without a red pencil to mark the colour of her eyes, there's no question.

I scream and throw the sketchbook across the room.

Octavia fucking Beaumont.

I hate her.

I snatch up the vial and drizzle a couple of drops under my tongue and sigh. When I glance at the vial it's empty. What the fuck? Did he trick me? Some kind of vanishing blood? There should be three-quarters of a vial left. I'll have to go back and demand a refund tomorrow. That's the last thought I have as I fall asleep; I don't even take my clothes off.

My dreams take me back to the club. The beat of the music thumping through my chest.

Beat. Beat. Beat.

Warmth at my back. Octavia fucking Beaumont.

"Don't. Get. Any closer. Most vampires this close to me end up dead," I say, repeating the words I said in the club.

Only the dream veers away from the memory. Octavia smiles against my neck, tilting her head into the crook, inhaling the scent of my skin. She spins me around, and this time, I'm slammed up against the wall.

The blade pointed at her gut is gone. Instead, it's my hand gripping her waist, a thumb skimming under the fabric of her top. It sends a pulse of heat to my groin. It's all so familiar...

No. No. No. I can't dream about her. Not like this.

"You want me," she breathes into my ear. Her words thrumming under the bass of the music.

No, I'm screaming silently. *I want to kill you.* But that's not what comes out. "Yes, I want your blood, Octavia."

She smiles, her full lips curving into a broad fang-filled grin. Her movements are quick, so fast I don't see the flash. I just smell her blood as it oozes from her wrist. She licks her lips, smearing the blood across her fangs with her tongue.

My pussy twitches.

"Use your words, Red. Tell me what you want."

But I can't. Because I shouldn't want this. It's wrong. It's immoral. It's everything hunters hate. Everything I hate.

Isn't it? But dreams aren't reality, so instead of slitting her throat as a good hunter should, an unexpected set of words slip out.

"I want to lick the blood off your fang."

This makes her eyes glint, a spark bursting to life. "Go on then, I dare you..."

I step up off the wall and into her personal space. For a cold blood, the space between us is ferociously warm. I slide my hands up and around the back of her neck. For a moment, we just hold each other in time and space. Her crimson eyes bore into me, pouring electricity and desire and something so molten and forbidden it steals the breath from my lungs and I stop breathing.

"Take it, Red. Take what you want from me."

I rise up on tiptoes, our mouths level now. Sharing the club's sticky air. She grips me suddenly. A vice-like hold keeping me balanced on my toes.

I lean in. My breathing restarts, faster now. Pumping blood around my body, throbbing between my legs. This close to her, the scent of oud and old spices mixes with the iron dribbling from her wrist. It's intoxicating. Messes with my head, I want everything. Her blood, her body. Desire swims through me. I lean in.

"Take it," she whispers as my tongue slides over my lips.

I do.

Our lips brush, a shiver runs down my spine so exquisite my eyes roll shut. Fuck. My pussy drenches my knickers.

So wrong.

My heart thuds against my ribs, making blood roar in my ears so much louder than the club's music. I can't hear anything except the rush of adrenaline and the screaming desire pushing me forward. Octavia is still as death. Allowing me to ease forward in my own time. The only reason I know she's alive is the intense grip of her fingers. A bruising hold on my arms that grows tighter with every second.

I lean in, let my tongue glide over her fang. It's cool and sharp, it nicks the fleshy pulp of my tongue. And yet it is consuming; my whole body fizzes to life as my blood mixes with hers. Her lips close over mine as her tongue slides into my mouth, caressing, dancing. Licking up every drop of blood I can give her.

She sucks my tongue into her mouth, locking me against her lips. Her eyes shut and she lets out a whimper as my blood reaches her taste buds. She snaps, releasing my mouth and lifts me off the floor and onto the table beside us. Her crimson eyes burn hot like molten furnaces.

"Delicious," she says.

"Fuck me," I say.

"You found your words," Octavia says.

I grab the buckle of her belt and pull her hard between

my legs. All my protests from the beginning of my dream have vanished.

She slides her hand behind my neck.

"I'll give you everything you want, Red... you just need to ask."

I unbuckle her belt, my heart pounding as I slip my fingers under the fabric.

A siren rips through the air.

Louder it screams. Louder.

The club lights flash on.

No. Fuck.

Not a siren. An alarm.

My alarm.

Shit.

My eyes ping open and the mortification of what I've just dreamt about sits heavy in my mind. I scream into my pillow and then drag myself to the shower. Much as I wish I didn't... I have to get rid of this lingering ache. My fingers slip through the water and between my legs.

"Fuck," I growl. I lean one hand against the wall as the other glides between my folds and up and over my clit. I grit my teeth, furious with myself, but I need to get rid of this... this... urge. It's wrong. It's probably the most fucked up thing I've ever done, touching myself like this after a dream like that.

I run the water over my face wishing the urge would leave. This is just one more reason to get rid of the addiction to blood. I wonder if the dealer sold me dodgy blood as well as some kind of magic vanishing vial. I'm definitely going to have words with them tonight.

When I'm out of the shower, watery light seeps through my window. My head throbs, a dull pulse reminding me that no matter how much I take, addiction means it's never enough.

I get dressed, make breakfast and eat in a silent fury trying to erase the dream from my memory. As I exit my flat, I bump into Lincoln.

"Red, hey. You sleep well?" he says.

"Morning," I say as he ruffles my already unruly hair. Lincoln is, without doubt, the best hunter and human I've ever met. Along with Bella, who lives in New Imperium, the closest city to us, they're my besties and I'd die for them both.

Lincoln slides an arm around my shoulder. It feels more like a tree trunk. The man is built like a castle, has a jaw that could cut diamonds and women falling at his feet twenty-four hours a day. Too bad for them, he doesn't date until he really knows a person. And I know what you're thinking.

But we haven't.

We wouldn't.

He's more like the brother I never had. Besides, I am, like, really, *deeply* into boobs. Just not boobs attached to a drainer... obviously. And don't you dare throw my dream at me, it was just a dream. Meaningless.

I pull a hand over my face trying to eradicate the memory.

"You ready for our birthday next month? I'm thinking a

huge party in that club in the Midnight Market. You know, the one that keeps all your secrets?" he says.

Lincoln and I share a birthday week. There's only three days between us, so we've always celebrated together every year since we joined the Academy. I stiffen under his grip.

"No?" he says, his voice hitching. "What's wrong with the club?"

Ahh, the Whisper Club... Octavia's territory. Of course he would pick there. But his face is so bright, his eyes twinkle at me in a way that I literally can't say no to.

"Nothing. It's a good idea. You happy to organise?" I squeeze his waist, which is like squeezing granite.

"Course. I was thinking we could invite your friend Bella and maybe some of the others from our year group, I think there's a couple of others with birthdays next month."

There's not many of our year group left, maybe a couple of dozen still working for the Academy, and we're the only two left from our specific squad.

"Sure, it's a big birthday for us all. Entering our thirties and all that. Might as well make a big deal of it." I smile, though I'm not convinced my poker face makes me look happy.

Lincoln and I came up through the Academy together but everyone else either died or moved on to work in other cities—or got bribed enough by the vampire houses to betray us and go to the other side.

Erin was the most famous of all the hunters who betrayed us, though she's a few years ahead of us. Apparently, she had a lot of potential as a hunter. But as I've learnt the last two weeks, since Amelia, everything always leads back to Octavia fucking Beaumont, including Erin.

We make our way through the castle corridors, the place is a maze. The first two weeks of any new cohort

60

we're basically support blankets for the lost and confused, poor pups.

"What are you teaching today?" Lincoln asks as we pass a new instructor and her eyes slide up Lincoln's combats and vest.

"Umm, I have the third years for defensive weapons training, and then I'm teaching basic hunter history to the new cohort until lunch."

"Sweet. I have the second years for PT for the whole morning."

"Five coins says you can't make that cocky lad puke." I grin. It's bad we do this. We probably shouldn't but sometimes the kids need to learn the hard way to keep their mouths shut.

"Six says I can do it in thirty minutes."

"Deal." I grin and shake his hand and he peels off, heading towards the PT gym.

I find my third years in the main training hall. The newbies start in the smaller halls and the longer they remain in the program, the bigger, badder and harder their training gets.

"Morning, Red," Winston, my favourite third-year, says. And yes, I'm aware favouritism is frowned upon, but get any trainer drunk and they'll confess who their favourite is. And if they don't, they're lying. Some of us prefer the ones that try hard, other trainers like the ones a little rough around the edges, those with a bit too much sass and attitude, and other trainers prefer the quiet underdogs. Those kids are always my favourites.

"Class is looking a little thin this morning, where is everyone?" I ask Winston.

The more I take Winston in, the more I realise he's looking more than a little off. He's a scrawny lad. But he's strong despite being eighty-five percent limb and bone.

He's lightning quick too, like a viper in the ring. And even though three-quarters of his squad are bigger than him, girls included, most of them don't want to train with him anymore because he's lethal.

What alerts me to the fact something is wrong are the dark bags under his eyes. The whites are shot through with capillaries. He's been crying? Even the curves of his nose are redder and raw looking.

My body is instantly tight, on alert. "What happened?"

"Chief sent a group out on a routine investigation of the border of the Montague territory last night. Sarge was with them. It was meant to be a standard recon. Practicing for the finals."

"Okay..."

"Three students are missing, presumed dead."

"Shit. What the hell attacked them?"

"We don't know," Winston says and his eyes well up. My fingers twitch. It's not really the done thing for me to give him a hug, but it hurts seeing him so devastated. I don't want my students in pain. I want to fix it.

He continues. "Sarge managed to drag Janie out and halfway back to the hunter territory before collapsing. They're both in the medical wing after the early morning patrol found them."

"Oh shit, Winston."

Winston shakes his head and wipes his nose. I can't watch him like this anymore. I pull him in and wrap my arms around him. I'm short at the best of times, and he's like two feet taller than me, but I hug him anyway. He buckles in my arms, a huge sob ripping from his chest as he trembles against me.

"My... my girlfriend is in the group that didn't make it back," he sobs into my chest.

And now I understand why he's cut up so deep. We all

cope with grief in such different ways. It's a strange, unpredictable emotion.

"I want to help. Do you want to talk? You need to hurt? Want to go to a different class?"

He lets me go and wipes his face. "I want to train so hard I can't feel anything, not even the ache in my chest."

"Okay, buddy. You got it. Get the group to run two laps of the grounds, I'll get the stakes. We'll do close combat weapons defence this morning."

He nods, his lips a thin line. "Thank you."

I wave him off and head to the gym cupboard. He's already barking commands and sounding more like his usual self.

I catch sight of the group as Winston swings the gym door open and they all, without exception, look various shades of shit. Red eyes, exhausted bags and sad expressions. But Winston sets off at a gruelling pace and not one of them complains.

I open to the storeroom and pull out a set of stakes, nunchuks and batons. Then I put the padded body suit on so they can batter the shit out of me until they feel better. I can't make what happened go away, but I can do this.

By the time I've clambered into the suit, they're back.

"First round is two of you against one of me. The first person or team to knock me on my ass wins," I say.

Of course, they're clumsy, both rushing me instead of working together to allow one of them to take the win. Which means I knock the first three groups down in about three seconds flat. I drill them until they're dripping with sweat and red-faced. But their expressions are lighter.

"Round two. Stake drills." I hand rubber stakes out and pair them up in front of the body bags. "Aim here, hit *hard* or you won't break through a drainer's ribs."

They practice till their training kits are soaked with

rings of sweat. When I think their muscles are nicely aching, I up the ante.

"Right. Round three. We're taking what we just learnt and now we're practicing it in one-on-one sparring." I demonstrate the throw down with Winston in one liquid movement. The second time, I slow it right down. "See here. Use the momentum of the takedown to push the stake through the vamp's heart."

The students line up.

"Five full three-minute rounds. Winner is the first one to get their opponent on the floor with a clear strike to the chest."

This is the clincher. Sparring usually is. The first girl spews on round three. I get another four students hurling their guts up after the fourth round. But finally, on the fifth round, Winston runs to the hall door, drops on all fours and hurls on the concrete. I half wish I'd bet Lincoln I'd be the one to get the students chundering. But never mind.

Despite the vomiting, all of them, without exception, seem a little brighter than they did at the start. Endorphins are an amazing thing.

As the class disbands, Winston helps me pack away the body bags and stakes. He pauses after handing me the last pile of batons as if he wants to say something.

"Just…" he hesitates and then nods. "Thanks. That's all. You're the best, Red."

"You're welcome. Stay safe, Winston."

I finish up in the gymnasium and head to see the Chief. But there's a commotion in the entrance hall.

I stop dead, all the air rushing out of my lungs.

Standing in the door to the Hunter Academy is Cordelia St Clair. The first, oldest, and most dangerous vampire in the city.

"What. The. Fuck?"

CHAPTER 6

RED

Cordelia St Clair, not only in hunter territory, but our fucking Academy building? It's unheard of. It's... There's no time. My instincts kick in.

I shove the students out of the way. Hollering at them to get back. This has to be an attack. Why the fuck didn't our guards detect her?

I smash my fist into the emergency alarm on the side wall and bellow at the kids to move the fuck back. More trainers pour into the foyer, now all doing the same. Shoving students back and forming a defensive line.

Cordelia hasn't moved. She's frozen in that unnerving way vampires have. How the fuck did she breach our defensive perimeters? Why the hell is she here in person? We have annual peace negotiations for this shit.

Lincoln swerves into position next to me, his arms out wide protecting the kids behind us. Finally, the Chief appears, breathless, clearly having run from her tower.

She skids to a halt in the hallway, her face darkening to

a violent shade of purple. The alarms cut out, but the after-burn of their ringing still echoes in my ears.

"What in the name of blood are you doing in here?" the Chief barks.

I cringe.

The balls of steel she has to speak to Cordelia like that. I've heard the stories about her. I hear she tears apart her staff for less than an incorrectly timed eyebrow twitch.

But Cordelia doesn't even flinch at the Chief's words. Instead, the vampire's eyes flick to the Chief, a snarl on her lips.

"I've come in peace, *Chief*. I bring an invitation," Cordelia says.

"And you didn't think to use the proper channels? The official ones that don't set our security screaming."

Cordelia's expression narrows. "There are no laws preventing my being here, and I've harmed no one... Besides, this is time sensitive."

"Oh. Well, that's okay then," the Chief drawls, her eyes practically falling out of her head.

Cordelia shifts her position, she moves so fast that a student behind us screams. Which unleashes another round of hysteria that takes the Chief and all the trainers bellowing at everyone to be calm before quiet is restored.

In Cordelia's hand is a claret-coloured envelope.

The Chief steps forward and snatches the envelope out of Cordelia's hand. "If I find out the students that died last night were at the hands of your vampires, I swear on the Mother of Blood herself, I will come for you, Cordelia."

Cordelia's expression twitches and shifts. Her head tilts to the side. "Were they lost in the Montague territory?"

The Chief's pallor deepens, red climbing her neck. "I knew it was you." She steps up to Cordelia, right in her face.

I think I might be sick. She's going to get herself killed

being that close, that confrontational. But Cordelia surprises me by stepping back.

She shakes her head, her features drooping. "Then this invitation is even more important than I first feared."

"What the hell does that mean?" the Chief asks.

"It wasn't me who took your students. I, too, lost several men last night. Good vampires. It appears that we may have a common enemy, Chief. I do hope you can find it in your heart to attend tomorrow. Despite our differences, I believe we can help each other here."

My mouth drops open and I blink. But by the time my eyes are open again, Cordelia has vanished, and the hall erupts into chaos.

The Chief barks orders. "Lincoln, Fenella, Keir... check the security gates and guards. I want to know exactly how the hell she breached our security." She turns to another set of trainers. "Talulla, take the others and get the kids back to their rooms, guards on all the dorm entrances and exits. Classes are cancelled the rest of the afternoon. If she's gotten in once, there's no telling if she will do it again. I want every student on lockdown."

She summons me to follow her. We head towards the west tower and climb up the stone spiral staircase. The receptionist waves us both through, and I follow after the Chief into her circular office.

This is the highest turret in the castle. Long rectangular windows, wider than a normal castle window, are carved into the circular walls. They shower the room in beams of light. A third of the walls are covered by tall bookcases, a ladder running across them. Three stakes with dried, crusted blood are mounted on a piece of decorative wood and line the wall behind the Chief's desk.

Each of those stakes killed a significant vampire, though the first stake's victim she doesn't talk about.

She sits behind her large oak desk and indicates I should join her and take the chair opposite.

"That was…" I start.

"Yes. It was. I'm going to need you to run a full diagnostics report on the Academy's security."

"No problem, I'll do that this afternoon. I know our wards were holding just fine yesterday."

"Yes, but there's very little magic in those."

She's right, of course. There's very little magic of any kind in our world now. There used to be, until vampires were created a thousand years ago and our dhampir healers were drained of power to do it. We use what little there is in the best ways we can now.

The Chief huffs and folds her arms. "Even a fresh drainer newly turned could get through those sodding wards without too much damage if they were really determined. It's the guards I'm pissed with. I want you to check the records of the patrols. The shift changeovers. Someone should have seen something. A millennia old vampire doesn't just get into the fucking Academy without anyone seeing."

"Unless she was so fast there was no way we'd have seen her?"

The Chief glares at me so I backtrack.

"Noted. I'll have a report ready for you by evening."

She flips the envelope Cordelia gave her over. "What the hell is she playing at?" she growls.

"Are you going to open it? Maybe you should let me, what if there's poison or something inside it?"

The Chief moves to hand it over and then pulls back. "No. In that case, I'll definitely open it. Cordelia can't mess with me, she knows I'd make her life a misery."

The Chief has one of those ageless faces. I'm not quite sure how old she is. Her skin is pure and wrinkle free. Her eyes, though, they hold a lifetime of stress and responsibility. They age her beyond the smoothness of her features.

She sniffs the envelope but seems satisfied so opens it and reads:

Cordelia St Clair cordially invites you to a ball in the Midnight Market.

All vampire nobles and senior hunters should attend. Consider this an additional peace talk. On my word, no blood will be drawn. I will be making an announcement that affects the entire city, and your presence is required at 9 p.m. sharp at the Whisper Club.

Yours in Blood,
Cordelia St Clair.

I whistle. "Well, shit."

"Have Lincoln run the security report. I need you to go straight to the Midnight Market and assess the Whisper Club. I need to know every entrance and exit. I want a full brief on the security forces we have."

"I don't think we should take every senior hunter either. This could be an ambush."

"Agreed." She pauses, looks me up and down and thrusts the card at me. "It's black tie. I'm assuming you're more of a suit than a dress girl."

I nod.

"Have the quartermaster see if they can tailor you a suit in time. One way or another, we'll know what the hell is going on by tomorrow night."

CHAPTER 7

OCTAVIA

Mother has turned the entire club into a farce. Instead of the usual dim lighting, moody rouges and dark furniture, the place is bright and full of fucking crystal chandeliers.

"Come now, sister, it could be worse," Gabriel says as he slides next to me on the mezzanine, a bag of books over his shoulder. He folds his arms.

"And how's that? Look at the state of my club."

"Oh, it could be worse, it could be in the library archive."

I glare at him. "Clearly that is not worse."

He shrugs, nonchalant, "It would be for me. I'm quite content with this."

"You're an arsehole of the highest proportions."

"Takes one to know one, Octavia."

I huff out a frustrated noise and leave him to read in one of the booths. I slide down the stairs, my hand unable to grip the rail for all the twinkling fucking fairy lights. At least these are red, I suppose.

Red. Fucking Red. I knew two weeks ago saving her sister was a mistake. It's happening all over again. I swore this would be the last time.

Someone barges into me. A decorator.

I growl, and the man startles, drops his box and dashes out of my way.

"Useless," I snarl.

Mother's decorators need executing. There are gaudy white and cream curtains draped across the usually black and maroon walls. Brightening up the place. Chandeliers have been drilled into my glass ceiling, everything sparkles and twinkles like a fairytale ball. It's disgusting.

The club's usual bass music is replaced with stringed instruments and an orchestral band. Xavier appears at the bottom of the stairs, his dark eyebrow set to firmly raised.

"This is…"

"A travesty?" I finish for him.

"Quite. Where are the donors? I'm hungry."

"Ugh," I tut at him. "Mother requested the removal of all cages. Then she gave all donors and all dancers paid leave. She said she wants this to be a civilised affair, and she didn't feel the hunters would be welcome if we had half a dozen vampires slipping into blood lust or fucking half drained humans on the dance floor."

"Gods, she's gotten boring in her age," Xavier says and that, at least, elicits a laugh from me. He glances down at me, the ballgown I'm wearing.

"Wow, you actually do scrub up half decent. You're looking ravishing this evening," he says and offers me his arm.

"Thank you," I say and jostle my outfit. My breasts are sat high in this corset, bulging over a little. The silk sheen of the skirts flows over my arse and thighs. There's a slit that is dangerously close to impolite cut over my right thigh. I like the way my leg slips out of it.

"No date tonight?" I ask him.

"Well, I thought I'd take one of the donors, but apparently not. I guess I'll have to find a nice hunter to debase. How about you? You're looking far too delicious not to get laid this evening."

"Thank you, Xavier, but no. I think I shall keep my modesty intact tonight. I'm far too preoccupied with A) getting my club back, and B) finding out what Mother is up to."

"It doesn't look like you've long to wait…" he says and points at the club doors as a mob of people enter, humans, hunters, vampire nobles alike, they all come pouring in. The orchestra ratchets up a notch. I spot Dahlia, looking actually rather tasteful in a deep navy dress suit and dicky bow. It's tight to her physique, her arms and shoulders bulging in the slim-fitting attire. Even if she's a prick, I'll have to remember to tell her she looks nice this evening.

"Where's Sadie?" Xavier asks.

I nod to a booth in the corner of the room. Sadie's wearing a shimmering, floor-length, deep maroon-coloured dress, a stark contrast to her white hair.

Amelia, Red's sister, appears, carrying a goblet of blood. "Evening," she says.

Xavier takes the goblet from her. "Thanks, I'm dying for food."

"Rude," she says and nudges him, then takes the goblet back and sinks the rest of the dregs in the cup.

The three of us have formed somewhat of an alliance. Amelia is still so fresh as a vampire I feel it my duty to ensure she doesn't fuck up. It's not something I usually consider, but then I very rarely Turn anyone. This was…

different. And what I value, Xavier tends to value, so he accepted Amelia immediately.

"She was here last night," Amelia says. "Wouldn't talk to me though."

"I know," I say and then fall silent because I'm not sure what else to add. Amelia knows... I told her everything last night after she saw Red. She thinks I should tell her. But I can't. It doesn't work like that. Not after what I did.

But that's a story for a different day.

When I turn back to my club, the dance floor is already full. Mother is on stage. I find myself scanning the room looking for Red.

I know she's found me before I've found her because my back itches like I'm being watched. Amelia shifts next to me.

"I should go," she says, her eyes drooping.

"You need to talk to her," I say.

"Don't you think I've tried?"

"Try again."

"Octavia..."

"Amelia."

Her jaw flexes, her eyes flaring bright. They're bluer than Red's, which are the most vivid green I've ever seen. But both sisters hold the same fire in their gaze.

"This wasn't just me. I might have started this cycle, but this started long before me. It's your responsibility to fix this just as much as it is mine," she says. She glances at the corner of the room and then vanishes up the staircase and out of sight.

I track across to the corner where Amelia was looking and find Red. I'm momentarily speechless. She's wearing a suit that's just as tailored as Dahlia's. While Red is short, the suit has tapered trouser legs that make her appear long and elegant despite her stature. Red's shoulders and arms are defined under the suit's shape. She wears a white shirt, nowhere near buttoned up enough. In fact, I can see her cleavage from here. I stiffen, uncomfortable with the way my body responds to this revelation. Uncomfortable with how familiar it is.

Our eyes lock.

My hand skirts to my own chest. My fingers tracing the scar over my heart...

The one she gave me.

The one that nearly ended me.

The one she doesn't remember.

"Excuse me, Xavier. I'll be back," I say and leave before he can stop me.

I move fast enough around the club Red can't follow me, but I follow her. The realisation that I've vanished spreads across her features in slow motion. *Too late, little hunter, I'm already behind you.*

Her heart senses me before her mind realises. The deep *thud, thud, thud,* the sweet scent of adrenaline filling her veins.

"Well, don't you look delicious enough to eat this evening," I whisper into her ear.

She startles, then tries to cover it by spinning on her heels to face me. This time, I'm the one backed against the club wall.

Her eyes drop to my cleavage, her tongue slides over her lips and then she shakes herself and steps back.

"See something you like?" I purr.

"Only a scar that should have been a cause of death." She smiles, a sour little thing on a mouth like that. It makes me want to do things. To push her to her knees and make her beg. "How'd you get that?"

I lurch off the wall, but she pushes me back against it.

"Such a vicious little temper you have. And to think I came all the way over here to tell you that you looked dashing, dapper even," I say.

She rolls her eyes and turns her back on me.

"Dangerous move for a hunter... turning your back on a vampire."

"You're not going to hurt me," she says, refusing to face me.

"And why's that?"

"Because you like playing with me, Octavia. This is just a game to you. All of it. The club. My sister. Every fucking spat we've had the last two weeks. It means nothing to you." This time Red does turn around but only to point a finger at me.

"You and your fucking family with all your power and your castles. You're surrounded by everyone and everything. Brothers, sisters. A Mother. You have land and titles, butlers and blood. Whatever you want is at your fingertips. And still it's not enough for you. You had to take the one thing I had left. You stole my sister and I'll never forgive you for that..."

"You think you're so alone... That I have ev—"

But I'm cut off by the sound of Cordelia's voice clearing her throat over the microphone.

How can she think I have everyone? She knows nothing. I have Xavier and maybe Amelia now. But I'm feared by most everyone in this city, hated by the rest. She thinks she's suffering, try a thousand years of isolation, of being told you're a freak, unlovable all because you were born different. A hardness settles in my gut. This isn't the end of the conversation.

"Good evening nobles, hunters, humans... If I may have your attention, please," Cordelia says and someone, Dahlia probably—kiss-ass—clinks a fork against a glass until the room grows quiet.

"I've asked you all here this evening as I fear we are in grave danger as a city. Humbly, as a servant of this city, I ask for your help. But first. I need to tell you a story..."

CHAPTER 8

CORDELIA

I'm doing the right thing, I know I am. I shift on stage. What choice do I have? This is the only way to stop everything from unravelling.

I take a deep breath, brush down my cream ballgown and look out at the crowd. It's show time.

"I've always been fond of antiquities. When you're as old as I am, memories fade, their edges fraying and blurring. It becomes difficult to hold on to them when their essence is slippery. Which is why I like antiques. You can attach a memory to the object, and it holds steadier, like an anchor.

"I was searching for antiques in the Montague territory thirty years ago. Many of you will remember that the city used to be fully accessible. There was no magical boundary preventing us from accessing the heart of the territory."

There's a murmur of agreement from the older hunters and most of the vampires. When it dies down, I continue.

"But what many of you won't know, is that I was there the night the boundary was created."

There's an audible gasp in the room. I close my eyes, letting the memories flood over me and begin to tell them my story.

Thirty Years Ago

Night washes over me, bathing my skin in pale beams only the moon and stars can. The Montague territory is peaceful this evening. The large lake in the heart of the territory is calm save for a few bubbles from the koi beneath the surface. I traipse through the maze-like streets towards the ancient castle at the heart.

I'm here because Isabella's heirs have a grimoire I want. Before she was turned, Isabella, the witch who cursed me, had dhampir apprentices, and this grimoire in particular is rumoured to have belonged to one of them. I'm not holding out hope that it will contain the cure to her curse. But anything could be a clue, so I'll treat it as such until I prove otherwise.

Unfortunately, as I step onto the grounds of the castle, I'm halted. I stretch my fingers out, testing and prodding the air, uncertain as to why I can't move forward. But there's no perimeter, no fizz of weak magic in the air. I'm just stopped and no matter how hard I try and push forward, I cannot.

Isabella's heirs stumble out of the castle and onto the driveway. All of them bearing the same startled expression I fear I'm wearing.

"What's going on?" I shout across the courtyard.

But my words are swallowed as if I never produced them. More of her heirs appear on the porch now. A cluster of ten or so. All of them wearing deep frowns.

The man at the front waves. His mouth moves but I

can't hear anything. I wave back and he turns to those behind him, but they're all nonplussed.

The air shifts, there's a crack of thunder and the ground rumbles as if it's tearing itself in two. And I suppose, in a way, it is. Between us, the courtyard fractures and tears, a thin fissure appearing down the middle, separating them from me.

Their eyes widen. My mouth falls open. This is no longer worth it. I care more for my life than the grimoire.

I step back, but my feet don't move. I'm frozen in place. My heart hammers in my chest. Blood pounds through my veins, I need to get out of here. I yank at my feet. Try to punch the gravel around my boots to force it to release me.

Nothing works.

The earth rumbles, shakes, and then through the widening cavern in the courtyard, creeping plants whip up, lashing at the air as they mat and intertwine. Her heirs stand aghast, some with hands over their mouths, others unable to watch.

The green stems twist and plait, interlocking. They're forming something, *growing* something. Faster now, more and more burst up through the earth and mesh with those already in place. It starts on the ground, as if the crack in the earth contains the roots.

A frame appears and I realise what the plants are making.

A door.

It's an enormous, ornate door. More and more vines erupt from the earth and slither their way towards the frame. They grow darker, harden into woody limbs and branches. The door has lower panels now, a handle, a lock.

But then something more. Words appear, etching themselves onto the door. A burst of light and sparks erupts as the words ignite and burn the wooden branches until the words are black scars upon the door. I pull a scroll and ink from my satchel and write as fast as I can, not wanting to miss a single letter.

And this is what it said:

Behold the Door of Destiny, forged in realms unknown,
　　Guardian of secrets, in its magic it is sown.
　　A portal bound by time, an enigma to explore,
　　Yet heed this warning, for thirty years it stands, no more.
　　Blood of the night, a child of two worlds' embrace,
　　A dhampir born, a dhampir turned. The heir to unlock this sacred space.
　　For millennia dormant, the door now stirs.
　　Only the worthy may approach,
　　Only the true heir.
　　In shadows they walk, with pulse of sun and moon,
　　The first of their kind, with fangs that hunger and a heart that beats,
　　They alone shall open the door and reveal the grimoire secret within.
　　The prophecy whispers of this sole chance,
　　For the rightful heir to undo the city's dance.
　　But heed, oh seeker, the sands of time are swift,
　　Thirty years' span, and then the door shall lift.
　　Open the portal, reveal the truth concealed,
　　Or lose forever the chance for Sangui's fate be healed.

Once the last word was scorched into the door, the earth stopped rumbling. The door was complete. My feet released from where they were being held. I took one step forward and the world exploded.

White blinding light burst from the heart of the door and expelled everything and everyone out of the vicinity. I

80

was flung, pushed, propelled out of the castle grounds. Further and further. Flung through the air like a rag. Yanked away from the door by a shimmering boundary pushing and pulling me away.

Until I was so far from the door, I could no longer see it.

There, the magic rested, sealing the door and the heart of the Montague territory behind a boundary that none of us have crossed in thirty years.

My story ends, and I come out of my memories, finding myself back in my eldest daughter's Whisper Club, the entire room stony silent. At least the story had the impact I needed.

I clear my throat and continue.

"Those thirty years are almost over. And that is why I'm here. And why I need us to work together. As a city, we must unlock that boundary and open the door because what lays behind it is the keeper of all of our fates."

CHAPTER 9

OCTAVIA

"Those thirty years are almost over. And that is why I'm here. And why I need us to work together. As a city, we must unlock that boundary and open the door because what lays behind it is the keeper of all of our fates," Mother says.

She pauses and I know what comes next is the bomb she's been waiting to drop. I tense.

Mother takes a deep breath. "During these trials, there will be a strict peace accord. There will be no war, no fights between our species under pain of death."

There it is.

Mayhem erupts through the club. Nobles are jeering and gasping in shock. The hunters are drawing weapons, confusion ripples through the dance floor, the humans are scrambling to leave. My mother has to be on drugs. This is insane if she thinks any of the hunters will buy this. Hell, I'm not even sure I buy it. Working together for some random door that no one but her knows about? She's lost her mind. But she also needs to get a grip on this situation before my club ends up destroyed because a riot breaks out.

The Chief marches onto the stage. But Mother raises her hands, a gesture of peace, and several of her guards step up to the perimeter of the dance floor. The hunters move fast; stakes drawn, their bodies form a tight circle in front of the vampire guards.

Red tenses like she's going to pounce. I grab her on instinct, my fingers pressing in above her elbow.

She glances back at me when I hold her in place.

"What the hell are you doing?" she snaps.

"Don't. This is... dangerous," I say under my breath.

Her features crinkle. "Exactly. I need to go help them."

"You could be hurt."

She tries to shuck me off her but I hold tighter, hard enough to bruise. "What in the actual fuck do you care?"

"Because..." but words fail me. How was I planning on explaining?

"Descriptive, Octavia. Well done for using your words."

My nostrils flare. "If someone is going to kill you, it will be me. And until then, I don't want you injured."

She shakes her head at me, I'm not sure if she's furious or suppressing a laugh. "You're the most fucked up vampire I've ever met."

This time Red spins into me and holds her stake right over my scar. "Now get the fuck off me, before I give you a scar that's even more permanent."

I lean into Red. Her pupils are blown. "So feisty, and yet your body is your traitor."

"Just the remnants of a dream I had last night," she growls.

"You're dreaming about me?"

"Only in my nightmares."

"So cute. Terrible liar, though," I whisper.

Cordelia's voice bellows over the crowd, "Peace. I demand peace or I will compel you into obedience."

That makes the room acquiesce into silence. Red releases me but stands by my side as Cordelia continues to talk.

"Guards, stand down. I do not want the hunters hurt. Hunters, I kindly request you allow me to finish explaining my plan before you decide on whether to slaughter my guards."

The Chief's jaw flexes. But she gives a curt nod and the hunters back down. "Get to the point, Cordelia." She's practically snarling stood next to her. The mic she's near amplifies the rage tenfold. Two vampire guards appear at the back of the stage.

"This is going to get ugly unless Mother hurries proceedings along," I breathe.

"What makes you think we won't enjoy that?" Red says, but before I can come back, Mother continues.

"Judge me as you may, but for thirty years, I've held this knowledge back, hoping I wouldn't have to share it. That the door would simply vanish after the years passed. But it seems that someone attempted to breach the boundary last night and both the Chief and I lost valuable men and women. We can no longer standby and do nothing. This is why I bring it to your attention now. We must breach the boundary before our enemies do."

"Why should we care about the door and what's inside it anyway?" the Chief says.

Cordelia's shoulders sag, her face drops and for a split second I actually buy the act.

"Because I'm tired. Are you not exhausted of this... this... charade?" Cordelia gestures between herself and the Chief.

The Chief narrows her eyes, trying to work out what game she's playing, what the real play is, and I do the same.

Red glances at me, confusion written in the lines across her brow.

Cordelia shifts position and turns to the crowd. "I am tired of war. And I am here to formally announce my retirement. It is my last wish to foster peace between our two species for the first time in history. And in order to do that, I formally request that the Chief also step down from her role."

A gasp rips through the room. The Chief takes a step back, her eyebrows practically climbing off her forehead.

"Did you know?" Red breathes.

"No," I whisper back. "I had no fucking clue."

"How dare you," the Chief says and her posture jerks forward as if she's going to attack. The two vampire guards behind Cordelia are on the Chief in seconds, swords crossed under her chin.

"Stand down," Cordelia says, touching one of them on the arm.

Reluctantly they shift back and release the Chief.

"Please..." Cordelia says, pleading in her tone and then turns to the audience, her face sweet and light. "I beg you to let me finish before you pass judgement. All our fates lie in your hands, Chief."

Oh, that canny bitch.

"Motherfucker," Red hisses.

"Come on, it was a good play. Even if it was manipulative," I whisper.

Red's teeth grind against each other.

"Fine. What are you proposing?" the Chief says, folding her arms a distinct expression of violence reflected in the hard lines of her neck and jaw.

Cordelia stands a little straighter and opens her arms. "Together, we break the barrier. Teams of two: one of my vampire children and one of your senior hunters. We run a series of trials to collect the items we need to break the barrier spell. And then..."

"Then..." Chief says, leaning forward.

"The winning team that reaches the door and opens it first, becomes our heirs."

The Chief bursts out laughing. "An-An-And what in blood's name makes you think we'd go along with such an audacious plan like that?"

Cordelia's face turns serious "Well, if new leadership and rolling in an era of peace isn't carrot enough, then how about this: *and reveal the grimoire secret within.*

The prophecy whispers of this sole chance, For the rightful heir to undo the city's dance."

She lets the words hang between them.

"The cure?" the Chief says.

Cordelia nods. "Behind that door lays a grimoire containing the curse that made me and the cure that will break me. Unbind... unmake all of our kind."

A shiver runs through the crowd. Through hunters, humans and vampires alike. This cure... it would change our world. Beside me, Red's shoulders tense. And I suspect she's thinking of her sister.

"Unmake?" Chief breathes.

"Indeed. I offer you the cure for vampirism. On one condition..." Cordelia says.

"Which is?" the Chief replies.

"That you let the vampires offer themselves voluntarily. Should they want to return to their mortality, then it must be their choice. Perhaps your hunters can even administer the cures."

"Their choice? Their fucking choice? You hypocrite. How many of my hunters, how many humans have you turned against their free will?" The Chief is snarling.

Cordelia smiles, a malice-filled expression that makes

her grey eyes sharp as blades. "All of them. But this is my condition. Or... you can just not participate, and I'll keep what I know to myself. That way, the door and the cure will be lost to us all in... oh, what was it?" She looks at her watch in the most dramatic fashion. "Ah yes, three weeks' time."

The Chief's jaw flexes so hard I can see the bones of her face grinding against each other. There's a long, heavy pause.

"Well played, Mother," I whisper.

Red is shaking her head. "No wonder she wanted to do this in public, she's backed the Chief into a corner."

I can hear the Chief's mind whirring from the back of the club. I'll bet good coin on the fact she's trying to find a way around this. I'm guessing she doesn't manage it because she slides a hand onto her hip.

"Explain the teams and whatever farcical nonsense you wish us to participate in."

Mother's grin is practically feral. "In order to access the door, we will work together over the next three weeks to collate the four items needed to break the boundary spell. Then, in the final days leading up to the door destroying itself, we'll challenge the teams to a duel of strength. The winners receive a time benefit when we set them off to reach the door. The victors who open the door become our heirs. Simple."

"And how do we choose the teams?" the Chief says.

"That is simple too. First, my five children will be the vampire half. Then, we'll need your hunters. Specific ones meeting certain criteria..."

The Chief's eyes narrow and gaze off into the back of the room. "*Blood of the night, a child of two worlds' embrace...?*"

"You're a quick study, Chief. The rest goes, '*A dhampir born, a dhampir turned.*' And then the next relevant lines are:

In shadows they walk, with pulse of sun and moon, The first of their kind, with fangs that hunger and a heart that beats, they alone shall open the door and reveal the grimoire secret within."

"You think the chosen dhampir is a hunter?" the Chief says.

"Oh, please." Mother rolls her eyes.

The Chief bristles. "Fine. I'll agree that there's some evidence to suggest hunters are born of the dhampir line."

"How magnanimous of you," Mother says, her features twitching as if she's trying to suppress the more impolite sentences. "How many hunters do you have that are almost thirty? My suspicion is that the door wasn't created spontaneously. I suspect the chosen dhampir was born that night..."

The Chief frowns and turns to the audience. "Hunters?"

"Shit," Red breathes next to me.

"Well, well, well," I purr.

She glares at me but steps forward into the light of the chandelier and raises her hand.

Another man built like a mansion slides up next to her.

"What the hell is going on, Lincoln?" Red says.

The man, Lincoln, scrunches his face up and shakes his head at her. Two more women step forward and raise their hands and another male.

"That's it?" Chief says.

"Would you look at that. Five for five," Cordelia says. "Then, I guess we have our teams."

CHAPTER 10

I've waited such a long time for this moment. For this game to finally play out. Such a fool waiting this long to confess your sins, Cordelia...

To confess that you've known about this door since its creation. And more of a fool if you think ten days is enough to break the barrier.

I thought you were better than this. I guess not.

Never mind.

Lower yourself to working with these peasants, but if you think you'll get to the door before me, you're mistaken.

Teaming up with your enemy?

Pathetic.

It won't last.

Ten days and then I'll win, once and for all...

CHAPTER 11

RED

I wake up the morning after the ball, my stomach lined with dread. One, because I need to go back to the Midnight Market tonight to clock the idiot who sold me weak blood. Two, because I need to pull the Chief aside and ask her what the hell she's thinking agreeing to let us partner with fucking vampires for some ridiculous set of trials for some cure that probably doesn't exist. And third, because Lincoln has left me a report on the security breach yesterday and there's no good news in there either.

I climb the west tower until I reach the Chief's outer room. Her receptionist waves to me and indicates I sit down.

There's a tray of cookies on the coffee table. I take one and bite it. They're warm, and it crumbles in my mouth, sending me back to childhood. Mama always used to bake cookies on our birthdays; it was a tradition and we got to decorate them in icing and sweets. Of course, Amelia would always make it descend into a food fight and Mama would always pretend to be mad as she scrubbed us in the bath.

She never was, I could tell from the smirk curled in the corner of her mouth.

But the last year before Mum died, we couldn't afford all the extras. So Mama baked one bigger cookie and the three of us shared it with hot lemon tea next to the fire. Even though there was only a third of a cookie each, it still tasted just as good.

My eyes well and I rub my face as the Chief's door opens and Fenella walks out.

She gives me a curt nod. Her reddish hair is braided in plaits and twisted into an elaborate up-do over the top of her head. It's pretty if a little inconvenient as a hunter.

"Red, morning, or I should say, afternoon now," Chief says as she checks her watch. I follow after her into her circular office. Warm midday light showers her desk and carpet as she sits behind her large oak desk.

As usual, I take the chair opposite.

"Any word from Lincoln?" she starts before I can even begin to question what the hell last night was.

I hand over the report he slipped under my apartment door. Her face crinkles, the lines growing deeper the more she reads. She groans as her eyes scan the final paragraphs.

"Make sure we have additional security on during guard shift changes. I want you to fortify the tunnels with the automatic stake weapons, line the barriers with silver."

"Done," I say and shift in my seat because the thing I'm really here to talk about is thick between us.

"Anything else?" Chief says.

"You know there is..."

"Out with it," she says and lays her hands on the desk.

I lean forward, searching for the right words. The right phrases to not sound totally insubordinate questioning her decisions. "I... er. It's about last night."

She huffs, her lips scrunching together. "I assumed it would be."

I decide to be strategic about this, I don't want to question her so much as the security issue... which is legitimately my job to do. "Well, from a strictly safety perspective, this is an unmitigated disaster."

"I disagree. There's only five of you that will have to partner with the drainers, and all of you are senior and highly qualified, highly trained hunters."

"Yes, and we're going to have to be left with five of the most dangerous vampires in the city. We barely get through the annual peace talks without someone getting staked or a hunter being drained. How do you expect us to partner with them?"

"I expect you to do your job. Think of it as undercover work. Get close, find out everything you can and report back."

"So you do think it's a ploy to get inside our ranks? You don't think the door is real?"

This makes the Chief scoff. "Oh, the door is real. I heard of its appearance shortly after the boundary was created. I'm certain that it's a ploy of some kind. Cordelia wouldn't just 'retire.' She's been head of the vampires for a thousand years. People like that don't just retire. They get power, they covet it, crave it and horde it."

"And when they can't get any more?" I ask.

"What does any leader do on their way out...? Burn it all to the ground."

That makes both of us pause.

"Shit."

The Chief nods. "But if we know that she either has no intention of retiring, or has an alternative plan, then maybe we can use this situation to our advantage. How many hunters have we lost over the years trying to penetrate through to the inner layers of Cordelia's house?"

"Too many."

"Exactly. But now we have a chance for our hunters, senior ones no less, to be inside her inner circle."

I don't like this. I run my hand through my hair. "We're not trained for undercover operations. We're trained for close combat and defence. What if they take the cure from the grimoire and leave us for dead?"

"Then we get to it first."

This time, I'm the one who scoffs. The Chief leans forward over her desk.

"Not only are we getting to that cure first, we're going to secure it and find a way to replicate it en masse. We could cure anyone, everyone. We could wipe vampires off the face of the city. Hell, Red, you could cure your sister."

I open my mouth. I shut it again. Of course I told the Chief the day it happened. She consoled me, let me cry it out and then took me to the gym and sparred with me until I passed out.

My sister? Fuck. I could really get her back.

"Isn't that what you want? To be able to cure her? Turn her back? Give Amelia her humanity again?"

That's the only thing I want. It's my fault she was turned. I didn't get there fast enough. Couldn't save her. Just like I couldn't save my mother from the drainers and couldn't convince my father to stay with us.

Maybe I can do this one thing. Maybe I can enter, accept the challenge and for once, actually save someone I care about.

"I'll have to work with the drainers, though."

The Chief nods, her face severe. "I know. There's nothing we can do about that. But perhaps we can see it as an undercover operation of sorts. You can report back anything you discover. We can make the most of this situation and gain as much intel on Cordelia's enterprise as possible."

I nod, sitting up in my chair, finally feeling more enthusiastic about it.

"Just don't partner me with Octavia."

The Chief frowns at me. "Why not?"

"Because I don't know if I can keep my hands to myself."

The Chief raises her eyebrow.

I roll my eyes. "Not like that. She's the one who turned Amelia. It will be hard not to stake her in her sleep."

"Ah, I see. I don't know how the partnerships will be established, but I will do my best to prevent that from happening."

"Thank you."

A sheen of sweat lines my brow, my hands tremble. It's been a while since I took any blood. Shit. I forgot I needed to go back and deal with the idiot who sold me half a dose. Now is not really the time for me to go into withdrawal in the Chief's office.

I slip my hands beneath the desk and grip them hard to hide the tremor.

"I need to go," I say. "Is there anything else you need?"

The Chief shakes her head. "Dismissed."

I shove the chair back and hustle out of there as calmly as I can and head back to my rooms to get the empty vial that idiot sold me. I grab two stakes and two blades for good measure, slipping them into the pockets on the side of my leather trousers. Exiting the Academy, I head out towards the Midnight Market, my body wracked with tremors and the heat of rage pooling between my ribs. Someone is going to get hurt over this.

CHAPTER 12

OCTAVIA

E rin slides a tumbler of vodka across the bar, then pours herself another and takes the stool next to me.

"What the fuck was that last night?" she grunts.

"I think Mother has finally gone and lost her mind."

Erin leans over the bar, her broad shoulders hunching as she swills the vodka in her glass. "Not that. I mean the disrespect she showed you." Her voice is kind of gravelly for a woman, like she ate stones for breakfast.

"Ah. That."

"It was..."

"Unexpected?" I say, taking an excessive slurp of vodka.

"That's an understatement. I thought it was clear. Given your status as one of the original three, I assumed if she ever retired, you'd be the one to take over..."

"Yes, well, it's clear that means nothing to her."

Erin scratches the back of her freshly shaved hair. It's shorn tight and all the way up the sides, the top is longer and slicked back neat. Her mouth pinches. "She's a bit of a bitch, if you ask me."

I snuff out a laugh. "There's not many people who would have the balls to say that about Cordelia."

Erin shrugs. "Well, it's true. You'd make an excellent queen."

"You know, over the years she's promised each one of my siblings the title. I think she does it to cause strife. She revels in it."

"Please. You're the only one with the kind of leadership qualities to make it work. I know that from how you run the club and your territory. Fairest territory in the city. Why do you think you have the most inhabitants?" She tilts her glass of vodka towards me, and I clink my glass with it.

"Thank you, but unless the city finds it in their heart to actually accept me, as well as my rule, I don't think I'm about to make queen anytime soon."

"They'll get over the fear."

"They haven't in a thousand years."

"Then you'll have to win the trials," she says, a grin tickling the corner of her thin lips.

"Oh, I'll win. But she should have given me the title of heir. It's mine by rights."

Erin turns to me, stands, downs the rest of her vodka, and stares me right in the eye. "When has anyone ever been *given* power? The greatest leaders always take it. So what are you waiting for?"

She leaves and heads towards the rear of the club, no doubt meeting the bouncers on shift tonight.

I roll her words over and over. Is she right? Do I need to mutiny against my own mother? No. It's not that. Cordelia is up to something. These trials, this rigamarole she's going to put us through, it's not what it seems, but I guess the only way I'll figure out what she's up to is if I play her stupid fucking game.

This whole conversation has irritated me. I know

Mother. What she wants is bloodshed. She's always been this way, trying to drive wedges between us and the hunters, drive wedges between her nobles, her children. Pushing us towards her twisted ideals.

Three hundred years ago she almost caused civil war between two factions of vampire nobles because she played favourites. At all the parties and dinners, she would whisper lies of secret alliances and deception. Lie upon lie she wove and all for her twisted sense of fun.

And then there's her children.

Where do I even start. Her eternal favouritism, constantly showering one or another of us with an inappropriate amount of attention and praise just to make the others jealous. Dahlia has been her favourite for the best part of the last one hundred and fifty years. It's growing tiresome, that's for sure.

Once, shortly after Xavier joined the family, he couldn't have been turned more than a decade or two, she convinced me that if I drained him, I'd bind him to me in servitude and secure the position of heir.

Of course, it was total shit and he nearly desiccated. It was only when I gave him my blood and slaughtered half a village for him to regenerate that I saved him, and that was when we swore allegiance together and against her. I haven't trusted her fully since then.

I should have known she wouldn't hand me the keys to the kingdom. That would essentially put me in place as the strongest vampire house in living history. And what is Mother going to do with the rest of her long life? I can't see her actually retiring.

Not when I'd own the entire city. The Montague territory has never had much about it, even more so after the boundary was created. None of us are even sure how the residents are surviving. Isabella—the original vampire who founded the territory, established her house and then vanished. The Montague heirs would never stand a chance against me. Not if I held Cordelia's territory too. It's everything I've ever dreamed of.

Fuck the humans and the hunters alike. No one would ever look at me like the freak they think I am again. I'd make them bow at my feet.

And if they refused?

I'd drain every single motherfucking one of them.

I'd dismantle the Hunter Academy, perhaps even restore the Montague territory. I could remake this city in my image, make it finally accept me.

Erin's right. If I want control of this city, I'm going to have to take it.

When sundown arrives, I leave the club. The Midnight Market is bustling already. Mist and steam rise off the canals as the cool press of night descends, eradicating what warmth the sun left.

The air is usually full of iron, what with the number of stalls selling blood. This is the only place you can get it legally unless you're inside the heart of the vampire territories.

But there's something else under the metallic tang of dinner on the breeze. I follow my nose and head into the warren of stalls, down canal streets with river boats gliding gently through the water.

I move faster, not vampire-fast but speedy enough that I knock over a couple of drunk shoppers.

"Oi," someone shouts as they nearly stumble into the canal.

"Apologies." I wave them off, hurrying over one of the stone bridges and veering into a narrow street with tall townhouses pressing against each other. I stalk through suffocating alleys where the houses all lean at strange angles and leer over me like drunk men. The cobbles are damp here, the canal leaking its watery bowels into the street. I'll have to keep an eye on it. A flooded market is bad for everyone's business.

My feet splash through the puddles as I turn into another, yet narrower street. The hum and hubbub of traders and sellers is muted now that I've meandered off the main thoroughfare. Though there's no lack of stalls; they are stationed in front of the townhouses, making the tight streets tighter. And these sellers' wares are less than legal, less than legitimate.

The night coils around me, the only reprieve the infrequent oil lamps. Not that I need the light, I see just fine without it.

And then I lock onto the smell.

It's rich, peppered with heat, the kind of fury that wraps around your throat and drills blazing flares of rage through you. There's something a little sweet buried in it. Like the sugary taste of revenge, and then something else I can't put my finger on.

I glide into the next alley and freeze.

"You give me my fucking money back or I swear to the three houses I will gut you where you stand and feed your entrails to the rats," a woman says.

A woman I am far too familiar with. "I—I—," the stuttering buffoon about to have his guts torn out says.

I should stop this, intervene or something. My little

hunter is about to get herself in a world of trouble. This is Peace Territory, we're not allowed to kill on this land.

But here is where I confess a secret... I know about her addiction. I've known about it for a while.

And I control the blood she drinks, in fact, I control every dealer in this city. And Red only drinks my blood.

She just doesn't know it.

I sigh inwardly. I knew this was all a mistake, I should never have gotten involved. Not the first time, I should have let her die. But I didn't...

Which means... her addiction is probably getting worse.

Shit.

"Well?" Red barks and grabs him by his collar. She picks him up and slams him into the building wall. I tilt my head, raise a single eyebrow. I forgot how strong she is despite her short stature.

I stick to the shadows and silently edge closer. She's at the end of the street. The chap she's manhandling is one of my local dealers. I recognise him, though his name escapes me. When you've lived as long as I have, remembering this Bobby, Alexis, Geoffrey from that one becomes a trying affair. But it doesn't matter. I've compelled all the dealers in the city. They all know if Red comes to them, they're only to give her specific blood and they're to come to me directly.

That's when I notice Red is sweating. She's pale too, paler than normal even for her usually fair skin.

She's having withdrawals.

"I swear, if you don't give me my fucking money back or a vial of blood replacing that half measure you gave me, I will—"

"It was a f-full measure," the dealer stutters.

Letting her continue to have my blood was a mistake. It's too much, too strong. Which means it's my responsibility to fix this and get her off it...

"My arse," Red says and pulls a knife to his throat.

Time to intervene. "I wouldn't do that if I were you," I say and slide out of the shadows.

"Isn't this just delightful," Red snarls. "A real-life drainer come to play. A snatcher of sisters and ruiner of lives."

"Highly-strung this evening, aren't we?" I say, the hint of a smirk on my lips.

The dealer is skittish as he glances between me and Red. Her head snaps to face me. She looks much worse than I expected. Definitely withdrawal. She won't like what happens next.

"It appears the hunter has a blood problem. Weren't you only here a day or so ago asking for blood?"

"He sold me a duff dose," she says and pushes the blade harder against his throat.

His beady little eyes widen, his Adam's apple bobbing against the knife just enough to nick his throat. Both Red and I snap to face him as the pungent scent of blood flows through the alley.

"Too bad for you, human blood doesn't cut it for me," Red growls at the dealer.

"Did you sell her a dodgy dose?" I ask the dealer.

He shakes his head, his whole body trembling against the wall. We both know he didn't. I personally hand my vials to them and compel each dealer to only sell those vials to Red.

"Liar," Red hisses.

"What's your name?" I ask the dealer.

"N-name?" he stutters.

"Yes, you know that moniker your mother gave you shortly after you sprung from her loins?"

"M-Morance."

"Well, M-Morance, why don't you trot along now while

this here hunter and I work out the issue. You can attend the club at midnight, and I'll resolve your issue. You owe me now, and I owe her."

"B-But..." he stammers, unable to actually look at me. But Red is already releasing him.

"Don't try and con me now, I've smelt your blood. I will find you if you don't attend the club."

He doesn't need telling twice, he scarpers without a backwards glance.

"You shouldn't save trash like that," Red says, and wipes her brow. There's a faint tremor in her hand. She's struggling. If she had her dose a couple of days ago and is reacting like this already, then I'd say it's a safe bet she's going to struggle to stay conscious.

Not that I want to feed her addiction. I genuinely don't. Honestly, most humans don't become addicted that quickly. This is my fault.

"I wasn't saving him," I say.

She rolls her eyes. "If you think stopping me wiping that waste of oxygen off the face of the city is going to eradicate the fact you turned my sister, you can think again."

"Lest you forget, Red. Your sister would have died."

Red snarls, baring her teeth at me. "Fuck you. You gave her no choice."

I take a deep breath, inhaling patience. I can't believe I'm here again... doing this again with her... "And yet you're hooked on the very thing you detest so much," I say.

That makes her falter. She looks away, her nostrils flaring, her shoulders heaving. "It was a mistake. One stupid fucking mistake. I don't even remember how it happened."

I remember.

She snaps up to face me. "But now I'm paying for it anyway."

"Quite the little contradiction, aren't you," I say, toying

with her. Yes, this is my fault, but that doesn't stop me enjoying the game.

"What do you want?" she says.

I shrug. "I'm just being helpful."

"You're never helpful, you want something."

Yes, to give you my blood so we can withdraw you safely. But such is the problem with Red, she never, ever takes it willingly, and so we go through the same dance we always do.

One day I'll let her remember. But then she'll hate me even more than she already does, and I can't have that.

It was always easier for her to hate me. Always easier for me to play her villain.

"Walk with me," I say.

"One, no. Two, fuck no. And three, you just let my only source of blood vanish, so you need to find me a new source or you can go royally fuck yourself and your walk."

That does make me grin. "I really do enjoy these encounters when you're so polite. Don't they teach you manners in the Academy?"

She opens her mouth to protest. But instead of an insult, her eyes roll shut and she sways. I lurch forward just as she collapses into my arms unconscious.

"For the love of blood." I sigh and scoop her up, suffering the bittersweet haze of déjà vu as I run her all the way back to Castle Beaumont.

CHAPTER 13

CORDELIA

A Thousand Years Ago

Mother stood in the doorway of our manor house, fury lining her forehead, her finger wagging in my face.

"What do you mean you left without getting the herbs? Why in god's name would you have done that?" she spits.

"Well, I... it's—"

"Spit it out, woman. How do you suppose you're going to attend the ball and find a suitable husband when you can scarcely walk on your ankle, let alone dance on it all evening? You must return to the dhampir witch immediately."

"But I—"

"No. You get back there and take some flowers from the garden by way of apology. Honestly, Cordelia, I don't know what you were thinking. That poor dhampir must have thought you were a sure bet for trade walking, or I should say hobbling, in the way you were." She spins on her heel and marches back into the house still berating me. "And then you go and hot foot it out of the apothecary without so much as a single coin donated, and I bet you..."

The words trail off as she disappears deeper into the manor. I suspect she'll continue her rant over my errors at Father for much of the afternoon.

I sigh, take a deep breath and ask the driver to ready the carriage again.

"Again, miss?"

"I apologise, but I require you to take me back to where we've just been. It appears I left too hastily."

"I see, ma'am. Not a problem. I'll ready the horses in just a moment."

I take my leave and wander, using Poppa's walking cane around the garden. I pick some flowers as an apology. I'm sure Mother will find out if I don't, and then I shan't hear the end of it.

I check the rose gardens first and find several exquisite white varieties blossoming. I open the gardener's shed, pick out a set of clippers and snip two snowy flowers. Then I see a clump of blue forget-me-nots and cut a handful of those.

I snip and cut, trim and shape. I add greenery to make it fuller, and within just a few moments, I have a full bouquet that I think is perfect.

It's not until I arrive at the apothecary again with the flowers in my hand that I realise I picked a bunch that matches her eyes almost perfectly. I stare through the glass door at her. If I were to put the flowers next to her, the ice blue and white of the flowers would set off the sea blue of Eleanor's eyes. Even through the glass, they're practically glistening like the crystal waters of the lagoons in Lantis Bay.

I shouldn't be noticing her eyes. It's not proper conduct.

"You're back again?" Eleanor says.

"I... um..."

"Did you decide better of the examination and return for your herbs?"

I nod and swallow, my throat thick and clogged. My words stick there, hiding. Like perhaps I am hiding a secret.

"I see. Well, would you care to take a seat again? I didn't quite manage to finish the examination."

She gestures for me to sit on a stool and to prop my leg up on another. I do as I'm told, my throat slowly loosening.

That's when I realise I'm still holding the flowers like a lovesick fool. Not that I'm lovesick. What a ridiculous notion. Honestly, these are just fleeting thoughts. Perhaps if I were to see to some self-care then I wouldn't be having them. I could focus on the gentlemen Mama wants me to marry.

"Excuse me?" I say, my voice barely above a whisper.

"Yes?" she says as she stoops to lift my skirts high enough to examine my ankle again.

"I brought these for you." I shove the bouquet at her. Her fingers brush mine as she takes it, a spark of static rushes through my fingertips. I hastily withdraw my hand, brushing it down my skirts.

"Why, thank you, that's incredibly kind of you, but if I may enquire... why?"

"Right. Yes. Well, you see, I got home, and Mother was quite furious that I'd not had my ankle attended to and thought me rather rude for abandoning you without first paying for the examination, and second, not bringing home the correct medicines or herbs to actually fix my ankle."

I'm babbling but she smiles.

"And so the flowers?"

"Sorry. I." I scratch my head and wipe a hand over my face, furious with myself for getting flustered for the second time today in front of this woman.

"I brought them as an apology. Because of my rudeness."

"Well, I don't think you rude at all. But the gesture is quite lovely. I think the bunch suits me beautifully, don't you?"

"Yes, actually. It wasn't until I'd returned here that I realised I'd picked flowers that match your eyes."

"You picked them yourself?"

Heat rises up my neck. I feel like I've been caught out, as if she's accusing and I should be denying.

"I did. It was the right thing to do."

She bustles around the shop, hunting high and low for a vase. In the end, she tips out a huge jar, chucking the herbs on the desk and walks out the back of the shop. When she returns the jar is full of water and she pops the flowers into it.

As she returns to stand in front of me, she presses her lips together. "Why did you flinch away from me this morning? Why did you run? Was it my touch? Would you prefer that I didn't examine you with my bare hands? I have gloves you see... I can—"

"No." I shake my head. "It wasn't that at all. Quite the opposite in fact."

"The opposite...?"

I shift on the stool, uncomfortable with admitting the real reason. Uncomfortable even acknowledging it to myself. I want to lie. To hide away from the truth, but it wells inside my chest, a growing swarm of realisation that needs to be released.

"I didn't hate it. I found it quite pleasing. And that... it, well. I was surprised by that because you're..."

"A woman?" she asks.

I nod and look away, suddenly embarrassed to have

made such a confession. She bustles around me. When I look up, she's arranging the flowers again.

"Do you know, I don't think I've seen such beautiful flowers in a long time. And more, I don't think I've been given such pretty things since... well... my ex, really."

"You have an ex-partner?" I say, shocked. That's not something that I've heard of. A woman without a husband having casual partners.

"Yes, she used to love giving me flowers. But unfortunately, she would only do it after we'd had an argument."

My world narrows to a pinpoint. All I can do is focus on her words repeating over and over in my head. Eleanor said *she*.

She.

She.

She.

"I'm sorry, your ex was a... a...?"

"A woman, yes."

I'm stunned into silence. I open my mouth but only a breathy whisper comes out.

"Is that... is that okay?" she says, her cheeks suddenly pink. "I'm sorry. Perhaps I shouldn't have been so free with the information. It's just that in our culture, that's not so much of an issue. I understand that for you the expectation is—"

My words return, surging like a tidal wave. I have to understand more.

"What was it like? You know... to be with a woman? If you don't mind my asking, that is."

She shrugs, her colour draining back to normal. "It was quite wonderful. To be so understood. To have someone whose energy flowed with mine. It's more intense, more intimate. Our connection wasn't just of the heart, it went as deep as our souls. It was simply, love."

I stare at her, my mind racing.

So she continues, "Besides, women are far more selfless and giving lovers than any man I've been with."

That makes my mouth fall open again. "You've been with men too?"

She nods. "Marriage isn't a sacred duty or expectation for us. Connection is more important. Now. If I may, I need to examine your ankle again. I suspect you've made it worse by walking on it this afternoon."

She nudges my skirts up and over my knee and I have to take a moment to steady myself against her touch. Her fingers are so tender and gentle as she presses and kneads my calf and foot. She slips my stocking off so that she can palpate my toes and apply pressure to my foot.

As her hands come around my heel and ankle, I wince against the pain.

"Okay, I think the issue is ligament damage. Unfortunately, that's not a quick fix."

"Oh no, there must be something you can do? Some magic you can give me so that I can dance for the ball?"

She folds her arms and looks at me hard. "Do you want a husband?"

"I need one."

"That's not the same thing."

"I want to please Mother."

"Do you?"

I take a deep breath. This woman is quite pushy and while part of me wants to tell her to leave me alone, the other has me leaning into confession after confession. How easy she is to talk to. How easily I seem to trust her.

I sigh, "No. Actually. I'm not sure I've ever really wanted a husband."

"Would you like a wife instead?"

"I... that's not possible."

"It is in my culture."

"How lucky for you."

She stands, leaves my foot and attends the back of the shop, clattering around, crushing herbs together and whispering words. She runs her hand along the back of the shop wall, and I swear the walls vibrate. There's a shimmering white thread that releases from the brick and then she pricks her finger, a drop of blood beads on the end. She touches her fingertip to the thread and it shivers and turns the colour of claret.

She winds the thread around her wrist and tugs it until it releases from the wall, and then she drops it into the bowl.

"What... how did the house give you magic?"

"All houses are magic if they've been built properly. But these new manors and castles, most of them aren't connected to the land. It's where their power comes from. But none of the magic is activated without blood in this city. It's actually a little different in every city in the land."

"That's fascinating."

"It is," she says. "I'd love to travel one day and visit the other cities so that I might learn their magic too. Here," she says and hands me a glass with an odd green-coloured substance in it. The shade reminds me of those trees that still have leaves in the winter, their evergreen hearts spilled into the mug. It smells like fish though, and I gag as she holds it out to me.

"Gods, that stinks something awful," I say, my nose wrinkling.

She laughs but pushes the glass closer.

"Fine," I sigh and hold my nose to down the lot.

"Well done. Wasn't that bad, was it?"

"It was vile."

"Baby."

"Cow."

She laughs out loud, throwing her head back. "You're quite something, calling your dhampir healer a cow."

I smile. There was no malice in my tone, and she knows it.

"I take it back. What's next, dhampir?"

"I've made you a salve to rub on your ankle, and I want you to strap it up tight for at least three weeks. I suspect you'll be able to walk just fine after that."

"Thank you," I say.

She applies the salve and binds my ankle. Her touch is as gentle and tender as always. By the time she's done and releases my leg, I'm quite disappointed, I'd grown used to her warmth.

She holds out her hand to help me up and I take it.

"Well, thank you again," I say.

"Was nothing."

I give her the coins and she hands me a bag with the medicine.

"Goodbye..." I say.

But she just smiles at me. "Maybe."

And as I leave, I wonder what she could possibly have meant.

CHAPTER 14

RED

When I wake, it's like being pulled from the depths of hell. Sleep was a void of nothing. And when I peel my eyes open, it's with a sharp intake of breath and the cold shiver of goosebumps crawling over my entire body.

I leap off the bed I was lying on. My heart drumming in my ears. Blood throbbing so loud I can't hear or see or think about anything else. A pounding headache claws at the inside of my mind like someone battered me in my dreams. I grip my temples and buckle, trying to remember if I got in a fight or was attacked by vampires.

No.

Worse.

This is withdrawal. That little cunt dealer did me over and Octavia fucking Beaumont saved him. Not something I'm going to let go easily. I stand up and glance down at my body.

"What the fuck?" I hiss. I'm in my underwear. And... and... What the actual fuck. I slip my hand in my underwear. I'm soaked? I pull my hand out and slide it over my painfully hard nipples.

Why am I so... so aroused?

I must have been dosed in my sleep. It's the only solution because the shivering sweats are gone and even the headache I woke with is receding. I feel far more myself. And whenever I've dosed, I've been unbearably horny for hours after. Half the time I end up busting my vibrator batteries or draining bottles of lube trying to get rid of what I can only describe as blue balls, only that sounds like the patriarchy. So blue ovaries? Blue pussy? Gross. How about a painful lady boner.

That will do.

There's a rustling outside the door. Shit. I glance around fast, hunter instincts kicking in.

Assess. Find the exits. Estimate the number of enemies.

Where the ever-loving fuck am I?

I'm in some kind of posh bedroom. I look over my shoulder, I was in a four-poster bed. I spot my blades on the bedside table. I lunge for them, grabbing one in each hand. But where are my clothes and who the hell took them?

And more disconcerting, why do I feel like I've been here before? This room... it's... familiar. It can't be though because I legitimately have no fucking clue where I am.

Dark maroon curtains drape and fall over the windows, their plush velvet looks soft enough to roll in. I consider hacking them down to cover myself up when footsteps alert me to an intruder.

I spring into action, my body moving for me, thank you muscle memory. My skin is unprotected, though, and I don't know where my leathers are or my armour. So I'll have to go on the offensive. Attack first, ask questions later.

The haze of a memory attempts to slither back into my consciousness. That fucking dealer.

I think Octavia and I were talking. And then everything went fuzzy. She probably compelled me, the fucking filthy vampire. I bet that's why I can't remember anything. She must have kidnapped me. I inhale, take a deep breath and confirm that the air stinks of iron-rich perfume.

Blood.

Shit. My head still isn't clear, my body riddled with the aftereffects of withdrawal. But I draw the best conclusions I can with the information I've got.

Octavia fucking Beaumont kidnapped me, and for what? Stored me in a private room just to drain me later so I can't compete against her in her mother's trials? Well fuck that.

I leap across the room and press my back to the wall beside the door, my blade raised to strike.

Attack first.

Question her after.

The door peels open and I lunge. I fling my arm down hard and aim right for the neck. I yank the blade out and arterial blood sprays all over me.

"Hnngsargggghle," the man says.

"Oh shit, oh shit, oh shit." My voice is high-pitched. Panic now leaking into my words. It was... he is a human.

Fuck, fuck, fuck.

I thought it would have been Octavia. Gods. I'm so fucked. I grab his throat and apply as much pressure as I can. But the arterial spray forces its way between my fingers. It's all down my arms, spraying across my face, down my chest and underwear. I help lower him to the floor as a shadow appears over me, looming down.

"What on earth?" Octavia says.

"Save him for fucks sake, don't just stand there."

"LENNOX," she bellows. There's a rushing sound and

another vampire appears in the doorway. "Quickly," she says.

Lennox's fangs drop and he plunges them into his wrist. He kneels beside me and nudges my hand away, letting the blood spray everywhere. Lennox holds his wrist to the dying man's mouth. The man's skin is pale, his gargled breathing short and shallow.

Gods, please, Mother of Blood, save him. The man gulps at Lennox's wrist. Slowly, his skin colour changes, from pale death to sickly green, and then when the first rush of pink floods back into his cheeks and his throat knits back together, I swear I breathe for the first time in three minutes.

"I'm so so sorry. I thought you were going to attack me. I—"

The man puts his hand on my wrist. His voice is cracked and gravelly. "I would love to tell you that this is the first time this has happened to me. But when you work for a vampire, getting wounded in the line of duty is an occupational hazard." I must have caught something in his voice box and it's still healing.

"That's why we have healers like Lennox on hand," Octavia says from above us.

Lennox puts his big hand around the man on the floor and hauls him standing. He slides his arm around him.

"I'm Wendell, Octavia's head of staff," he says and holds a trembling hand out to me.

My cheeks are flame red and not just because I'm covered in his blood, but the sheer embarrassment of the fact I could have been so reactionary.

I take his hand, but the act makes me blush even harder. I'm suddenly grateful to be smothered in blood. "I truly can't apologise enough."

I realise then that my clothes are strewn across the floor. Wendell catches me looking.

"Ah, yes. I was bringing them back for you all laundered."

I grit my teeth. It's even more humiliating that he was doing me a kindness too.

"Gods. I am mortified."

"Think nothing of it," he says, and nods to Lennox to help him out. "I'll have the chef bring you a tray of breakfast. I'm afraid after we dosed you, you slept the whole night. I appreciate that an addiction isn't exactly what anyone wants, but if you're choosing to withdraw, there are safer ways and means than cold turkey. Octavia took the liberty of ensuring you didn't die in the night."

He nods to Octavia and Lennox helps him unsteadily out of the room.

Wait, what? I replay his words.

Octavia took the liberty of ensuring you didn't die in the night.

Octavia?

Suddenly, Octavia is inside the room. She's closed the door behind her, turning the lock at her back. Her nostrils flared.

I realise then, I'm half naked and covered in blood.

"Why did you help me?" I say.

"You wouldn't believe me if I told you. Now. Get in the bathroom."

"You don't get to boss me around."

"Would you rather I licked the blood off of your naked skin?"

My mouth drops open, a short, sharp gasp escaping. My skin heats. I find myself taking a step closer.

Fuck.

Do I?

No. I can't. A nervous laugh bubbles up and out.

"Something funny?" Octavia says.

"I—er... no. It's just..." I can't form words; my whole body is warm. Desire pools between my legs. For fuck's sake, if Octavia saved me, then it must have been her blood she gave me. Which means... Mother of Blood, I do want her to lick it off me. I wipe a hand over my face and realise I'm still holding the blade.

She steps closer.

I move on instinct, sliding a foot back, holding the blade up and under her chin.

"That's close enough, Beaumont."

Her blood might be coursing through my system, bringing an intense need for her, but that doesn't mean I need to act on it.

I can fight this.

She tilts her head down at me, arrogance pouring through her expression in the quirk of a perfect black eyebrow, the pout of those full lips.

Why am I objectifying her like this? It's the blood. It has to be.

She shifts another inch closer.

A tease.

A test.

A fucking dare.

I shove the blade tighter against her throat. "I said that was close enough."

"Is it though?" she says and a smile peels across the plump rouge of her mouth. Her fangs drop. Either she's hungry or horny. Given I'm covered in blood I assume the former.

She draws in a breath, her nostrils flaring wide. Then those crimson eyes pierce mine. "Something tells me you'd prefer it if I was much, much closer." She practically purrs the words.

Did she just...? Oh my gods. She can smell the excitement in my knickers.

I swallow.

"You can't hide when you're turned on, *Red*... In fact, you can't hide anything from me." She steps so close to me that we're sharing air. The heat of my body wraps around us.

She leans in, my blade digging into her skin, a line of blood rolling down her neck. But it doesn't stop drawing her tongue down my cheek, swiping the blood right off it. I swear I nearly collapse as a bolt of pleasure shoots straight to my clit.

I know what she's done, but I need to hear her say it. "Who's blood did you give me last night, Octavia?"

She stands back, letting the cool air rush between us.

"Get in the bath or I'm going to lick every drop of that off you." She glances down, my eyes follow hers. There's arterial spray on my thighs, my knickers, over my pussy.

Fuck.

My thoughts are running away, my mind slipping into the idea of her drawing that tongue over my entire body. I don't want that.

Yes I do.

No.

I can't. But... but... the way my body is reacting, the fact I'm straining every muscle I have not to leap up and jump into her arms tells me I already know whose blood she gave me.

"It was yours, wasn't it?" I say.

She holds my gaze but remains silent. I open my mouth to threaten her, shout at her... do what... I don't know.

But she cuts me off. "You're the only one..."

"Only one what...?" I say getting tired of this and desperately wanting to be away from her before I do something I regret.

"...Who will look me in the eye."

"Oh," I say, surprised that that's what's on her mind. Her statement hangs between us, and I feel like I'm missing the importance of it.

She steps back again, and the air turns icy, shivers wracking my body.

"The bath is already drawn. I had it run while you were sleeping." Her breathing is as ragged as mine. Is she struggling to hold herself back as much as I am?

Her eyes flick to the bathroom door and then she speeds out of the room, leaving me in my underwear, covered in blood and with a raging lady boner that I'm wondering if I can casually masturbate away in her bath.

CHAPTER 15

RED

The bath has bubbles, and I won't lie, I let out an excited squeal. It reminds me of when Amelia and I were little and Mama would make magic bubbles in our bath. They were purple, and we used to build purple beards on each other's faces until it devolved into flinging handfuls of the stuff at one another. And every time Mama made the bubbles, we filled the house with the sounds of glee.

I lock the bathroom door and strip my underwear off, place my blades on the table next to the tub and slip under the water. It's gloriously warm and someone must have put oils and shea butter in the bath because the water glides off my skin like it's made of silk.

I wash myself down, there's an array of products for me to use, and then I just lay in the bath, wondering why she bought me to her house of all places. Why she fed me her blood. Couldn't she have used Lennox? Or basically any other vampire other than her? Is she trying to torture me on top of taking my sister?

And this *is* torture. It's how I know she gave me her

blood. Because I'm drawn to her. It's compulsive, a need filling my entire body. I'm not even sure I want to resist it anymore.

If she dosed me while I was asleep, I'll never know how much she gave me. But given the way I wanted to climb her face and fuck the horn away, I'd say it was definitely more than a drop or two.

I sink under the water and groan. When I surface for air, I jolt. The door is opening. I lurch up, grab my blades and try not to slip in the bath as I form a fighting stance.

Raven-coloured hair appears first, then Octavia's form slides into the bathroom.

"What the fuck. I locked the door," I snap.

"This is my house. No doors are locked to me."

"How did you get in?"

"Same way you get into any vampire-owned mansion. I paid the door a drop of blood and it gladly opened for me."

I throw my hands up. "And why did you feel the need to come in here? Was the locked door not a clue? I'm in the fucking bath. A bath you made me take."

Her eyes drop.

Wherever she looks, heat erupts over my skin as if it were her hands touching me instead of her gaze. First my shoulders, and then heat trails down my chest, my stomach, my pussy, my thighs. It's the first time I truly appreciate just how naked I am. Sure, bubbles cover at least one of my nipples and half my stomach, and my calves are still fully submerged. But that's about it. And her blood is one hundred percent not out of my system. I know because my neck muscles are taut, preventing me from flinging myself at her.

Her lip twitches, then she drags her eyes up to meet mine. "Oh, do sit down, Red. You're making the floor wet."

"Am I safe?" I say.

"From me? Yes. The ahh…"—she wafts a hand in the air —"heat you're experiencing is shared."

"The h—? Oh."

"Unfortunately, while I knew of this phenomenon, it wasn't something I factored into the decision. Which I should have, given our close physical proximity."

I lie back in the bath with a smug sense of satisfaction that she's also suffering. "So, what you're saying…" I drag it out, watching her squirm in the doorway. "Is that because your blood is in my system, you want to fuck me? Oh, that is too bad. That will teach you to feed your blood to a human then, won't it."

Her eyes narrow at me. "You are the first."

My mouth forms a tiny 'O' and makes me look away.

"We have a problem," she says, putting a hand on her hip.

"I think that much is evident," I say, trying not to roll my eyes.

"Not the arousal. Though that is an uncomfortable issue right now." She adjusts her bra, no doubt her nipples are as hard as mine. Though the warm water is easing that.

She leans against the wall. "The trials. This… whatever this thing is that Mother is making us participate in. Have you given any consideration as to who you will partner with?"

"Not fucking you. That's for sure. Why the hell would I want to partner with a sister killer."

She rolls her eyes at me. "Oh, and I suppose you'd rather be partnered with… who exactly? The beautiful Xavier? I didn't think cock was your thing."

"Careful, Octavia, you almost sound jealous."

I bring my fingers to my lips. My words hit me. The familiarity with which I speak to her. No one else would dare speak to one of the original three the way I am, and yet... it feels so... natural.

So strange.

She ignores my teasing and returns to the point. How dull.

"Or would you rather be bored to death by Gabe? Hmm?" She folds her arms and leans one of her feet against the wall for support. She looks like every fictional book boyfriend Amelia has ever fawned over.

Amelia.

The bubbling pit of fury simmers up again in my gut. And yet, her fucking blood is a pull I cannot resist despite how fucked off I am with her. Despite how my fingers twitch on the edge of the bath, desperate to grab a blade and fling it at her.

I lean back in the bath, the tip of one nipple rising above the water, the cool of the air making it stiffen all over again. I watch as her eyes flick to my breasts. I know she's seen. I know she likes it.

What the fuck is wrong with me? I shouldn't be teasing her like this. I hate her. She took my sister away from me. Destroyed both our lives. Maybe the Chief was right. Maybe I'm exactly where I should be. I can partner with one of the vampires and investigate all of them. Maybe I'll find evidence of Octavia's wrongdoing. Hell, maybe I can be the one to execute her. Maybe this won't be so bad after all.

"Well?" she asks.

"Well what, Octavia?" I was clearly too busy plotting revenge to catch what she said.

"Would you rather partner with Gabe, who will be utterly useless in any trial other than a history-based test? Or is Dahlia more your thing? She is butch... and she loves pussy even more than I do. But perhaps your masc tendencies wouldn't marry well. I guess that leaves you with Sadie."

"The sister with white hair?"

"That would be the one."

"Doesn't she have a reputation for being more blood-thirsty than even you?"

She nods at me.

I grunt in frustration. Octavia has a point. "Maybe Xavier wouldn't be so bad after all," I say, mostly to get a reaction out of her.

And I do get one.

Her nostrils flare and she stands upright again. I sink under the water, grinning. There's nothing sweeter than pissing her off. I pull my hands through my hair, washing the soap out. When I rise out of the water, I startle. She's right at the bath's edge.

My hand is already on my blade and pointing it at her chin.

"So quick to react, little hunter."

"My name is Red."

She tilts her head at me, "Is it?"

"What is that supposed to mean."

She stands up, her back straight, looking down at me from above the bath. There's a smile curling the corner of her mouth, and I can't work out if it's a sneer or something a little smugger.

She spins on her heel and walks to the door, setting her hand on the knob. She glances over her shoulder. "Because I thought your name was *Verity*."

My mouth drops. My body erupts out of the water. No one calls me that. That name was lost when my mother died. Heat floods my cheeks, rage and lust and desire to make her pay for so trivially spilling my truth.

"How the f—"

But she cuts me off by wrenching the door open. I throw the blade at her head as she walks out, screaming, "How the fuck do you know my name?"

But the door slams shut and my blade lands exactly where her head was a millisecond prior.

CHAPTER 16

RED

I leap out of the bath, snatch up my blade and grab the towel. My feet slip as I race to the door, but I gather my balance and charge after her. I stop. I never, ever go anywhere unarmed. And right now, I am completely butt naked save for the towel and the single blade. I back up and grab the other one so I have one in each hand. I don't trust a soul in this godsforsaken mansion.

Especially not now.

No one, and I do mean no one, save Amelia knows my real name, and even Amelia doesn't call me Verity. And she certainly wouldn't have told Octavia fucking Beaumont it. No matter how mad I am at her right now. The day I changed my name I'd gone home from the Academy. Neither of us were of age to drink, but she'd persuaded me to celebrate in style. So we snuck half empty beers from the local pub and poured them over my first red tally mark tattoo. She was so proud of my first kill tattoo, she vowed to call me Red from then on. And that's how it stuck. We spent the rest of the night watching the stars and stealing dregs of beer together until we fell asleep in the pub garden.

She wouldn't betray that, no matter what.

So how the fuck does Octavia know?

I rip the bathroom door open, but Octavia is already walking out of the bedroom. I chase after her, wrapping the towel around me tight.

"Wait, for fuck's sake."

She doesn't. Of course she fucking doesn't. She just walks, or swaggers is more accurate, out the room and down the hall. Her hips swing in this delicious curve through the air. Half of me wonders if she's doing it on purpose or whether it's just her blood in my system that makes me aware of her every moment.

But I can't take my eyes off of her hips.

Her ass.

It's curved and round in all the right places.

She veers left despite my protestations. I skip and jog to keep up. But my little legs pale compared to the length of hers. And I'm barefoot.

She's speeding up too. Totally on purpose knowing I'm struggling to keep up.

"OCTAVIA," I shriek.

This time, at least, she cocks her head over her shoulder, giving me a devious grin. Wendell, the head of staff, pops his head out of a door on the right. He opens his mouth to speak but closes it again and shuts his door when he sees me with a blade in my hand and wearing only a towel.

Octavia turns right, into a new wing, which is quieter. Not just quiet, but silent. There are no staff, no people anywhere. Almost like it's a private wing. I wonder if it's hers.

Finally, she reaches the end of the wing's corridor, turns left and there she vanishes through a leather-studded door.

"What the hell?" I mumble and open the door.

And there I halt.

"Ah, shit." This is very definitely a sex room.

The walls are dark, the kind of blood red that's not quite dried but isn't liquid anymore. The lights are low, a dim ember colour like a dying fire. From the ceiling, chains and handcuffs hang. On the walls there are countless toys, straps, floggers, dildos, and fuck knows what else. There's a four-poster bed in the middle of the room, rich black curtains hanging from the gilded, gothic frame.

Well, this is all rather uncomfortable. I came to find out how the fuck she knows my name, and now my pussy is throbbing with want. Just looking at the toys in here is enough to make me wet, let alone thinking about using them.

"I said..." I start trying to stay focused and ignore the very appetising room. "How the hell do you know my real name? No one knows it."

She smiles. But says nothing.

"My blood is in your system."

I shrug and have to grab at my towel as it drops a little. "And?"

"And?" She huffs. "And... Verity, I don't give my blood freely. That's why Lennox is here. To fix any of my humans who get sick."

I bristle at my name in her mouth. It's so foreign hearing it that it doesn't even feel like it belongs to me. "So? Bravo, you're a saint. A real white knight vampire not dishing out your blood."

Fire burns hot in her eyes. She snarls as she speeds across the room and into my personal space. My nose fills with the scent of her. Of oud and spice, and winter nights.

She takes a step closer to me. So close that I can smell her perfume. Like winter hugs and city nights. Like desire and bonfire smoke and kisses from soft lips.

"Do you know why I don't indulge humans with my blood?"

"I don't know, Octavia, but I bet you're going to tell me."

"Because, when another has my blood, it creates a bond. The kind of bond that creates certain feelings."

My breath hitches. "What, like the need to fuck? I'm sure we will survive," I say as the first hint of flutters drift through my stomach. This is so fucked up. Nothing I feel is real. It's just the blood.

Just. The. Blood.

When it's out of my system, things will go back to normal, and I won't care about her anymore. I won't want her because this is temporary.

"No. This isn't about you or your human feelings. This is about the feelings it creates in the vampire."

Oh. I take a step back, the flutters shifting to unease. "What do you mean?"

"Feelings of... ownership. You see, you're mine now. I own you. You belong to me."

I take a step back.

She steps with me.

"No one owns me. I own myself."

She smiles, the first hint of a fang dropping. "Really? Then why can I smell your excitement? Why can I taste your desire in the air? There's no one else here, Verity. Just me. Which means all of that... it's all for me."

"I..." My heart pounds, my breath is short because she's right. I do want her. I want her to fuck me against the wall, on the bed. I want her to hang me from the ceiling and fuck me until I can't walk. But worse, I want her blood. More of it. It is liquid gold and fire and glistening ecstasy.

"What do you want, Verity?"

The way she says my name, it curls around her tongue, like magic, a purr and a secret. She says it like it's hers. Like she does own me. Like she's always owned me.

"My. Name. Is. Red."

Her eyes drop to my arm and the red tallies that gave me my nickname.

"So many dead. So many kills."

That gives me a shot of confidence. A reminder of who I am. I stand taller. "Yeah? And how does it make you feel to know one day all that will be left of you is a red mark on my arm?"

"It sounds like you'll be keeping me forever. Like either way I win."

Motherfucker.

She steps closer.

I step away.

Again and again until my back is pressed against the door. My legs quiver with want. I'm desperate for her to rip my towel off me. To take me where I stand and yet some quiet region of my brain is screaming *no*. The conscious part of me is louder.

"What do you want, Octavia? You've made your point."

"I want you. I want you to be a good girl and drop that fucking towel already and let me make you come all over my face."

I can't speak. All I can do is suck in short sharp breaths and stare into those crimson eyes. If the pull I've been feeling between us is really as strong in her as it is in me... This only ends one way.

"W-what?" I say.

"You heard me. I'm going to make you come. We both know it's what you want."

And she's right. It is. The excitement is already sliding down my thighs. The more she speaks to me like this, the more I am struggling to stay focused. To remember why I hated her, why this is such a bad idea. Especially when my clit is aching with desperation.

"Are you a good girl, Verity? Good girls get rewarded."

"What kind of reward?" I say, switching into the role she's giving me.

"Whatever you want. Do you want to touch me?"

No.

Fine, yes. She leans in, her lips brush against mine, the softest caress like the kiss of a melting snowflake. It sends shivers down my spine and all the way to my cunt.

"You want more of my blood?" she whispers against my earlobe.

Gods yes.

"No. No more blood. You'll be able to track me."

She smiles, leans into my neck, drawing her teeth along the delicate skin. "See, I think you want me to chase you. I think, Verity, that you want to be owned by me. Fucked by me."

"No..." I breathe but it's weak and makes her laugh.

"Yes," I say, stronger this time.

"Good. Now... Drop your towel." She kisses my neck, sucking at the flesh and drawing her tongue down the curves of my body.

I have no self-control left, no willpower. So I do as she says and drop the towel. And then I'm standing against her door naked with nothing other than the blade in my hand. Her arm reaches around me and locks the door. She doesn't touch my knife. She must know I need it. Even if her blood is flowing through my veins and changing everything I know and think and believe, I'm still not ready to trust her. My hand clenches around the hilt as she scoops me into her arms and carries me to the bed, dropping me on top of it.

She looks me up and down. Her eyes are like feathers caressing my skin everywhere they skirt. "You really are quite the work of art."

She climbs on top of the bed and kneels in front of me. "Open your legs."

"D-don't feed from me," I managed to stutter out. "You can fuck me, but don't bite me."

She hesitates. Something washes over her expression that I can't read, but she doesn't argue. She nods and then glances down. "Legs."

I draw my knees up and spread just as she's asked.

She licks her lips and slides down between my thighs. Her long raven hair tickles my thigh. But I like it and it only serves to make me even wetter. She kisses my knee, down my leg, sliding her tongue over my flesh. Her fangs drop and I catch sight of the pure white. My fingers grip my knife a little tighter. But I don't react when I normally would. Perhaps she's right, she does own me in this moment.

What the hell am I doing allowing a vampire to have me in such a vulnerable position? Her teeth and fangs graze my thighs but she's careful. Gentle enough that she doesn't break the skin, and the tingling sensations make my hips buck.

"Octavia. Please."

But I don't really know what I'm asking. Please stop? Please more?

The word elicits a hummed noise of appreciation from her. "I like it when you say please," she says and kisses down my leg quicker.

My free hand scrunches the silky duvet as a bolt of pleasure finds its way straight to my clit. She draws her mouth over my pussy, kissing her way across me to my other leg.

"Octavia, stop teasing me and fuck me already," I shout.

And there it is. The truth. I do want her.

She halts and returns to my centre, sliding her tongue from my clit to my hole, and I can't help the moan that rips from my chest.

It's raw, carnal.

Her tongue is cool and thick as it slides inside my entrance. My back arches off the bed, as if the blood pumping through my body can sense its owner. It responds to her, calls to her, makes me desperate to have more.

My clit swells as she draws her tongue up and down as if she's summoning her blood, drawing it into my cunt from wherever it was drifting around my system.

"Oh fuck," I moan.

And she sighs in appreciation. My pussy heats, slick and wet and I swear the more she draws long lavish licks down my slit, the more blood she's drawing into my cunt. Every sensation heightens, far more than when I've had sex with anyone else. Bolts of pleasure erupt, shimmering out from my clit all the way across my thighs. Pleasure rides up to my nipples and down to my toes. It's like my clit is everywhere. Like she's controlling every ounce of my pleasure, wringing it not just from my pussy but my entire body.

"Fuck. Fuck," I cry.

But that just encourages her. She focuses on my clit, sucking and licking it in delicate circles, then flicking her tongue over and over, faster and faster. She takes me into her mouth, sucking just hard enough to make me cry out as a shiver of ecstasy fires out and around my body.

"More, please. More," I say.

Her finger drifts to my entrance and circles me, teasing, tempting but not pushing inside me.

"Octavia," I say. This time my voice is a growl. A warning.

I can hear the smile in her breathing.

She enters me, and I nearly come undone. She slides one finger in and then pushes another in beside it. She's rough, brutal, almost not giving me time to adjust. But fuck, do I feel full, and she feels amazing.

It's everything she said. Like my pussy is hers, she owns it and will do with it exactly what she wants.

Her fingers grind in and out, thrusting and pumping as her mouth ravishes my clit, drawing long, luscious licks down my pussy.

I'm panting, crying out her name. I've always been noisy in bed. But every whimper that escapes urges her on.

"What do you want?" Octavia says as if she knows I want to tell her, to say everything in my mind,

"I want you to fuck me harder," I say and even uttering the words makes my pussy throb.

"I want you to make me come and lick up every fucking drop I give you."

The pleasure of my words makes her eyes close. So, she wants to own me, but she likes me telling her what to do? I can play switch better than anyone.

"Curl your fingers," I say. "Fuck me hard. Own me like I know you want to. Fuck me like the good little bloodslut I am."

Octavia's free hand releases my thigh and slips between her own legs. Oh, she really likes it when I talk.

She licks me harder, faster. Her fingers curl until they find my G-spot, and then as my walls clench, she thrusts harder, rubbing exactly where I need, making me soak her fingers.

"Fuck, I'm going to... Octavia. You're going to make me c—"

My words die in a strangled moan of pleasure as an orgasm rips through me, sudden, unexpected and totally mind-blowing. My eyes close, my back arches off the bed and my clit pulses, flooding my body with bolt after bolt of delicious ecstasy.

I lay there a moment, my body still twitching as I try and come back to reality. Fuck, that was intense.

As I sit up, I realise I've cut her bedding. The knife in my hand is still gripped tight, and I've made a hole in the sheets where I was writhing around in pleasure.

"What was that? How did you make the orgasm so intense?" I ask.

"My blood calls to me. I can make it move anywhere I want inside you. And if I push it into your clit, it makes things... well... a little extra."

"I'm going to fuck you now," I say.

"Oh no, that wasn't part of the deal," she says. "This was about me owning you."

"I think you'll find that's not the game we're playing." I move fast. Faster than is possible for me, even with my heightened hunter abilities. I put it down to the fact I have her blood in my system. I shift, lurch forward and slice two giant gashes through her top. I'm careful not to cut her skin. But I absolutely shred the garment.

It falls away, piece by piece floating to the bed.

"That was one of my favourite tops."

"I'm sure you're wealthy enough to buy another one. Now get on the bed, before I put you on the bed," I say and this time, I'm the one in charge. I realise that perhaps we're both switches. Neither of us really willing to let the other always take control.

She doesn't move.

I take a deep breath and I jerk fast, moving the knife up

and under her bra and yanking forward, parting the fabric and wrecking the bra too.

"You're going to be expensive, I see," she says.

"This is a one-time deal. When your blood is out of my system, we can go back to hating each other. This will all be one giant memory. It will be dreamlike and neither of us will really know if it happened."

"Is that so?" she says. "Do you want me to compel the memory away? Do you regret me so already?"

"No. Never compel me. I can't think of anything worse than having my memories stolen."

Her eyes flicker, as if she's shoving a memory away.

"Then I guess this time, you need to find a way to not regret me, *Verity*."

Her words are odd, but I'm too engrossed in stripping her to figure out what it is. "That name," I breathe. "How *do* you know it?"

But just like last time, she closes her mouth and refuses to confess her secrets.

I reach out to her shredded bra, though it's still cupping her breasts. I peel away one cup then the other and slide the straps down her shoulders. Her skin is tanned, a deep olive I could only dream of having, and yet it's as cold and smooth as marble. And to my delight, both of her nipples are pierced. I press my mouth to them, flicking my tongue over one, then the other. My hands desperately trying to hold their ample size and failing. Under my tongue, she hardens. Sucking in a hissed breath, she moans something inaudible.

"Pardon?" I say.

"I said"— and this time she's gritting her teeth— "you will be the death of me."

"I doubt that, you're immortal."

She slides her hand to the back of my head, winds her

fingers in my hair and yanks back until I'm staring into those crimson eyes.

"There are other ways to ruin a woman than just killing her."

I smile. Hate. Desire. Rage. All of them cloying in my gut, in my chest, fogging my mind. "Then I promise you, Octavia Beaumont, I will ruin you in each and every one of them."

I put my arms around her and swing her around and down onto the bed. "Do I need to shred these as well?" I ask glancing at her trousers.

She unbuckles her jeans and wrestles them over her hips and off. Before she can do the same to her lace underwear, I have already slipped the knife between her hip bone and the lace.

She gasps. And the flash of fear in her expression makes a sick sort of pleasure twist through me.

I'd be nervous with a weapon that close to me too. Especially in my hands, even I don't know what I'll do with it.

It's a fine line I'm skirting between desire and rage.

I jerk the knife and her lace panties part, shrivelling and splitting as the fabric pings apart. I rip through the other side just as fast and then I peel the underwear away to reveal her exquisite core. I nudge her bent legs open so I get a full view of her pussy.

My mouth waters, my own cunt soaking all over again. Fuck. It disgusts me that I want a vampire this much. She's everything I hate, and yet, I've never wanted anything more in my life. I must have a masochistic heart to put myself in this much agony.

I switch the blade to my left hand and crawl up to meet her mouth, placing my balled fists either side of her head.

"What are we doing?" I whisper.

"I think that's obvious. We're both crazed with blood lust and there's only one way to get rid of it."

"Why does it feel like more than that?" I ask.

She hesitates. That same strange expression drawing across her features.

"What aren't you telling me?" I say, holding the blade under her chin.

"That's becoming a nasty habit you have, threatening me with a knife. Maybe you should follow through?"

The temptation is real. And yet as I kneel above her, my heart beating a rhythmic symphony between my ribs, I don't want to hurt her. Every thud in my chest is the music of her. Of desire. Of need.

Gods dammit.

I slip the tip of my blade to her lip, gently pull it down, displaying the ends of her fangs.

"I'm not the only one aroused," I say, staring at the sharp white points.

"I'm not the one fighting it," she says, never taking her crimson eyes off me.

"What if I don't want to fuck? What if I want something else?" I whisper, glancing at the blade. How easy it would be to just slice. Stab. Kill.

"I know what you want. Take it," she says and like a viper, her hand lashes out, gripping my wrist, forcing me to push the tip of the blade into her scar above her heart.

"So stake me, Verity. If that's what you really want."

The blade slips beneath her skin, a well of blood pooling at its tip.

Fuck.

Rich iron fills the air. It fills my head, swims in my vision, makes my body hot and my nipples hard.

I need it.

I want it.

"You fucking temptress. I don't think it's me that will ruin you. I think it's the vampire princess that will be the death of me," I say.

She grips my wrist so hard I know she's going to leave marks. "Take. It."

So I do.

I snap and throw the blade away. I drag my tongue over her scar, mopping up all the blood, and then I rise to meet her mouth, sucking her lip into mine and biting until her blood wells in my mouth. I suck hard enough my mouth fills with the sweet iron nectar.

And then my whole world comes apart.

Everything is bright, exhilarating. The air kisses my skin, my veins are alive with electricity and my pussy throbs.

I move my mouth over hers, our tongues caressing and gliding over each other, the taste of me on her lips, the taste of her blood in my mouth.

It's too much. I can't breathe, my body is covered in goosebumps. I'm not even sure if I'm in my body anymore.

I slide my hand down her body, tweaking her nipples until she moans. I break off the kiss. I want more of that sound. I need it.

I shuffle lower, kissing and licking her breasts until she's pleading with me.

"Touch me, please," she begs. Her voice sounds fragile, vulnerable. It's the first time I've ever seen her show weakness and I crave it. Not so I can hurt her, but so I can hold her, let her know I'll keep her safe in this moment.

I slip my hand between her thighs, one finger either side of her clit rubbing up and down slowly. I will take my damn time. She doesn't get to own everything. Her pleasure is mine.

I squeeze my fingers a little tighter and slide down her

centre, bringing her slickness up so I can move faster. I shift quick, my finger finding her hole and push the tip inside. I pull out. Tease the tip in again. Over and over until she's soaked my fingers and bucking her hips. She's fucking with my head. Shifting everything I know, everything I should want. I take a second to lean against her stomach because I can't believe she's this wet for me. I need to take all of her.

I shuffle down. She looks at me, catching sight of me between her legs.

"I wish you could bite me," she says.

"I have a knife for that."

She grins at me, and I nip at her thigh. It's not a vampire bite, but it's the best I can do.

"Harder," she says.

I sink my teeth in a little more. Not enough to draw blood but enough to leave a little imprint. It elicits a filthy moan from her mouth.

I drop to her pussy and draw my tongue down her centre, savouring the delicious taste of her. I lap it up, I want more, I want all of it. My mind is crazed with need. I circle my tongue around her clit. Lap fast and slow and fast and slow until she's whimpering and gripping at what's left of the sheets.

I slide a finger inside her and she breathes my name like she's praying to the Mother of Blood and I swear I nearly come on the spot.

"Verity," she moans.

I slip another inside her and that draws another equally filthy sound from her. She's swearing and crying my name.

"Your clit is mine. Ride my fingers till you make yourself come, Princess."

I curl my fingers into a better position and the twitch of her legs tells me I hit the right spot. She grinds her hips against my mouth as I focus on her clit, licking and lapping and worshipping her pussy.

Her walls tighten, I thrust my fingers a little more, helping her ride them faster, deeper, harder. Her pussy clenches so hard around my fingers I'm sure she's going to break them. Her back arches, lifting off the bed. I make my tongue stiffer, flicking it as fast as I can, and then she breaks, screaming my name as wetness drenches my fingers, my face, the sheets. Everything soaks as she squirts all over me.

Fuck. Fuck. This is amazing, I've never fucked anyone and made them squirt. I hold my mouth to her pussy taking everything she gives me. Licking and swiping my tongue, cleaning her up.

"Octavia…" I say when I still haven't pulled my fingers out of her.

"Yes?" she pants.

"You need to relax, I can't pull out."

She laughs at the top of the bed. "Sorry, I… give me a second."

I hear her try to take a couple of deep breaths, and as she loosens, I inch out, which only makes her twitch and tighten again. It takes another couple of breaths before she releases me, and I crawl up the bed and lay flat on my back.

"Wow," I say.

"Yeah," she says.

"Now that we've both come, our heads should clear. The effects of the blood lust will ease off," she says and strokes my cheek. I lean into her palm. "When your mind is free from the hold of my blood, you will feel very different. You'll go back to hating me."

"I know. This was just blood lust. Just sex. It doesn't change anything," I say.

"No. Things changed a long time ago."

I roll onto my side to face her. "What does that mean?"

She shifts to face me, her eyes soft and sad. There's a secret hidden in the blink of her lashes, and I can't quite reach it.

"It means that sometimes it's easier to hate someone than love them."

But her words feel distant and slippery, like they're already leaking from my mind as my head shifts back to clarity and all I can focus on is the horror of realising I'm in bed. Naked. Having just fucked one of the original three vampires.

"I... I need to go," I say, wiping a hand over my face. Octavia's face hardens, though underneath it there's a crack, but it's too painful too look at.

"I'll have Wendell draw you a carriage," she says.

And then she's slipping out of bed and pulling on a robe, and I am swimming in a toxic cocktail of confusion.

INTERLUDE

OCTAVIA

I lie in bed knowing two things:
Verity is mine, and she hates me.

I just hope when she finds out what I did, she understands. Why I had no choice but to do it.

I still remember the first time I met her.

Three Years Ago

I was in the Montague territory. Honestly, I was minding my own business. Inspecting some of the villages for Mother. I knew it was a mistake sending me. I'd pleaded with her to send Xavier, he's the friendly face of the family. But she insisted.

The Montague region isn't like mine or Mother's territory. At least there they either revere or fear me. I'm only too happy to play leader or villain. All our residents receive our protection as long as they toe the line. In my territory, my word is law and one day, my word will be law for the entire city.

I was in a small village called Elysium. It was close to midnight, and I was patrolling the minor villages near the border of the Peace Territory.

Red must have been working or training, I don't recall now. But I was attacked. A group of villagers took it upon themselves to try and outmanoeuvre me.

I was down the end of this village, cornered by the local pub and an alley. I'd seen a kitten haphazardly trying to catch a mouse and considered helping it, given I was much faster and the youngster was clearly starving, when someone attacked me from behind.

"Filthy drainer," he spat and swung the wooden bat at my head again.

At this point, I don't believe he knew who I was. I think he just saw a vampire and decided to attack. Unfortunately for him, I am not just any vampire.

I was knocked to the floor, a drizzle of blood oozing from my already healing temple. I pushed myself up, turning to him. That's when he saw my eyes.

There was a moment of hesitation. He froze, a trickle of piss leaking down his trouser leg as he realised exactly who I was.

"That was a mistake," I snarled.

But such is the curse of humanity; in moments of danger, they freeze, flee or fight. And for some reason, this mistaken fool decided the latter was the right option. He snapped out of his frozen daze, his eyes changing from their wide-eyed panic to the narrowed squint of a man staring at a target. A man in possession of a goal and a hunger akin to a death wish.

Perhaps the fact he'd gotten a successful swing in gave him the boost he needed to attempt to beat me.

"LADS," he shouted.

Now, I am strong. I can take half a dozen men at once

without breaking much of a sweat. But twenty on one? That is a lot even for me. Vampires have their limits no matter how old we are. Not that we let the public know this, but our immortality can be taken, look at Mother's cure she's chasing.

A swarm of drunken louts rounded the corner. I glanced behind me, there was a wall surrounding this village, a kind of protective stone battlement that you could walk around. The Peace Territory had a similar one, keeping the humans that lived there in, and everyone who didn't want to behave, out.

I could make it if I ran and leapt, it wasn't that high, but it was high enough that it would hurt with the headache that was now forming.

The group of men drew closer. Some were holding pints that sloshed over the side, others spades and bats and pitch forks. This was going downhill rapidly.

I was standing in a flash, my feet sliding into a defensive stance. I poured all the arrogance I have into my voice.

"You do realise who I am?" I snarled. Of course he did, that's why he called his friends. "You're making a mistake."

I made myself stare into his face, and yet the fucking coward couldn't bring himself to look me in the eye.

Of course he couldn't.

"Pathetic. You dare to challenge me, and you won't even deign to look me in the eye?" I shout.

"Those filthy crimson eyes? You're a freak. Good for nothing. Born an abomination. Someone needs to put you out your misery."

I laugh, I can't help it. "Do you know how many men have said that to me over the years? And you think one little drunk piece of shit is going to scare me?"

The crowd of men spills into a semi-circle around him. The air is potent with stale beer and cigarette smoke. The essence of regret. And I would make them regret this.

"Not just one of me though, is there? All you drainers are the fucking same. You're a plague, a virus, and you... you're the fucking worst of them all."

"You don't even know me."

"I don't have to. And thankfully, now, I won't have to. Lads... GET HER."

They run at me. I brace myself, let my fangs drop, and ready for the ambush. They're fast, but they're also drunk. I am decidedly faster.

A punch wallops me in the stomach but I'm spinning out of the way, flinging my fists into jaws hard enough the bones crack and break, echoing in the alley like a symphony. And fuck is it glorious music.

Someone slips underneath the tangle of limbs and delivers a kick to my knee. Pain explodes up my leg as my kneecap wrenches out of place. I stumble back but manage to keep upright as I swing my leg the opposite way despite the excruciating heat searing through my bones. My knee locks back in, the muscle fibres and ligaments already knitting back into place as I throw a punch so hard it drives right through the perpetrator's rib cage. His eyes flare wide. But it's too fucking late.

"N—" he starts to screech but I've already torn his heart out of his chest. Warm blood spatters my face. He dies standing, watching it beat its last beat. Then he drops to the floor. I lick my lips, the blood urging me on, giving me strength they'll never possess.

But the confidence is short-lived. I'm knocked forward, crashing to the cobbles with three men piled on top of me, screaming and hurling obscenities. They clear off me, but another three take their place, battering me with spades and bats. Then one of them slams the pitchfork into my gut and that...

It hurts. Like really hurts. The kind of pain that shoots white across my vision and then explodes in a burst of fury.

"Oi," a woman's voice screams from behind me. The men freeze their assault. That was their second mistake. I tug the fork out of my gut and slam it into the side of the man who wielded it. He drops like a stone to the cobbles. It focuses the others' attention back on me.

"What in Blood's name is happening?" the woman screams. But the group doesn't care, they're focused on me. On taking me apart piece by piece. This is why I hate humans.

"YOU NEED TO STOP. IN THE NAME OF THE CHIEF, I COMMAND YOU TO STOP." Her voice drops an octave as she bellows and my heart sinks.

Just what I didn't need. A fucking hunter meddling in this business. She will probably finish the job.

"Fuck off," someone shouts at her.

A growl rips from a man's chest, I can't tell who, and then one of the guys stops his assault on me and heads towards the voice behind me.

"I said stop," she bellows. There's a crunch of fist on body; a hollow, cracking thwack joins the echoes of bone breaks and spluttered cries of pain. I don't know if it's her or the guy who was attacking me, but I can't spin around until I've dropped these last two idiots.

Something clatters behind me, like a body landed against a dumpster. The hunter girl moves like water through the air, graceful waves and flows of her limbs as she disarms man after man, knocking each one out.

The man charging at me draws a knife. My jaw flexes. I'm tired of this. I spin out of the way as he lunges at me, then I spring forward, sinking my teeth into his neck and bite down and tear. A chunk of his neck comes away with me. I'm showered in blood like the warm splatters of monsoon rain.

I close my eyes, savouring the taste and sensation of blood as it coats my skin when a gasp rips me from my reverie.

I open my eyes as the hunter girl screams, "Watch out!" She flings a blade at the man whose fingers are inches from mine. I spin out of his reach as the knife sinks into his chest.

She saved me? Or at least stopped me getting knifed.

A hunter?

What the fuck?

I turn back to the girl, wondering who the hell this hunter is, and why in the name of sacred blood she would protect me. But the attacker she flung into the dumpster has gotten up and thrown himself at her. He raises his hand and plunges a knife into her gut.

I move instinctively. My body flinging itself through the air at vampire speed. I sink my fingers into his arm, my nails plunging through his shirt and straight into his skin and I yank, tearing his arm out of its socket, detaching it from his body.

He screams, but I halt the sound as I sink my mouth over his throat and tear it out. I fling his carcass away and drop to my feet, cradling her body. She's warm, her green eyes pierce right through me, as if she sees something in my soul even I can't.

The hunter girl lurches, curling into me as she holds her stomach. A strange smile on her pale lips. "Ironic isn't it... a hunter dying to save a vampire." She laughs.

Laughs? As if dying is nothing. Then she looks down at her hands, and her face pales as she pulls them up and blood pours from her gut.

"Shit." I put my hand over her stomach and apply pressure.

"Let go, I'm finished," she says and then she catches sight of my eyes. "Oh." Only she doesn't flinch, she doesn't recoil, she just smiles. "It's you..."

"And now you understand why they were attacking," I said.

She shakes her head. "It... It was unprovoked."

I stare at her, shocked that she's not displaying any kind of fear.

"You're not afraid of me?" I whisper.

"Why would I be?" She says it so casually, as if *not* being afraid of me is the most normal thing in the world when it's as far from the truth as possible.

Her skin pales, her lips turn blue as a dribble of blood oozes out of her mouth. I'm suddenly not ready for her to die. I need to know why she's not afraid, why she defended me.

"Why? Why did you help?" I say.

"Because... hunters are trained to protect."

"Yes, humans, not vampires."

She shakes her head, her eyes rolling back. "No," she says and then the next words she utters carve my world in two. "We're trained to protect the innocent."

Her head rolls back, her eyes flutter shut.

I make a decision. Maybe it was wrong, maybe I shouldn't have done it. But she'd saved me...

No human had ever done more than given me a passing sneer. And she'd not only saved me but taken a blade to the gut and was going to lose her life over it.

A human... sacrificing themselves for me?

I shove the sleeve of my shirt up and sink my fangs into my wrist. The movements are automatic, my body reacting on instinct. I hoist her up and into my arms. I drag my teeth

149

across my wrist until my own blood pools in my mouth and spills over. Then I place my wrist over her mouth.

My blood flows in long throbbing pulses into her mouth. She's already unconscious so I just pray enough of it reaches her stomach and seeps into her system to make a difference.

I shred her top, ripping the fabric over her stomach so I can see the gash in her belly. It's an ugly, raw wound, the flesh rumpled and torn, blood crusted over her skin. My wrist slows to an ooze, but she hasn't woken. I pull it away and sink my teeth in again, re-tearing the flesh and push her lips open further, hoping more blood will pour down her throat.

"Come on, come on," I plead.

I glance back at her gut; the blood has slowed to an ooze but I'm not sure if that's because mine is healing her or if I'm too late and she's too far gone.

She spasms under my hold, then her hands find my arm and she grabs hold, plunging her mouth over my wrist.

"Fuck, easy now."

But her eyes snap open, something feral passes through her expression and she gulps down my blood. The harder she sucks on my wrist the hotter my body grows.

Oh shit.

I've never allowed anyone to feed from me. Xavier's told me about the side effects, but in my panic I'd forgotten. Warmth drops to my crotch, heat pools between my thighs, my underwear sticking to me. Mother of Blood. She's taking too much. I glance at her stomach, the wound is sealed shut. I pull my arm away, but it's too late, she's taken too much, and I am consumed by her. By the scent of her blood, the scent of mine thrumming through her veins. My clit pulses between my legs.

I have to get away from her before *I can't.*

"You're…" she says as she climbs out of my arms.

"Octavia Beaumont," I confirm.

"Beaumont," she whispers and then her eyes flare wide as she takes in the sight of her shredded clothes.

"What did you do…? Oh, no. No. No. No."

I frown. "You're welcome, by the way."

"Welcome?" she snaps. "You just fucking fed me your blood. You're a vampire and not just any fucking vampire. You're one of the original three."

"Yes, I've known that for quite a while," I deadpan.

"I am so completely fucked. I'm a hunter. I can't drink vampire blood."

I sigh, "What's your name?"

"Red."

"Your real name."

She raises an eyebrow. "Red."

"Don't make me compel it out of you."

"Compel it out of me and I'll take your life instead of those village men…"

I raise an eyebrow.

"You get to know my name when you've earned it."

"And how do I do that?"

She grins at me, the smile lights up her green eyes. "I don't know yet, but I'll be sure to tell you when I do…"

"Well, *Red*… thanks for… for… you know. Stopping that guy."

"You're… welcome?" she says. "Gods, what is… why do I feel?" She slides her hand over her chest, gripping where her breasts sit. She glares at me and then scrambles up. But she doesn't back away. Instead, heat rushes up her neck.

"Fuck," she says and buckles over. "Why do I…? What… what is this?" she takes a step closer to me despite the confusion sprawled across her face.

Shit, she drank too much.

"Have you ever drunk blood before?" I ask.

"Obviously not. I'm a hunter, it's my job to prevent drainers like you taking blood illegally, why the hell would I drink the stuff?"

"If you hadn't, you would have died."

"Oh my gods, maybe you should have let me. Shit, if anyone in the Academy finds out—"

"They won't."

"Why, because I can trust you not to tell anyone?" Her face scrunches like that's the last thing she would ever believe.

She wobbles on her feet. She had lost a lot of blood and even though I saved her, she's going to need to rest. I slide my arm around her waist.

"Let me assist you home."

"I cannot go home like this. If anyone realises it's not human blood on me. If they knew I'd drunk... Gods, I am in so much shit. Next time, let me die, yeah?" She pats my shoulder, her face strained as if she's not sure whether to run away or sit on my face. "Why the hell did you save me?"

The words slip out before I can stop them. "Because you're the first person in nearly ten centuries to not look at me like I'm a freak."

Her brows knit together, and then I scoop her up and I'm running her through the villages. I run so fast the wind whips her straggly short hair away from her face. Her pupils blow wide, and I know my blood is seeping into her system. That the urges crawling through her body aren't real. She may have been willing to help me, but none of this is real. It never is. No one ever wants me. Not really. Eventually they all find a way to be afraid.

I need to get her back to Castle Beaumont and into a private room before I find myself unable to leave her. I run through the forest, trees and branches whipping at my arms.

She clings to me, the pads of her fingers pressed against my neck, the faintest thud of her heartbeat against my skin.

I can sense my blood in her body as it ebbs and flows through her veins. The further is drifts through her body, the calmer I grow. It infuses with her essence, her soul.

It makes her mine.

In blood.

In bonds.

In life.

And law.

We're connected in the most intimate way, our life-forces united. The smell of us is euphoric. It peels off her arms and chest like perfume and fills my nose like a drug.

Shit. I can't leave her now. I don't want to.

She is *mine*.

My thighs burn with the speed at which I'm sprinting through the territory. Her fingers wind through my hair, she tilts my head towards her. No. I cannot do this. I will not.

I need to get away from her. I can't trap her like this it's not fair. She doesn't understand what she's asking of me.

Finally, finally, when I can't take the scent of us mingled together for another second, I burst through the castle doors. I race across the ground floor and up to my private wing.

That was my second mistake. I should have dropped her in the guest quarters and fled to my wing. I just needed her off me, away from me. So I could set her free.

I need you to believe me when I tell you that I tried. But blood lust already had its claws in me. I thought I was doing the right thing taking her to a place to fully recover.

But I failed her. The urge to take her, make her mine, too much.

I could smell my scent all over her. She smelled like my domain. Shit. I drop her in my master bathroom and push her, fully clothed, into the shower.

I flick on the showerhead and warm water streams out. I plead with it to wash away the scent.

It doesn't.

I was too late.

The scent of her, of me, pools inside the shower, mixing with the steam. Cloying in the air as a smoky euphoria.

She is already mine. The shape of us hardens inside me, the bond blooming in my heart. I was never going to let her go. I owned her now. And much as I didn't want to admit it, she owned me.

Her lips part. "I'm going to take my clothes off now," she says as she pulls the remnants of her top off, letting it drop and splash in the basin of the shower.

Her skin is so pale compared to the tanned olive of mine. Blood streams down her stomach, a faint silver line dividing her stomach the way it's divided our lives. Before tonight and after.

"We shouldn't do this," I say, unable to peel my eyes away from the hard plains of her abdomen.

"I want to," she breathes.

"It's not real, it's blood lust."

"Never heard of it."

"Probably because you've only witnessed humans drinking from common vampires. If you feed from me, or any of the original three or our direct sires, like Dahlia and Xavier who mother turned, then it does something else to you. It…"

"Arouses us?"

I nod.

"Well, Princess," she says, a commanding tone running through her voice. "You're the one who fed me, so I guess you better get on your knees and do something about it..."

She unbuckles her trousers, her eyes never leaving mine. And that, in itself is a drug. To have someone look at me. Really, truly, stare in my eyes and not hate me, or fear me, or want to flee from me.

It is so surprising. My entire life no one has looked at me like this. No one has ever wanted me.

I know I shouldn't. Every rational thought is screaming at me not to do this, that when the blood lust vanishes, she'll hate me, she'll run like the rest of them. Fear will leak into her bones, and she'll be just like everyone else.

But the way she's looking at me, the way it warms my blood and heats my bones and fills the cavity in my chest...

I can't let it go.

I can't walk away.

I step into the shower. One foot. Two.

She smiles and reaches for my wrist, her slender fingers pulling me closer until my fingers find the buckle of her trousers. She nudges me until I slide the zip down.

"You don't want this. You will regret me," I say.

"You don't get to tell me what I want." She wriggles her arse, pushing her trousers down over her hips and stepping out of them.

This is why I've never let a human feed from me.

The water drenches me, blood pools in the basin, running off our clothes. I pull my sopping top off and fling it out of the shower. Her fingers find my trousers, and she unhooks the button, slowly drawing the zip down.

My entire body is alive.

"Are you okay?" she says.

I nod because I can't bring myself to confess, to tell her

how alone I've been. That she's daring to do something no other human would.

She stands under the showerhead, letting the water pour over her short hair, rubbing her hands over her face and pushing the shaggy locks back. I pull my trousers down and throw those outside the shower too.

Both of us stand there in our underwear. She's wearing boxers and a cropped sports bra. I'm wearing black lace.

Her eyes draw down my body, tracing the curves, I can feel them on me. The way she stares at me heats my entire being. I step closer and she pulls me in, sliding her hand up my back, sending a shiver of pleasure down my spine.

In a single swift movement, she's unhooked the clasp of my bra.

"Fuck," she hisses. "You're stunning." She bites her lip, the same heat spreading through my body drawing into her expression, her lids becoming heavy.

My cheeks flame as hot as the air between us. Water pours over my hair, the long locks sticking to my back.

She draws my bra straps down and tugs until my breasts are free.

"I..." she starts. "I need to touch you."

"So touch me already."

Her eyes flick up to meet mine. She holds me there, steam billowing around us.

"Your eyes..." she says.

And this is what I was dreading. The moment she realises I'm the city's freak, the only vampire born. The only one with crimson eyes the colour of death.

But to my surprise, she reaches up and caresses my cheek. I lean against her palm, waiting for the disgust.

But instead, she breathes, "Wow."

"Eyes the colour of blood and death..." I mumble.

"No," she says, "they're the colour of love and life."

I'm struck silent. To have someone really truly look at me, to see me how no other has ever seen me. I wasn't sure if I wanted to cry, bite her or wrap her in my arms and never let go. I think maybe a little of all three.

She reaches up for me, stretching on tiptoes, she's at least half a head shorter than me, and she pulls me down to kiss her. Our lips caress, warmth pooling between the gentle brushes. I lose myself in her touch. The way her mouth moves over mine, claiming me. I slide my tongue against hers and she moans.

It makes me instantly wet and crazed with need. I reach my arms around her back, hook my fingers under her sports bra and yank, splitting it in two.

She gasps against me, and then laughs as she pulls away and lets it drop to the floor. She swings me around until my back hits the shower wall. I hiss against the cool press of the tiles.

"Do that again,"—she grins, pointing to my lace knickers—"only to them..."

I grin in response. I can't hold myself back anymore, my fangs drop. I expect her to shrink away or slide into a fighting stance. But she doesn't.

Who are you, little hunter?

There's a part of my mind screaming at me to be realistic, to recognise that all this will go away when my blood's thrall fades. But she has me mesmerised, I cannot walk away. I will not.

Not until she realises she's mine.

I slide my fingers into my knickers and rip. They fall away.

Her expression darkens with desire. Her tongue slides over her lips. "I'm going to fuck you now," she says.

And all I can do is nod because fucking me is exactly

what I want her to do. I crave the feel of her inside me, the way my blood is in her.

"Spread your legs, Princess," she says, so demanding.

I don't.

Just to see what she'll do.

Just to play the game.

She steps into me, "I said..."— she shoves one of my feet apart with hers— "Spread. Your. Legs." She nudges the other apart until I'm bared wide.

No one else would dare speak to me like this.

But the way she barks the order, it makes me wet.

She lowers her mouth to my skin. Caressing my neck, licking and nipping as though she were the vampire and not me. Her lips run over my collarbone sending waves and sparks of pleasure over my skin. She bites my neck, not hard, but hard enough to make me moan and wish she were sinking her teeth in.

She kisses every inch of my body, taking her sweet time, her hand roaming over my waist, skimming over the dip and up to my breasts. Her thumb brushes my nipples until they harden into nubs. Her fingertips glide down my curves and rounded tummy until she finds my centre.

"You're already wet for me," she says.

"It's the blood," I pant as her fingers draw between my folds and glide up and over my clit. Over and over until I'm a panting mess.

"Liar." She smiles into my chest and then her tongue swirls over my nipples, and I know I'm losing myself in this moment. Losing myself to her.

As she tips me over into bliss, the only shadow marking the night is the fear of what happens after...

CHAPTER 17

OCTAVIA

When I wake the following afternoon, Red has long since gone. I considered compelling her. It took every ounce of control I had not to do it. I didn't because something shifted between us. She wasn't as hateful or regretful. I wonder if it's the quantity of blood she had or something else. She felt... different.

But I can hardly explain that to her, can I? Not without a series of confessions I am far from ready to give.

In fact, it was a mistake to call her by her real name. But I couldn't help it. The pull of my blood coursing through her system fucked with the clarity of my mind. Normally, she's in the hunter territory when she takes it, and I am far enough away I can't sense her. But last night. I was consumed, irrational, possessive.

I'm faced with two choices, neither of which I particularly like: Tell her how I know her name and why she has no memory of that night. Or lie and hope that she never finds out.

Like I say, neither of these feels particularly appealing. I cover my face and groan. At that moment, Wendell walks in, carrying a tray of breakfast.

"This is one of the finer breakfast delicacies from the cellar. A vintage blood with essence of jealousy. I know how you like to start the day drinking something a little spiteful," he says, not quite meeting my gaze. It makes a piece of me shrivel inside. Wendell cares for me, I know this. But no matter how hard he tries, he is still wary of me, he probably always will be. It's inbuilt in them—the humans, I mean.

"Oh, you're too good to me." I take the goblet and cradle it. He does raise his eyes briefly to glance up at me but pulls them away just as quick.

"You warmed it too?" I say and clasp my hand to his in gratitude.

"But of course." He smiles and nods and then says, "You have an hour before the private carriage will be ready to take to you Castle St Clair."

"What does Mother want now? I thought we'd be sent the trial information and get on with it," I say, frowning.

"I believe she's referring to it as the partnering ceremony. It appears Cordelia is pushing quite hard with the timeline on this. She wants to begin the trials immediately."

"Ugh." I lean back against my pillow and take another sip of the delicious blood, B negative, I think. Not my favourite but certainly not the worst tasting, and the vintage quality makes the iron particularly rich. I close my eyes, savouring it.

"I'll draw you a bath while you enjoy your breakfast."

He leaves and fusses in the bathroom while I sip on breakfast.

Several hours later, I am in a long queue of carriages trailing up the winding mountain path. I stick my head out of the carriage window and all I see for miles are carriage upon carriage of vampire nobles and hunters alike.

It truly is a strange sight to witness, for the second time in a week, so many hunters and vampires in close proximity without any bloodshed or fighting.

I shut the window and ponder. What is Mother up to? She's spent ten centuries fighting hunters and suddenly she wants to partner with them? I don't think any of us believe her bullshit about retiring. But I also don't agree with how she rules; she has her own best interests at heart rather than the city's.

Her fear and furious hand, I understand. So rarely do people obey unless you give them a reason to toe the line. But this partnership I find curious because the only reason she would do this is if she is getting something out of it. But what?

I intend to find out.

Finally, we reach the castle courtyard. One of Mother's staff opens the door.

"Miss," she says, realising who I am and paling. She steps out of the way, giving me a wide berth. Xavier steps out of a carriage on the other side of the courtyard. I make my way to him.

"Favourite," he says and bends to kiss my cheek. He's wearing a luxurious, long black gentleman's coat, his chin-length locks wavy and coiffed to perfection. He looks dashing as usual.

"Fetching attire, darling," I say and kiss his other cheek. "Shame about the personality attached to it."

He gives me a dirty look. "You look different. Did the little hunter pity fuck you? I saw the way you were looking at each other in the club."

"One, how dare you. Two, no."

He huffs out a laugh. "My, my, Octavia, we are defensive this fine evening. Methinks the lady doth protest a little too much."

"Remind me why you're my favourite again?"

"Because of that summer of blood and whiskey and the fact we fucked our way around three cities and never got caught?"

I open my mouth to contradict him and decide he's probably right. While we've had hundreds of years together, that summer really was the one that bonded us.

"So much carnage." I sigh.

"So much blood," he whispers.

He offers me his arm and walks me across the courtyard and up the porch steps to the front door. Mother's door is an ornate, imposing arch. It's dark wood, lined with dapple hammered wrought iron framing and studs. It's ajar, but the gargoyle door knocker jerks forward closing it.

"In a mood this morning I see, Rumblegrit," I say but he doesn't reply. He just sticks his engorged tongue out. There's a spike on the end ready and waiting for my offering.

I dutifully place my index finger on it and press until a single bead of blood rolls down the spike and absorbs into his silver tongue which shimmers red briefly.

"Thank you. Human blood is vile," he says, his features softening. The door swings open and we walk in.

The house acknowledges my payment, and for a few short seconds, the hallway walls ripple with veins spreading down the corridor like bloodied tree roots. They fade just as quick and vanish into the wall, only to reappear as another vampire noble enters behind us.

"The house will be in a delightful mood by suns up," Xavier says.

"No doubt. I don't think it will have been fed this much blood in at least five decades." Mother's staff are dotted down the corridors, dressed in their finest, polished maroon uniforms. They guide us towards the heart of the house and the main ballroom.

When we enter, I halt, surprised at the changes in here. Usually, it's a sweeping cavernous space dedicated to balls and parties, with glistening chandeliers. But tonight, it is quite different. Around the edges of the room is a bank of tiered seating. It covers three walls, leaving the wall to my left free for a small stage.

In the middle of what was the dance floor are two plinths. The seats are about half full, but it doesn't look like there's a seating plan, for hunters and vampires are sitting wherever they choose. Though there's a natural divide occurring.

Vampires occupy the seats against the far wall, and the hunters fill the seats closest to the door—that, at least, makes sense.

But in the middle, where the two species meet, there is a little crossover and as far as I can tell, no fights have broken out.

"What oh what are you up to now, Mother?" Xavier says under his breath.

"Octavia, Xavier," Cordelia shouts from the stage, opening her arms as she spots us walking into the room.

We veer towards the stage, climbing the steps and embracing Mother.

"Shouldn't be too much longer. We're just waiting for the Chief and the other challengers.

"This is most unortho—" I start. But a sensation stops me speaking.

My body heats up, my cheeks flush, electricity shoots to my pussy. Oh no.

Oh shit. Red.

She's in the house, I can sense her. Or more accurately sense my blood nearing. But that doesn't make sense. It should be mostly out of her system by now.

"Excuse me a moment," I say, and before Mother can be annoyed that I've fled, I'm off the stage and exiting the ballroom.

I spot her coming down the corridor. Her posture stiffens when she notices me. I cock my head at her, she presses her lips together but nods and breaks off from the tall handsome chap that is one of the five, I forget his name, Lionel? Larry? Whatever.

I pull her into a drawing room two corridors away.

"Hi," she says, but she's rigid, holding herself away from me.

"Is everything okay?"

She shifts on the spot, her eyes falling away from me. She takes a deep breath, gathering herself and says, "I mean, yes, fine."

I raise an eyebrow. "Fine? Really? I don't need to be a thousand years old to understand that 'fine' means you're anything but."

She hardens, her shoulders tight as she rounds on me. "If you really want to know, then no. I am very much not okay, as it happens."

"I see. And what is the matter?"

She throws her hands up. "You. You're the problem, Octavia. You ruin everything."

I won't lie, that stings. After last night I thought we were moving forward. I thought things might be different this time.

I recoil a little as Red stares up at me, her eyes so cold, the green sliding from warm forest to icy lake. She steps into my space, only this time instead of the heat of the night prior, it's all corded neck, tense muscles and an expression that could stake a weaker vampire.

"I get that you were trying to help..." she says through gritted teeth. "But you fed me so much of your blood last night, the withdrawals are even worse today. I had to dose before I came here and I never. Ever. Do that. Not when I have to leave the hunter territory, and certainly not when I'm going to be in the presence of other vampires."

That explains why I could sense her. My heart stops.

"Whose blood did you take?"

"Yours, unfortunately. I took the vials you had couriered to my apartment."

The relief makes me sag. I cannot allow her to drink from anyone else. If I caught her drinking another vampire's blood... I'd slaughter the entire city.

She is mine.

The thought makes my blood pulse. It must do the same to her because she steps a little closer, her chest heavy with each breath.

"And how do you feel now you have my blood in your system?" I say, daring to edge a little closer.

She edges forward, forcing me to take a step back. We move like ballroom dancers.

Step. Step. Step. My back crunches against the wall.

"How do you think I feel? The closer I've gotten to you, the worse it's screwing my head up. I need to fuck your blood out of my system. Fuck the woman who murdered my sister. You think that fills me with joy? It makes my insides burn. It makes me sick to my stomach and hate the skin I wear. You took everything from me."

"I took nothing."

"Lies. You left my life in pieces and for what? What did you even need Amelia for?"

"She had a choice, *Verity*."

"Stop fucking calling me that," she shouts and kicks a stray chair beside us halfway across the room. It shatters, the pieces tumbling like accusations on the carpet. It seems the longer she suffers with blood lust, the more it twists into rage. Too bad for her, because that little act of frustration sends the most exquisite bolt of pleasure straight to my pussy. Do I like her angry? This could be a fun game to play.

She must sense the temptress in me because her expression hardens even further. The muscles in her neck are straining as she paces back and forth.

"You want to fuck me," I purr, fluttering my eyelashes like the little vampire vixen I am. She glares at me but continues pacing as if she thinks walking will erase the blood lust. We're going to fuck all right. I'm going to wind her up enough she fucks the anger out of herself.

"What I want... What I've wanted for two long weeks... Is to stake you." She leans so close to my face that I can smell the aged leather of her hunter uniform, the oils used to weather her stakes, the metallic tang of our blood mixed together.

Delicious.

Our breath mingles in the millimetres between us, and I want to drink it in as much as I want to sink my fangs into her neck and guzzle her iron-rich blood.

But better than that, I can smell the excitement pooling in her knickers. The same wetness clings to mine.

This will end the same way it ended last night. Her hands twitch. There's a stake in both, silver threaded through the wood like veins, and I know I'm playing with fire, with the devil, with death.

But the risk... the danger, it just turns me on. My breathing increases, and heat blooms at my centre. This is the problem with blood lust. It only grows stronger the closer we are to each other.

I stare her right in the eyes, offering myself on a plate. "So stake me."

"Don't. Tempt. Me," she spits.

This is my chance.

This is how I get her to embrace the fury. I know she'll feel better afterwards. She just needs to take it out on someone and lucky for her, I'm strong enough to take it.

I want to take it. I want to give her everything she needs no matter what it is because she is mine. And I would burn the city to the ground if it made her love me again...

"I turned your sister," I say, the words like silken blades.

"Shut up," she grabs my shoulders and shoves me back against the wall. I like it when she's rough with me. I like the fact I'm controlling her emotion, controlling her. Giving her exactly what she needs. Then, now, and forever.

"I took Amelia, and I sank my fangs into her neck and drained every drop of blood in her body."

"I SAID SHUT THE FUCK UP, OCTAVIA. I'll do it. I'll stake you." She puts her head in her hands pulling them down her face. The thought occurs to me then that something is definitely wrong. She shouldn't be suffering this bad with blood lust, or blood rage or any withdrawal.

She's panting, her torso heaving at the pressure building inside her. I hold my hands up against the wall, stretching my body tall.

An opening.

An invitation.

A temptation.

"She tasted delicious," I purr.

She screams and slams one of the stakes through my hand and into the wall.

It hurts. Fuck it hurts like nothing else. Searing white hot pain radiates out where the wood has punctured my hand and fixed me to the wall.

And yet, my skin flushes, my pussy throbs in time to the pulsing in my hand...

And. I. Want. More.

I laugh at her. I know this is dangerous. The scar over my chest tingles a warning. *Don't piss her off too much.* Don't stray over the line, not when I know what she's capable of.

She tried to stake me for real once when I snuck up on her while she was doing security rounds. Only she missed. She said it was an accident. I think she missed on purpose. That invisible bond between us, the one she doesn't remember, always tying us together.

"Is that all you've got? Pathetic. No wonder you couldn't save her," I sneer.

She slams the other stake into my other hand pinning it to the wall. The pain is enough to make my eyes water, but I refuse to let them spill over. Because as much as it hurts, I am now so wet that I'm certain I'm going to soak through my knickers and into my trousers.

Besides, I could pull my hand off the wall whenever I want, I'm choosing not to. To stay pinned here because this is what she needs and what I'm getting off on.

"Now what?" I say and take a big inhale of air. "Do you feel better?"

"No."

"I didn't think so. I told you the only way to rid yourself of the blood lust is to fuck it away and given I am your current object of desire, I'd say you need to fuck what you just pinned to the wall."

Her face heats, angry lines sink into the sharpness of her jaw and across her forehead. "I hate you," she snarls, and rips open my shirt, displaying my bra and the scar she gave me five years ago.

She points a finger at it. "One day."

I just smile, all this bravado for nothing, she couldn't stake me last time, she's only playing at staking me today. And she won't be able to do it next time either. I know her. I know what's in her heart.

"What do you want, my little hunter?" I say.

"YOU," she barks.

"Mmmhmm. So take me. Make me yours."

She pulls a blade out of her back pocket and unhooks my trouser button. With brittle, agitated movements she pulls my trousers off and then uses the blade to shred my underwear.

"That's the second set of underwear you have destroyed."

"Well, if you'd stop feeding me your fucking blood, maybe they'd stay intact."

She leans forward, pressing her fists either side of my waist, resting her head against my chest.

"This... what we're doing..." she starts.

"Yes...?" I purr. I shift against the wall, forgetting about my numbed hands until a searing bolt of pain erupts through my palm. It soon settles into a deep aching throb, one that morphs into desire.

"I can't. Not with—" She glances up and then reaches for the stake to remove it.

"Leave it, a little pain never hurt an orgasm."

"Fine. Then what's a safe word?" she asks.

And suddenly her voice is softer, calmer, knowing her prize is near.

"Seems I'm very good at playing your villain, so why

don't we go with that."

She glares at me. "You use it the minute it gets too much. I know you'll heal in seconds once I rip them out."

"I swear to gods if you don't fuck me this instant—"

She leans across my body, her nose millimetres from my wrist where the blood oozes down in glorious red ribbons.

Her tongue swipes up my arm, stopping just shy of the crimson trails. Part of me wants her to take it, ingest more, but it's the blood lust talking. And I won't force her, not when we need to get through the evening.

Without warning, she pulls away, a grunt of frustration escaping her lips. Those eyes never leave mine as she staggers a few steps back.

I'm left at the mercy of that delicious gaze, half naked and staked to the wall, quivering with need.

She drops to her knees before me. "I hate you. But I need you just as much," she says.

"I'm yours," I say, the words an echo of a life lost. She lowers her mouth onto my pussy.

I rock my hips forward, tilting my cunt so she can access as much of me as possible. My punctured hands burn with every movement, the heat transforming instantly into desire as it mixes with the bliss of her tongue.

She's feral as she licks my clit. Her tongue swipes long and luxurious strokes down my pussy and between my folds. She moans her own pleasure into me.

"Red..." I moan as the first intense wave of pleasure grows at my core.

She shifts, one of her hands disappearing into her own trousers.

"What are you doing?" I say, trying to get a better view.

"You don't get to touch me," she says, pulling off my pussy. "Not today. Not with how pissed off I am."

"You'll pay for that later," I snarl.

"So be it," she says and then resumes licking my cunt. Her tongue sweeps up and down. Over and over, she massages my clit. She brings her free hand to my entrance and pushes a finger inside me.

Her other arm rocks furiously between her legs. The faster she moves, the quicker she licks my clit until we're both building.

"I love looking at you on your knees for me," I say, wishing I could run my fingers through her hair and yank her harder to my cunt.

"More, Red, I need you to fuck the rage into me. I want you to punish me for everything I've done. Hate fuck me the way I know you want to."

My words topple her over the edge. She moans into my pussy, her back and shoulders arching as she makes herself come.

"Fuck you," she cries into me. Then she tears her hand out of her trousers and resumes her licking. She pushes another finger inside me, both of them thrusting hard.

"How much do you hate me?" I say, tempting her, teasing her to fuck me even harder. It's not enough. I want all her rage. I can feel it surging in her blood and that is like a drug to me. It's rippling off her in waves and it bleeds into my system like a siren call.

"I will always hate you for what you did," she says and thrusts a little harder.

"Show me," I say. "Or maybe I should drag your sister in here and show you just how I drained her all over again."

She snarls against my pussy and roughly shoves a third finger inside me. My head rolls back till it hits the wall. My hands sear with every thrust she makes, the continuous grinding of bone and tissue as it tries and fails to heal against the stake.

The pressure from her fingers filling me and sliding in

and out over and over makes me want to come apart. I moan in time to her thrusts as she curls her fingers and rubs just in the right spot. Her tongue licks and laps at my pussy as if she were starved.

I whimper her name when my walls clamp with a rising orgasm. She pumps her fingers into me harder and harder until my back rocks against the wall and my hands shift against the stakes, the searing pain radiating down my arms, mixing with the pleasure of her mouth on my clit, I can't take it. I'm going to crash over the edge.

She thrusts once more, a second time, and then I fall into bliss.

The instant I come, Red calms. She pulls her fingers out and kisses my clit with a tenderness I didn't think she was capable of.

Slowly, she presses my hand against the wall and then waits for me to say I'm ready. I nod and she pulls one stake out. It stings like a bitch, but in a single heartbeat, the wound begins to mat itself back together and heal over.

She waits for me to nod again and then tugs the other stake out. By the time I've pulled my trousers on, both my palms are already healed.

I start to leave, but Red stops me with a hand on my wrist.

"Wait," she says.

I frown. "What's—"

She pulls me into her arms and forces me to the floor. Her back rests against the wall and her arms are around me. It's ridiculous really, I'm far taller than her, but I get it. She needs to take care of me after what she did, after that scene, it's her duty to make sure I'm okay.

I twist and lean back, cradled in her arms instead of having my back to her chest, then I reach up and push some of her shaggy locks behind her ear.

"You don't need to——" Her finger over my lips silences me.

"I do still dislike you," she breathes.

"Not hate anymore?"

She gives me a glare that makes me smirk.

"But what we just... it's not like me to be like that... I need to get the addiction under control. I don't want to be that person."

I lean in, brush another lock away from her forehead and then place a kiss on it.

"You asked my safe word, you're looking after me now. But... I pushed you, I wanted to see how far you'd go."

"You don't need to take responsibility..."

"Actually... I really do. You have no idea what I've done."

She frowns at me. "What's that supposed to mean?"

This is my chance, my opening. I could tell her... But what do I say? Where do I start? And what happens if we're on opposite teams and she uses it all against me to win? I can't take the risk. Not yet.

"Nothing, just vampire shit," I say. "Speaking of which, you don't get to feel bad about the stakes. If only you knew how much I get off on a little bit of pain. I'm a vampire, we like things, well, a little more."

That makes a soft smile appear amid her concern. She leans closer and then hesitates.

"I think I want to kiss you."

"You fuck me like you hate me and now you want to kiss me like you love me?"

"Don't push your luck, Beaumont."

I laugh.

She smiles against my lips, and it is the most tender caress I've ever had. For the first time in my life, my stomach flutters, the twirling ballerina dance of adrenaline spiking in my belly, and I wonder if this is what they mean in fairy tales.

Her fingers make their way to the back of my head, and she tugs, pulling me closer as if she can't quite get enough of me, as if she wants to drown in me, and fuck, I want to let her.

I kiss her back, our lips moving slow and sensual, so different to the crazed fucking earlier. I don't quite know which I prefer. The way her fingers wrap through my long hair is so tender and gentle I lean in. I want more. Need more.

The door cracks and someone walks in behind us.

"Fuck," Red says and springs away from me.

I glance up at Xavier, who is wearing the smuggest, most entitled shit-eating grin I've ever seen.

"Favourite," he says.

"Xavier," I reply. He leans down giving me a hand to help pull me up without saying a word. But his eyes glance at the two puncture marks in the wall, the blood-covered stakes and the dried blood on my palms.

"I'll explain later," I say.

"See that you do," he says.

"This is..." I start.

"Red," he says and holds out a hand to shake. She hesitates, her hunter instincts telling her he's a predator not a friend.

"He's my brother and the only decent one between the lot of us," I say.

She nods and steps forward.

"A pleasure," he says, the faintest hint of compulsion under his words, a rumbling vibration that makes a human want to close their eyes and drift into an unconscious obedience.

"Xavier," I growl.

"Sorry, it's habit," he says to me, then turns to her. "A pleasure, as I say. I've heard lots about you. But I'm afraid I must break up whatever this was. Mother is ready for us to begin the partnering ceremony."

He exits, leaving the door ajar.

"We should talk. In fact, you should talk to your sister too," I say.

"Yeah," she says, but her eyes wrinkle in a way that makes my chest ache.

It's clear that all of my blood has drained out of her system and the walls have gone back up. This time, though, the resentment I'm used to has dissipated a little. She's not quite as cold, not quite as distant.

I hate it, but the first bloom of hope swells in my belly and I wonder if this time... this time I'll be able to keep her.

"Yeah," she says again. "This is a mess."

"Well, I fear it's about to get a lot messier." I hold the door open for her and do up the final button on my shirt wondering what chaos Mother is about to throw us into.

B y the time we enter the ballroom it feels more like the auditorium of a sports tournament. The tiered seats are alive with shouted conversations, team vampire on one side and team hunter on the other.

Xavier whistles, "This is more vampires and hunters together in the same room than I've ever seen before."

"And I thought there were a lot the other night in the Whisper Club," Red replies.

Cordelia steps up to the microphone of a lectern at the edge of the stage. "Welcome, vampires, hunters, nobles, and honoured guests," she says, clearing her throat.

There's a tussle in the central seats where a vampire is hissing at a hunter who's drawn a stake. Two bodyguards

—one vampire, one hunter—step into the stands and restrain the pair of aggressors. They're hauled out of their seats, cuffed at the bottom of the stairs, and dragged to either side of the room.

Behind Cordelia on the stage, the Chief's ocean-blue eyes are hard, her posture tense. Like the rest of us, this is the last thing she wants to happen. I can hear her heart beating from here, the heavy thud echoing against her ribs.

"This is dangerous, there's too many humans in here for the number of vampires. It's only going to take one of them who didn't drink breakfast to snap and we're all fucked," I whisper.

Thankfully, Mother continues.

"I've asked you all here to formally start the trials. To welcome you and thank you for your continued willingness to participate in this joint venture. I appreciate that this is a very unorthodox situation. We are not used to working together. But this is, I hope, a fresh start. An opportunity for us to wipe the slate clean and begin again."

Lord Berkeley, one of Mother's least preferred nobles on the vampire council, stands up in the seats. He's tall, bald and sinewy, but what really makes him stand out is his beard. There aren't many vampires who keep a beard; it's too messy.

Lord Berkeley screams, "This is a joke. You're a disgrace to vampires everywhere. You're the one who led us to this point and now you renege? You fucking hypocrite."

He launches a glass bottle full of blood at the stage, and of course, because of his strength, it flies the entire way across the ballroom and smashes against the lectern.

Chaos erupts as the scent of human blood thickens in the air. All of the hunters stand simultaneously, each one of them drawing stakes, blades and knives.

"Shit," Xavier says.

He's about to launch into action when Mother leaps from the stage, springing up and flying halfway across the ballroom. She jumps again and lands right on top of Lord Berkeley.

Her fangs sink into his throat.

His eyes bug wide. He tries to grip her shoulders. But she's wrapped her legs around his waist, and he only has one arm free. He squirms and shoves trying to push her off.

The vampires around them lean back, edging away. The nobles would jump to his defence if it were anyone else attacking him. But this is Cordelia, and her word is law. They stare, slack-jawed and silent.

Lord Berkeley lets out a garbled cry.

He coughs, choking out another screech, then his face pales to grey and blood dribbles out the corner of his mouth. He sags back into his seat with Cordelia still clinging to him.

A moment later she detaches from his throat, throwing her head back and gasping for air. She stands; Lord Berkeley slumps in his chair.

Mother snarls, then she punches her fist right through his chest and rips his heart out.

Black veins splinter across his face and down his neck as his skin shrivels and wrinkles into desiccation. Give him an hour and there'll be nothing left of him but the ashy remains of his outfit. It's an ugly affair and to have been ashed so publicly is deeply embarrassing. I feel for his heirs.

Still holding the heart, Cordelia steps off the stands and leaps into the air, making the same jumps back across the ballroom. Her outfit is a mess of dark blood, it's smeared across her face and dribbling down her neck.

She doesn't even attempt to wipe it clean—something I suspect she does for effect. Back behind the lectern, she raises his heart and takes a noisy bite. Blood trickles out of the flopping arteries.

She swallows and lets the heart fall to the floor. "Does anyone else have anything they'd like to say before we begin?" she says into the mic.

It's the most silent the ballroom has been.

CHAPTER 18

Everyone can see through this pathetic shamble of a ceremony. Lord Berkeley just said what every vampire in here was thinking.

Dissent. Chaos. Mutiny.

They will fester in your ranks, and I will sprinkle them with turmoil and watch as your own kin slowly poison your ranks, seeding disloyalty and instability.

These partnerships are a shambles. You could have the strongest vampires in the city, the sharpest hunters. It won't matter.

I'm coming for you.

I'm coming for your children.

I'm coming for what you stole from me.

And piece by piece I will dismantle your reign and take everything you care about.

I've been planning this for far too long to falter now.

If you think this ridiculous attempt at peace will help, you're sorely mistaken.

Even if the vampires don't, the hunters will see through your pathetic ruse.

And while you're wasting your time with your enemies, I'll be quietly pulling the border down. I will reach the cure before you.

And when I do...

I will come for you.

CHAPTER 19

OCTAVIA

"Lovely," Mother says, the sweetness and light back in her tone now that Lord Berkeley is quietly desiccating. "Then let us begin."

I notice Sadie, Dahlia and Gabriel, they're sat at the back of the stage. The Chief and the chosen hunters are on the opposite side. Only Xavier, Red and I remain by the door.

Cordelia detaches the mic and steps off the stage. She gestures to the Chief and together, the mortal enemies walk side by side across the ballroom.

"So strange," I whisper.

Cordelia spins around, observing the room. "Tonight, we welcome you to Castle St Clair for this prestigious and unique occasion. For those of you who didn't make it to the Whisper Club, the Chief and I are retiring. We are running a competition in partnership with the hunters for the first time in history to choose our heirs."

Mumbles drift around the room. Mother stands a little straighter as if the attention feeds her as much as the blood did. The Chief gives her a furious glare, those ice blue eyes piercing through her expression.

"Today we will be choosing the partner pairings for our set of trials which will culminate in us breaching the boundary inside the Montague territory and securing the cure."

The murmurs rise into a crescendo of jarring noise, from those squarely on the side of finding the cure cheering to those against growling and jeering.

"Silence," Cordelia bellows into the mic and the room settles down.

She hands the mic to the Chief to take over. "Good evening, you all know me as the Chief of the Hunter Academy. In order to ensure the fairness of the teams, we are going to be using these bowls to pick the partner pairings."

"WHAT?" Dahlia says from the stage. She stands and marches down the stairs and over to the plinths holding the bowls. Her face trembles with fury as she glares at Mother. Dahlia drops her voice, but I'm close enough I can still hear.

"What the fuck? How is this fair? We should be able to choose our own partners, make the most tactical pairings so that we stand the best chance of winning," she whines.

Cordelia clasps her palm to Dahlia's cheek in a loving embrace. "The Chief and I agree that this is the fairest way to do it. There can be no accusations of cheating or favouritism this way."

The Chief and I agree? What the ever-loving fuck. I glance at Xavier, whose eyebrow is trying to crawl off his brow.

The Chief raises the mic to her mouth again. "If the five chosen hunters and five vampires can make their way to the ceremonial bowls, we need you to scribe your names on these pieces of parchment paper so that we can drop them in the bowls."

Gabriel and Sadie give each other a sideways glance but they dutifully stand and step down off the stage.

The hunters on the other side of the stage rise in unison like the well-trained, brainless soldiers they are.

Red, Xavier and I meander over together until ten of us stand surrounding the bowls.

"This bowl is for the vampire names," the Chief says, pointing to the maroon bowl. "And this one is for the hunters." Her hand moves to the navy bowl on the right.

Cordelia hands out ten needles and ten quills as the Chief continues to explain.

"Draw a drop of blood and use it as the ink to scribe your name. Then fold the parchment three times and drop it into your respective bowls."

It takes a moment, but all of us do as requested, and then the Chief indicates that we should step back. She collects the vampire names, and Mother collects the folded parchment from the hunters. They both drop the collections into the respective bowls and step back.

The Chief turns to the audience. "To begin this partnering ceremony, I will pick one vampire name from the bowl and Cordelia will pick one hunter. This partnership is binding and irreversible."

Dahlia huffs and folds her arms. Gabriel isn't even paying attention, he's a step back, glancing at an open book he's holding.

Red catches my eye but there's nothing I can do now. Of course, I wanted to be partnered with her. The thought of her spending time with anyone else is painful.

But if I made my preferences known, then I'm sure Dahlia would find a way to make Red her partner just to piss me off. I figure silence is the only way forward.

The Chief lowers her hand into the bowl and pulls out a piece of folded parchment. Cordelia steps forward and does the same. Slowly, they unfold the strips of parchment.

The Chief speaks first. "Sadie St Clair."

Cordelia unwraps her parchment and reads the name, "Fenella James."

Fenella's fine features draw into a strained smile, her red hair twisted and braided into an ornate pattern on top of her skull so different to the sharp white of Sadie's. The pair of them eye each other, both giving the other a stiff nod before one of Mother's staff members strides over and takes the two pieces of parchment, indicating the pair should follow him. He leads them into a space and makes them stand side by side.

The Chief steps forward and picks the next name. "Xavier St Clair."

Mother pulls, "Talulla Binx."

"I'll take that," he whispers under his breath and winks at me.

He's winking because any fool can see Talulla's hour-glass figure and voluptuous curves, defined lips and fluttery eyelashes are mouthwateringly attractive. She looks like she's got some sass about her, though. Her deep brown eyes carry a distinct lack of fucks and an edge of no bullshit that match the rounded bulge of her shoulders, which frankly look like they could crush a small child.

Oh, Xavier is going to have his hands full.

"Bottle of vintage Sanguis Cupa says you can't bed her before the end of the second trial," I say, leaning into him.

"Two bottles says the end of the first."

I slide him my hand, and he shakes it and then trundles after the member of staff organising us.

I glance at who's left: Dahlia, Gabriel and I for my siblings part. Red, that large fellow from the club, Leonard? Lincoln? And another chap I don't know.

Mother goes first this time. She drops her hand into the bowl and pulls a name, "Keir Thomas."

The slender hunter with a shaved head and several tattoos down his arms and up over his neck raises his hand. My gaydar pings and I secretly hope he's paired with Gabriel. He's exactly the kind of man Gabe would feast on for days. Not that that is what we're supposed to be doing. But vampires will be vampires.

The Chief lowers her hand into the bowl and my stomach turns. There's only three of us left. My gut twists, praying to the Mother of Blood that even if I can't be partnered with Red that Dahlia isn't. I whisper silent prayers, *pick Dahlia, pick Dahlia.*

The Chief announces, "Gabriel St Clair."

Shit.

Though I'm gutted, I do smile to myself when I catch Gabriel's eyes lighting up. I suspect he's caught a whiff on his gaydar too.

It's only me and Dahlia, Red, and Lincoln left.

As if Dahlia can sense my nerves, she steps close to me and lowers her voice enough that only I can hear. "Why you looking so nervous, sister? Scared I'll get the man-tank for a partner? Worried he'll help me win the crown?"

I turn away, refusing to engage. But that was a mistake. It's like she can smell the connection I have with Red.

She tilts her head at me, her eyes narrowing as she scans my face. "Oh no, it's something else entirely... Does the hunter mean something to you?"

I go still, vampire still because it's the only way I can prevent the anxiety from crossing my features. But that, too, is a mistake.

She sneers, "If you think stilling yourself is enough to dissuade me, you're sorely mistaken. In fact, your very lack of response is answer enough, sister."

I reanimate myself, slow my breathing to ensure I give her as little ammunition as possible.

"Is that a threat, Dahlia?"

"Only if you plan on getting in my way of the crown. Something we both know I deserve more than you."

Fuck her. The only thing this bitch deserves is my ripping her throat out of her neck. I jerk suddenly, scruffing her by the collar and speeding across the room, slamming her into the wall.

"Octavia!" Mother shrieks. But it's too late. Dahlia takes a swing at me, driving her fist in an upper cut between my arms. She crunches into my chin, pain splintering deep into the bone, rattling my teeth.

I'm knocked back, dazed.

Dahlia is nothing if not viciously strong. But she can go to hell before I let her get away with that. I charge forward but she dances out of my way. I've fought with her enough times to know her moves, though.

I duck low, kicking my leg out, and catch her knee, knocking the joint out of place. She yelps and hits the deck. I jump on top of her, swinging fist after fist. But Dahlia snaps her head around, catches my fist and sinks her teeth into my wrist.

I cry out and punch my other fist through her gut, grabbing a fist full of intestines. She screams as big arms wrap around me.

"Let. Go. Tave," Xavier says.

I growl at him. But he uses his big arms to clench and squeeze until I feel like my ribs are going to crack under the pressure.

"Xavier," I say, his name is barely above a whisper.

"Let. Go. Both of you. I won't tell you again."

I do as he says, releasing her innards as she dislodges

her fangs. He yanks me off her and drags me away, back to the plinths and the remaining group.

"What on earth do you think you're playing at?" Mother hisses at the pair of us as Xavier, still holding me, deposits me in front of Cordelia. Lincoln helps Dahlia up and she hobbles next to me in front of Mother.

"Do you wish me to punish you publicly?" Mother snarls.

"No, Mother," Dahlia says, and it takes every ounce of my willpower not to roll my eyes at her and call her out as the arse-licking suck up she is. But I bite down on my tongue until I can taste iron to keep the words from spilling out and igniting another fight.

"I swear to the Mother of Blood, if you so much as whisper out of line I will hang you both from the castle dungeons and drain you dry for three days. Do you understand me?"

I nod. Dahlia grits her teeth and nods too. Mother turns to the Chief.

"I do apologise," she says. As if apologising to the fucking chief of all the hunters is a common place courtesy. It takes even more self-control not to drop my jaw and pass out with shock. What the actual fuck is she playing at? I decide I'm going to pull Mother aside this evening and see if I can draw a confession from her.

"I believe it's your draw," the Chief says to Mother.

Cordelia steps forward and pulls a name. My heart is in my mouth.

"Lincoln Landry," Mother says.

Lincoln stands a little taller. Red's eyes bug wide, her face draining a little of colour.

I lean close to her. "Friend of yours?"

"One of my closest."

The Chief reaches into the bowl and the action makes

my chest tight. My breathing increases. This is it. Much as it would be awful for Red's friend to be partnered with Dahlia, it would be so much worse if Dahlia was paired with her. She'd kill her just to spite me.

I swear the Chief is taking her sweet fucking time just to annoy me. Her fingers slide into the bowl and at last she tugs out a name.

"Dahlia St Clair."

Thank fuck. Red's gaze flickers between Lincoln and Dahlia. Lincoln nods and moves forward to follow the staffer herding us into place.

Dahlia's eyes narrow, but a nasty sneer peels across her lips. She's obviously delighted she got Lincoln as a partner.

And truth be told, so am I.

But I realise I'm being selfish. There are more ways to hurt a person than death or physical injury. The more Dahlia smiles, the more Red chews on the bottom of her lip.

It's a mere formality now, but the Chief's hand pulls my name out of the bowl. "Octavia Beaumont."

And Mother follows suit. "Red... Oh," she says flipping the card over as her expression darkens. "There's no surname."

"Don't have one," Red says and winks at the Chief.

Except I know she's lying. Her name is Verity Fairbanks, and the night she told me was the night she broke my heart...

INTERLUDE

OCTAVIA

One Year Ago

There is a strange phenomenon in cities. You can go your entire life and never bump into a person who lives just two streets from you. But once you do, the city conspires to bring you together, like waves to the shore.

That was how it was with Red and me.

I was the moth, and the city set light to her flame. For a year, we met in passing, casual occasions and coincidences. I saved her from a rowdy vampire protesting the cure at the Festival of Blood, she was on a night out with hunters in the Whisper Club.

On and on it went until she relented, or perhaps I finally charmed her.

"Happy anniversary," I say, holding a glass of vintage Sanguis Cūpa out to clink against Red's.

"Happy anniversary, I can't believe it's been a year," Red says and cuts a sliver of steak, which elicits those delicious sounds of pleasure when she chews and swallows.

The restaurant we're in seated us at the back relatively out of the way to prevent me terrifying the other guests.

But it's filling up, a busy night for expensive dinners it seems, so Red and I swap seats, putting my back to the restaurant so that I don't scare the customers away.

"I bought you a gift," Red says, and slides a small rectangular package across the table.

"What is it?" I ask.

She shrugs, her eyes glinting at me.

I unwrap it and find a remote. "What is this?" I ask, poking at the buttons.

Red gasps. Sits bolt upright. Her cheeks flame pink.

I frown at her, then glance back at the remote as the realisation dawns on me. A slow smile spreads across my lips.

"Are you wearing what this controls?" I ask.

"Maybe." She presses her lips together trying to hide the grin.

"Oh, I am going to enjoy this evening very much."

She giggles at me.

I lean forward, "Are you wearing any underwear under that skirt."

Her eyes bug wide but she nods.

"Take them off," I whisper.

"Octavia!"

"Take. Them. Off."

"Shit," she says. But she obliges, wiggling under the

table as discretely as she can. Then I feel her foot slide between my thighs as she deposits a G-string.

"Happy?"

"I will be when you tell me your name."

"Never," she says.

My eyes narrow and I hit one of the buttons.

"Eek," she squeals and then slaps her hand to her mouth. "Octavia," she growls.

But this is too much fun not to see it through. I take a sip of blood from the goblet I've been served. It's O negative, and a vintage, I think, 21-day aged.

"We're going to play a game; I'm going to make you come and you're not allowed to make a sound. And if you do... you tell me your real name."

"And if I don't?"

I shrug. "I don't like your odds."

"If. I. Don't?"

"Then your name can stay secret forever."

"Deal," she says and holds out her hand. I shake it and use my elbow to hit one of the buttons. She jumps, knocking the salt over and turns what would have been a moan into a hiccup.

I laugh, loud and delighted. I am definitely going to win this.

The waiter comes to retrieve our plates. I instinctively turn my head so he doesn't see my eyes, and he sets about gathering up several knives and forks.

I hit one of the remote's buttons, not having a clue what any of them do. I press it three times in rapid succession. Red jerks back in her chair, her knee kicking up and hitting the underside of the table so hard the water in her glass ripples.

The waiter glances at her but resumes clearing the

plates. When he's holding them all, he turns to us just as I decide to hit three more random buttons.

"Would you like the, er—" he raises an eyebrow at Red, who's gripping the table so hard her knuckles have gone white.

"Are you okay, miss?" the waiter says.

She presses her lips together so hard they lose colour and manages to nod at him.

"Would you like the dessert menus?"

I glance at Red and gesture an open palm at her to indicate she should answer. Gods forbid I turn and stare at the boy with his hands full, the plates will end up smashed and broken on the floor.

Red's nostrils flare. She gives me the darkest stare I've ever seen and utters a breathy, "Y-yes."

I stifle a laugh knowing full well that yes was rather too breathy and far too close to a moan for her to win this game.

The boy glances between us and then makes a hasty retreat.

"Ready to tell me your name?"

"Fuck you," she says, laughing.

"I do hope so."

"I will pay you back for this..." she manages as I turn off some of the buttons. She sags in her seat, but this is only round one.

I ruffle my bangs, pulling my hair in front of my face, and I slide around to sit next to her. I tuck my chair in, blocking the underneath of our table from potential onlookers.

"What are you doing?" she says, her eyes wide.

"Upping the ante."

"That wasn't part of the deal."

"Upping the ante is always part of the deal, Red, you should know that. Now, be a good girl and spread your legs for me."

"What? People could see."

I shrug. "Then they'll enjoy me making you come, won't they."

"Octavia..."

"Yes, Red?"

"You know damn well I can't resist being watched. You're cheating."

"No, I just know how to win. There's a difference. Now. Spread your legs. I want access to that pretty little pussy of yours."

She grits her teeth but hitches forward spreading her legs. I edge as close as I can get and then I slide my hand between her thighs.

She inhales a sharp breath.

"Remember... don't make a sound..."

I hit a few buttons and if I strain my vampire hearing, I can just about make out the buzzing noise of whatever is vibrating inside her. I slip my finger over her clit, and she bounces in the seat.

Her body is instantly hot, a bead of sweat forms on her brow just as the waiter returns.

"Here's the menus," he says and lays them down.

"Lovely, thank you," I say, careful not to look up at him. I flick Red's clit once, twice, then I push my finger between her folds, drawing her excitement up and over her clit. She sniffs in a sudden breath and sits bolt upright.

"You sure you're okay, miss?" the waiter says.

She nods frantically but doesn't open her mouth. I rub her clit faster. Her eyes flutter shut.

"I actually think I know what I want to order," I say.

"Super. Oh, crap, I'll just go grab a pen," he says and vanishes back to the counter.

I hit another button. Then hit it again just for shits and giggles.

Red's cheeks are rosy, her forehead beaded with sweat and her chest rises and falls so quickly I'm sure she's about to hyperventilate.

She glares at me.

"Something you want to say?" I purr.

She gives me the birdie. So I press the same two buttons again and whatever is inside her kicks up another notch.

Her lips press tight again. She can't even hide the fact she's panting as the waiter returns.

"I'll have the blood cake, please, and Red... what would you like?"

She fires me the filthiest stare, so I increase the pace of my finger, rubbing her clit faster and faster, then I slide down to her entrance, coating my finger with her wetness. I pull my hand from her hot core, lean back and bring my finger to my mouth.

She gasps as I slide it in my mouth, sucking her juices off my finger right in front of him.

"Mmm, delicious," I say. I push the button one last time knowing she's about to go over the cliff. "She'll have the same."

"Oh fuck, fuck," she moans, and then she leans back and comes apart, twitching as her orgasm wracks her body.

The waiter, his face totally crinkled with confusion, scribbles on his pad and scurries away.

"You win. It's Verity. Okay? Verity fucking Fairbanks."

"At least the orgasm was worth it." I grin.

She pulls herself upright, and I push a straggly strand of hair away from her face. "Totally worth it. You have to promise to keep it safe. Never tell anyone."

"I promise," I say.

And I did keep her name safe, even after that night ended and she broke my heart. I never told a soul.

CHAPTER 20

OCTAVIA

When the partnering ceremony is over, we leave the ballroom swiftly. The hunters exit first, scrambling out in a less than orderly fashion. The vampires speed out even faster in a rush of pissed off mutters. Though from what I could discern, all of their comments were directed at the hunters, no doubt to save themselves from being ashed like Lord Berkeley.

Cordelia gestures for the ten of us chosen ones to follow her along with the Chief. None of us move, each giving the other surreptitious glances. We might be standing next to our partners, but our partners are still the enemy.

No one wants to make the first move.

The air is as tight as our bodies are stiff.

"Now," Cordelia says sticking her head back through the door.

Red glances at me and nods, we move first, united in a way the others are not.

We make our way through the imposing castle. It's cold; the evening chill outside seeps through the cobbles and thick stone walls. The moon shines bright tonight, showering the halls with beams of dust motes and shafts of pale, glistening light.

The corridors are peppered with wall lanterns interspersed between the numerous portraits. She takes us to one of the wings and up into her office turret.

Red makes a huffing sound.

"What?" I ask under my breath.

"The Chief's office is in a turret remarkably similar to this one. It must be a leadership thing. Wanting to be at the top of the castle."

"I've no doubt. There's a reason Castle St Clair is situated on top of the highest mountain in the city. Mother likes to be above everyone."

"You sound bitter."

"I sound right, and maybe a little tired," I say.

"Tired of...?"

I consider not telling her, keeping my shame and secrets locked away. But it's Red, and she's always known how to nestle into my heart. "I'm tired of being hated because I was born this way and everyone else was turned."

"Have you ever thought that maybe instead of isolating you and making you different that it sets you apart because you're special? Because you're meant for something more? Because you are unique in the best way possible?"

I'm silent as I blink at her, digesting her words.

"I didn't think so. Not everyone hates you, Octavia."

"You do."

"I dislike your actions because you took my sister's life. You as a person? I'm not sure what I think anymore."

I desperately want to correct her. To tell her I didn't *kill* her sister. I want to explain what really happened that night, but it's not my position to get between sisters. I know how much hurt she carries over her family, and I don't want to step in the way of that. Even if it means playing her villain a little while longer...

After all, I did actually turn her sister, she witnessed it. So even if I do try and explain, she wouldn't believe me anyway.

I wipe a hand over my face, frustrated that I can't convince her otherwise, that she needs to have a conversation I can't be part of. But I respect it for what it is and tell her the same thing I've always said.

"She would have died."

"Maybe she was meant to." Her eyes are soft, distant, watery.

"You don't mean that. You need to talk to her. She spends much of her time either in the Whisper Club or Castle Beaumont. I will happily arrange a dinner—at my expense—for you both. I know she would love the chance to talk to you properly."

She smiles, but it's strained and doesn't meet her eyes.

"Thanks," she says, but that's the end of the conversation because she walks off at that point, and fast enough that without my speed, I have to trot to keep up with her.

"Can you not forgive her?" I ask.

I know before she answers it was the wrong thing to say. I've stepped over a line I shouldn't have.

"Are you fucking kidding me?" she growls under her breath, nudging us away from the rest of the group. "Amelia nearly killed me too."

"I... I know, I'm sorry, I should have gotten control of her."

"Control? You shouldn't have turned her in the first fucking place. And don't even think about telling me she had a choice. She chose *your* side, Octavia. Despite everything I've done for her... Despite everything your kind has done to us. She chose vampires and then she nearly killed me because of it."

Her voice falters on the last syllables and I'm certain she's about to tell me to go fuck myself or shut up or to fuck off out of her business. But instead, she sags against the hallway wall and stares up at me.

"After our parents, I can't believe she..." she lets the words drift off, not finishing the sentence, and then sighs. It's the kind of heavy breath filled with stories and memories laced with hurt. I've seen and felt that pain so many times. You don't live for a thousand years without centuries of that pain buried in your marrow. Sometimes I wonder what it would be like to just end. To be human and have the ability to make everything stop.

Of course, I've wondered if that is what the Morose Mourning period feels like. I glance up the corridor, the rest of the group have left us behind already. We're alone.

"Father left. He chose work over us... chose some vampire noble over his own flesh and blood. When he left, we thought he would come home at the weekends, send coin to help our mother. He did for a while. But eventually he stopped coming home, and then he got completely embedded in vampire culture and just stopped contacting us at all, stopped sending money."

"I'm sorry," I say, and I mean it.

"He left us destitute. Mother always worked but she didn't have much of a choice. She tried to keep us on the savings she had for a while. But it wasn't enough."

"It never is. Our society is designed to drain you. Keep the wealthy rich and the poor struggling."

She nods at me, her expression all hard lines and cold glares as she wipes a hand over her face. "When the money ran out, she had to do something that would earn more."

I reach out for her but hesitate. I want to hold her, pull

her into my arms or do something to make the pain carving lines into her forehead stop. But she shrinks away from me, so I step back.

"She sold herself for her blood," Red says, and she turns away.

I can't hold back anymore. I reach for her chin and pull it around to face me so I can look into her eyes. "Your mother was amazing. She looked after you, made the ultimate sacrifice so that she could continue to care for you alone. Single mothers are incredible."

"I begged her to stop. All donors suffer the same ending. But what choice did she have? She worked for a couple of years. But they were draining her too much. Too frequently. She had one of those blood types that vampires love."

"Does she have residual magic?"

"Only a little. I think way back, a few generations ago, like before magic was eradicated, we must have had dhampirs in the family. But that's not unusual for hunters. Most of us can trace our lines back to a dhampir if we look hard enough."

"What happened to her?" I ask.

"The vampires used to pay top whack for her, but the donor pimps would take most of the profit and leave her with only a little. And they didn't look after her. They made her buy her own iron supplements."

"Shit," I say. Iron is not cheap and especially not when you need it in the quantities donors do. We supply our regulars for free.

"She fell into the cycle of needing more money... so she let them take more blood. And then one day, one of the vampires took too much and they ended up draining her completely."

"Who was it?" *Because I will hunt them, find them, carve their heart out and drop it at your feet if it made you feel better.*

She shrugs. "I don't know. Vampires protect their own. I'll probably never know."

"Well, I will pray to the Mother of Blood that you do. Everyone says revenge isn't sweet. But I think there's something utterly delicious about retribution."

"Careful, Octavia, you may chip some of my hate away after all."

CHAPTER 21

OCTAVIA

"OCTAVIA?" Dahlia's voice screeches from the top of the corridor.

"We should go," I say and wave Dahlia off. Mother is obviously impatient to start this meeting and tell us what we need to do in these blood forsaken trials.

We make our way to the end of the corridor and up the turret steps and into her enormous office.

It's a gorgeous circular room with leather walls and Chesterfield furniture. Conference tables surround two dancing poles in the centre of the room. Rather distracting if you ask me, but Cordelia has a penchant for the taboo. Speaking of which, there are two men fucking against one of the poles, one a vampire, one human.

Not illegal, but not exactly encouraged either.

One of the meeting tables is full of people. Three vampires from the looks of it and half a dozen humans. All of them naked. Two humans are sat on the laps of two of Mother's vampire guards. They're fucking in long, slow rocking motions. Another two vampire guards sit at their feet, their fangs sunk into thighs and breasts draining the humans.

Oh, this is not good.

The Chief leaps across the room, silver stake in hand as she rips one of the naked girls off the vampire's cock. She straddles him, pointing a stake right at his heart.

The vampire goes deathly still.

"CHIEF," Mother screeches. "Please. They're all here consensually."

The human, suddenly aware of how many of us are in the room, covers her modesty. But blood drips down her torso and between her thighs, and I can tell Dahlia is struggling to hold herself together. Her fangs have dropped, her nostrils are flared.

Xavier leans against the door frame looking handsome and cocky as if this is all just entertainment for him.

Gabriel is already relaxed in an armchair, his head in a book, not giving a single fuck what everyone else is doing.

Sadie sits cross-legged on Mother's desk. The rest of the hunters are busy pulling the humans away from the vampires and finding their clothes.

This is deeply awkward.

The Chief doesn't move. Mother speeds across the room and places her hand on the Chief's arm.

That single movement makes the entire room stop. Even Gabriel peers over his book to see what's happening.

I haven't seen Mother that close to a hunter, let alone the Chief, in years. In fact, the last time they were in each other's personal space was twenty years ago. They gunned for each other and ended up tearing up half the Midnight Market in the process. I forget the details of what set them off, some cuss or badly taken joke and before we knew it the pair of them were fangs and fists drawn, blades and stakes, tearing chunks out of each other.

I do believe they caused enough damage for one of the canal bridges to need repairs, which they both ended up coughing up for out of their personal funds because the market people were so pissed off with them. They had to pay for the loss of goods too.

Honestly, sometimes Mother scolds us for being childish, and her own behaviour isn't exactly becoming of a thousand-year-old vampire.

I focus on where Cordelia's hand is on the Chief's and brace myself to have to intervene. If Mother is right and we only have three weeks till the door eradicates itself, then we don't have time for them to fight, sulk and make up. But to my surprise, the strangest thing happens. The Chief snaps out of it and her eyes drop to Cordelia's hand.

"It's okay. They are here consensually. You have my word," Mother says.

"The word of a drainer."

"The word of your enemy, if you like, but a word of honour no less."

Mother's eyes darken. There's a pregnant pause, the room as thick and heavy as the stake in the Chief's hands.

And then, just like that, the Chief drops it away from his chest and the vampire beneath her breathes. He speeds out from under her lap, knocking her off balance as he races from the room. Cordelia catches her, one hand landing on her back and the other gripping her arm.

The Chief's eyes widen as she rights herself, pulling out of Cordelia's grip. There's a moment where the pair of them stare at each other. They hold each other in a vice, a thousand things passing between them. Secrets, memories, hatred and something else. I'm still not sure whether they're going to go for it and kill each other.

"Thank you," the Chief says, though it's through gritted

teeth. Cordelia merely nods, as if them being civil is commonplace.

The room is now empty save for us ten, the Chief and Mother, who makes her way to her desk as if nothing happened.

Even I am surprised by this exchange. I glance at Red, whose mouth has parted like she's catching flies as she surreptitiously glances at Lincoln. I tap her chin closed, pleased to know that I'm not the only one shocked here.

Mother takes a seat on a throne-like chair at one of the meeting tables. Sadie stays where she is, quietly observing us like normal. Our hunter partners dutifully sit next to their paired vampires, Fenella moving to stand near the desk with Sadie. The Chief takes the seat opposite Cordelia.

"Well, that was a little distracting," Xavier says, taking a seat next to me.

"I enjoy the entertainment," Mother says.

"It made me hungry," Dahlia whines.

"And me horny," Gabriel adds, winking at Keir.

"Get a room, Gabe," Dahlia says.

"Oh, I will later," he replies, making Dahlia roll her eyes and the Chief give him a nasty glare, which he ignores to continue berating Dahlia.

"Oh, sweetie," Gabriel starts, "don't be bitter just because your vagina is a perpetually barren landscape of death. If you weren't so angry, darling, maybe you'd get laid once in a while."

"I think the problem is that she keeps draining everyone she fucks. Makes it a little hard to form a relationship when you have the self-control of a four-year-old," I say.

Dahlia picks up the mug in front of her and launches it at my head. "Don't be a cunt, Octavia, at least I'm not in love with a fucking hunter."

Xavier catches the mug millimetres from my head.

I'm standing, about to launch myself across the table when Mother's voice cuts through me.

"You will sit down now, Octavia, or I will disqualify you both. We will not have any more squabbling this evening, you two have embarrassed me quite enough for one night."

I want to scream that Dahlia is a lying cunt. Instead, I'll plot my revenge, knowing that when I am done making her life a living hell, she will willingly walk into the sun and ash herself.

Dahlia leans back in her chair, folding her arms over her chest as if she just won a prize.

"Now, we will have calm before we begin, or I *will* lose my temper, and we all know me losing my temper isn't good for anyone."

"How do you want to begin?" the Chief says.

"With an understanding between us, that the most important thing in this competition is securing the cure. This will be a political minefield. There will be many who don't want you to secure it. But it's vital for the safety and legacy of this city that it's found," Mother begins.

"That goes for us hunters too," the Chief adds. "We've dealt with enough protests and riots over the years to know that whatever the result of this, the city is divided. Which is why we must work together."

Mother folds her hands in front of her. "The first trial is the trial of the map. Your task, teams, is to find an ancient map."

"What map?" Gabriel says, closing all his books and sitting upright.

Of course, he's affronted that he hasn't heard of this map, for he knows everything about everything important —as long as it hasn't come from this century. The man is a literal vault of historical records. If we're hunting for an ancient map, we're all fucked because he will clearly win

206

this round. I'd assumed the trials would play to my strengths. But Dahlia is twitching in her seat and I'm wondering if I shouldn't have been quite so cocky.

"The map is the lost amulet map, which means this is a two part-trial."

"The amulet of the dhampirs?" Fenella says.

Everyone turns to Mother's desk where Sadie and Fenella are. Mother's eyes narrow, not with suspicion, but curiosity.

Another piece of my ego shreds, this definitely won't be as easy as I thought.

Mother nods. "That's right, would you like to tell everyone the myth that surrounds the amulet?"

Fenella shakes her head. "I've only heard of it, I don't know much about it."

The Chief takes over, "Millennia ago, our myths say that the witch-gods gave the dhampirs a magical amulet. The amulet was kept in a secret location. Stored as one of their most precious gifts and most powerful of magics. Only a few knew its location."

Cordelia is nodding like they're old friends recounting a story together, and it is the weirdest thing to witness. It's like the very fabric of the city is shifting and I truly wonder whether this was Mother's plan. Is she having her second Morose Mourning? Is she really so tired of life that she wants to retire and make peace with the hunters?

I find it difficult to swallow that thought, but the way she's acting is in accordance with what she's saying. Except vampires don't change. Or maybe they do, but they don't do a one-eighty shift overnight. And just the other day, Mother was planning battle strategy against the border cities to take more land back from the hunters.

No. This is just exceptional acting from Mother. I need to get her alone and find out what's going on.

The Chief continues. "The amulet is said to be the most powerful magical device in existence."

"Why? What can it do?" Sadie signs.

Gabriel relays Sadie's words.

The Chief turns to Sadie and talks to her directly, "It's said to preserve whatever it holds. It has a compartment inside it that is magically protected from everything, anything. From the elements, war, magic. It's impenetrable to weapons and diamonds and anything you can throw at it. It's the safest place in the world."

"But...?" Dahlia says.

The Chief sighs, "But the amulet was lost. It was lost during one of the wars centuries ago."

"So how the hell do we find it?" Xavier says, running a hand through his mop.

Mother opens her arms, her eyes bright. "That is where the map comes in. The amulet map was spelled. Connected magically to the amulet. The illustration on the map changes as the amulet's location changes. If the amulet stays where it is then the map's image remains static. It's essentially able to track the amulet no matter where it is. No matter the city or body of containment, the map can always locate it."

Red frowns. "How come we never knew about this? It sounds like it's part of our history and an integral part of it."

"It's part of the dhampir's history," the Chief says.

"And how do you know about that?" Gabriel says, his tone accusing.

"Gods, Gabriel, you don't own history," Xavier says.

"Fuck off, Xavier, at least I have a brain."

"At least I've been laid this century."

"CHILDREN," Cordelia snaps.

The other hunters in the room, Lincoln, Tallula, Keir, all

give each other the side-eye. They all have stiff backs and wild gazes that are constantly scanning the room as if expecting sudden movements and surprise attacks.

I don't blame them.

I'm well aware that my siblings and I squabble like we're teenagers, but honestly, this is our love language. I think we'd all be a lot unhappier if we didn't bicker. I don't think any of us know how to show affection in any other way.

Sniping, bickering and fighting is what we do.

"Right, you know the history and you know what you're searching for," Mother says.

"Well, no. We know that we're hunting for some lost map that leads us to an amulet," I say.

"Exactly," Mother says.

Lincoln finally breaks the hunters' silence. "That doesn't exactly give us much to go on."

"No, but I'm sure you'll figure it out. If I were you, I'd try the library," the Chief says.

That makes Gabriel lean back and sneer a nasty, smug smile, "And to think brawn and beauty are the only skills valued in this family." He glares at Dahlia and Xavier in turn.

Xavier gives Gabriel the middle finger and Dahlia elbows him in the ribs.

"But you're going to help me, right? Twinny?" she says so sweetly I'm almost sick in the back of my mouth.

"Ohhh, sure, *D*. I'll help you. I'll help you right out of my library and all the way to go-fuck-yourself land. This is a competition, darling. You're not getting shit from me."

Her mouth drops. Oh my gods, did she really think he would help her? I can't help but laugh. The look of shock on her face from her twin dismissing her is utterly priceless, I wish I could paint it and keep it forever. That sweet, contorted agony.

"Braun and naivety, Dahlia. Good mix," I say.

"Go to hell," Dahlia says. "Are we done, Mother?"

"No, we're not," Mother says.

Dahlia grits her teeth, massaging her knuckle joints.

Mother folds her hands together and takes in each and every one of us sitting around the tables.

"Now, we need to discuss the most crucial factor. During the ball, I told you the story of the door's creation. I told you about the prophecy. I'm sure you understand that it is no coincidence that there are five hunters all in close age to one another sat around this table.

"You're saying one of us has the potential to become the first dhampir in a millennium?" Talulla laughs, but her eyes are skittish, flicking to each of us.

"Why couldn't it be one of us?" Sadie signs.

Mother answers, "It can't be one of you because you're already vampires. Dhampirs are halfway between a vampire and a witch. They're a hybrid species. You're too much vampire and have been for too long. And according to the hunters, they can trace their genetic lines back to the dhampirs. Can't you, Chief?"

The Chief nods her agreement.

"The door was created because that chosen dhampir was born, so we can safely assume that it is one of you. How we establish which one I do not know. Nor do I know how we... for want of a better word, activate you."

Keir pipes up for the first time. He rubs a hand along his arm. "What happens when one of us becomes this dhampir?"

"That's a good question," the Chief adds.

"You'd be a new species," Cordelia replies.

"Society doesn't like new things," Fenella says.

"It's more than that, dhampirs have the ability to wield magic," the Chief says.

Oh shit.

Red's eyes widen as the realisation dawns on her too.

I shift in my seat, drawing everyone's attention to me. "So they're not just a new species, they're a threat. If they can wield magic, they can bring magic back. They'll become the most important person in the city," I say.

"I think that's it for today. You have forty-eight hours starting at sundown tomorrow to return with the map. Take a day to strategise. You're dismissed," Mother says through gritted teeth.

Dahlia, clearly still pissed off from earlier, shoves her chair back and speeds out of the room before the rest of us have even stood up.

Lincoln looks at the place Dahlia was standing, and then to the door. There's a rush of air and Dahlia's head pops back in. "Lincoln, follow me."

He mouths "Good luck" to Red and then he traipses off after Dahlia. The Chief follows them out.

Keir turns to Gabriel, "Would you care to show me the library?" he says.

Gabriel positively blushes and inclines his head, and they leave.

Sadie and Fenella walk out together in silence. Xavier gives me a wink and then turns to face his partner Talulla. "I'd like to show you the castle before we begin strategising, would you do me the honour of accompanying me on a walk?" He practically purrs the words, and it makes me shake my head; that man is something else. I suspect he'll trounce me in the bet.

"I guess that just leaves us," I say to Red.

"I guess so." She shifts on the spot, mostly examining

her feet instead of looking at me. "Do you want to spend some time strategising?"

"I do, follow me. We can discuss it in the carriage. We'll go to the Whisper Club. Would you mind waiting for me by the carriage, though? I need to speak with Mother."

She looks as though she's going to protest and thinks better of it. "Sure."

When it's only Mother and I left, she narrows her eyes at me from her throne.

"What are you playing at, Mother?" I ask.

"I have no idea what you're talking about." She smiles.

"Don't bullshit me. The others might fall for your charms, but you forget, I am as old as you are. I was born a matter of days after you were turned. And I know you better than anyone here."

"Then if you know so much, why are you asking what I'm doing?" She smirks at me, but all she's doing is confirming that I'm right. There is more at play.

"What's the Chief got to do with this? Why are you suddenly so pally-pally with her when you were plotting strikes on the borders a matter of days ago?"

"Your partner is waiting, Octavia, you only have two days to complete this trial."

"So you're giving me nothing?"

"I already told you everything you need to know. The enemy of my enemy is my friend. And that means right now, we're at a truce. You forget how far we go back, how deep this curse goes. I am not the only one who wants control of the cure. So, moth to flame, darling. My reasons are simply different from the Chief's, but we share the same goal. And sometimes, that is enough."

I leave frustrated, churning her words over and over in my mind. Mother plays games, I'm certain she's telling me more than I'm realising.

On my way out, I catch one of Mother's human members of staff. I whisper a request of him. He raises an eyebrow.

"But I don't have any standing at the Hunter Academy," he says.

"I appreciate that. But I think the command is better coming from you than me, don't you think?"

He sighs. "Yes, I can see how it would be better from me. Fine. I'll do as you've requested."

"Thank you, I do appreciate it." I slip him a bag of silver coins for his troubles and smile to myself, wondering what Red's expression will be like when she finds out what I've done.

CHAPTER 22

RED

The carriage rocks us as we travel back down the mountain. It's still fairly early evening, most of the city's revellers won't be out yet. I'm not even sure if Octavia's Whisper Club is open this early.

We descend into the underground carriage tunnels, not because it's daytime, but because they are, generally speaking, the fastest routes through the city, being far more direct and having no traffic. But not everyone can afford these routes.

The carriage is so smooth and the tunnel so dark that I don't realise until we pull into the Midnight Market station that I'd fallen asleep.

"Good evening," Octavia says. "Was your nap restorative?"

I wipe my face. "Did I snore?"

"Terribly," Octavia says, smirking.

"Oh my gods, did I actually?"

"No," she laughs. "A little light breathing, occasionally

on the loud side, but that was it. You're quite beautiful when you're asleep. Far less angry, anyway."

Beautiful? Hearing that word in her mouth makes my insides squirm.

We make our way through the Midnight Market hunting for the Whisper Club door.

We pass through the main square at the back of the heart of the market, and it's packed full of people. Humans and vampires alike, the air is palpable. Thick with unease and skittish glances. The square is divided in half, though the division isn't vampire versus human. It's cure versus anti-cure and neither side is happy to see the other.

Those opposing the cure have hideous signs that depict a person being burned at the stake.

"Is that supposed to be a dhampir?" I breathe.

Octavia nods and then closes the space between us. Goosebumps rise up my arms.

"They're awful. Why would they want to kill the first dhampir in a millennium?"

"Humans can be awful."

"Do you think they'll actually try and kill the dhampir when they're activated?"

She glances at me, her face grave. "I think humans generally try and kill anything new and different." She walks half a pace in front of me, her body edging across mine like a barrier.

"You don't need to protect me, I'm not some defenceless weakling," I say.

"You're on my team, which means you're my responsibility, and this gathering doesn't look too healthy," she says, scanning the crowds.

There are banners and placards. People jostling, shouting and jeering at each other. A dozen hunters and a dozen vampires line the front of the crowds, keeping them back and contained. In the middle of the square is a lectern and two queues of people, one stretching from each side of the square.

"It's just a rally," I say.

"Rallies quickly turn nasty, and I don't want our win jeopardised."

She's not wrong, and I'll give her that these crowds, while usually here, are bigger than normal. I wonder if news of the competition has spread already.

"So this isn't about me but the win? I'll try not to be offended by that."

She tilts her head at me. "You want me protective, you don't want me protective. Make your mind up, little hunter."

What I want is to ignore that line of questioning. "Come on, let's get out of the square, there's an alley down there."

We veer back towards the heart of the market. I notice a few market stalls I've been meaning to stop at, so I touch Octavia's arm and tug her to a stop so that I can peruse. I need more art supplies. It's been a couple of days since I drew anything or painted anything and half my supplies in the apartment are low anyway.

It's cold tonight; the chill makes mist roll off the canals. It drifts in bubbles and billows through the air, making my breath plume out every time I breathe or speak. I wrap my coat tighter around me.

We stop at my favourite seller, and I have a nosy through the items, picking up a few sets of paint tubes and a brush or five, several pencils of varying strengths, some charcoal, and oil pastels.

"You draw?" Octavia says, a note of surprise in her voice.

"I do. I'm an amateur really. But that tiny bit of magic in

our family I mentioned mostly materialised in the form of party tricks. But both Mum and I loved using it for art."

"How can you use magic for painting?" Octavia asks.

I give her a devious grin, "She could forge, make copies of anything with a bead of blood mixed in the paint, and she taught me how to do it too. It sort of became our family trick. I don't have any other magic though, unlike her. She could do a small handful of things."

"That's still more than most people have," Octavia says.

I shrug. "It's something a little different, I guess."

"I should like to see your work sometime. Do you only forge or do you paint your own stuff too?"

"A little of both, but honestly, they're not worth seeing."

"All art is worth viewing, Red. It's the most beautiful gift a creator can give to the world. It's a little piece of their soul wrapped in the work."

I pull up, staring at her. Such words... I find myself swallowing, my eyes stinging a little. I don't think anyone has ever made me feel like my work is special or meant for something, and yet here she is casually throwing out compliments like they're true.

I hand the market seller the correct coin for my purchases and follow after her.

"We'll see," I say, my skin heating at the prospect.

"I need to discuss a matter with you," she says, her expression suddenly serious.

"Okaaay?" I say, drawing out the syllables with the snarkiest suspicion I can muster.

"You're moving in with me."

"I beg your pardon?" I say, halting where I am.

"I said, you're moving in with me."

"I'll do no such thing."

"You will, Verity, and you'll be okay with it."

That makes my blood positively boil. Who the hell is

she, dictating to me what I can and can't do, let alone where the hell I'm living.

"It's not permanent. It's for the purposes of these trials," she says, her voice so calm like this is trivial. Like it's nothing but a simple conversation.

"I don't think you're hearing me. NO. Are you out of your fucking mind? And would you stop fucking calling me that," I snap and start power marching through the market, not giving a shit if she's keeping up.

Which, obviously she does, because vampire speed. So I start talking, knowing damn well she can hear me from behind.

"The fact I drank enough of your blood you could track me for a while was enough of an issue, I'm not living under your roof. You are a threat to me and always will be."

She grabs my hand pulling me to a stop again. She makes me face her, her fingers finding my chin and tilting me up to meet her gaze. Her crimson eyes deepen to a delicious maroon that makes me want to lean up and kiss her lids. What the fuck is wrong with me? She's pissing me off and suddenly I want to kiss her eyeballs? Gods, I need help.

My heart thuds against my ribs in my chest, my breathing ragged. And where her fingers graze my chin, my skin is alive, tingling. I wonder if it's some kind of vampire compulsion. Whether I should shut my eyes so she can't convince me.

"I will never. EVER. Be a threat to you," she says.

"You took my sister. Your kind took my father. My mother. Your kind will always be a threat. Whether it's you or someone else. I will never trust you, Octavia. I am not moving in with you."

"You are."

"You're not listening. I said no."

Her lip curls, and I'm not sure if she's going to kiss me,

growl at me or bite me. Heat fills the space between us, and my body urges me to close the gap. Memories of the overpowering need to fuck her from earlier fill me and my body responds. Every time she's close. The danger of her. The threat. Instead of setting my hunter skills on fire, it sets *me* on fire. I don't understand her. The effect she has on me.

"What are you going to do? Compel me? Force me?"

She recoils at that, releasing my chin. "I prefer consent," she says.

But I note that she says 'prefer' and not that she was promising not to compel me. Together, we resume a more normal pace, allowing my lungs the chance to calm down.

We turn down another aisle of market stalls, Octavia slows and runs her fingers over the rich silks and fabrics on display at one stall.

"Give me one good reason," I say.

The Whisper Club door comes into view, finally revealing its location to us. Octavia leads me towards the door. It's an enormous arched wooden door, dotted with aged silver studs and painted the kind of black that absorbs light and secrets and memories.

The gargoyle on the club door opens its mouth and sticks its spiked tongue out. Octavia presses her finger down and the goyle shivers in delight.

"Evening," he says, and she gives him a polite nod. He's kind of ugly but has sweet eyes. What a cutie.

"What's your name?" I ask.

"Broodmire," he says, raising his eyebrow at me.

"Well, Broodmire. Would you like another drop?"

He practically pants at me, nodding excitedly and sticking his tongue out for more. I place my finger on his tongue, giving him the promised drop. His eyes light up with delight and as we enter, the mansion walls ripple, the veins of the house accepting the blood.

The gargoyle smiles at me, so I stroke his cheek then follow after Octavia.

"You charm him like that every time, and you'll be treated like a queen," Octavia says.

"Even though the goyles are ugly, I think they're cute," I say.

Octavia shakes her head at me, a bemused smile on her lips.

We enter the main club room and take a seat at one of the enormous round sofa booths. While it's evening, the club hasn't opened yet and won't for another hour or so, I don't think. So the place is empty save for the bar staff and a few of the entertainers. There are two female dancers practicing on the poles.

Octavia kicks her shoes off and folds her legs under her. I find the movement so shocking I halt where I am. It's so informal. So relaxed I'm not quite sure what to make of it.

"What? My feet don't smell," she says.

"No. I. Never mind. Anyway, why are there no paintings of you hanging in Castle St Clair? I noticed when I walked in, there's ones of your siblings but not of you."

"I don't like them."

"Why not?"

"Because they can't help but paint me like a demon, okay? Now. Let's settle this discussion. You're moving in."

"You didn't answer me. I want a reason why I should temporarily move in with you."

I take a seat opposite her, tucking my leg underneath me and pulling out the charcoal and sketch pad I bought. I figure I'll just sketch something while we talk, maybe the dancers on the pole.

She waves her hand at the person behind the bar, showing him two fingers, and they nod. A moment later, they set down two tumblers of drink. It's a greenish colour and I've no idea what I'm accepting. "Reason one, we only have forty-eight hours and I want to win," Octavia says, taking a sip from her drink.

"That doesn't explain why I should move in with you. Why do you even care about winning anyway?" I say.

"If I lose, the only one of my siblings I don't want to take the crown is Dahlia. Unfortunately, she's just vicious enough and invested enough to do whatever it takes to get it."

"The masc looking one?" I run my fingers over my pencil markings, smudging this area, blending that and then set about making more marks.

Octavia leans over trying to see what I'm doing, but I pull back, tilting my sketch pad away from her. I'm not sketching for her, I'm sketching for me, and I'm not ready to share.

"Yes, she's... well. Let me put it this way, our values do *not* align."

"And what? You think she might cheat?"

Octavia shrugs and takes another sip of her drink. "My relationship with my siblings is complex. We are all hungry to win in our own ways and each of us is as vindictive as the other."

"You seem to get on with Xavier well enough."

She nods. "I favour him over the others. But Mother chose her children. And for very specific reasons. We all have something she wants. A skill, a value, an ability. But the thing we all share is our ruthless competitive vision. Each of us is desperate to get the thing we crave most."

"And what is that?"

She smiles. "Different for all of us, but I'd take a guess that the thing Dahlia values most is strength. Gabriel values our history and knowledge."

"The one always carrying books and wearing crisp-cut red suits?" I ask, still staring at my sketchbook.

"That's the one. As for Sadie, I think for her, she values religion, spirituality. That's why she's head of the Church. There's something about magic and the gods that calls to her, and honestly, I think it's been healing for her."

"And Xavier?"

She laughs. "Beauty. That man is the vainest son of a bitch I've ever met. Shiny things, wealth, beauty, popularity, tits. He wants them all. The most delicious, exquisite things you can find. That's the key to his heart."

"Which just leaves you," I say.

"Which just leaves me." Her voice drops, it's smooth and melodic. The kind of tone that leads to compulsion. I want to look away but there's nothing to compel me over right now anyway. So instead, I just enjoy the sound of her voice and the conversation.

"What do you value most, Octavia?" I say. When her lips close and she glances away from me, I realise she's uncomfortable. She's sharing a piece of herself she must usually keep private, though I'm sure if I spent enough time with her, I'd figure it out, and honestly, I have my suspicions given she's hell-bent on winning the title of heir.

I want to know though, so I return to my sketch pad and continue drawing. The minute I take my eyes off her, the tension in the air eases.

"I suppose I value power."

I was right. But the thing I really want to know is why. "Why do you want power when this city has vilified you? When they've discriminated against you and pushed you aside."

She exhales a sharp huff. "That's exactly why."

"What do you mean?" I ask, adding some darker lines, and then moving to etch wisps of hair on the edge of the

222

page. But she doesn't respond, so I look her in the eye once again. "Tell me the truth."

"I can't," she says, looking away.

"Why?"

"Because... because I'd have to let you in. Tell you something that makes me vulnerable. I'd have to trust you—someone who hates me—with a piece of me that I keep locked away."

"Then what if I make a deal with you?" I say, an idea forming. As ridiculous as it is, I really do want to know. I want to understand her. Understand what makes her tick. Maybe I'll never be able to fully forgive her for what she did to my sister, but I can certainly understand her. That might at least give us enough of a working relationship to get through these sodding trials. Because right now, nothing is more important than getting the cure for my sister.

"Tell me this one truth about you, let me sketch you, and I'll agree to move in."

I know I've won because her jaw flexes and her eyes flash at me. A second later, her expression relaxes, she smiles so broadly the tips of her fangs poke out from the curve of her lips.

"Devious little cunt, aren't you?"

That makes me laugh. "I do try."

"That's two things for you and only one for me."

"No, the sketch is for you."

"And yet, you're the one who wants to do it."

"So you agree?"

"Fine. I'll tell you and you move in." She holds out her hand and we shake on it.

There's a beat as if she's drawing up the courage and then she says, "Because if I hold the power to this city, they won't be able to ignore me or leave me out or push me away if I'm queen. If I win, I prove I'm good enough for the city. They'll have no choice but to accept me for who I am."

That makes me stop drawing and really look at her.

"You're lonely?"

"I didn't say that." She snatches my sketchbook out of my hand. "Oh, you cheater," she gasps and then blinks a bit too rapidly as she stares down at a pencilled image of herself.

"You'd already drawn me..."

I grin. Yes, yes I had. "What do you think?"

"That's... This is..."

"It's rubbish," I say and snatch the sketchbook back. "I should have used forgery magic."

"No," she says and places her hand on mine. "It's the most beautiful thing I've ever seen."

And this time, I blush furiously.

CHAPTER 23

RED

As we're walking out of the club and down to the carriage tunnels, I spot Amelia. My heart seizes.

"Hey," she says.

Her skin is porcelain, and smooth in a way that reminds me of marble. So unlike the soft, cuddly Amelia I grew up with.

"Hi," I say, and edge back. I still haven't gotten over what she did to me. My fingers reflexively reach up to my neck.

Amelia's eyes drop away from mine. Her hands knead and rub each other, just like she used to when she was little and unsure of what to do. But I can't be her big sister right now. I can't tell her what to do anymore, she broke that bond when she chose them.

"We should talk. I need to apologise to you, and..."—she looks over my shoulder at Octavia—"there are things I need to tell you."

She reaches out, arms open.

Flashes of fangs and being pinned down rush through

my mind. I can't breathe. My whole body is cold. I'm choking on my own blood. Everything is white, and static races across my eyes. My mind is screaming at me to fight back. But I won't. I can't. I refuse to hurt my sister, no matter what she's done.

I step back. Again. Again. My back hits the exit door.

"Not... Not yet," I say.

Amelia's eyes well, she bites down, her lips shutting, "Okay. I love you, R—"

But I'm already out the door running towards the carriage tunnels.

Octavia catches up to me in the tunnels as I reach the platform. She slides her hand into mine to slow me down as we stand and wait for the next carriage to appear. She wraps her arms around me and pulls me into her body.

"You're okay, Verity. It's okay."

"It's not. I miss her so much. But I... What she did."

"I know," she says and rocks me in her arms until my heartbeat slows back to normal and my breathing settles.

I nestle in against her chest. "When we were younger and I visited at the weekends, every Sunday night she would stand like that, rubbing her hands together because she wanted to tell me not to go."

"She loves you," Octavia says, her voice reverberating through her chest.

"I know." I peel myself off and look up at her. "I do know that."

"But?"

"But what she did..." My fingers skim the scar on my

neck. The only reason it's healed is because of the herbs the Academy used. Beneath the surface, I'm still wounded. "I nearly died, and I know she didn't mean it, but that's not something you just forget."

She nods. "Would you like a distraction?" She opens a carriage door for me to step into.

I narrow my eyes as I sit in the corner of the carriage and lean against the wall. "What did you do?"

"I have a confession to make... I'm glad you agreed to move in," Octavia says.

The carriage jerks forward and rocks us from side to side as the horses clip-clop along the underground tunnels.

"And why is that?" I say, raising an eyebrow. From where I sit opposite her, I put my feet up on her seat, and she tuts at me and flicks them off.

"Heathen." She glares at me.

"What, I'm tired. And you did it in the club. Stop prevaricating. Why are you glad I agreed?"

She huffs at me as I'm about to put my feet back on her seat and yanks my shoes off. "Now you can tuck your legs up."

She flips around and leans her back against the sidewall of the carriage and takes her shoes off, resting her shoe-less feet on a pillow at the end.

"I'm glad because, for one, you are potentially a dhampir, and we don't know how the city will react when the new dhampir awakens."

"And for two?"

"Two, the city is on edge. Look at the market just now... didn't you feel the tension?"

I did. I can't disagree with her.

She continues. "I'd rather our team stuck together."

"Why do you think anyone will have a problem? We're only returning our city to what it was."

She laughs, a barked thing all hard around the edges and gravelly. "And you think those vampire nobles and Cordelia are really going to be okay with a shift in the political power lines?"

"Then why is she even doing it?" I swing around and nudge Octavia's feet out the way so I can put mine up on her side of the carriage.

She moves but by the time she folds her legs over each other, her toes are so close to mine that the air between us warms, and I have to drag my eyes away from the distraction.

"I don't know. I tried to ask her before we left. But she gave me some bullshit about the enemy of my enemy is my friend."

"Meaning, she's made some kind of agreement with the Chief?"

Octavia nods and scratches her cheek, her eyes going wide. "I've been wracking my brains to work out why she isn't strategising with me. We always work together to plan attacks and defensive moves."

"Should I be listening to this as head of security?"

"You're not the head right now, you're my teammate."

I huff, but she continues.

"I plan with Mother, Dahlia implements with the army. But as far as I can tell, she's blocked us both out. Which means she's worried. I don't think she knows who the enemy is. That's why she's being evasive. There's someone else out there more powerful than her, and it's unsettled her."

"Shit," I say.

"And she would never admit that publicly because it would damage her reputation, make her look like she's not in control. She said 'moth to flame' and she slipped it in so subtly I didn't even notice. I think she's using this competition as a cover to draw out whoever is trying to take the boundary down and hoping we get to the cure before them."

The carriage jerks suddenly, and my feet knock into hers. Her eyes flick to where our feet now touch but she doesn't move away and neither do I.

"Dhampirs are magical. They represent a threat because they have the best strengths of a vampire and the best of witches. Theoretically, they could be more powerful than Cordelia is. I was born as magic drained away, so I don't remember what they were like, I only have secondhand stories. But she was already an adult. And I can assure you, she won't take too kindly to someone being more powerful than her."

"So do you think she's really doing this to find out who the dhampir is before anyone else? To what? Kill them?"

Octavia takes a deep breath, a sigh rippling through the air. "You know what? No. I think she wants to get to them first so she can control them. She wouldn't want to lose access to that kind of magic. But she also wouldn't want it in someone else's hands."

"Well, I'm still not convinced that's reason enough for me to move into your house."

"Castle."

"I'm sorry, does your ego need to be told how big your house is?"

She fires me a dirty look. "The point is, we don't know anything. And we are a team, therefore, you need my protection."

I frown at her. "No, I do not. I'm perfectly capable of looking after m—"

She uses her fucking vampire speed to bolt across the carriage and pin me in place by straddling my lap and forcing my arms up and above my head.

Her chest heaves up and down as she stares at me, "Really? Is that so? You know what every vampire is going to do, do you? You can anticipate everything? Defend yourself from every move and strategic play?"

The scent of oud and spices and crisp winter winds wraps around me. But it's more than that. I can smell her blood under her skin. The sugary iron, the taste of delirium and hysteria and ecstasy. I swallow a thick lump, my tongue skittering over my lips.

She narrows her eyes at me.

"How long have you had a problem with blood?" she says, reading my every thought.

"Not long. It's gotten worse since Amelia tried to drain me to be honest. I started using a couple of years ago. But my addiction seems so much worse than most people I know."

"I'm sorry," she says as if she's trying to solve all my problems.

"It's not for you to apologise, it's not your fault I'm addicted."

She stiffens and rises off me, returning to her seat opposite. But the carriage draws to a slow halt as we have entered her castle's courtyard.

"Home," she says, smirking at me.

"Not. My. Home."

"It is for now." And with that she whips her shoes on and speeds out of the carriage, holding the door open for me.

"Oh, and that's the other little confession I should have told you earlier."

"Hmm?" I say as I take her hand and step down from the carriage.

"I took the liberty of having your stuff brought here already."

"WHAT?" I shout. "But I hadn't agreed."

She just smiles at me, those crimson eyes glinting like she has not one fuck to give about what I wanted or not.

"Octavia fucking Beaumont," I growl, but she's already turned on her heel walking away from me.

"Don't walk away from me, dammit."

She's not listening. She's waltzing to the door and sticking her finger on the gargoyle's tongue. Which I do just as quickly and run after her. Fucking vampire speed making it difficult for me to catch up when she wants to piss me off. That's going to get old real quick.

"Octavia," I bark.

"Yes?" she says, stopping only momentarily to raise a sarcastic eyebrow at me.

"I said... oh my gods... do you know what, it doesn't even matter. Don't do it again."

"Can't promise that. Follow me."

She leads me down various stone hallways to a wing of the castle. Much of the décor here looks similar to her mother's. I have no doubt the opulent artwork hanging on the walls is indescribably old and hideously expensive. Though, just like at her mother's castle, no portraits of her grace the corridors. Intermittent lanterns cast warm glows of orange and muted light over the hallway flooring to guide our way.

We weave from hallway to hallway. Some have sculptures, some have jewels and other interesting pieces of art.

Then we reach the private residences.

"I don't need to be down here," I say.

"You're staying in my room."

"Abso-fucking-lutely not."

She grits her teeth at me, "Must we go through this again?"

"Listen. I agreed to stay here, but that's as much as you're getting."

"If you get killed, I am fucked. Don't you understand that? This isn't just a game for me. This is about me protecting the future of this city."

"You think this is a game for me? I can cure Amelia if we win. I can get my sister back. Fix what you fucked up. This is just a power grab for you," I snap a little too sharply.

She recoils. Her eyebrow flickers, then her expression hardens.

"You think that's the only reason I'm doing this?"

"You told me as much in the club."

She throws her hands up and walks off muttering to herself. "And this is why I didn't want the conversation."

"Okay then," I say, running after her. "Then tell me."

"Because Dahlia will tear this city in two. She'll drain it of every drop of blood and then she'll move onto another city. If she wins this, it's not just about me having control. Though I admit that is deeply appealing. It's about saving this city from that fucking monster. She's a plague and she will destroy the city I love. And I can't have that, even if the city doesn't love me."

I look up at her, seeing her differently for a moment. I had no idea that she cared so much about Sangui City. I had no idea that she could care that much given how the city has treated her.

"Don't fucking pity me," she snaps.

"I wasn't."

"And don't lie to me either. I don't need to be a vampire to smell the pity in your blood because it was written all over your face. Your poker expression sucks. There—" She points at a room on the right. "If you're so insistent on being away from me, sleep there."

"That's not—" I start but suddenly she's a hair's breadth from my face. She continues moving.

Step. Step. Step.

I move back. Back. Back.

My back hits the doorframe. She leans in, her hand above my shoulder.

"Do you think I asked you to stay in my room as a joke?"

"I... I don't know what you mean."

"The problem, *Red*... is that it's not just you that's addicted. It's incredibly difficult for a vampire to have a human take their blood regularly and not feel the pull towards them. It's why we don't allow the same humans to feed on us."

"Then how come I haven't had other vampires coming after me? You know, given how long I've been taking blood."

Her eyes narrow. Her lips part like she's about to tell me a secret. But she doesn't. Instead, she leans in until her lips brush my ear lobe, sending a shiver down my back and straight to my pussy.

Fuck, I want her even though her blood isn't in my system. It must be a residual thing from the last couple of times I took her blood. Maybe it just doesn't fade the more you take it, and I've lost count now of how many times I've had hers. Two? Three?

It's two or three too many.

"The problem," she whispers against my ear, making my eyes roll shut as her words trickle down my neck like a caress. "Is that I *want* you to take my blood." Her breath quickens as her hand grips the doorframe above me. There's a creaking wail and then it cracks.

"I would cut myself open and let you bleed me dry if it meant you took another drop of my blood. It's not just you fighting this. Don't forget that."

I reach up, tilt her chin down to me, "But you hate me," I whisper.

She smiles, but it's soft, her eyes watery. She shakes her head once. "I think you'll find, you're the one who hates me." She backs up, cold rushes into the space between us. She slides her hair back behind her ear.

"Good night, Verity."

"It's Red. And you still haven't told me how you know that fucking name."

"And perhaps I never will."

"What if I made a deal."

"Don't play games you can't win."

"I'll drink a drop," I say.

She halts halfway across the corridor.

I'm playing with danger. If I take a drop... Even half a drop, we'll end up fucking and that is not what either of us wants. When she cocks her head back to look at me, her nostrils flare like she can smell her blood coursing through me. Her fangs lower, peeking out between her lips. But her neck strains.

"Good night, Red," she says, and then she walks into the room opposite and closes the door behind her.

I sag against the doorframe. Part of me is relieved that I was refused and she didn't give me her blood, and the other part is desperate to rip the door open and sink my blunt little human teeth into her neck and guzzle what I know she wants to give me.

I shake it off and enter the guest room.

There, next to the bed is a suitcase I recognise. I laugh to myself. She knew I'd never agree to stay in her room after all.

Dammit, Octavia.

I pull out the belongings I need for the night. A towel,

my wash stuff and pyjamas and slide into the bathroom. It's similar to the one I was in when I hurt her butler.

By the time I slide into the bed, dawn is only a few short hours away. I'm exhausted and tomorrow will be an even longer day.

But still, I dream of her.

CHAPTER 24

RED

O ctavia slips her cool hand between my legs. She's in my bed, her long body pressed next to mine. Her breasts hang heavy against my chest, they're so much larger than mine. My fingers find their way to them. I thought she was clothed, but now she's naked, and I can't resist tweaking her nipples.

It makes me wet. As if she can tell, she slides her hand higher up my thigh until her palm finds my pussy and she nudges me to grind against it.

I let out a moan of pleasure.

She leans into the crook of my neck. There's a sharp sting as she sinks her fangs into me. A pulse of pain followed by an instant orgasm shoot through my body and into my clit.

My eyes fly open, I'm panting as I sit up. My heart is hammering so loud in my chest I swear I can hear it echoing around the room. I scan my surroundings trying to remember where the hell I am when the promises of last night filter back to me.

The Whisper Club.

The sketch.

The deal.

"Shit." What the hell was I thinking? Of course I'd be safer in the Hunter Academy. This was a stupid idea.

Then the dream that shocked me awake moments ago flashes in my mind, vivid and carnal, and I groan. A fucking sex dream? Really? I slide my hand inside my knickers, realising I'm drenched. My pussy kind of feels tender like I did actually come over her in my dream. Is that even possible?

I groan again and get out of bed. I find a sports bra and jumper and slide them both on and decide to go for a walk. I check the clock; it's 4:45 a.m. Not quite morning, but not quite nighttime anymore either.

I pull some socks on and find my trainers. Maybe I'll go for a jog. I slip out of the guest room and try and find my way back through the insane rabbit warren that is Octavia's mansion.

Unlike Cordelia's home situated at the top of a mountain, Octavia's castle is hidden in a forest, nestled against nature like it's meant to be here. Green and claret-coloured ivy trails up the outer walls. Honeysuckle intersperses it, making the exterior of the castle smell sweet and edible.

I'm lost. I backtrack up a corridor, then a second and realise where I first went wrong, then manage to locate the central staircase.

I head downstairs and out into the garden. There's a beautiful stillness at this time of night. The nocturnal animals are almost ready for bed, they're quiet, their hunting for the night done, and the birds aren't quite ready to wake up yet.

The sky is still dim, the depths of midnight giving way to a heavy navy and purple haze stroking the horizon like a paintbrush. I jog through her gardens, building up a nice sweat relatively quickly. I double back on myself, taking a different route through the gardens this time and admire the fact that someone obviously takes good care of them. They're all pruned and preened and shaped neat. Some are square or rectangles. Two evergreen trees form an arch leading into a rose garden, but the trees are bent and trimmed to look like a set of fangs. It's impressive even if it is gaudy.

Something heavy shifts behind me. I glance around but see nothing. Must have been a bunny.

But my skin prickles like I'm being watched. As my hand swipes my thigh, those prickles grow bigger as I realise I didn't bring my stakes or blades. What the fuck was I thinking? I should know better than that. I *do* know better than that. I never go anywhere without some kind of weapon.

I lean against a bush and press my back into it while I squint into the darkness. But it's not quite light enough for me to be able to see more than fifteen feet or so. I'm a sitting duck here. My back tingles.

Shit, shit.

I have enough experience with ambushes to know there's definitely someone out there watching me.

Part of me wonders if it's Octavia fucking with me. Trying to prove that there's a reason I should have stayed in her room. That this is why I need her protection.

But I just don't think she'd make that kind of joke.

So, I have two choices. I can stand and make it a fight. Call the attacker out and make it known I'm here.

Or I try and escape.

If I run and they have a weapon they can fire or throw, I'm screwed. But if I stay and have to fight without any weapons myself, I'm also fucked, unless I can disarm them.

Tick tock, Red. What are you going to do?

Fight.

The answer is always stand your ground and fight.

"Come out, come out wherever you are..." I say. "Games up, Fuckface."

Perhaps antagonising the enemy before I know who they are isn't the smartest idea, but then I always had a big mouth.

A laugh spills through the air. It's deep and throaty.

Male then. *Great.*

And by the sounds, a big male. This is when I'm grateful to have Lincoln as a bestie. We've sparred so many times, I've learned how to use his body weight against him.

I scan where I am, how far it is to the courtyard where the exterior lights will turn on and I'll get a better view of the attacker. It's maybe thirty metres. Good job I have trainers on then.

I don't think. I just move.

I bolt fast and unyielding, swinging my arms and pumping my legs at breakneck speed. But I hate running on grass. My ankles wobble, the uneven surface playing havoc with my balance.

"FUCK. COME HERE YOU LITTLE CUNT," the voice rumbles behind me.

But I'm gone. Fuck stopping to see who it is because it's definitely not Octavia. I skid onto the courtyard driveway, slipping on the gravel because of the speed I hit it with.

"Fuck," I yelp as I tumble headfirst onto the ground. I tuck my head in and manage to spin into a roll and end up back on my feet. Thank you, hunter training. But my jumper rode up, and my sides are grazed and stinging.

The attacker charges across the grass, but even as he comes into the light, I can't tell who it is. He's wearing a black mask that fully covers everything save for his eyes and mouth. In which, I can see his dropped fangs.

Brilliant. So vampire then. Gods dammit, I'm really cursing myself for not bringing my stakes and blades.

I brace myself for the attack and keep stepping back until the front porch lights blare on. Bright spotlight beams fill the courtyard. The porch is only twenty metres or so away but there's no time to reach it. Sweet Mother of Blood, the attacker is a big boy. His shoulders and biceps look more like balloons.

He sweeps onto the gravel, and I steady myself as he charges right into me, his fists swinging.

I block the attack and kick out with my foot.

But he senses it coming and leaps up and out of the way. As he crashes back to the gravel, he reaches out and grips my hair. Taking a fistful and yanking me forward and onto his other fist.

His knuckles slam into my ribs, and I groan as he socks all the air out of my lungs. He pulls back and swings again, smashing his fist into my ribs so hard I scream as I hear the bones crack beneath his power.

He lays a brutal series of punches on me. My face, my chest, my stomach. Bones splinter and crack under the assault. My face immediately bloodies. I can feel it dripping down my chin, my vision blurring where my eye swells. My jaw burning where it's probably cracked if not broken.

I need to get out, get away before there isn't enough of me left conscious to attack back.

I kick up, the movement causing a ricochet of pain to splinter up and through my chest. But I don't care. This prick will kill me if he continues his attack at the ferocity he is. My foot makes contact with his balls, and he instantly releases me.

Good, stupid prick, I hope you're impotent now.

Before he can gather himself, I reach up and grab his

shoulders and yank him down as I drive my knee up and into his groin again and again.

Sure, it's a low blow, but fuck this guy. Who the hell is he? Where the fuck did he come from and what the fuck does he want?

I can't keep the kneeing up, though, my ribs are screaming. Despite the adrenaline suppressing the pain, I know something is really wrong inside me. As I cough, blood splatters over his jacket. Shit.

Internal bleeding.

That is not good.

He takes my hesitation as an opportunity to steal the upper hand. He drives his fist at me in a savage uppercut. It's so vicious, I'm thrown several feet backwards and crash down to the gravel. The pain that lances through my face is excruciating. My jaw is broken for certain. Static and stars smatter my vision, everything goes dark and then I rear up, spitting blood on the floor.

My whole body is hot. I glance up, realising the sky is lightening. Thank the Mother of Blood, I have never been so happy to see dawn. I just need to keep myself away from him long enough that he has no choice but to flee.

"Suns up, fucker," I splutter.

As he glances around at the sky, the glorious orange orb rises over the horizon. A melting pot of colour smears the clouds. Not enough to force him to leave, certainly not if he's an old vampire, but enough that if he's young, he'll only have a few minutes to get to shade despite the fact he's fully clothed and all his skin is covered. Either way, he doesn't have long.

I snarl at him.

And he growls back. We're like two dogs standing off against each other.

"This isn't over," he says and bolts.

Thank fuck. I collapse back on the ground silently praying to the Mother of Blood.

I glance at the castle and those twenty metres of space between me and the porch suddenly feel like a marathon away. I haul myself up. But I can't get the air deep enough into my lungs. My breathing is shallow and rapid, with every staggered step forward, static rips through my vision.

I manage three paces and stop.

I can't do this.

The door opens and Octavia's face appears.

"FUCK," she screams. "WHAT THE FUCK?"

She races out from under the porch, her skin immediately lights up, smoke hissing from her arms.

She screams and steps back under the porch.

Her breath hitches, she's panicked, her eyes wide. She glances out from under the porch cover and up at the horizon. Shit. It's too late even for her to come out, and I'm not sure if I can make it there.

Her chest heaves up and down. Then she stills herself.

"Look at me," she says, her voice suddenly calm, controlled, assured. "You need to look at me, Red."

I do. I crane up, my hand on my knee supporting myself. Being bent over is so much better than standing upright with how my ribs feel.

"I—" I start.

"Just one step. Take one step and then another. I want you to walk to me."

I try. Really, I do. I take one step, then another. The image of her moving towards me last night washes through my head. The way she pushed me into the door. If only I could move like that, use the heat and energy of our desire.

But there's only searing, throbbing heat racing through my body this morning. And every step is fucking agonising, bolts of pain and blistering anguish tear through every inch of my body.

I sag. Drop to my knees.

"I can't," I say. But the words are garbled.

"Let me compel you. Look at me and I'll make you come to me. I can get you to me."

"No," I shriek, finding my voice. "Never. Ever. Compel me."

"This isn't the time, Verity. I can hear your heart rate, it's slowing. You NEED my blood. You'll die if you don't take it."

"Said. No," I gasp and finally look up to catch her eyes. There are lines across her brow, furrowed deep like scars.

Even though my vision is smattered with grey, I still recognise that it's odd that she's worried about me. I'll be fine, I just need to walk a bit more.

I push up onto my feet, pain lances through my ribs so sharp I can't catch my breath. I'm panting. My lung must have been nicked, I can't seem to get my breath deep enough.

"That's it, keep coming, it's only another ten metres," Octavia says. Her eyes frantically looking from me to the dawn sun rising above the horizon.

"HURRY, VERITY. PLEASE."

But a cough spills from my lips, filled with blood that showers the gravel in a pretty splatter of red.

I look down thinking it's a pretty mosaic and then I collapse to the ground. I know now that this is how I die. Vampires got my entire family and there's nothing I can do about it.

"VERITY," Octavia is screaming. She turns back into the house and bellows, but her voice is fading in and out of focus.

I glance up at her and say, "Sorry we didn't win."

"Fuck," she spits and shoves one of her arms into the sun. Her arm hisses and her skin immediately blisters. Smoke rising off her arm and drifting into the glimmering light, she yanks it back inside the shadows of the porch and a string of obscenities leaves her mouth.

"You owe me for this," she growls and then I don't hear anything else because I black out.

When I come too it's like I blinked. Like there was a flash and suddenly I'm inside and the pain has gone.

Oh gods.

Oh gods, no.

The pain is very much gone but my knickers are sticking to me, and I'm acutely aware of the need for sex. I slide my hand over my ribs and poke, but they're fine, barely a dull ache beneath them.

Someone definitely healed me, which means a vampire gave me their blood. And given the level of arousal I'm feeling that person has to be near.

Octavia.

I groan as I roll over.

"Good morning," Octavia says looking at me from across the bedroom. She's sat on an armchair, her luscious long locks are squiffy and mussed. Her face is splattered in blood, the crust of it around her wrist.

It was definitely her then, because as I gaze at her from the bed, the urge to stride over and sit on her face is over-whelming.

Fuck's sake.

"How long have I been out?"

"Only an hour or two."

"You fed me blood," I say.

"You were going to die."

"Was it yours?"

She turns away. That's when I really take in her appearance. Her whole body is smothered in burns and blisters.

"Shit, look at you. What the hell happened?"

"I ran into the sunlight to get you and got burned to shit."

I sit up, push the covers off me and get out of bed. While the injuries are gone, the ache of what was there hasn't left. I wince as I move across the room trying to find my balance with the healing injuries.

"Here. Take my blood. It's the least I can do." I hold my wrist out to her.

She slaps it away.

I stagger back, my forehead creasing. "Am I not good enough for you?" I snap a little too harshly.

She hisses as she stands, picks me up by the thighs and throws me back into the seat. "Do you think I'd give just anyone my blood?"

She's told me this before. I know she doesn't and that it's a big deal, what I don't understand is why.

"Then why did you?"

Her jaw flexes and she looks to the bedroom door. It opens and Wendell comes in bringing a tray of blood bags. He pops it on the bedside table, glances between us once, twice and on the third time, he realises the level of tension and makes a hasty retreat.

Octavia goes to the blood bags, uses her fangs to tear one open and drinks the whole thing down. Her skin reacts immediately, the blisters and puss weeping from them reduce. She tears another and drinks that too.

"I'd have given you my blood," I say again, though this time it's weaker and I feel like I'm a needy idiot for offering again, especially given our history.

She looks over the bag at me as she guzzles it down.

When she's finished, she screws the plastic up and shucks it back on the tray.

Her words are softer now. "Yes. I know you would have. But we cannot. You've had my blood too many times, besides, it's still in your system."

"Right." I scratch my mind trying to remember why that was such an issue when it comes to me. Ah, fuck. "The bond?"

She nods.

"What's so bad about that again?"

"You don't want to know."

I go to get up out of the chair, but Octavia puts her bare foot on my chest to pin me to the armchair. "Did I tell you to get up?"

How dare sh— "Be a good girl for once in your life and stay the fuck where you're told."

This is a role reversal from the last time we were in this situation. It was all me in charge and her submissive. I didn't think I'd like being in this position. Beneath her, under her control. But her blood makes me do and think and feel ways that I wouldn't normally.

And I just want more.

More of her touching me, so I obey and ease myself against the back of the chair.

"I wouldn't have asked if I didn't want to know," I say, putting my hand around her foot and kneading the sole. She groans in pleasure as I dig my thumbs into her arch.

"If I drank your blood when my blood is in your system, given the number of times you've had mine, it would create a mating bond." She sucks in a deep breath and shakes her head then she continues.

"I can't do that to you. This has to be a one-way thing. You think I'm possessive over you now. You have no idea what would happen if we bonded."

"I see."

She leaps on top of me, straddling me in the armchair. "And I know how much you hate me. How much you'd despise being owned by me. Being mine."

I can't quite breathe. The air seems to have locked itself in my lungs, so instead I shake my head. Wait. That means no. So I stop and nod. But then I'm confused as to whether I've said yes or no.

"You do hate me, don't you?" Octavia says.

I nod.

"And you don't want to belong to me, do you?"

I start to shake my head but she grabs my chin so I can't. "While my blood is in your system you do, in fact, belong to me, Verity." This time, her words are less purr and more growl.

"I hate that you call me that. I hate that I have no idea how you know my name."

She smiles, and her eyes drop to the corner of my mouth where I realise some of her blood must have settled. She leans in and draws her tongue over my lips, licking up what remains of her blood.

Mother of Blood.

It sends electric bolts straight to my cunt. I want to groan, to lie my head back and let her fuck me right here. The closer she gets, the more the pull and yearning need for her pulses through my veins.

"Look at me," she says, suddenly serious.

I pull my head up, my expression crumpled at the rude interruption to the pleasure I was hoping to receive.

She scans my face, her eyes dancing over my skin. "I need to know who did this to you? Who attacked you?"

"I—" but I don't know how to answer. "I don't know. He was masked up and I couldn't see him."

"I will scour this city and tear down every mansion,

247

castle, and building to find him. And when I do, I will drain him dry and tear his limbs from his body. Do you understand me? You're mine, Verity, and no one gets to touch you but me."

I knock her hand away from my chin, "You're like reverse blood drunk. The scent of you inside me is driving you wild."

She holds my gaze for a moment, it's a hard tense stare and then it breaks. "I will eviscerate anyone who touches you. Do not forget it."

My whole body is alive with her words. It's always been me caring. Me responsible for Amelia, for keeping us safe and sending enough money to keep her fed.

"Octavia?" I say, unsure of what is about to pop out of my mouth.

"Yes?"

I'm leaning forward. "I'm going to kiss you."

I need her. It's the blood, the connection and pull urging me to fuck the blood lust out of my system. But also, maybe it's not only that.

"I think that I'm alone, as alone as you are, and maybe we don't have to be if we're together," I say.

A tear spills over her lids. I wipe it away with my thumb, wondering why I've made her sad.

I brush my lips over hers and she slides her hands around my neck and into the short, shaved bits at the back of my head. I press my lips to her cool mouth, our tongues caress each other, her fang scrape my tongue but not hard enough to cut.

She moans. She's as desperate as I am for her to cut me, fuck me and take me for her own.

I may have drunk her blood more than once, but she's right. This is a one-way thing. I don't want to be connected to a vampire. Mated. Bonded. This is just sex. Very fun, very delicious sex.

"You risked your life for me." I breathe the words into her kiss. And then my fingers find their way to her pyjama slacks, and I slip my hand beneath the fabric. She's not wearing underwear, so I go straight to her pussy. I rest my flat palm against her and rock back and forth, enjoying the wet soaking into my fingers as she grinds into me. I angle my hand so I apply the most pressure to her clit.

She breaks off the kiss and gasps, throwing her head back to expose her neck. My eyes drop to exactly where I wish I could sink my teeth in, and then I wonder what the hell I'm thinking. I'm not a vampire, of course I don't want to sink my teeth in.

I slide a finger inside her and she shivers against me, moaning out a breathy, "Fuck."

I push another finger inside her and curl them around to hit the soft fleshy mound of her G-spot.

"Oh my gods," she breathes.

"Use me. You won't take my blood, but you will let me make you come. So use me, Octavia. Ride my fingers until you come all over my hand."

She rolls her head forward. She pulls me up so that we're sat on the edge of the chair and she can ride me faster. Then she's rocking herself on my lap, my fingers stroking her G-spot, palm rubbing her clit. I use my other hand to pull her pyjama top off. She has to help me, but we get it off.

Her long raven-black locks cover her breasts as she stares down at me, my fingers still inside her. Those crimson eyes everyone fears so much, and yet I find myself lost in them. They are the richest sunset and the beauty of a rosy dawn. They're the colour of life and love and the oldest roses. Her plump lips part as she pants, rocking faster on my lap.

I gently brush her hair over her shoulder and lean in to lick her nipple. I suck it into my mouth, and she whimpers against me, arching her back to push her breast deeper into my mouth. I apply a little pressure, let my teeth graze her hard peak, her pussy reacts, her walls tightening around my fingers.

"Fuck, yes. Harder. Bite harder."

I do as she says, licking and drawing my tongue over her hardened nub and use my teeth to scrape her nipple, the swell of her breast. I bite and suck and lick her breasts, her torso, her shoulders.

She arches back so far I have to lace my arm around her back to keep her on my lap, but she's not in control anymore. Her eyes are shut as she's crying out my name. Her pussy clenches my fingers and then she's moaning and swearing and screaming obscenities as she comes.

When her body stops trembling enough I can detach myself, I move my hand from her back to her neck and I pull her down to kiss her.

"That was delightful," I say against her mouth. "But it could have been better."

I grin as she frowns at me.

"I could have had my mouth on you, your taste on my tongue. Mmm, I think that would have been much better."

"I think you already have enough of my taste in your system. Now it's my turn."

She slides off my lap and sits between my knees. Fuck. The sight of her beneath me, her legs folded underneath her, her hands turned upright in submission. My mouth waters at everything I want to do to her. The way I want to wrap her hair around my fist and drag her face to my cunt. Hold her there until I come all over her lips.

Her hair drifts over her breasts as she stills, her softened nipples peek out as she inhales and her chest rises.

She doesn't look at me, she just waits for my order. How easily I switch into the position of command. How easily she submits.

The sight of her in the submissive position makes me wet.

"What's your safe word?" I ask.

"Villain."

"Good. Now come here and take my trousers off." She does as she's told and deposits them on the floor. I pull my hoody off and sports bra and lean back in her armchair.

She's already sitting back in the sub position. My tongue slides over my lips.

"You could have died rushing into the sun like that."

"I didn't wan—"

"Did I tell you you could speak?"

Her jaw flexes as she closes her mouth, her cheeks flashing pink, her nipples hardening as I control her.

"Your skin is healed now, though," I say.

She nods but stays silent because I haven't given her permission to speak. Fuck I love how we've switched roles. That one minute she's in charge and the next I am. I've never had a partner willing to play to my desires like this and it drives me wild. Heat builds between my legs.

"Eyes on me, Octavia."

She raises her head.

"I think you deserve more than just one orgasm for that," I say.

She grins at me, those crimson eyes glinting all the way into my soul.

"Touch yourself. Touch your clit and tell me how much you like me controlling your pleasure."

Her fingers slip between her legs as I sit and watch her sliding her fingers over her core. But I can't see enough.

"I can't see your pussy. That displeases me. Move. I want to see how wet you are for me."

I give her the pillows from the chair, and she leans back on them, lifting her knees up so that she's spread wide and bared for me. She slips her index finger and middle finger either side of her clit, squeezing it as she rubs up and down, up and down. Then she dips her fingers inside herself and draws the excitement over her apex. She leans back against the pillows, her mouth parting, dragging harsh breaths in.

"Fuck, you're so beautiful. How does it feel?" I ask.

"So good," she says.

"Fuck yourself, Octavia, I want to see you fuck your own fingers this time."

She leaves her clit and pushes her fingers inside her pussy and the glorious sight of how wet she gets nearly makes me come on the spot.

My heart pounds heavy in my chest, my own breathing matching her pants as the ecstasy of controlling her pleasure seeps into my body the same way her blood has.

I want to fuck her until she can't walk. Fuck so much pleasure into her that it makes me come.

I wipe a hand over my face, trying to push the confusing emotions aside.

Her pants are louder, heavier. But I'm not letting her have this orgasm without my mouth on her. Not again.

"Stop," I command. She stills immediately. "Good girl. Now, spread your legs wider, and move your arms to the side."

She does as she's told, and I lay my stomach on top of hers, shuffling back until my cunt is millimetres from her mouth.

"Fuck," she moans. "Please can I taste you?"

"No," I say and lean down to lick her swollen clit. I draw quick flicks over her until her hips buck and she moans, twitching and gasping.

"Red, fuck, please," she whines.

I smile against her pussy, inching my body back until my wet hole is touching her mouth. Her body tenses underneath me.

I rock up and down, dragging my soaking cunt over her closed mouth. I can hear her ragged breathing in and out through her nose.

It's agony having what she wants and not being able to take it. I pull off her clit trying not to smile. She wants me so bad, but I won't let her until I'm good and ready.

"Did you have something to say?" I purr. I tilt my hips so that my pussy comes off her mouth. I can hear the slide of her tongue over her lips licking up every drop of my excitement off her mouth.

"FUCK, please, please..." she begs.

"Please what, Octavia. Use your words."

"Please let me touch you. Let me make you come..."

"Hmm," I say. "You have been a very good girl. You can take your reward."

Her mouth lowers to my pussy, and I slide my tongue over hers. She's feral against me. Having been denied the orgasm and denied my pussy, her tongue now swipes this way and that, licking and lapping like she wants to drown in the taste of me.

It's making it increasingly difficult to keep fucking her. My pussy throbs. Deep carnal waves of pleasure pulsing out from my clit.

My core is electric as wave after wave of bliss wash over me. She sucks my pussy, draws long strokes of her tongue from clit to hole as she drags her nails down my skin, making me break out in shivery pleasure.

Together we moan, each of us riding the other's face, our tongues sliding between folds, our hips bucking. Her hands grip my ass, pulling me down harder on her mouth. She raises her hand and gives my cheek a soft slap.

"Fuck," I cry out, lurching off her pussy as my clit responds to her slap.

She sinks her nails into my ass cheeks, and it hurts just enough it sends another bolt of pleasure to my clit. But I'm not going to come before I give her another orgasm.

I bend to her clit again, taking her hard nub in my mouth. I hook a hand around her thigh and slide two fingers inside her.

Her mouth slips off my pussy as she tenses under me. "Shit, I'm going to—" she tightens and comes immediately, her body shivering under me.

I crane over my shoulder to look at Octavia. She nudges me off her body, then suddenly she's lifting me up and setting me back on the armchair. She looks up at me from between my knees, the stare from her crimson eyes so intense I can barely breathe. She slides her fingers through mine and whispers words full of promise.

"You might not be mine, but this time, I'm not letting you go either..."

I replay her words, wondering what she means, and then her tongue glides up my thigh and to my entrance and nothing else seems to matter after that.

CHAPTER 25

OCTAVIA

I lunge for Verity's pussy. I slide my hands along her thighs and yank her arse to the edge of the chair. Then I push her legs wide. She might have taken control when she was pleasuring me, but it's my turn now and her cunt is mine.

I draw a lazy finger down her slit, her excitement coating me. I pull it away, making sure to look at her, hold her gaze as she sees the pleasure it gives me to suck her wetness off my finger. I pull my finger into my mouth, my eyes rolling shut as I draw her juices off and swallow them down.

"Fuck," she hisses.

"There is nothing sexier than knowing I've made you wet."

She sucks in her bottom lip, spreads her legs wider, pushing her pussy towards me. I narrow my eyes at her. "Impatient," I say.

"If you don't hurry up and fuck me, Octavia, I'm going

to wrap your hair around my fist and pull you to my cunt and keep you there until I come, do you understand?"

I gasp, desire darkening my gaze. My clit tingles at the thought. I think I might want her to do that. Maybe I'll antagonise her into it. Wind her up, drive her to the point of punishing me.

There's nothing quite like being a brat and getting what I deserve.

I slide another finger over her clit and down her centre, hovering at her opening but not moving a millimetre deeper.

"Octavia," she warns.

I slide my finger back up her pussy, she twitches as I glide over her clit.

"Octavia, this is your final warning. Tease me again and I will take control."

"Mmmm," I say and give her the naughtiest look I can from under my lashes. Then I swipe right down her centre to hover over her entrance and stay where I am.

Her jaw flexes, a flash of rage washing through her expression. "You're being a brat," she says.

And I nod, unable to keep the grin from my lips as I suck my finger back in my mouth.

"Brats get punished."

"So punish me."

She lunges for me, sliding her arm around my neck and looping my long locks around her fist. She holds my hair tight in her grasp. So tight that it tugs a little on my scalp as she tilts my head back. It is divine, the slight sting, the heavy grasp. My pussy is slick, again.

"I warned you," Red says.

I'm soaked. It's too much, I may end up coming sat here, her controlling me.

"What's my punishment?"

"I'm going to fuck your mouth until I'm spent, and then you're going to clean up every ounce of my come from my pussy. Do you understand?"

I try and nod but forget that she has my hair wrapped tight in her fist and it pulls against my scalp. It stings just the right amount to make me moan and the slickness to seep down my thighs.

"What's your safe word?" Red asks.

"Villain... what's yours?"

"Elysium," she says. "Now, be a good girl and make up for what you've done."

She yanks me between her legs, crushing me to her cunt.

I draw my tongue down her pussy one last time. One last rebellion. She might be punishing me, but that doesn't mean I'll stop being a brat.

But she tastes too good, so instead of misbehaving, I do want to lick her clean. I lap at her entrance, drawing my tongue between her folds. I drag up and down her pussy as she moans against me.

The more excited she gets, the harder she presses me to her cunt. I can barely breathe. She holds me there, her hands trembling beneath the pressure and pleasure.

I focus on her clit, licking and sucking and nibbling, running the risk of grazing my teeth over her hardening nub. She lets out a gasp and bucks underneath me as my teeth stroke her hood, my tongue sliding over her pussy.

"Fuck," she breathes. "More, again."

So I do, and I know I'm playing with fire. If I don't concentrate, I could nick her skin, slice the flesh and draw blood. Even a single bead would be enough to bond us. Heat rushes to my cheeks at the thought.

I want it.

I want her.

The scent of my blood coursing through her veins is only the start. Though as I inhale a deep breath, I realise is faded so much I can scarcely smell it. And yet, I still need her to let me drink her.

But I won't. Not against her will. Never against her will. So I stop and move my lips over my teeth to protect her.

"Why did you—"

"It was too close. I could've cut you," I say.

Red seems to understand because she doesn't question it. Instead, she tugs my hair. "Fuck me with your fingers." She loosens her grip enough to let me bring my hand up.

But I have different ideas. "I have something better," I say and suck her whole clit into my mouth. A throaty moan erupts from her lips.

I release her and disappear to my wardrobe, looking for the new toy I bought. I bring it out. It's a strapless strap-on, I insert the anchor end in myself. It makes the other end appear like I have an erect cock, only this one is a deep maroon. I flick the button to make it vibrate inside me.

"How do you feel about str—" I start.

"YES," she says. "Fuck yes."

I grin. "Oh, good." I slide between her legs again and this time I guide the cock to her entrance and push it in just an inch.

She leans back against the chair, her eyes already rolling shut, her nipples hard. I push the cock in and hit the button to make her shaft vibrate too.

"Sweet Mother of Blood," she breathes, and she couldn't have said it better.

Waves of rhythmic pleasure spill between us, from clit to core, washing from one body to the next.

"Give me your hands," I say.

She holds them out and I use my strength to lift her up and into my arms and carry her, still joined to me, to the dresser where I deposit her. This is a much better angle than the armchair.

"A thousand years is hell on the knees," I say, and she laughs.

The funny thing is, I can't smell myself on her anymore. I think we fucked the blood lust away. But she hasn't asked me to stop. Hasn't pushed me away, not like all those other times.

I falter, wondering if this is the night I tell her the truth. But she grabs my arse and pulls me forward, forcing the cock inside her deeper.

"No more fucking around, I need to come. I need you to make me come," she says and swipes her mouth over mine.

I grind into her, slamming the cock deep into her pussy. She moans against me. Gripping my shoulders to keep balance.

"YES," she says. "AGAIN. MORE."

I stop thinking, analysing, obsessing, and I just fuck her.

Hard, and raw and full of memories and fury and all the unspoken secrets I'm keeping.

I drive into her harder and harder.

The photo frames on the dresser fall off. The jewellery box knocks onto the floor and spills its contents, but I ignore it all because the way she cries my name is like a drug. It's almost more intoxicating than the smell of my blood mixed with hers.

She digs her nails into my shoulders where she's holding on so hard. Her hips rock against mine where she pushes back and tries to drive the cock in deeper.

She moans my name again and again, the rhythm matching the vibrations inside me. It makes my own pleasure build. She releases one of my shoulders and slips her fingers to her clit.

"No," I snarl and slap her hand away. "Mine."

I stick my fingers in her mouth. "Make them wet," I demand.

She obeys, licking my fingers and dribbling enough saliva that I can drop them to her pussy. I squeeze her clit and then rub slow circles, fast flicks. She bucks against me, again and again we move together like the ebb and flow of waves.

Pulses of pleasure begin in my clit and vibrate all the way to my core.

"I'm so close," she pants. "Harder. Fuck me harder."

I pick her up, pulling her off the cock and throw her clear across the room to the bed. She lands on her stomach, and I leap the four metres across the room and onto the bed. I drive the cock into her engorged pussy from behind and reach around, pulling her up onto all fours to massage her clit.

"Fuck, Octavia. Fuck," she says just as she comes apart for me, her body wringing out every ounce of orgasm it can.

It's only later as she's falling asleep nestled in my arms that I say, "I told you you'd move into my room."

"No," she says, but her voice is already being carried away by dreams.

"Why?"

"Because there's only one bed," she mumbles.

"Yes, and you'll find it's the most comfortable in the house." But she's already fallen asleep. And I am already smiling.

CHAPTER 26

CORDELIA

One Thousand Years Ago

The sun beats down on the Midnight Market. It's roasting this summer, far more so than in any summer I can remember past. I'm in a thin dress; I fought Mother hard not to wear the layers of skirts she prefers. It was far too warm for such a plight.

She relented when I pointed out she herself wasn't wearing them. Her argument was that I was meeting a man for a walk and therefore I needed to be dressed appropriately. I told her a summer dress *is* appropriate for the weather and for once, Father came to my rescue.

The carriage drops me in the centre of Sangui City. The heat is worse in the market. All the bodies and people milling around in such a small space. There's no breeze either, and the mist won't rise off the canals until the coolest part of the night. So I'm to suffer the rest of the day, which makes me even more thankful Father intervened with Mother.

I notice the gentleman I'm supposed to meet perusing a clothing stall full of jackets and hats. I wait patiently for him to notice me so I can wave him over. But a prickling heat rises in my chest. Why should I be the one to wait? To do as I'm told like a proper young lady?

It's such an unfairness. I hate that Mother won't allow me to make my own choices. Why should my worth be attached to that of whomever I take as my husband?

I've thought myself into such a mess by the time he turns around and catches sight of me that the wave I give is stilted, and my features, I should imagine, are lined with fury.

Indeed, as he comes upon me, he's hesitant as if I'm the one to fear.

"Good morning, or perhaps I should say afternoon now, Lady St Clair."

"Good afternoon, Lord Fenwick."

I try hard to soften my features but it's difficult. I pick up my picnic basket and nod to indicate I'm ready.

"Would you care to accompany me for a stroll? I was intending to wander around the markets, and your mother said you were free this afternoon. I'd be honoured if you joined me." He holds out his arm for me.

I slide mine over his, albeit reluctantly. Of course, Mother said I was free. I'm free for anything that involves moving me closer to marriage. Honestly, I'm sick of it. Sick of her, the control she has over me and this ridiculous pursuit of marriage, like my only goal in life is to bear children.

"So, Lord Fenwick. How are you keeping? How is business?" I ask, trying to think of something appropriate to say.

"Delightful. I'm rather successful in my particular line

of work, even if I do say so myself." He smiles and inclines his head at one of the market sellers as we walk past.

Why is it that the wrong sort of arrogance is so unappealing? The right sort though, someone who deserves to be praised and knows their worth, now that is the most arousing thing of all in a person.

"It's your father's business, am I correct in my thinking?"

"Indeed, you are, Lady St Clair. I inherited it just this past six months. Father decided to retire."

Right. So definitely not deserved then. His father built the business and he's been handed it on a plate.

"And what changes have you made to your business since taking over? It's steel rebar, is that correct? I'm sure Mother mentioned a metal of some sort."

"Oh, aren't you the clever lady for remembering. Yes, you're quite right," he says, his chest puffing out.

My fingers stiffen against his arm. *Clever lady?* Why, that patronising imbecile. I want to rip my arm from his and storm off.

"Yes, well, I'm quite educated," I say, my grip now a little stiffer on his arm.

"How unusual. Most women don't need education. Of course, their place is in the home. Making children and serving the husband, you understand."

That's it. I don't care what Mother thought he was, I'd rather have my teeth pulled than listen to another moment of this utter drivel. I direct him towards the medical streets where the witch, dhampir and apothecary shops are.

Though why I find myself down here I'm not sure. Perhaps because the streets are narrow and busy, and I think I can lose him. But it's not until I notice Eleanor's apothecary that I realise why my feet led me here subconsciously.

"Would you mind? I just need to pop in here for a moment. I shan't be long and then I'll be right back out," I say.

"Of course, I'm happy to wait here, it's quite lovely having the shade."

I untangle my arm, the relief instant, and wrench open Eleanor's door. The room is empty though. Damnation. I check the door sign but it's definitely open.

"Hello?" I call, the urgency must be clear in my voice because Eleanor immediately pops her head from around the door to the back of the shop.

"Oh, hello. How delightful, Cordelia, it's nice to see you again," she says.

I cut straight to the point. "You must excuse me barging in here, but I need an urgent favour," I say, and my expression must show how desperate I am because she drops her herbs and the jar she was carrying on the counter and wipes her overalls down.

"What's wrong? How can I help?"

"Right. Well. It's an unusual request but I need you to... umm... hide me. Please. If that's okay."

"Pardon?" she says, her bright blue eyes crinkling with amusement, fine little lines appearing around the corners. They make her quite beautiful. I realise though, she's older than me, perhaps eight years, maybe ten.

"My mother set me up with this pompous buffoon outside, and I'm meant to spend the afternoon strolling the market with him. But if I have to spend another moment with that man, I will intentionally pluck my eyes from my head and jump into the canal."

"He's that bad?"

"Utterly intolerable."

"I see. Well, I can't possibly let my favourite customer down, can I?"

It doesn't pass me that she said "favourite" nor how my stomach responded—with flutters and butterflies that danced like I was meeting... No, I shan't think about that.

"Thank you," I glance over my shoulder and notice Lord Fenwick twitching and glancing at his watch and then the door.

"Could we hurry? I fear the Lord himself will come chasing me shortly."

"Follow me," she says and holds out her hand. I glance down at it. My hesitation must worry her because she pulls away. I throw myself forward, slipping my fingers in between hers.

Her hand is warm and soft and the strangest feeling washes over me, like I never want to let go. I'd be happy standing here holding Eleanor's hand for the rest of the day, maybe the week. I frown, pushing the thought away.

She tugs me through the back of the shop and into her store's cupboard, then winds me through the back to a secluded door. She pulls an iron key out of her overall and unlocks it. It opens onto a canal street that leads to the river. "Oh, I know where I am. How odd, I didn't realise the medical street was so close to the river, I thought—"

"It isn't. I'll explain in a minute," she drops her finger to a nail poking out of the door frame and a bead of blood rolls down the nail and disappears into the wood as if the door itself swallowed the blood.

"Wow," I say and then she's staring at me hard. "Wait here for me. Okay?" she says and turns back the way we came when I nod.

I glance around and find a stone boulder to sit on situated next to the shop wall just a few feet away. I lean back against the wall and close my eyes, calming my racing heart. The sun beating down is pleasant, warmth fills my body and tingles against my skin. So different from the insipid heat of earlier. I can breathe easier now, my mind calmer and lighter.

After a few minutes, the door cracks and tinkles as Eleanor opens it. Her overall is gone, revealing trousers and a light linen shirt.

"Oh," I say, "You look positively radiant."

"Thank you," she says, smiling. "I persuaded him that you'd gone and he must have missed you leaving the shop."

"Thank you," I say, leaning back against the shop wall once again.

"That relieved?"

"You can't imagine. He was a pompous fart, it was tiresome to say the least. Oh, watch out—" I say but the shop door swings shut.

"No matter," she says, glancing over her shoulder. "I'm taking my lunch break. Thought I'd keep you company seeing as your mother expects you to be out of the house for the afternoon."

"Don't you have customers to attend to?"

"No clients booked in this afternoon. I'll only be missing the odd walk-in. I have a suspicion this will be much more fun."

Heat climbs my cheeks. "Well. I... I have this picnic. Perhaps we could walk along the river?"

"I'd be delighted."

And so we take a stroll beside the canals, until the canals turn into locks that turn into rivers, and suddenly we've walked three miles out of the centre of the city and haven't stopped talking the entire way.

"Here," Eleanor says. "This is my favourite spot."

We're in a little field with summer daisies and buttercups, a fallow field untended by the local farmers.

"Shall we sit?" she says.

I pull the picnic blanket out of the basket and lay it out

flat. She helps straighten it while I arrange the food: sandwiches and some crinkled, crispy potatoes, cooked sausage and meats, and some wine.

She reaches for the sausage at the same time I do, our fingers brush.

"Oh, beg your pardon," I say, frustrated that every time she nears me, I erupt in a flush of blotchy skin.

"You're fine," she smiles. "It's not the first time our hands touched today." Her smile is so warm it reaches her eyes and melts the deep ocean blue into crystal waters and beaches. Gods, I want to swim in them. Swim in her.

I shake the feeling off. It's a silly childish notion. I'm not like her. I can't just *be* with another woman. Mother would disown me. It's not the done thing.

"Where did you go?" she says, her fingers find my chin and pull it up so I'm looking at her. But whatever she sees makes her let go suddenly.

"Nothing. Sorry. How rude of me," I say.

"Tell me what's wrong. If we're to be *friends*, we should be open with one another," Eleanor says. And the way she emphasises the word friend makes bile claw up my throat.

I stare at the river, the grass, the daisies, anywhere but at her. "I was thinking about how free you are. To live and love whoever you like, however you like. That's something I'd rather like."

"Perhaps it's not so far out of the realm of possibility."

I shake my head, "I don't think so."

"Come on, Cordelia. It's not like you come from the St Clair family."

I look away. Her words sting like blades to my heart. Because, of course, that's exactly the family I am from. One of two families that run this city. One of two families that demand a pure line, that demands heirs.

"Actually..." I start.

"Nooo," she says, her eyes wide.

"Unfortunately, I am Cordelia St Clair, firstborn and heir to the St Clair legacy."

She pulls back. The warmth in her eyes evaporates.

"I see you've heard of my family," I say.

"Gods," she breathes. "Open the wine."

A strange request at the revelation of who my family are. But I do as she asks and uncork the bottle.

When we've both taken a sip, she glances at me, strain wrought through her brow. She glugs an entire glass of wine and then takes my hand in hers.

"You like me," she says as if it's fact.

"Of course, I find your company very pleasant."

"No," she shakes her head. "I mean, you *like* me. Don't you?"

"Why I... Um..." My words are all jumbled on my tongue. They won't come out in a proper order.

"Just tell me," she says and squeezes my hand.

"I mean. I certainly have some unusual feelings. I find myself quite flustered around you, but I'm not experienced with what that means."

"It means that you like me. I should like to kiss you now," she says.

"I...Pardon?"

"A kiss. I'd like to take a single kiss from you, and if you feel something, if this is what I hope it is... then, well... We shall have to cross that bridge when it comes."

"I see."

"So... may I?" she says the words so softly, so tenderly that I find myself desperate to say yes. Desperate to taste her lips and see whether I can savour the sweet wine from her mouth, her tongue.

"Yes," I say. "Kiss me."

She cups her hand around my jaw and leans in, pulling me to her. She brushes my long, black locks behind my ears and looks into my eyes. "You really are beautiful, you know."

And then she closes her eyes and presses her lips to mine. They're so soft, so tender. As if she holds all the silk in the world on her mouth. My stomach comes alive. Butterflies race and dance and twirl at a rate that make me breathless. I want to clutch my chest for fear of losing the ability to breathe.

Her touch fills my mind, her hands claim my body, my shoulders, my neck. She consumes me as if her kiss has swallowed me whole and I fell into paradise.

Her lips move over mine, my eyes fluttering shut as she presses herself against me. Her fingers wind their way into my hair, stroking the back of my head and threading it through her fingers. It is a delightful sensation, I'd love her to stroke my hair and run her fingers through the silken threads the rest of the afternoon.

She pushes my mouth open, sliding her tongue past my lips. I've never been touched like this. Never had a man kiss me the way she is. Only lips to knuckles and the backs of hands. But as her tongue moves into my mouth, I find myself pushing my own tongue over hers until we're locked in a swirling snowstorm of caresses. Mouths and teeth and lips and tongues. A moan must escape me because she stops and smiles into my lips, kissing me with a peck, once, twice.

But I'm not done.

She has unleashed something and now I'm hungry.

Starving.

I want my fill of her.

So I pull her tighter, I grab her shoulders and draw her

down onto the blanket with me. The food goes everywhere, the glasses spill. Everything trickles over my dress, her trousers.

Both of us stained and dirtied.

But neither of us care.

Our legs entwine and she rolls onto her back, pulling me on top of her. I crush my lips to hers trying to savour every mouthful of her sugary skin.

Just as I thought, she tastes like sweet wine, like summer breezes and clouds made of gold. She tastes like a hint of iron and magic and like the hottest desire I've ever experienced.

She tastes like I want more.

Like I never want to let go.

She tastes like a thousand years of history and a thousand more to come.

And I know in that moment that I can't give her up.

That no matter what my mother says, no matter how much she pushes and chides. There is no going back from this.

I will not marry a man.

I cannot.

For a woman has stolen my heart, ripped it from my beating chest with a single kiss. And I can tell from the way she's staring at me, that she has no intention of giving it back.

When I finally pull away, I remember she had a confession.

"What was that secret you needed to tell me?" I whisper, running my finger along her rosy-pink swollen lips.

She lowers her eyes, as if she's afraid to tell me.

"You told me your surname, but I didn't tell you mine..."

"What is it?" I ask, frowning down at her.

"Randall. My name is Eleanor Randall, and I am the heir to the Randall estate."

The daughter of my enemy.

And there, in a summer field, my heart cupped in her hands, my world falls apart.

CHAPTER 27

OCTAVIA

I actually slept. I rarely sleep. We don't really need to. Or at least, I know I don't, being born this way. I think Mother does a little more than me. The ones she's turned too, they sleep more than I do.

But I rarely sleep. Once a week? Once every couple? There's just no need for it. I live forever, my brain function doesn't slow or suffer, and my healing comes from another part of my biochemistry. Sleep, then, becomes indulgent, an utterly pointless exercise. A waste of life—despite the fact I have ample amounts of that.

But sleep I did, and I have an awful suspicion that I slept because of her. Verity wrapped herself in my arms, curled in tight like I was her comfort blanket. It was too hard to keep my eyes open. I shut them against the pleasure of having her with me.

It reminds me of before.

I wonder where she is, but when I lean over the bed and look for evidence of her having been here, the only thing I find is the discarded strap-on and my clothes. Hers have vanished.

I sigh and pad to the bathroom, showering and applying lipstick and getting dressed. When I'm ready, I exit my room and find Red by the door, hovering just outside, her suitcase beside her.

"You're moving out?" I say, raising an eyebrow, trying not to let the tinge of irritation seep into my tone.

"In. Actually. You said I should—" she points inside the room.

"Oh." I relax instantly, I'm so used to her telling me she's leaving that moving in was the last thing I expected.

A surge of adrenaline rushes to my stomach at the prospect that maybe, maybe after all these years I could be winning her over.

"Hey, what's up with your skin?" I ask.

"What do you mean?" she says.

"I'm not sure, you just seem... more... I don't know, flushed? Bright? You kind of look like you do after you've had my blood."

"Well, I did have a ton of it last night."

"Yes, but we got that out your system, or it should be by now."

She shrugs. "What does it matter, it's trial time. We should hurry. We don't want to waste any of the two days we have."

Wendell appears with a tray of food and a goblet of my favourite blood. I thank him and drink it down. Red's eyes skirt to the goblet, a stiffness peeling across her shoulders.

"You okay?" I ask, taking the last gulp.

"Fine."

The most un-fine response I've ever heard.

"Come on, let's go," she says, eyeing the goblet again and marching out of the room.

A driver meets us by the carriage outside the front of the castle. It's a beautiful evening. The sun has just dipped below the horizon, enough that us older vampires are safer even though there's still a little light. Twilight is much safer than dawn because the sun is dying and losing strength rather than gaining it with every passing second. Purple and navy daub the sky like smears of dripping blood. It's glorious.

Red carries her sketchbook and a pencil case with what I assume are pencils, paint and brushes. We board the carriage, and she sets about opening her case and pulling out what she needs. I cross my legs and watch.

"Stop staring, you'll put me off," she says.

"Just curious."

She pricks her finger, the scent of iron fills the carriage. I jerk back, my eyes wide.

"What the hell are you doing?" I shout.

"What? Chill out, it's like a bead of blood, it's not like you haven't just had breakfast. Me having drunk your blood a handful of times can't be enough to make you hunger me that much."

But it is. Because it's not just a handful of times. It's not the fourth or fifth or even twentieth.

She has no idea.

This is it. Amelia will have to deal with me telling Red first. I don't think we can continue down this path without me coming clean and confessing what I've done. Not this time.

Things are different between us. This time she's more open, she hates me less, our communication is different, and for the first time, I really believe she could love me. "There's something I should tell you," I start.

"Later," she says. "Now, stay still. This is really cool."

She drops the bead of her blood onto the palette. I stop

breathing entirely so I can't smell her blood. I am so rigid with the tension of trying to stay in my seat and not leap across the carriage and sink my fangs into her finger that when she looks up, her eyebrows lift off her forehead.

"You okay?"

I shake my head.

"Damn, you must be hungry this morning. All that sex, no doubt."

I try and laugh off the suggestion. But to my relief she sucks her finger and then pads it against her jeans until the prick clots and the scent of iron eases.

"I need you to stay very still for me, okay?" she says.

I nod. Not a problem. I'm still getting over the smell of her blood. It's infused the carriage, slipped inside the fabric of the walls and into my veins.

I force myself to take a steady set of breaths and relax. Her finger must have fully clotted now because the tension eases out of my shoulders.

I lean my head against the carriage wall and watch the artist work.

She opens her pad and draws her hands through the air. Her fingers bend and contort and if it isn't the most incredible thing I've ever seen, I don't know what is. The paint whorls through the air spinning and twirling like colour-filled ribbon.

It splatters onto the page, but she moves her fingers above the pad of paper faster and faster until the colours blend and merge and take a shape. She lifts the pad up, using her knees to hide the sheet from me. Then she furrows her brow as she stares at the page, shaking her head and moving the pad this way and that. Then her fingers jerk in a flurry of movements.

She pulls more paint from the palette without ever touching it.

"Why the need for brushes?" I ask, confused.

"Sometimes I like to go old-school, and sometimes I like to use a little magic."

She takes her time and after an hour or so as the carriage pulls through the Peace Territory and towards the Midnight Market, she hands me the pad.

"There," she says.

It takes my breath away as much as it did the first time. Only this time, it's fully in colour.

"Mother of Blood, you're so talented," I say because there before me is my castle, my home. And in front of the towering turrets is a beautiful woman.

Tall, hourglass figure, long, luscious hair, tanned skin and rich crimson eyes. She smiles back at me, the hint of a fang between her lips.

"You made me look stunning instead of like a monster."

"You're not a monster, Octavia. You never have been."

I huff; it's a short, barked huff full of snark. "Just wait till you see what happens when we walk through the library and then you tell me how much of a monster you think I am. Or at least how much of a monster other people think I am."

"Well, maybe they just need someone to show them otherwise."

The carriage pulls up outside the library and I help her step down. "You have the shortest legs of anyone I've ever met," I laugh as she has to jump the last step.

"Piss off, just because you're super tall," she says, but she's smiling.

I lead her towards the enormous library building. It's not like the castles Mother and I own. This building is square and old. Four round turrets sit on each of the corners. Windows pepper the front and sides. The door is huge, towering over us, made of oak and peppered with ageing studs.

We approach the front of the building as Gabriel and Keir appear. The gargoyle sticks its tongue out for Gabriel and as he deposits a drop of blood it smiles at him. They exchange a few words, and the goyle continues to grin as the door swings open and swallows the pair of them.

He's not smiling as I approach, though. Rude.

"Hello. I'd like to enter, please," I say.

He glares at me, but dutifully sticks his tongue out, and I pay the toll of a bead of blood. He shivers as it seeps into his tongue. And then he realises who I am. What my blood represents.

"Satisfied?" But he just looks away as if he can't bring himself to talk to me.

"You see, Red? I told you, even the gargoyles hate me."

She tuts and then pays him an extra bead, giving his chin a tickle. "He's not all bad, are you?" she croons. "What's your name?"

"Grimstone," he says.

He ruffles up, smiling, and then she bops him on the nose. "Now, you listen to me, Grimstone. Stop being mean to Octavia. She's a person just like the rest of us. Do you hear me?"

His eyes widen, he trembles as she raises her finger to scold him again. But he nods and glances back up at me, dipping his head in deference.

I'm about to walk off when I realise that perhaps I should try to meet him halfway. I reach back and offer him an additional drop.

"I'm really not that bad," I say. Then I lean down and give his bopped nose a kiss.

His bronze cheeks flush and he flutters his lashes at me

as the door swings open. The walls pulse where our blood races through the mansion's veins.

Doors swing open as we pass as if they're grateful for the additional drops we gave, and I wonder whether part of the problem with the citizens has been me rather than them all along.

But I don't think I can accept that. I've faced too much abuse. I don't want to be lured into thinking that after a thousand years everyone will suddenly accept me and let everything be bygones. No, the goyle was a one-off.

"Octavia?" Red says, catching my arm.

"Yes?"

"Can you call me Red? Like in front of everyone else? I know you know my name, but no one else does. I'd like to keep it that way."

I'm about to protest but I figure that's the least I can do given she singlehandedly turned a goyle around for me.

"Of course."

"Thank you," she smiles, and we make our way through the library's maze of hallways. We traipse down corridor after corridor, past rooms and rooms of books and archives. Some filled with records, others with books, others still with maps and scrolls.

"Gods, how does Gabriel find his way around here?" I mumble.

But as I start to complain, we approach the heart of the building and a central foyer. Off to one side is the grand library and there, when the doors swing open for us, are the other four teams.

The grand library is positively mesmerising. A huge chandelier the size of a carriage hangs from the ceiling. Little book-shaped crystals dangle from the structure alongside candles, sparkling and glimmering in the low light.

Around the edges of the room are towering shelves that reach so high I have to crane my neck to see the top. Along the walls are row after row of mahogany shelving units, each one with their own ladder. It's spectacular. At the head of the room in the centre of the library is a circular reception desk, I suspect where you order books and deposit loaned ones.

The air is rich with the scent of old leather, musty paper and the tang of spilled ink. I smile to myself; I've always taken the piss out of Gabriel for his incessant love of books and history, but standing in here immersed in his world, I can see why he loves it.

"Lincoln, SHIT. Are you okay?" Red sprints across the grand library entrance towards him. I catch up and realise the problem.

His face is smashed to pieces. He has a black eye and split lip. As I look around the rest of the hunters, none of them look much better.

Fenella has stitches through one of her eyebrows and bruises to match Lincoln's. Her red hair is matted and clotted with crusted blood.

Keir's hand is bandaged. Only Talulla doesn't look too worse for wear. I suspect Xavier either fed her blood or forced another vampire to give her some to keep his partner beautiful.

"Were your partners attacked?" Sadie signs.

"Yes," Dahlia says as she saunters in behind me. "All of them were last night."

"And we're doing what about this?" I ask.

"Nothing," Xavier says.

"Nothing?" Mother says as her and the Chief stride into the library. Mother looks furious, the Chief looks practically apoplectic.

"This is a travesty. I will not allow you to be under threat."

"We're all under threat?" Red asks.

Mother's lips thin. "Maybe not immediately, but as word spreads, those on the side of anti-cure will likely have a problem with what we're doing. I suspect that's who attacked you all last night."

"But those who are pro-cure will be out to support us," Lincoln shrugs.

Gabriel's fingers toy with the spine of a book. "If we succeed, we're going to change the course of our city. We're going to divide opinion even further than it already is. This is going to create anarchy."

Next to him, Keir shakes his head. "Even if we don't do this, we've already been attacked. Enough people know what's in that boundary, enough know that there's a prophecy about the cure... Chaos is coming, so no matter what, we can't back out now. Because if we don't find it... someone else will. We're all targets. Even you vampires."

"I agree," Sadie signs and Dahlia translates. "No matter what, nothing is going to be the same in this city after these trials, regardless of the result."

Beside him, Talulla rubs her jaw, her wide eyes tell me everything. She looks how the rest of us feel.

"We should increase security around the hunters and your children," the Chief says.

Cordelia huffs. "Please, if the hunters are with my children, then they're safe."

The Chief's expression darkens. "I don't care whether you believe your children are heaven-sent from the Mother of Blood herself. My hunters were attacked last night and look at the state of them. Besides, you are still vampires, and we are still hunters. I'm going to be assigning more guards to protect them."

"And what do we do in the meantime?" Fenella asks.

"We carry on with the trials," Sadie signs. "We have to push harder than ever now that other people know what's going on, they'll be trying to get there before we do."

"Sadie's right," the Chief says. "You only have two days before the next trial. We will be investigating these attacks while you continue with the trials. Good luck, everyone."

Mother and the Chief walk out together, side by side.

Lincoln glances down at Red, "You look okay, how are you not more injured?"

She shifts, realising that while I know that she's an addict, no one else does. This is a precarious position to be in given the rest of the hunters aren't faring too well. Had I realised that the others would be attacked, I may not have given her quite the amount of blood that I did. I'd have left her at least a little injured.

I step forward ready to jump in with any lie I can think of. But she puts her hand on my arm.

"I was just quick with a blade," she says, but her eyes don't meet Lincoln's and I'm not sure he buys it.

"Okay," he says, but I know from the increase in his heart rate that he hasn't bought it and that he will question her later. I wonder if this is the start of how it all unravels. If all the secrets I've kept are going to unwind.

I decide that no matter what, I'll tell her tonight. We're spending way too much time together for me not to tell her. If she found out some other way...

"So, we're going to find out who did this and attack, and slaughter them, yes?" Dahlia says, cracking her knuckles.

"I don't think we should," Keir says, scratching at what looks like a new tattoo, a little piece of scab flakes off it.

"And why the hell not?" Dahlia says glaring at him.

It's Lincoln that speaks up this time. "Because we're on

a time crunch. You heard your mother and the Chief. We only have two days. And that is already trickling by. If we want to stand any chance of breaking that boundary, we need to stay vigilant but carry on. There will be more attacks I've no doubt. But would you rather lose?"

"Exactly," Keir says. "Gabriel and I are going to hunt for the map, and you can do whatever you want."

Dahlia gapes open-mouthed at the hunter boys. It's not often she's spoken to like that. Vampire nobles tend to treat us with absolute deference, and I can't imagine Dahlia hangs out with too many hunters.

She springs forward but Gabriel steps in the way. "Not today, sister."

"Did you hear how he spoke to me?" she snaps.

"I did. But he's also correct. Each hunter has a vampire partner. They are arguably as trained in combat as we are."

"More so in some cases," Xavier drawls.

"What's that? Too pretty to train in case you break a nail or nose?" Gabriel snarls.

"At least mine is straight," Xavier quips.

Gabriel rounds on Xavier, but this time Dahlia stands in front of him. "Lincoln and Keir are right, this is wasting all of our time."

Gabriel stands a little straighter. "Fine. And to show there are no hard feelings, I will give you all a clue as a head start. I will be heading to the archives. Where all the most lyrically written books and maps lie. But that is all the information I am willing to give you. You're on your own for the rest of it."

With that, he rounds on his heels and places his hand on the small of Keir's back, pushing him out of the library and down the corridor.

There's a beat where we all gawp at each other, and

then like a starting gun was fired, we all move at once out of the grand library and after Gabriel before we lose him.

Gabriel turns down several corridors, leading us through the warren of hallways. Finally, he slows and enters another room that honestly is almost identical to the grand library. Except this time the books are enormous. They come up to my hip and I am not short. The leather smells a little older, the paper a little mustier. It reminds me of happy childhoods and infinite worlds lodged in fairy-tales. Maybe I could get used to being in a library more often.

"Map archives," Gabriel announces. "And that is where I leave you." He grabs hold of Keir and speeds out of sight.

"Well, fuck you. Bye then," Dahlia says. "Come on, Linc, we've got some losers to beat."

I glance at Red as Dahlia shortens Lincoln's name and I don't fail to notice the twitch of her expression. Honestly, I wouldn't want him to be friends with Dahlia either if he was my bestie.

The rest of the teams peel off leaving only Red and I.

"Where do we start?" she asks.

"Here is as good a place as any, because I have absolutely no clue."

We traipse down the aisles. Pulling out book after book. The maps all pertain to cities. Some I know of, others are lost, and others still are so obscure I can't believe they exist.

"This is ridiculous," Red says. "We'll never find anything in here. We have to think differently or we'll be walking these aisles for the next century."

"I agree. Gabriel gave no indication of what he was looking for either, just that he was starting in here."

Red stands up straight. "Didn't he? What was the exact phrase he used?"

"Umm, he said 'I will be heading to the archives, that's all the clues I'll give you' or something."

"No. He said something else about the archives. That sly bastard. He did give us another clue. He said, 'Where all the most lyrically written books and maps lie.' What the hell does that mean?" Red says.

"Let's walk down a few aisles and see if we can find anything that suggests music maps? Or, or... Gods, I have no idea. There have to be records of dhampir maps," I say.

"Records? Like music records? I wonder if that was his clue," she says.

"Good thinking. Let's search for them first."

With that, Red walks back out to the main aisle and crisscrosses her way through the library. I keep pace with her, watching her move: the hard lines of her body, the way she walks a little heavy on her heels, the fact her fingers dance at her sides like she's twizzling a stake. I wonder how many times she's practiced, how many stakes she's flung at walls and mannequins. How many times she's imagined killing me for what I did to her sister.

We check the records section, searching through various books and documents but find nothing. We continue to schlep through section after section.

After an interminable time, we decide to try a new area, so we walk for what must be half an hour through various aisles, some lit with lanterns, others electric lights, others not lit at all. We reach a corridor where all the maps are behind glass.

"Where are we?" Red says, suddenly pulling up to a stop.

The room around us has changed, we're no longer in the main area of the archives. The walls are darker here; instead of mahogany wood panelling, the walls are made entirely of bookcases. It's dim, scarcely a light in here.

"I have no idea, I was following you," I say, my fingers trailing the spines of the leather-bound books behind me.

"What was that?" she says, spinning on her heel to face down the corridor.

"What was—"

"Shh," she cuts me off by placing her hand over my mouth.

"Donth doo s'thing you'th mmgret," I mumble into her palm.

She glares at me. "I neither have your blood in my system, nor do I want to fuck you. Now, silence." She removes her hand. But I can't help the wind-up.

"Liar," I whisper.

"Don't make me gag you."

"Yes, please."

She cracks a smile, shaking her head at me and places a finger over her lips. She closes her eyes and tilts her head one way and then the other. I want to ask what she's hearing, but she scrunches her closed eyes in concentration, and I know I'll get walloped if I speak again.

"There," she breathes. Her eyes snap open and she charges forward down the corridor. She marches left down another hallway and then comes to an abrupt stop.

"Do you hear it now?" she asks.

"Hear wh—"

She puts her hand over my mouth and then tugs my ear. I close my eyes and listen. There under the creaking of the wooden floors, the rustling of feet in the main rooms, the opening of pages and slide of leather against leather as books are pulled off shelves, is a whisper.

It sounds like crinkled paper and sliding sheaves of parchment. Like secrets and stories and the murmured promises of tales to come. But more than anything, it's the lyrical sound of a book, as if it were singing.

I pull her hand off my mouth. "What is that?" I whisper.

"I have no idea, but that clever son of a bitch tricked us, he meant lyrical literally. I think it's coming from this corridor. Help me look."

We set about scanning the shelves but see nothing obvious. I pull books out, tug at the giant maps and run my fingers down leather spines.

I bend to the lower shelf, catching the hook of a whisper. I lean down further, brushing my fingers against the spines and then I find it. "Red," I call.

She appears, looking down at my arse.

"Oh," I say, standing up and pulling the book with me.

She drags her eyes back up my body.

"Sorry," she says, a hint of pink brushing her cheeks.

"Enjoying the view?"

She glares at me and tugs the book out of my hand to hold it up to her ear.

"You did it," she says. "And it's saying something. Here, listen."

She holds the book up between us and steps into my personal space. I'm suddenly very aware of how close we are. The fact that, even though we've fucked multiple times now, we're so rarely close. We're not tender, our connection is forged in rage and hate and stolen memories. But standing this close to her in the dim corridor, my fingers find their way to her jaw, brushing along the soft skin.

She tenses and then relaxes, moving even closer.

"I—" I start, realising that things are shifting between us again and that I am going to have to confess the truth. Tell her what I did and why. "I need to tel—"

She cuts me off, her lips crushing against mine in a bruising kiss. The book falls somewhere behind me onto the bookcase shelf. Her hands twine through my hair as she deepens the kiss.

My arms slide around her waist, pulling her tight against my body. Our tongues slide over each other, and I realise that this is the first time we've kissed outside of blood lust. She pulls back, runs her thumb over my lip, leans in and sucks it into her mouth. When she releases me, she smiles.

"You taste like cherry balm," she says.

"And you taste like you belong to me."

She narrows her eyes at me, but I just smile.

"I do believe," I lean into her, kissing across her cheek towards her ear. "You're falling for me, Verity Fairbanks."

She breaks away, leaning back, her eyes wide, her lips parted. But before she has a chance to respond, Dahlia and Lincoln appear.

Lincoln's eyes dart between Red and I. She springs back, grabbing the whispering book.

Dahlia's eyes narrow. "Oh, it's you. Well, I was hoping you wouldn't have found the talking books, but seeing as you have, you'd better follow us. We found something."

CHAPTER 28

RED

Falling for her? She's insane. Of course I'm not falling for her. She turned my sister, who nearly killed me because of her. Besides, it would be suicide in the Hunter Academy to fall for a vamp, look at how Erin was excommunicated.

No. She's being ridiculous.

We make our way back through the rabbit warren of corridors until we find ourselves in an alcove of the main library room.

Gabriel and Keir are stood at the head of a table. Gabriel's long, slender fingers are pressed against the leather of a tome. Around the table, each of the teams is clasping a book.

Xavier, I note, has his arm around Talulla, who doesn't seem to mind one bit. So much for being excommunicated for your vampire associations. Talulla's taking a bit of a risk being so open about it.

Keir's tattooed fingers drum against the table. "It

appears that we're at a stalemate. Each of us is holding a whispering book, and it's our belief that together, the whispers will give us a location for the amulet," Keir says.

Talulla places hers and Xavier's book on the table, her fingers holding it down. Protective, possessive.

She clears her throat. "A truce then, we share our books' whispers and then it's up to us to figure out where the location is."

Lincoln goes to put his book on the table, but Dahlia places her hand over his and he returns the book to his chest. "What's the guarantee you won't try and take our books?"

"Sister, please," Gabriel rolls his eyes. "There are five teams, five books. There's no way one team of two can take on four other teams. Four to one are not great odds."

"Then what do you propose? Because I'm already weary of this game," Dahlia says, eyeing each of our books in turn.

Gabriel scratches his jaw and then pulls a pocket watch out of his top jacket pocket.

"Everyone will place their books on the table. I will set a timer and we get twenty seconds to listen to each book's whisper. Then we move one place around and repeat. Everyone understand?" he says, setting the pocket watch.

Sadie signs at Fenella to find a pen. She scurries off and when she returns, she's holding a handful and Sadie has sourced several scraps of parchment off the tables.

Octavia leans into me. "You listen and whisper to me, I'll scribe, I can write faster," she says.

There's some jostling as we find paper and get into position. "Right, given that we'll be keeping our original books, everyone step to the right in three... two... one..." Gabriel says.

We do, though there's a beat of pause before we all

move in unison. I don't have to be a vampire to know that everyone's heart rates are elevated. It's the skittish eyes darting between each other that give it away.

"Quite the game of trust," I say. And an odd one, given I'm now questioning my fellow hunters over my vampire teammate.

I note the tension in each hunter's body. The way they're ready to pull out weapons and stake anyone who moves wrong.

Gabriel displays the pocket watch. "Open books in three... two... one..."

In unison, we open the books. There's that familiar scratching of paper and rustling of parchment scraps. I lean close to the book and whisper the words I make out to Octavia. She scribbles them down fast, glancing at Gabriel's pocket watch the entire time.

I close the book just as the time ticks down.

"Move in three, two, one," Gabriel says.

We step to the next book and the cycle repeats until we're back to our original book.

"There. That wasn't so difficult, was it?" Xavier says. "But on that note, Talulla and I are out of here."

He picks Talulla up, swinging her onto his back and speeds out of the library in a blur.

I open my mouth to tell Octavia she has another think coming if she dares to do that to me, but it seems I'm already on her back speeding out of the library, the wind rushing through my hair as I cling wildly to her shoulders. She races me all the way through the Midnight Market, running faster and faster. I dig my nails into her shoulders but it's not enough, I have to slide my arms around her neck as I fear I'm going to slip off.

She brings me to her club, stabbing her finger over

Broodmire's tongue. As her blood rolls down the spike and onto the goyle's tongue, my nose twitches. I realise it's been almost twenty hours since I last dosed.

I can't think about that. I need to ween myself off, not worry about where the next drop is coming from. Especially after I had so much of Octavia's blood. But even as I think it, the first hint of withdrawal shivers course through my body.

She slips us inside. The club is in full swing, and as we race through the corridors and past the main club room, I notice dozens of people fucking in varying states of naked and the distinct scent of iron in the air.

She races me around the dance floor and up the stairs to a mezzanine floor and in through a door that was blended with the wall.

She slams the door behind us and barks an order at a boy sat in a chair to the right of a desk.

He scrambles up, "Yes, I'll get that immediately."

I notice how he flinches when he passes Octavia, how he never brings his eyes up to hers. I knew Octavia was treated differently, but I don't think I really saw it until now. How easily my privilege kept me blind to her experience.

He disappears and I take a seat. Octavia pulls out the parchment she wrote on and uses a knife from her desk to cut it into pieces. She gestures for me to come to her desk. I join her, staring at her swirling script and the scraps of paper.

She moves a couple, switching the order. The young man returns carrying a tray. He deposits a goblet, a wine glass, a bottle of wine and a warmed bag of blood on the table and then darts to the furthest point of the room.

"You're dismissed," she says, and he doesn't need

telling twice. He scarpers but Octavia stands bolt upright. "Wait," she says, and he halts.

Her shoulders sag a little and she turns to face him.

"Yes, Lady Beaumont?" the boy says.

"Frank, is it?" He nods, edging back.

"Thank you, Frank, I appreciate your service."

His face crumples, washing through about four different emotions in the space of three seconds and then slowly, a smile spreads over his lips. He chances a quick glance up at her and bows deeply. "My pleasure."

Then he hotfoots it out of her office.

A smug smile curls in the corner of my mouth, but I say nothing, and by the look Octavia is giving me, that's a wise move.

"Anyway," Octavia says and leans back over the scraps of paper to examine them. She reads the strips of riddle out loud as I pour myself a wine.

"In twilight's shroud, where shadows dance, Beneath the gaze of stone's grim trance. Seek the spire, where secrets seep, Where echoes whisper, and secrets keep.

Amidst the ancient city's hush, Where winged sentinels guard the rush. Stony guardian, with eyes of night, He guards the passage, veiled from sight.

At the crossroads of the spectral hour, Where silence reigns and veils devour. Speak the cipher of the midnight air, To the stony keeper standing there.

When darkness weaves its cloak profound, And moon-light's tendrils touch the ground. Utter the language of the night, Unlock the path veiled from the light.

Where serenity and mystery entwine, A clandestine union in the shadow's sign. Pursue the whispers through the night, To secrets veiled in silent light."

I listen as she speaks, turning the words over. "Hmm," I say.

She nods, "Hmm indeed, I've no idea what this means."

"Me neither."

Octavia's eyes fall to my wine. Reluctantly, I slice the bag of blood and pour it into the goblet for her.

There's that burning scratch in my chest again. It's not like it bothers me that she's drinking someone else's blood. She's already told me the consequences. It's just that it feels uncomfortable to watch it. Obviously, that's my hunter tendencies. The fact it's so unnatural. The fact that until a couple of days ago, I'd have staked her if I could, and now I'm partnered with her, and it's messing with my head. And that's without my own hypocrisy of drinking her blood.

She takes the goblet, our fingers brushing.

"You don't need to look at me like that. Would you rather I drained one of the club-goers?" she says, her voice a little huffy.

"I'm not looking at you like anything. It's fine. I know you have to eat. Shall we focus on the challenge?"

Her lips twitch. "Oh, you're jealous?" she says, her voice lowering, lust threading through her tone.

"Don't be ridiculous," I snap.

But she's walking up to me, this dance we play over and over. One of us prowling toward the other.

I step, step, step until my back hits a wall. I shift against it as she paces closer and realise I'm not against a wall at all but a curtain. Her arm reaches up beside me and she pulls a cord, the wall vanishes, the curtains shooting into crevices.

Her office wall isn't a wall at all, but a giant window allowing her to look down upon the club. Or the club-goers to look up at her.

She tugs her office chair around and picks up her goblet,

taking a sip from it. Watching my reaction the entire time. Her chair is more like a high-backed black and red throne, ornate filigree twirling up the edges and over the seat arch.

She sits in it, reaching up and pulling me onto her lap.

"We need to figure out what the riddle means," she says, wrapping her arms around me and lacing her fingers into mine.

I'm stiff in her arms, my palms are sweaty where I'm trying to suppress the need to dose. But she tugs at me until I relax.

"This is my favourite place to think," she says. "There's something mesmerising about being up here while they're all down there. The only thing that helps clear my mind better is sex."

I choose to ignore that statement, or the fact that it's true for me too. I notice several platforms with poles and half-naked dancers. One woman of whom is grinding her pussy against a fellow male dancer's thigh.

She must catch me because she says, "Remind you of anything? A certain canal bridge perhaps? Little exhibitionist that night, weren't you?"

"Or maybe everyone on the boat was just voyeuristic."

"A little of both, I think."

My head is fuzzy, I'm having trouble focusing on her words, on the room.

She taps my thigh to stand me up and slips her hand back in mine, pulling me to the window so we can look down. But she narrows her eyes at me instead.

"You're sweating, and your heart rate is elevated," she says, a blunt fact.

"Yes."

"Why?"

"I don't know why," I lie. I don't want to have to

vocalise it, but my fingers have started to tremble, and my stomach is churning.

"You're lying," she breathes and lowers her mouth to my neck, kissing down towards my collarbone.

"We don't have time for this. We only have a day and a half."

"We won't win if you're in a state of full-blown withdrawal. Though I must say, I've never known an addiction like this. Your tolerance is so much lower than most addicts."

"Yes. Thank you. No need to remind me I'm weak."

"I didn't say weak."

"It was implied," I say, my blood heating, fizzing through my veins.

"Not at all. I just find it curious."

"I find it irritating," I snap, a little harsher than I mean to. I pull a hand over my face, wiping the sweat away.

My stomach churns, stars smatter my vision, I might actually be sick.

Octavia's fangs drop, she raises her index finger and presses it to the razor-sharp tip. I step back as a bead of blood wells on her pad.

"No," I say and shove my hand over my mouth, stepping away.

She grabs my wrist, yanking it off my mouth. "Listen to me. You are going to get worse. You'll go through full-blown withdrawal. Your organs could shut down, you could fall into a coma. You could die, for fuck's sake. Do you want another team to win? To take the cure from your sister?"

"Obviously not."

"Then take the blood and let's focus."

"If I drink that, focusing is the last thing I'll want to do."

"Then we deal with that and focus after."

"You make *fucking* sound so romantic."

She snaps, pushing me against the window. Pressing me into it. "Drink. The. Fucking. Blood."

"We can't keep doing this," I whisper.

"You're not drinking anyone else's blood. It's mine or nothing, or would you rather fall into a coma?"

I grit my teeth and grab her index finger bringing it to my lips.

"Fuck you," I spit and then I suck her finger into my mouth, my eyes rolling back as the metallic liquid spills over my tongue, seeping into my bloodstream and instantly calming my body. My mind re-focuses, the sweating stops, the shivers cease.

Shit. The addiction is bad.

I gasp as she pulls her finger out. My mind is already addled by her blood. Hers is addled by the scent of us mixing.

This endlessly toxic cycle needs to stop. But I am utterly focused on her. The way her body curves into a tiny waist, the way her hips round into the perfect ass. Her long, thick thighs I want to wrap around me.

"I'm beginning to think you only want me for my blood and my mouth."

I shrug. "It's an expert mouth."

She rolls her eyes at me. "After this is over, once I win the trials, this little blood and sex thing... it's over."

I'm not sure what pushes me to do it, but I reach up and pull her down until she's looking at me. "You keep telling me I'm the one who's jealous, the one who's falling... but I think it's you."

Her plump lips press together, thinning.

"I don't want to like you. I don't want to need you. But the more blood you take from me, the harder it's becoming to let you go. And that is a problem because you don't want me. In fact, you've made it quite clear you don't even like me. You only ever kiss me, want me, or fuck me when you're high on my blood."

"And whose fault is that? Who keeps giving it to me?" I say, pushing up onto tiptoes. Heat spills between our bodies as we edge closer. "You just pushed me to drink!"

"Yes, because I'm trying to keep you alive. You do need to quit, but not in the middle of this chaos."

"That's not only it, is it?"

"No. I deserve to be wanted. For me, for who I am. Not for what I can give you."

"All these assumptions you keep making and yet how easily you forget, I'm the one who kissed you in the library."

Her blood flows through my system, pooling between my thighs and we both know where this is heading. Whether she's right or wrong about what we are to each other, we need the release now, talk after.

"Fuck me," I whisper against her lips.

"No," she says.

My eyes bug wide. "You're going to hold out on me? You need this as much as I do."

"Yes. But you're not mine. And I only fuck things that are mine."

My teeth grind against each other. My clit throbs between my legs, and I know she's suffering the same intense need that I am.

"Fine," I snap. And pull my top up and over my head. I unbuckle my trousers and yank the zip down until I'm standing there in my underwear.

"What are you doing?" she says, perching on the edge of her desk. Lazily, she takes a sip of blood from her goblet and pops it on the desk, folding her arms instead.

"I'll make myself come instead. I'll sit here and fuck myself in front of you until you're all out of my system and I can focus."

Her entire body is rigid, her nostrils flared wide. "You wouldn't dare."

"Try me."

She shakes herself off, clicking her neck, then she eyes me hard. "When are you going to learn that you belong to me. You always have and you always will."

"Prove it. Fuck me in front of your minions. That's what this is about. Isn't it? You want to own me? So fucking own me. Prove I'm yours in front of your club. No one in the city will touch me if they know you're fucking me. Hell, maybe they'll see you the way I do."

"Oh? And how is that?"

"As more than a crimson-eyed monster, Octavia. As a leader, a woman with vision, as a woman who loves art and beautiful gardens. As a woman who, despite being treated like shit, has a heart of gold and is always willing to change and grow and try and give those that have hurt her a second chance."

That last one takes her by surprise. I'm not sure if she's going to cry or break something, but her knuckles are white where she grips the edge of her desk. There's a crack and the ledge splinters off and drops to the floor, making her slip and have to stand.

There's a flash and then I'm pinned to the window.

"What's your safe word?" she says.

"Elysium."

She reaches above my head and pushes a button. She speeds back to the desk and grabs her goblet and is back beside me as the wall judders. I yelp as she grabs hold of me. The floor rumbles and shifts and lowers as the glass comes away from the wall, music flares to life, the bass beats pounding around us.

The strip of floor we're on detaches from the rest of the office. It lowers like a platform over the edge of the dance floor. It's just us, the throne and a tiny balcony keeping us from falling over the edge into the crowd.

She slides into her throne, flicking a lazy leg over the arm of her chair as the platform grinds to a halt. She sips from her goblet, a little blood staining her upper lip. Every sip she takes irks me further. She knows it too as her eyes rake over my face, my every movement and expression.

"Take off your underwear," she says, her tone completely different. It's full of the power I know she has. The command. The control.

I do as she says, sliding off my briefs and pulling the sports bra over my head. My heart rate increases, there's nothing hotter than being watched, than everyone knowing you're swimming in pleasure. But this is an entire crowd. And I've never been watched by this many people. Adrenaline kicks around my stomach, and an idea forms. Octavia doesn't get to control everything, two can play at this game. I fling my underwear over the side of the balcony.

Her mouth twitches. Her jaw flexes. I know what she was thinking. They were hers to keep. Hers to give away. Not mine.

It was unexpected. But I like that I can keep her on her toes.

"How do you feel about being watched?" she says.

"Like everyone can drool over what they can't have… and no one will be able to tell a soul." I lower to my knees and crawl forward.

Her eyes narrow. "That's right," she says over the beat of the music. "You belong to me, and everyone will know after tonight."

"Submit," she says.

I halt, and ease back, sliding my feet under me, and

resting my hands, palm up, on my knees—the same way she did for me the other night.

She smiles, her fangs dropping. She drains her goblet and drops it to the platform floor. She stands, paces around me, examining me.

"Turn around, face your crowd," she says.

I do. Inching around to face the dancers beneath us. She steps in front of me, peering down from beneath her long, dark lashes.

"Spread those legs wider, and show them what's mine," she says.

I obey and realise that several of the people beneath us have stopped fucking, dancing, and gyrating to watch us.

My skin warms, blood rushing into my cheeks as my breathing increases. I want to touch myself, I can feel the wetness pooling between my open legs, the air cooling it against me. The more their eyes crawl across my body, my breasts, my cunt, the harder my nipples form.

My mouth falls open, my breathing ragged.

"You like being watched?" Octavia says.

I nod and her grin deepens.

"Stay there. Don't move an inch."

She speeds off and when she returns, she's naked, her pierced nipples peeking out between the locks of her hair. But she's also harnessed up, a thick cock bouncing between her legs as she walks.

"Fuck," I say, a little hiss escaping my lips.

My body is already vibrating with need. She sits on the chair, her legs closed together and beckons me forward. I rise, and she spins me around and sits me on her lap, facing the crowd. I slide my legs over hers, leaning my back against her, the cock pressed against my ass.

Slowly she opens her thighs, pushing my legs open and baring my pussy to the crowd below.

More people have stopped to watch us, and it fills my body with electricity. Her hand slides around my abs, drifting along the hard edges of my body.

"I'm going to touch you now," she whispers against me.

"Yes," I say.

She slips her fingers between my legs and over my pussy. It's instant pleasure. My head sags against her shoulder as I let out a moan.

Her fingers glide between my folds, drawing up and sliding down over and over until I'm rocking my hips to make her move faster. She spreads her legs wider and slips a finger inside me, her other hand massaging my breast and tugging at my nipple.

Everyone beneath us is motionless now. They've ceased their own fucking, dancing, and drinking to watch us. And the more eyes I see on me, the more excited I get.

"So wet for me," Octavia says.

"Yes," I whimper. "I need more," I pant, as she slams her finger inside me, and I arch back.

She pulls out of me and shoves me forward. She pulls my chin around and slides the finger that was inside me into her mouth. She bites down, her fang re-piercing the finger I drank from earlier. My body warms, my mouth fills with saliva and the desperate need to drink her. She pulls her finger out and offers it to me, with everyone watching. This is how she makes them see, how everyone will know I'm hers. The only thing she could do to seal it further is drink from me, and that isn't happening.

I take her finger in my mouth. There's a drawn breath beneath us and I know they've seen.

She has claimed me.

No one can touch me now. And yet, this secret stays inside the walls of the club. A moment shared, a memory kept locked away.

She pushes her finger deeper into my mouth, the taste of my juices and her blood mingling together into a cocktail of bliss.

She lifts me up by the thighs like I weigh nothing and hovers me over the cock. Then she lowers me on to it, spreading me so wide I gasp.

Lower and lower she plunges me, filling my pussy.

I'm seated back on her thighs, facing away from her and toward the audience. When the cock is in me to the hilt, she moves, slow at first, tilting her hips and drawing the thick shaft in and out of my cunt.

I moan, waves of pleasure pulsing out from my core. She reaches around to play with my clit as she rocks harder, bouncing me on her thighs, urged on by the slap of our legs as we crash together.

"Octavia," I whimper.

And hearing her name moaned like a curse makes her snap. She rears up, holding me to her body and rushes us to the edge of the balcony. She bends me over, my hands grip the rail.

"You're not allowed to let go," she says.

My legs tremble both from the thrusting and from the adrenaline of being so high, having so far to fall.

"Fuck," I cry as she drives into me from behind.

"Harder," I plead.

She slams into me, driving the cock deeper and deeper. My vision whitens as I lose myself in the motion of her pumping into me.

She leans in and whispers next to my ear. "I'm going to bite you."

I tense up, but before I can protest, she continues.

"I won't draw blood I promise, but I need them to think I own you. So no fangs, okay?"

"Okay," I say.

She leans back, a roar ripping from her chest, her fangs drop. Fuck, she better not, then she tips her head forward, her hair covering her face and she lowers to my trapezium, just far enough back, the crowd wouldn't be able to see any blood if it were to drip from the wounds. Clever.

She sinks her mouth over my skin and the crowd beneath us explodes in a roar of cheering. Her teeth nip me, but it's gentle and her tongue swipes over the spot, caressing the skin immediately after.

No blood.

No bond.

She pulls off my back and continues thrusting into me. I reach down, slipping my fingers over my clit to rub yet more pleasure into me.

But she notices and growls, "No."

She pulls the cock out of me and spins me around so my back is against the railing. She kicks my feet out wide and drops to her knees, plunging her mouth over my cunt, his time owning me in a whole other way. She laps at my pussy and replaces the cock with two fingers, curling them up and into me, finding that spot that has me screaming out her name for the entire club to hear.

I buck against her mouth, she licks long, luxurious sweeps over my pussy. She focuses her mouth on my clit, her fingers thrusting hard. The tingles build and build, pleasure washing through not just my body but my mind, knowing everyone is going to watch me come apart. Watch her make me come apart.

I realise the music stopped at some point, there's only my moaning her name and the hushed whispers of the people below us.

And that thought, along with her tongue flicking faster and faster against me, tips me over and I cry out as a blinding orgasm rips through me.

And through the bliss of the post-orgasm rush, and the continued whispers of the crowd, I realise Octavia was right, maybe sex is the best form of thinking.

"I know where the riddle is leading us," I say as my exhausted but thoroughly satiated body drops into Octavia's arms.

CHAPTER 29

RED

I'm out of her arms, running down the platform back into her office and picking up my clothes. I scramble to get them on, hopping on one foot, when Octavia, still very naked, strolls back into her office.

"What's going on?"

"The riddle, I was thinking about it, and I know what it's saying."

"And?"

I pick up the scraps of paper she cut up. "Think about the words: Seek the spire, where secrets seep, Where echoes whisper, and secrets keep."

She looks at me blankly, so I wave a different scrap at her. "Stony guardian, with eyes of night, He guards the passage, veiled from sight."

She continues staring at me, but the faintest hint of confusion sweeps across her brow.

"Octavia, dammit." I hand her the next piece and hop on my foot trying to pull my boot back on. "'Utter the language of the night, Unlock the path veiled from the light. Something, something, 'Pursue the whispers through the night, To secrets veiled in silent light.'"

Octavia's eyes widen.

"The Whisper Club?"

"Exactly. And the stony guardian?"

"The Broodmire?"

I nod. "And one of us has recently charmed them, so I'm betting he might be willing to give us what he wants."

"Let's go," she says and makes to move out of her office.

"Octavia..."

"What?"

"You might want to... um..." I point at her still extremely naked body.

"Oh. Right. Right." She vampire speeds around the office reclothing herself and is ready in about three seconds. Fuck, that's annoying when you're unable to keep up.

I follow her out to the front of the club and find the door empty, "No one else has figured it out yet."

"Doesn't look like it," she says and turns to the goyle. "Hey, Broodmire."

"Good evening," he says his scratchy gravel of a voice ebbing through the night.

"I would like a favour," Octavia says.

"Would you now?" he narrows his eyes at her and sticks his tongue out for payment. She presses her finger down onto his spike and a bead of blood rolls down from her index finger.

"Perhaps we could sweeten this deal..." I offer, shoving her out of the way and adding a bead of my own blood.

He shivers when my blood slides down his spike and touches his tongue. I catch Octavia frowning at him, or maybe my blood or maybe the whole situation. Broodmire ruffles himself and settles back, satisfied as he chews on the blood. He says, "What can I do for you?"

"We're looking for a map," I say, having a feeling that he may respond to me more than Octavia. I'm not sure what makes me think that other than his reaction to my blood. So I leap at the chance. Act first, think later.

"What sort of map?" he says.

"An ancient one, it's a dhampir map. It will take us to the amulet that's been missing for centuries."

"Hmmm," he says, chewing on his teeth like he's got gum. "I can help," he says.

And I positively beam.

"You know where to find the map? Or could you tell us where we can get it?" I ask.

"Mmm, I can give it to you," he grumbles.

"How?" Octavia says.

"Because it was right here all along. This club keeps many secrets, the mansion was built on sacred ground where secrets were sown into the earth. It's how we got our name."

The door swings open. But before we enter, I pull Broodmire's lip down, his eyebrow rises but he lowers his tongue and I push my finger down on his spike once again, a little thank you.

He bristles then sags, "Maybe there's hope for us yet," he says and then he promptly falls asleep in what I assume is a blood-addled coma.

We step back inside the club. The corridor walls are beating. They pulse like they have a heartbeat. Veins appear. But as I stare at them closer, I realise they're not veins but marks. Marks on a map.

"Did you know the house could do things like this?" I ask.

Octavia shakes her head, her eyes wide with fascination. She reaches up to touch the wall. It shivers and pulses faster.

"I think it likes you."

"Well, so it should, I've owned the place long enough." She traces the edge of the map and then she gasps as her fingers sink into the wall.

"What the f—" She yanks her hand out but comes away clasping a roll of parchment the same colour as the wall. And to my delight, there's a map drawn on it. The corridor wall returns to its usual blank colour.

"Holy fuck, that was cool," I say.

She's grinning like an idiot. "We can win this. How much time is left?"

"Just over twenty-four hours."

"Then I'll get a carriage ready. We need to make a trip to the Montague territory. The amulet is in there."

The club door swings open, Gabriel and Keir are standing there and next to us the wall begins to vibrate.

Gabriel's fangs drop, he hisses at his sister. She rounds on him. Fucking territorial vampires. I grab her arm.

"We don't have time. Leave them."

She steps back, rolling the parchment up so Gabriel can't see it but it's pointless, the wall is showing him the same map that it showed us. Only he hasn't realised he needs to peel the map away from the wall.

"Let's go," I say, tugging her arm and then we're running through the club back to her office.

By the time the carriage is readied, Dahlia and Lincoln are outside the Whisper Club and Sadie is disappearing from the carriage parking area holding a scroll. I can only assume that she already got the map and Dahlia is about to.

"Only Xavier left," Octavia says as the carriage jerks forward and powers through the night.

"He won't be far behind. He might not be the brightest of my siblings, but he's not a fool. He'll figure it out quickly, and I suspect he won't even have to pay the blood toll, he'll just charm the map out of Broodmire."

I smile. "You love him."

She nods. "I do. He's been my brother longer than the others, he came first, and we were together while Mother went through her Morose Mourning period. It was... tough."

I nod. "Tell me about him."

I take my shoes off and tuck my legs up underneath me.

She narrows her eyes at me.

"You don't have to if you feel I'm prying."

"No. It's fine. It's just that no one normally asks. He's a softie behind his charming exterior. He really cares, you know? He's a total man-whore. But when he loves someone, gods. They become his entire world. He'd fall on a stake for them."

"What's he interested in?"

"We both like chess. It was one of the things that kept us sane while Mother lost her marbles for a few decades. We'd play over and over. He liked it because he tried to trick, charm and corral the win out of me. Talking at me, trying to draw secrets out of me while I was distracted. I suppose it was practice for him. And I'd try and win by strategy, by playing the best sequence."

"He would make an amazing right-hand man, you know... if you were to lead the city."

"I would change this city so much," she says, staring out the carriage window.

"For good or your own benefit."

She glowers at me from the corner and crosses her legs. "I like to think that I'd change the city for good. I'd stop the segregation the territories create. We'd become one united city. I'd impose more laws protecting humans."

That catches my attention. "Why? Why do that when they've treated you so badly?"

She opens her mouth and then closes it, choosing instead to stare out of the window. After a moment she turns back to me.

"I think... because of you."

"Me?" I say, touching my chest.

"I have always led with a hard hand. Forced my club-goers to bend to the mansion's magic. Forced their kindness towards me. If they come into the club, they can't ignore me or treat me like a freak. It goes against all of their natural instincts, of course, and it hasn't worked."

"They all flinch away from you. They don't catch your eye if they can avoid it. Which brings me back to my original question. Why the change?"

"Because I treat everyone around me with derision. Even the goyles. And yet, you treat them with kindness and generosity, and they behave differently towards you. So, I suppose you have become my muse, Verity. Your kindness is something I think I should try to emulate. And perhaps, the humans may in turn come to see me for more than the monster they've made me."

I smile. "I think that's a beautiful thing to do. And I have a good feeling that you'll find they do come around to you. Hell, apparently, *I* don't hate you anymore."

"You don't?"

I shrug. "I don't."

She laughs, it's a soft tinkling sound that makes me smile because it's so different to the husky tone of her voice.

"I like your laugh. You should laugh more often."

I lean forward and glance out of the window and whistle. While it's tough to see far because we're in the depths of the night, I can make out the woods nearest us. I must have lost track of time, we're deep into the Montague territory. The carriage rocks unsteadily from side to side as the horses struggle to make their way through the overgrown forest paths.

"Wow, this part of the city is neglected," I breathe. "It's kind of creepy."

Octavia gets up and comes to lean beside me. Her face is so close to mine, warmth bubbles between us. The now familiar scents of oud and spice and winter nights wrap around me. Her long locks drape over my shoulder, and I have the urge to lean in and smell her hair. Curl a lock around my finger.

My heart kicks up. She faces me, "Your heart..."

"I know," I nod.

"Are you okay?"

I shake my head realising I'm far from okay. I want to kiss her, only there's no blood in my system driving the desire. It's just me and my wants and realising that is making me dizzy. My legs tremble. She slides her arm around me.

"Verity..."

"I'm okay, I just... I think I wanted to kiss you." I cover my mouth shocked that I let the words out.

"So kiss me," she grins.

I do. I lean up onto tiptoes and press my lips to hers. It's tender, compared to the wanton fury in the club; this kiss is fuelled by desire and want and need. We stand there, locked against each other, drifting in the blissful taste of each other's mouths, her hands roaming my back, tugging at me and pulling me closer.

My lips slide over hers, I suck her bottom lip into my mouth, and she groans against me.

"You don't have my blood in your system," she says.

"No, I don't."

"You actually wanted to kiss me?" she says, pulling away. Her eyes grow watery.

"I guess I did. Is that okay?" I ask, realising that she's trying not to cry.

"Fuck. I've made a mess of this." She sinks down onto the carriage seat.

Outside, the horses whinny. The carriage jerks and I frown, glancing out the window but assume they must just be spooked.

"I need to tell you something. I tried before, but I think it's time now," Octavia says, putting her hands in her head.

"What's wrong?" I say.

"I did something. Well, we both did. But I think really it was just me, and I need to explain because this has gone too far, and I don't know how to come back, and I'm scared that it will change everything and... Mother of Blood this is a fucking mess."

I slump down in my seat, my eyebrows cinched together. "Octavia. What in the hell are you talking about? You just said an awful lot without saying very much at all."

"I know. Sorry. I... Okay..." she says and takes a deep breath. But she never finishes the sentence.

There's a blast, an explosion that booms around the carriage. And then we're flying through the air. The carriage is spinning.

Spinning.

Spinning.

Spinning.

Our bodies are in the air.

Gravity has vanished and the carriage is upside down. We slam into the ground and our bodies smash against the window.

Screams split the stunned silence, and I'm not sure if it's us, the horses or the driver.

"SHIT," Octavia screams. "Are you okay? I don't smell blood."

I groan against the floor but use the now upended seat to pull myself standing. "I'm fine, just bruised, I think. What the fuck happened?"

Another booming explosion tears through the air.

"Attack. We're under attack," she says, scrambling up. "Get out of the carriage. We need to get to safety."

I pick up my bag and find my blades and look back at Octavia to see her fangs have dropped and her eyes darkened. She reaches up and rips the carriage door right off the hinges.

She springs up, leaping out in one blurred move, leaving me to clamber my way out of the wreckage.

I stick my head up and shriek, immediately lowering it back inside the carriage as a disembodied arm nearly careens into my head.

"Gross," I moan and then kick off the carriage wall and jump out myself. I land with both feet on the ground, stake and blades drawn.

Someone in a mask is on me instantly. Fists fly at my head. I block, lunge, but he's lightning quick.

Vampire.

His fist catches my thigh and I yelp as I stumble back, my leg feeling dead. Fuck, it's hard to move with a dead leg. He takes the opportunity and lands a crushing blow to my cheek. It makes me see stars, but I'm not giving up that easily. I'm trained for this. Even with the welt swelling on my cheek, I duck over and over, making him miss the next three punches.

I dance around him, my face throbbing, leg pounding. But I move as fast as I can, I'll worry about the ache after. A loose horse wheels and bucks besides us, it distracts him. I use it to launch a savage attack.

Fists. Stake. Block. Swing. I move almost as fast as him.

Turning kick, reverse side kick, tornado to the head. He staggers back, concussed maybe. Hopefully.

Who the hell is attacking us?

I don't have time to think about it though, he's already recovered and is charging at me with a spray of kicks and punches. I block. Spin out the way. Lunge back.

That's when I spot Octavia, her mouth attached to another attacker's neck, blood pissing out of his throat.

My attacker lunges for me again, but I spin out the way and land my boot across the back of his knee. He bellows and crumbles to the ground. I grab him and spin him onto his back before he hits the deck. And then I leap on top of him and plunge the stake right into his heart.

He desiccates instantly.

I scrabble off him. No time to stop and work out who he is because there's still one more attacker to get. Octavia is prowling, circling him, her face smothered in blood, chunks of human flesh scattered over her clothes, limbs at her feet. Her fangs drip with gore, eyes blazing, and this is when I see the monster the city thinks her to be.

But I also see through the mask she's wearing to the terrified vampire trying to defend herself and protect me.

I wait a beat. The man's back is to me. Octavia spots me a split second before I move. I lurch, crouching and springing forward onto his back. She's ready and she swings her fist, landing a savage upper cut to his chin. He sways and with my weight on his back, he staggers and collapses. I scramble off him, my stake drawn and ready to plunge into his chest.

But Octavia is way ahead of me. She slams her fist right into his chest. The man screeches but it's too late.

She roars and rips his dripping heart from his chest, and he falls still.

We're both breathing heavy, panting loudly in the darkness.

That's when we survey the damage around us. Our human driver is dead. There are three dead and dismembered vampires by our carriage. In the distance behind us, there's another overturned carriage.

"Whose carriage is that?" I ask.

Octavia speeds up the forest path and is back before I can take a breath. "Gabriel's. He's alive, so is his hunter, though Keir is looking a little worse for wear. Behind them is Dahlia's carriage."

I suck in a breath.

Octavia waves me off. "Lincoln is fine, Dahlia is more covered in blood than me. She had fun by the looks of it."

"Then I suspect Sadie and Xavier have been attacked too," I say.

"I don't think it's *us* that's being attacked," Octavia says, bringing her hand up to my cheek and stroking.

"The hunters?" I mumble.

"It's more the potential dhampir. That's who they're looking for."

"Someone doesn't want one of us turning, activating and becoming the dhampir. Shit." I wipe a hand across my face, frustrated. "If these attacks continue, we might not make it to the boundary, let alone the door."

Octavia hardens. "I'm not going to let anything happen

to you. I'll kill every human and vampire in the city if I have to. I will keep you safe no matter what."

"You don't hate me...?" But I'm grinning because it feels more like a joke, we both know it's me that's the problem.

She smiles, soft and tender as she strokes my cheek. "That's the thing, Verity. *I* never hated you..."

CHAPTER 30

RED

I lunge for Octavia, sinking my mouth over hers in a bruising kiss. She tastes like iron and sweat and the hint of blood—the other vampires she killed, not hers. She's drenched in it, all over her face, neck and body.

But I don't care. They're dead, consuming their blood because I'm kissing her won't make a difference.

Besides, I want her. Right now. Here in the woods and I don't give a shit if anyone is around us. I need to take her right now.

I push my lips over hers, and her hands glide around my waist. "We shouldn't," she gasps as she pulls her mouth off mine and glances at the carnage around us. Dead vampires desiccating, a missing horse. Human driver without a throat, and bits of wooden carriage splintered all over the ground.

"Fuck shouldn't. Who's going to complain if we fuck? We killed everyone."

She smiles and swings me around, popping me on top of the carriage wreckage.

"Oh no, not this time." I hop down and turn her body instead. I put her hands on the carriage.

"Don't move. This is all about me pleasuring you."

I slip underneath the bridge her body has made leaning against the carriage and crouch down so I can unbuckle her trousers.

I slide them down her thighs and pull her shoes and socks off so she's naked from the waist down. I move out from under her and turn her head to face me.

"I'm going to make you come before we leave, okay?"

She nods at me.

"What's your safe word?"

"Villain."

I slide my hands up her legs, from ankle to arse, and then I pull my hand back and slap her cheek hard enough I know it stung.

She groans, "Again."

This time I slap a little harder. Hard enough she shunts forward against the carriage almost stumbling into it.

I rub my hand over her cheek soothing the sting. Then I pull back and slap again. She whimpers, her knuckles whitening as her fingers push against the section of carriage frame.

I slide my hand around her hip and down between her legs where I glide my fingers over her clit. It hardens beneath my touch.

I pull back and slap her other cheek hard enough it stings my hand this time. She moans as my other hand rubs her clit faster.

I use the palm of my hand to apply pressure over her arse and then I use the delicate trace of my fingertips to glide over my handprint. The pressure shift and sensation change make her groan and lean forward, sticking her arse out further for me.

She's wet, my fingers are drenched where I slide down her warm core and tease her hole. But it's not enough, I want to taste her, have her in my mouth and savour every drop of come she gives me. So I kneel behind her.

"Spread," I say.

She does, shifting her feet out wider, but keeping her hands on the carriage at all times.

I kiss her skin, my lips peppering the red prints. I draw my tongue between her perfectly rounded cheeks and down over both her holes. She bucks up when my tongue touches her arse. But she doesn't resist, doesn't stop me. So I continue exploring her sensitive places and enjoying the exquisite view. I circle one opening with the tip of my tongue and then drop to circle the other.

Just the tip.

Just a tease.

Teasing her this way only makes me want to taste her excitement more. When I can't hold back any longer, I swipe my tongue over her cunt, then focus on her clit. I draw neat little circles, feeling the bud swell on my tongue.

She twitches every so often, her hands gripping the carriage so hard the wooden frame cracks and groans under the pressure.

But I want to be inside her. This isn't enough. I spin her around, pushing her till she can lean against the carriage for support.

Then I spread her legs again and resume lapping and swirling my tongue in long, delicious licks over her pussy. I push a finger inside her, thrusting up until her legs shake against my shoulders.

"Fuck," she moans. "Fuck, more. I need more."

I slide a second finger inside her and her eyes drift close. She tilts her hips forward, giving me easier access and I lick faster.

I drive my fingers up inside her, and she moans my name into the woods In between pleading and swearing as her thighs tremble and threaten to give out.

I focus my tongue on her clit, and thrust my fingers in and out, curling them as she begins to tighten around me. Her hands find their way into my hair, and she grips so tight it tugs at my scalp and makes me moan with pleasure.

She bucks her hips, grinding into my face as I lick quicker, pump into her harder. She arches against the carriage, her legs buckling as she comes, and coats my face in her excitement.

I lap at her pussy, cleaning her up before I pull my fingers out. Each flick of my tongue makes her twitch with pleasure.

"Gods," she says. "You'll ruin me if you keep making me come like that."

"Here," I say, picking up her trousers. "We need to go."

"What's the hurry? It's my turn now."

But I glance up at the horizon and shake my head. "There's not enough time. Dawn is only an hour or so away, and now we don't have the carriage we'll need to find shelter."

She gazes up at the sky. "Shit." Then she's speeding around the carnage, pulling her trousers back on and untethering the remaining horse. I dive into the carriage and pull our bags out.

"There's only one horse," she says, looking apologetic.

"Just get on it," I roll my eyes, we're way past me being difficult for the sake of it. The horizon is already a purple haze. "We need to hurry."

I pull the map out and figure out where we are. "We'll have to ride fast."

She nods. "Especially since it looks like the rest of the group aren't far behind us now."

In the distance back down the path, I realise Gabriel's righted his carriage and Dahlia's drawn level with him.

"Let's go."

CHAPTER 31

OCTAVIA

I sit Red in front of me and hold both reins in one hand so I can grip her around the waist with my other. This way, I can see over her head. Plus, I want her in front of me and not behind unprotected.

Not when this is the second attack we've faced.

The forest here is thick enough it could be jungle.

We find a half broken shack that's just about sturdy enough that it will provide shade for the worst of the day.

We tie the horse up, giving it enough rein slack that it can move around and forage.

"I'll take the first shift," Red says.

"Like hell, you actually need the sleep, sit down and rest. I'll keep an eye out."

Red folds her arms and glares at me. "Gods, you're so stubborn."

I slide down the shack wall, and she nestles next to me, leaning her head against my shoulder. She's asleep before I can even ask if she wants a jumper rolled under her head.

And so that's where I sit for hours, waiting for the sun

to set, nothing but the melody of her breathing and the song of the forest birds to keep me company. It's the most peaceful I've been in decades.

By the time the sun is low enough in the sky and the tree canopies provide sufficient shade, I am itching to move.

We bring the horse with us, though this deep in the forest, we're forced to walk it rather than ride it. We leave the shack a little too early though, and the odd dying sunbeam catches me. Thankfully, it's not enough to do any severe damage. I only get one blister on my hand before the sun drops low enough to not be a problem. As the oldest vampire in the competition, I want to take advantage of the extra few minutes we'll have.

"This forest gives me the creeps," I say.

"Don't the humans think you're the monster they should be afraid of?"

"There's always someone worse."

The deeper we go, the more the forest becomes a dead zone. There's no ambient noise at all now, almost like a we're in a vacuum. The only sounds are the cracking of twigs beneath our feet and the horse's hooves, the rustling of our clothes and the horse's nervous breathing.

I grab Red's hand.

"You afraid?" she whispers.

"No. But I don't want anything to happen to you."

Moments later, we step into a giant clearing in front of a building. It's made of huge boulder-like standing stones, the light grey stark against the dark tree roots that weave between them and the green moss and foliage that adorns their edges and the ground.

The building towers up into the trees behind it.

"What was this place?" Red whispers.

"Looks like a temple or some sort of religious building."

"Not recent though. Not the Mother of Blood," she says under her breath.

I shake my head. "No, this is much, much older. It has to be for the witch-gods, the dhampirs." I check the map again and locate the structure's entrance to try to orient the page to the building in front of us. But it's so derelict it takes me a second to figure out the right angle.

"There," Red says, pointing at a half collapsed opening about twenty feet away.

We rush across the clearing. She attempts to go first, but I pull her behind me. "No. I can't die. I go first."

"We can all die, you told me that yourself."

"Yes, but it's considerably harder to kill me than it is you," I growl, wishing she would just let me protect her.

"Fine," she relents and lets me pass in front of her.

I step into the darkness and pause knowing it will take a moment or two for Red's eyes to adjust. Mine, of course, are far more adept at seeing without light.

We creep through the broken entrance into a corridor, the walls a mess of damp moss, tree roots and strange markings on the stone.

The air is cool and sticky, an odd sensation on my skin.

"Are we going to remember the way out?" she says, her voice a little higher than normal.

"I'm remembering."

"You better, this is the kind of shit in my nightmares."

We wind our way through the building until we find ourselves in a circular room. An occupied circular room.

"Fuck," she hisses behind me as we come face-to-face with the rest of the teams. "We're late."

"Apparently so."

Before us, the other four teams are spread out in a standoff. In the centre of the room is a plinth formed of the same stone boulders as the building. And on its surface, raised on a silver stand, is an amulet.

Despite the years it must have spent here in isolation, the talisman shines bright. A green crystal rests in the centre of the shiny onyx metal. It's only when I step up to the same point the others are at, I realise the metal isn't plain. It's inlaid with a delicate filigree style pattern shaped with keys. The green stone isn't a crystal either, but some kind of vial containing green liquid.

"Well, well, well, this is a problem, isn't it?" Dahlia snarls.

Besides her, Lincoln's eyes meet Red's. His face is harder than I've seen before. Normally, he's chiselled and handsome, but now he seems sharp and hard.

"Lincoln?" Red says.

"Red," he nods, but his expression isn't the friendly one he usually gives her.

She glances up at me, worry written in the frown creasing her forehead.

I lower my voice and whisper, "This competition is making all of us crazy. It will be okay."

Her shoulders sag.

Gabriel coughs, and everyone turns to face him. "I will happily step down, I have no wish to fight for the amulet. I believe I can win this competition in other ways. I will leave you to it."

Keir glares at him, but together they step back out of the circle.

"Xavier?" Dahlia says, her eyes boring into him.

He glances at Talulla, "You know, I think this face is far too pretty to smash up with your petty sister quarrels. I'm out too."

Talulla hesitates but then they, too, step back.

"Just leaves us three," Sadie signs.

"Well, I'm not standing down," Dahlia snarls.

"Neither am I," Sadie says.

"Not a chance," I add.

"Then I guess it's game on," Dahlia spits, and then she lunges for the plinth and chaos erupts.

The hunters lunge forward. Fenella dives onto Dahlia's back. Red grabs for Lincoln. Everyone shrieks desperate pleas for everyone else to stand down.

Dahlia roars in fury. Fenella is flung backwards off her and she slams into the wall, her head colliding with a stone. The air immediately fills with the tang of iron.

Red's head snaps to the wall. Lincoln's eyes follow hers and it's as if the shock of what he's done cuts through the haze he was in.

"Fuck," he screams and bolts to Fenella's side. He holds his fingers to her throat, places his hands on her chest and pumps multiple times. He breathes into her mouth, but the pool of blood surrounding her head tells me everything I need to know.

I squint at her pupils, and they're blown. She's already gone.

Red charges Sadie. I want to scream at her to stop. But I can't. I don't have a chance to because Dahlia is swinging her fists at my head. She throws her leg out and it connects with my stomach.

I bend double, the air rushing out of my lungs as she pummels me with hit after hit. I drive my fist up into Dahlia's gut hard and she stumbles back. It's the only thing that makes her stop for long enough I can catch my breath.

But she's back on her feet, and this time she's using her legs and arms. Kicks fly at my head.

I am not a fighter. Not really. I can defend myself, but I've not trained to the extent Dahlia has. She was born fighting.

But I make a mistake. It's Sadie I should have been looking for. Dahlia is loud and brash and all swinging fists. Sadie, though, is sly and silent. She slips between our bodies and kicks Dahlia's legs while we aren't watching.

Dahlia ends up on the floor, and I faceplant the ground. My nose, I'm pretty sure, is broken. Though as soon as I think it, I can sense the bone and cartilage knitting back together.

Dahlia shrieks in frustration as she stands and wipes the back of her head. A smear of blood comes away.

"You'll pay for that, you little bitch," Dahlia snarls. But Sadie just smiles, her sharp little fangs dangling like shark teeth.

That woman can be terrifying when she wants to be.

Dahlia steps to Sadie, but I know for all Sadie's dancing between us, she's thin and sinewy. She won't be able to take Dahlia out. Not when Dahlia is solid muscle. So I launch at Dahlia instead, knocking her over before she can get to Sadie. She'll kill Sadie if she's given the chance—especially if it means she can secure the position of heir. It's the only thing she wants.

And yes, maybe power is the only thing I want too. But I like to think my reasons are far more justifiable than hers.

The pair of us drop to the floor. We roll around, scratching and biting and kicking at each other. Dahlia pulls a blade. Not a normal one either. It's silver. It will hurt, badly.

Xavier sees it too. He darts forward. "Stay back," I shriek.

327

But it's too late, he throws himself into the fray, trying to pull Dahlia off me, but she's screaming at me and throwing punch after punch at my head, the knife held in her fist.

This isn't going to end well. I use my forearms to block the blows. But Dahlia is savage. She grabs me and rolls me over before I have a chance to stop her.

"Shit," I hiss.

Xavier launches himself at us, but Dahlia sees it coming. She leaps up and flings the blade right at his throat. It lands in the side of his neck, and he drops to the floor.

"XAVIER," I shriek, but Dahlia is wrenching the blade out of his neck and a halo of blood is pooling around him. He holds his hand to the wound but it's not healing. Not fast enough.

"WHAT THE FUCK DID YOU DO?" I shriek at Dahlia. But she's laughing and revelling in the fact her brother is laid there unable to heal himself.

I spot Red out of the corner of my eye, running for me. "NO," I bellow. I don't want her anywhere near Dahlia when she's in this state. She'd kill her just to spite me.

Lincoln hears me scream and reaches out for Red's ankle. She hits the deck with a loud thump, the air knocked out of her lungs. She squirms and clutches her chest, coughing, trying to get oxygen. Better that than dead.

Dahlia's punches grow more savage. I swipe at her face, my nails carving through her skin. She hisses at the sting of it and then drives a flurry of hits at my body, my face. I splutter blood out. She's obviously bruised something vital inside me, and if she doesn't give my body a chance to heal, it will be serious. Especially without blood in here.

As she pulls back to slam her fist into my face, I rear up, grab her throat, and I squeeze with everything I have. Her face instantly purples, her eyes bulging as I cut off her air supply.

"We can both play nasty, Dahlia," I snarl.

Her face darkens and I'm not sure if it's with rage or the lack of oxygen, but as I'm about to pierce her throat with my nails, Sadie appears in the left of my vision and swings an enormous rock at Dahlia's head.

The crunch on contact makes me gag. I'm sprayed with blood and brains and shattered fragments of bone.

Dahlia sags in my arms and I drop her to the stone floor. I'm up in seconds, holding Xavier in my arms.

"SHIT. SHIT," I repeat over and over. I sink my teeth into my wrist to rip a gash in my arm and hold it to Xavier's mouth. He drinks but it does nothing. His neck doesn't heal.

"What the fuck was on that blade?" I cry.

"Well, this has been lovely," Gabriel says, "but I'll be going now." He picks up the amulet off the plinth and drops it into his pocket.

His face is splattered with blood the colour of his suit. But it's his smug grin that really pisses me off.

"GABRIEL. Do something," I plead.

"No. Don't think I will. Xavier's a big boy, I'm sure he'll be fine eventually. Besides, we have a trial to win. And *I am* going to win, thanks to you lot squabbling like children. I told you fighting was never the way. Toodles now."

He takes Keir's hand and speeds the pair of them out of the temple.

"BASTARD," I shriek after him, but it makes no difference. He's gone. The amulet's gone and Xavier is growing pale, the first signs of desiccation seeping into his brow.

"Here," Red says. "Let him feed. He needs human blood, right? That's the only way to save him?"

"NO," I say. "Absolutely not."

"Would you rather he died?" she says, squeezing my arm.

"No, but..."

"Will it bind me to him? You said when you drink my blood..."

"No, you haven't fed from him, you haven't consummated the binding, it won't affect you like that."

"Then let him feed." She tugs at my arm. "Let me help him. I know you don't want him to die. Please? Let me do this for you..."

"For me?" I breathe. But she's already rolling up her shirtsleeve and opening his mouth. She slices her arm on his fang and the cut is deep.

My nostrils flare; her blood smells delicious. It makes my fangs lower. It's like summer and sex and the heavenly smell of iron, desire and warm winter fires.

"Fuck," I bark. I scramble back, trying to force my fangs away and stop myself grasping for her arm.

I'm panting and breathing heavy. I've never had such an unconscious, automatic response to someone's blood. But we've obviously gone so far that we're already connected in ways I hadn't anticipated.

The colour runs back into Xavier's face at the same time it drains from Red's. She sags a little against him, but I can't go to her with her arm still bleeding out like that.

"Lincoln," I shout. "Help her. He can't take too much more."

Lincoln gets up from where Fenella lays motionless and wrestles with Xavier's jaw, slapping his cheek until he unlocks his fangs and releases from Red.

Xavier sits up gasping. "What the fuck was that?" he says, his eyes are wide and feral, bloodshot like he took drugs rather than blood. He's panting as hard as I am.

"Shit," he says, gathering himself as he glances at Red.

"I'm sorry, I think I took too much. She's going to need your blood, Octavia."

I shake my head, my fangs still dropped. He frowns. "You've fed her before?" I nod.

"Ah," he says, realising the problem. Then he scrambles up. "Lincoln, hold her arm." He hands my wrist to Lincoln, and then he wraps his arms around my body, pinning my other arm to my side and going vampire still so he's locked in place.

Lincoln pulls out a switch blade and draws a short cut across my wrist and raises my arm to Red's mouth.

She laps at my arm, her skin colour shifting rapidly as the blood feeds into her system. But the more she takes the more I need her.

I need to feed.

Drink.

Own.

I need all of her. I don't know what's come over me. I fight against Xavier, but he's granite-like and I can't get out of his arms.

I scream in fury, but it's useless. My neck is corded with the strain but still, Xavier holds me. Finally, Red detaches her mouth, and we all sit in absolute silence. The only sound is the four of us panting. Then Dahlia groans, slowly waking up as her skull knits back together. The knowledge that Fenella is dead and Gabriel has won this round crashes over us. These trials are going to cost all of us more than we thought.

CHAPTER 32

CORDELIA

One Thousand Years Ago

It will be no surprise to you that I fell for Eleanor. Fell hard and fast. She quickly became my entire world and the prospect of marrying one of Mother's favoured men filled my dreams with nightmares.

We've been meeting for some months now. I spent much of the summer evading Mother's parties and balls and engagements with various lords and suitors, but autumn is establishing itself and the crisp chill of winter is in the morning air.

Today is one of those rare autumn days when the sun decided to show itself in a waning attempt at warmth. So I decided to organise a get-together and sent a note forward to Eleanor to meet me for a late picnic.

I trundle to the apothecary street where Eleanor's store resides. She agreed to meet me for a late lunch. She's closing the shop early so that we can spend the afternoon together in our favourite spot by the river.

I open the shop door, the bell tinkling, just as she's closing the register and writing in her accounts book.

"I won't be a moment," she says.

She's wearing a dress today, it takes me by surprise. I've never seen her in anything but men's trousers.

"Oh, gosh," I say, my mouth falling open at the sight of her. The way the dress curves around her bosoms and shapes her bottom. It's cut just above her knees so that a little thigh is on show.

I swallow hard trying to draw my eyes up to her face but finding myself rather preoccupied with her waist.

"Hi," she says grinning, clearly aware that I'm rather flustered. I press my fingers to my cheeks, the heat spilling into my hand.

I fan myself trying to calm down, but I'm unable.

"Do you need to sit?" Eleanor asks.

"No, it's just. You... I, umm..."

She laughs, "What on earth has come over you? Shall I get you a tonic?"

"No, for goodness' sake, Eleanor, it's you."

"Me?" she says, her face falling.

"Oh gods, I'm making a mess of this. It's just that you look rather fetching and I wasn't expecting it, and I was rather taken aback by how... by how... well, how beautiful you look. That's all."

She beams. And I swear on the witch-gods, the universe comes to an abrupt stop. My vision narrows to only include her gloriously blue eyes, the pale crystal water and dark pupils. I lose myself in her gaze, the way her smile radiates warmth.

"I wore it for you," she says.

"You did?" I gasp, more heat flooding me.

"I did." She smiles. "It felt like an important day."

I'm not sure what she means by that, but I'm delighted she dressed the way she did, I can't pull my eyes away from her. In fact, I'm drawn to her ample cleavage and would rather like to see what she looks like without the dress on, but that's probably not appropriate.

We have kissed, on more than one occasion actually, but that's as far as it's gone. Though, she has educated me on the ways of her love-making and how it's different, and I'm quite thrilled at the idea, but we've yet to have an opportunity to try anything more than a surreptitious kiss.

She hurries around the counter, putting jars of herbs and ointment away, then she grabs her coat and the shop keys and locks the door behind us.

We walk to our favourite spot, taking us out of the city and far away from anyone who would know us, to the safety of the river and the fields and the knowledge that we're at least three miles from anyone who could cause us a problem.

When we arrive, my mouth falls open. Someone has constructed a stone pavilion-like building.

"How... what?" I say, completely incoherent for the second time today.

"I had a friend build it for us."

"A friend? But, Eleanor, what if..."

She shakes her head. "He's like us."

"I see. And that means we can trust him? I don't much

trust anyone other than you, truth be told. I'd prefer no one knew about us."

"He doesn't know about us, only that I asked him to build this for me for someone I care about." She tucks a loose strand of hair behind my ear.

"Well, it's the most beautiful thing I've ever seen," I say, checking around us before I place a kiss on her lips, pull her to me and wrap my arms around her.

The pavilion has several marble pillars around which three-quarters of it is walled off. It will keep us protected from sight from anyone behind or approaching. The only way we'd been seen is from across the river, but in all the months we've been coming here, we've never seen another soul on the opposite bank. And that's when I realise why she did it. What this building is for.

I glance down as we enter to see swathes of fabrics and pillows lining the ground making it soft. And a small stove burner in a corner that she's already attending to.

My air catches in my throat. She wants to... we're going to have...?

I can't bring myself to consider it. I've so desperately wanted to make love to her and yet, I am absolutely terrified.

"Here," she says and pulls me down onto the bedding. We eat our picnic, and gaze over the river watching the swans float lazily with the current. We chat about magic and her witch-gods and how she uses blood and its power to pour into her spells.

Thankfully, we avoid discussing our families. Save for the odd complication of trying to visit each other, we try not to discuss the politics our families engage in. We hear enough of that at the dinner tables every evening.

She lays her head on the pillow next to me and threads her fingers through mine.

"Cordelia," she says, serious.

"Yes?" I say, unable to prevent the hitch in my voice.

"I need to tell you something..."

"Okay?" I roll over onto my side to face her, lines already etching their way into my brow. "What's wrong?"

She pulls me forward, laying a gentle kiss on my cheek, my nose, my lips. She's soft and warm against the late afternoon air.

"If I don't get to touch you soon, I think I might very well die," she says.

"You're already touching me," I say, squeezing her hand.

"Not here..." Her eyes drop, drop, drop until they focus on the spot on my dress covering my core. "There."

"Oh," I squeak out. "Well, I. Umm."

"Oh gods, sorry. You're not ready. I shouldn't have. No. Forgive me, I—"

I cut her off with my mouth. Rolling her onto her back and sliding on top of her, I plunge a kiss over her lips and force my tongue into her mouth. Because gods, I am ready. I am desperate for her to touch me everywhere, taste every inch of me. As desperate as I am to do the same for her. I wore a light summer dress today despite the temperatures, daring to hope for just this to happen. I break off the kiss and pull the dress up and off my body.

I wear no bra and my nipples immediately harden in the cool air.

Eleanor falls silent. I'm not sure I've ever seen her stunned into silence. It's normally me flustered.

"Oh. I'm... is there something wrong?" I glance down at my breasts, worrying that perhaps I'm abnormal or hideous, but this time it's me being thrown onto my back and lain on the pillows.

"Wait there," she says and her whole face is alight. Like

the sun's own rays beam from her expression. She digs in a box beside the stove and pulls a log out, shoving it into the stumpy burner. Heat kicks out immediately and the goose-flesh that coats my skin dissipates.

"Now, where was I?" she says, and this time, instead of bright sunlight, there's something dark and hot trailing through her gaze. She licks her lips.

"I have never wanted something so much in my life," she says. "May I have you?"

"Yes, always. Now and forever. Today. Tomorrow and for eternity."

"I love you," she says. And I know in that moment she doesn't mean the type of love between friends.

But between lovers.

The smile that peels across my lips is infinite.

"I have loved you since the first moment I saw you. Since I stumbled into your store and ran away because you made me feel alive and breathless and like the whole world was in your smile."

She gives me the very same smile and I swear my heart ceases beating.

"If you want me to stop at any point, just tell me. I want to pleasure you, make you happy. Not scare you or push you too far too fast," she says, stroking the back of my hand.

But I shake my head, "I want to give all of me to you."

"Okay," she says and leans down to remove my underwear.

"Wait," I say suddenly. She freezes, her hands having only tugged them down an inch.

Her face falls as if I stole her toy. It makes me laugh.

"There's a problem," I say.

"Too quick?"

I shake my head.

"Too slow?" she frowns.

"No. That..." I point at her dress and as the realisation dawns on her, she bursts out laughing and slaps my thigh. "Oh, you're terrible, you frightened me."

She hoists the dress up and over her head and lets it fall to the bedding.

"Oh, my gosh, you are... exquisite," I say as I take in her curves. The bulge of her breasts, the neat slit between her legs. My mouth waters and suddenly I'm not sure I'm happy for her to be the only one having everything.

"I..." I start.

"Yes?" she says, raising an eyebrow at me, a mischievous little glint in her water-blue eyes.

"I think I should like to kiss you right there."

"Oh, you will," she says. "But me first." And with that she pushes me back to the bedding and pulls my knickers off, flinging them out of the pavilion so that I can't change my mind.

She draws herself level with my mouth and lays her body on mine. Her hand cups my jaw as she tilts my chin up to kiss me, her other hand sliding between my legs and finding that precious space between.

"I'm going to touch you now," she says, and I nod into her kiss as she slides her tongue over mine and her hand nudges my thigh.

My legs fall apart then, and she presses her palm to my core. I draw a quick breath in. The shock of someone touching my most intimate place for the first time is enough to take my air. But then I settle as she draws the flat of her hand over my mound and down, and the pressure she applies is simply divine.

My hips seem to move on their own, tipping and rocking. And then her finger parts me and slides up and down, over my apex, which tingles and makes my whole body twitch every time she touches me.

My heart races inside my chest, my breathing increases. Her finger is wet, I can sense the slick as she slides faster between my legs. She grips my apex between her fingers, giving it a light squeeze which drags a deep carnal moan from my throat that is so unexpected I break off our kiss and clap my hand to my mouth.

"I'm sorry," I say.

"Never apologise for the sounds you make when receiving pleasure. It is most delightful for me to hear."

"It is?" I frown.

She grins at me. "Give me your hand."

I do, and she pushes my fingers between her legs to discover the same slick substance coats her entire core.

"Your moans did that."

I bring my hand back up and find my fingers edging toward my mouth. She smiles and nods that it's okay. I slip my fingers into my mouth and the taste makes my eyes roll back.

"Fuck," I say and then blush at the curse that slipped from my lips.

"You can have it all, but first, I'm going to make you see stars."

She shuffles down the bedding, stopping briefly to suck my nipple between her teeth and flick her tongue until it hardens, and then she slides between my legs and there's no more talking.

She draws her tongue down my wetness, sweeping it up and down my core until she finds a spot she's happy with and focuses there. I twitch and moan as she works at my nub.

I can scarcely breathe for the panting she's drawing out of me. My back leaves the floor, arching as I cry out. But still, she's relentless. She slides a finger inside me, and it hurts.

I wince, and hiss, the pleasure evaporating momentarily.

"You're untouched?" she says.

"Not anymore." I laugh.

"Oh, this is everything," she says and then she's back to kissing my apex. Licking and swiping that wicked little tongue until I relax and she's able to work her finger in. This time it doesn't hurt. It brings pleasure like nothing else.

She pushes her finger in deeper, then pulls it out in a rhythmic movement, all while focusing on that spot that has me shivering and gasping as waves and pulses of electricity spark through my body.

I'm trying to focus on the sensation, to understand what she's doing so that I may do it back to her. But I can't. My eyes squeeze shut, and I swear my soul leaves my body as I grasp my nipples, pinching them hard to ground myself. My hips rock, she moves her finger faster, faster, and then I come undone. Piece by piece, my world falls apart and all that's left are the stars and the sky and the ripples of pleasure soaring through my body.

She holds me for a long time after that. She tells me that I bled a little but that it's normal, and that it won't happen again.

Once my body is calm, and I've recovered, we swap positions. She tells me again that I don't have to if I'm not ready. But I have never been more ready for anything in my life.

I nuzzle between her legs and try to mimic the movements she made. It's a mess. I catch her with my tooth, and she flinches. I can't find where to slide into her with my hand.

But she's patient the entire time. She tells me where to move and I inch myself up.

"A little softer, yes. YES," she cries as I find a rhythm that works on her apex.

She guides my finger inside her and then says, "Use another."

So I do and I find it so much easier with two.

"Harder," she pants, and I can tell she's enjoying it because my hand is wet and covered in her delicious excitement. It makes me lap faster and quicker and that makes her moan louder.

And then like a spell, she tightens around my fingers, and I realise she's experiencing that magic sensation that washed through my body too and that makes me grin with delight.

When her body calms enough to release me, I pull my fingers out and clean up every drop of what she gave me. I collapse in her arms, watching the fire burn low and the sun drop beneath the horizon. It's the most beautiful moment I've ever experienced.

And nothing else matters for a long, long time.

But like so many things in life, nothing ever stays the same.

There's a rustle in the reeds on the other side of the river. We glance at each other, the blood drains from both our faces. A cloaked figure in shadows rushes away through the night and our world falls apart all over again.

CHAPTER 33

RED

The following day, we're all gathered at Castle St Clair for the presentation of the amulet and the point awarding for the first trial, back in front of the nobles and non-players. All of us have recovered from both the attack in the Montague Forest and the fight in the temple, but the atmosphere is tense. No one dares relax their guard.

Octavia is still smarting from having lost the challenge. She's furious that Gabriel could have been so underhanded. We were so close to winning the trial, but he was clever and played to his strengths and she can't disagree with that. She doesn't have to like it either, though, which was her point.

We're stood again in the main ballroom. The seating that surrounded the room for the partner pairing ceremony has gone, and instead, there are banquet tables dotted around the room full of groups of vampires or hunters. There is a little more blending of species, but not much. The stage has a space for Cordelia, the points display of five glass vials, one for each team, and a series of bloodstones in a bowl to the right.

Last, there's an orchestra. Though they're sat with their instruments between their legs, their backs straight against their chairs. As tense as the room then.

There are balconies furnished with lavish curtains and chandeliers dotted around the room. Vampire nobles occupy most of them, watching the proceedings and drinking from goblets of wine.

"I expected more of him," Octavia mutters, still unable to let it go.

"Stop being a sore loser, we've plenty of time to win. Besides, he was clever, you can't deny him that. While we were all distracted, he took advantage. And you would have done the same," I say.

"I also won't underestimate him again. Sadie neither. That boulder she smashed against Dahlia's head was savage. I know there are rumours about her, but I guess I didn't expect her to be so... so..."

"Violent?"

Octavia nods.

"You're all vampires. Even those that seem gentle in their humanity acquire the vicious killer gene once they're turned. You're all capable. Why do you think the Hunter Academy exists? We're not here for nothing."

She nods, her lips pressed thin. "I think that I need to reassess my view of just about everything. These trials are going to be far harder than I anticipated but I am not willing to lie down and hand them to my siblings. I am one of the original three, and if anyone should rule this city next, it's me. I am enough. Just as I am."

"Yes. You are, Octavia."

She turns to me, a soft smile on her lips, her eyes glinting as she looks at me. "How did you cope coming down off my blood without me fucking it out of your system."

"Well, my wrist aches today, let me put it that way," I say.

She laughs so hard her head flies back as she cackles.

"Perhaps I can find a way to make it up to you."

But there's no time right now because Cordelia steps onto the stage.

"Ladies, Gentlemen, hunters and noble vampires, welcome back to my home for the end of the first trial celebration. We have a winner in our midst, and an announcement to make."

The Chief steps up onto the stage next to Cordelia. The pair of them are rigid, stood next to each other. Both radiate tension. But somehow, Mother is a little less tense than she was the first time they stood on stage next to each other. Perhaps peace or the semblance of it is possible after all. Cordelia hands the mic to the Chief.

"Thank you," she says, and Octavia shakes her head in astonishment.

"It's never going to sink in, is it?" I say.

"I don't think so, the manners are the most shocking part to me. I'm so used to violence and aggression between our kinds. I still feel like there's something else at play here."

"Oh, I've no doubt," I say. "I'm convinced it's all for show."

Before we can deliberate any more, the Chief clears her throat.

The hall settles into an expectant silence.

"Unfortunately, we lost one of our hunters yesterday during this trial. It is with great sadness that we confirm the loss of Fenella James back to the Mother of Blood. We thank her for her service and send our condolences to her family. There will be a ceremony tomorrow evening where we will burn her body and celebrate her life. But for now, we will proceed with the award ceremony."

She hands the mic back to Cordelia, her demeanour colder, sharper, carved like icicles now she's had to confess the loss. She's pissed; I can tell from the way her eyes blaze like blue fire. I'm not surprised. It's unlikely any of the vampires will die during these trials. Though, I say that, and if it weren't for me, Xavier could well have desiccated in the temple.

But the hunters are taking a far greater risk than the vampires in these games.

Cordelia moves to the centre of the stage and brings forward the bowl full of bloodstones. She wafts her hand over the bowl and five stones hover in the air, one representing each of the teams.

"Now, if the holder of the amulet would come forward, we will award the points," Cordelia says, and the glee in her expression is evident.

She beams, her fangs even drop a little over her lips when she can't contain the excitement. *What are you hiding, Cordelia?* I decide I need to talk to Octavia about it. There's something more we're not seeing. This all seems... too easy, too staged, too civil.

Gabriel steps out of the crowd, Keir following in his wake. He's wearing an ornate red suit tonight, it's embroidered with a filigree pattern. And Keir is wearing a matching black and red suit. They actually look kind of good together.

They kneel at the foot of the stage, and Cordelia raises her hands for them to ascend the stairs.

Keir goes first, Gabriel in his wake. To my surprise, it's Keir wielding the amulet. He takes it from his pocket and hands it to Gabriel, who drapes it across his palms and presents it to his mother.

Cordelia takes it out of his hands and stares at it. She's practically vibrating, the glint in her eye is the most terrifying thing I've ever seen.

"Ladies and Gentlemen, the amulet..."

A cheer erupts around the ballroom, vampires and hunters alike clapping and shouting.

"This is the first artefact we need to drop the boundary and reach the door and retrieve the cure. Congratulations, Gabriel St Clair. You are the first trial winner."

"As is Keir," the Chief says, her voice like a blade.

"Of course," Cordelia says, correcting herself. She shifts on her feet, aware of the error she just made. "Gabriel and Keir, you are the winners."

She waves her hand in front of the glass vials and all five of the bloodstones drop into their jar. Then the Chief steps up to the points pots.

"There are additional points to be awarded to the other teams in the following order. For coming second, Octavia Beaumont and Red receive three points."

There's a muted clap, so the Chief continues. "In joint third place, is Xavier St Clair and Talulla Binx and Dahlia St Clair and Lincoln Landry who both receive one point. And for the loss of half of her team, Sadie St Clair is in fifth place with no points."

There's another round of clapping and then the crowd falls silent. Cordelia picks the mic back up.

"We will have a day of rest, to allow for the hunters to grieve tomorrow and the teams to recoup their energy. The second trial will begin the morning after. For now, enjoy the ball, and enjoy the evening. Hunters, my thoughts are with you."

The orchestra strikes up a fast beat made for dancing. I glance at Octavia.

"Come on, we have to talk..." she says, her face grim and takes me by the hand leading me out of the ballroom.

She winds through several corridors and then we climb a set of stairs and stop when we reach a door.

"I don't want you to be mad at me, but there's something I've been trying to tell you for a while, and it's to do with your sister. So... I'm sorry, and I hope this is okay, I know how you've struggled with what happened. And this is messy and complicated, and I don't exactly know the right way to explain. But I do need to apologise, and I figured that there was only one person who could really explain this part of it."

"I don't understand," I say, frowning. But then my mind flashes back to the carriage in the forest and that she was going to tell me something before we were attacked.

"What you're about to hear is only the start... But will you please hear your sister out?" she asks.

I go what I can only compare to vampire still.

"Red? Please? I'm sorry to spring this on you, but I cannot go on any more without explaining this to you."

She leans down and places a kiss on my forehead. "You don't need to be afraid of her, she's fed recently, and I will be right by your side. But she loves you so, so much. She's desperate to see you..."

"Okay." I nod. "Okay."

Then she opens the door to the balcony, and I come face-to-face with my sister.

"Amelia," I gasp.

"Hello, sister. It's been a while."

CHAPTER 34

RED

Amelia.

      Amelia.

Amelia.

She stands in front of me, the closest she's been since she turned. The balcony sways under my feet. My body freezes, flashes of the night my sister was turned race through my head. Her teeth sinking into my neck, darkness growing over my vision. My whole body cold.

Someone screaming my name.

Someone grabbing me. Someone feeding me.

"Red. RED?" Octavia's squeezing my arm, wafting her wrist in front of me, the stench of iron in the air.

I snap back to attention, gripping her wrist. She yanks it away, taking her blood with her.

"Where did you go?" she says.

"Flashbacks, I... I keep getting flashbacks of that night."

Amelia's eyes well, "I am so sorry, Red. I didn't even know who I was when I... when I..."

"When you attacked me?" I say.

She drags her eyes away from me. "Yeah, when I attacked you. I was mid-transition, but now... I'd never. I hope you realise that I'd never ever do it again."

She steps forward, her arms open, but I shrink back, hold my palm out to stop her. "Not yet," I say. "I'm not ready yet."

I remain standing, preferring to be able to escape fast if I need to. Octavia sits in one of the balcony's velvet armchairs.

"Okay, okay, I understand that," Amelia says and pushes her blonde hair behind her ears. While her eyes are green like mine, they're a different shade, and tonight they're closer to blue. It makes her alien to me. Her porcelain skin, she was always young-looking but she holds an impossible permanence in her features now, as if she's sculpted from marble instead of the squishy little sister she used to be.

My throat clogs.

This is pointless.

"What could you possibly say to make this better, Amelia? You're a vampire, and I'm a hunter."

"Yes, and by the looks of it, you're in love with a vampire too."

My mouth falls open. How is it only your fucking siblings can talk to you like this?

"I have n—" I say but she speeds across the balcony and slaps her hand over my mouth. I freeze, my body rigid and hard. Her palm is cool where it used to be warm, but her skin still smells like her, and it makes my stomach ache and my eyes sting. Fuck, I've missed her. I flinch against her touch, but she doesn't let go, she also doesn't try to hug me. She just stays, holding her hand to my mouth until I stop trembling.

And when I do, she says. "Don't even try and deny it. But that's not what I wanted to talk to you."

I drag her hand off my mouth. "Yeah? And what do you have to say that's going to make up for this?"

She puts her hands on her hips. "Octavia saved my life, Red. You need to stop being shitty with her."

"She TURNED you, *Amelia.*"

But Amelia shakes her head at me, her eyes full of pity. "I was going to die."

"Yes, because *she* drained you." I stab an accusing finger at Octavia and all the rage I used to feel bubbles back into my body. I start shaking, my heart hammers in my chest so hard it aches. And once again, I'm not sure if I want to stake Octavia or fall into her arms. I wipe a hand over my face trying to remove the cocktail of confusion, but it won't pass.

"You're not listening. Octavia didn't drain me," Amelia says.

My head snaps up to face her. "But that's impossible, she turned you. How else would she have turned you? She... She..." But I'm no longer sure what I'm going to say, so instead, my mouth hangs open with nothing but air exiting through it.

"You don't remember that night..."

My jaw hardens, my eyes flick to Octavia, but she's intentionally looking out over the balcony. "What do you mean 'I don't remember'?"

Amelia sags. "I'll tell you everything, I'll explain why you don't remember, just... hear me out first."

My eyes flick to Octavia again, a burning in my chest telling me I already know why.

Amelia sits down in one of the balcony chairs. "We'd argued earlier on that night. You were worrying about me as usual."

"Let me guess, you put up a fight about it? Saying I was being overprotective."

She nods at me, her lips pressed together. "You were so mad at me, Red. I'd pushed too far. This was one party too many. You found out that Derek dared me to break into this vampire noble party and you let rip. You kept screaming about how easy it is to get addicted to blood. How anything can happen at these parties, and of all the stupid things, a vampire party... on and on you went."

My insides coil at the hypocrisy of what I'm hearing. But I know myself, I was trying to prevent her falling to the same fate I have.

"I was drunk. Honestly? I was probably also on drugs, I can't even remember now. But I snuck out and we broke in."

I slump down into an armchair opposite Octavia and lean my forehead against my hand. Derek was her dickhead ex who I hated. Awful influence, but the more I hated him, the more she fell.

I can't take this. I don't think I want to know where this story is going. Everything is shifting and it's leaving me unbalanced.

"But the thing is, the mansion I broke into, it was on the St Clair estate. It belonged to Dahlia..."

She's said enough. She doesn't have to finish this story for me to know that everything I thought was wrong. Two straight weeks I've avoided this conversation. Maybe somewhere deep down I knew it couldn't have been Octavia, I knew and didn't want to hear it.

"I thought we were being quiet, that we'd dance around a couple of the rooms and then get out before any vampire noticed."

Octavia grits her teeth. I glance up at her, but she looks away. This story is painful for her too.

"But Dahlia isn't just any vampire. She heard, Red. She heard us, and she came, and she killed everyone."

Amelia is crying now, big fat tears roll down her cheeks. "I managed to hide, but I saw everything as she tore through all of my friends. Derek, Sandra, Elijah. She drank them all dry, torturing them, making them think they could escape. She let Derek run, then hunted him like a mouse. And I watched from the cupboard, trying not to scream. I thought I was safe, that I couldn't be heard. But I was wrong."

"What happened?" I ask, my voice nothing but a whisper.

"I let a sob out when she dropped Derek's body to the corridor floor. She sped to the cupboard, ripped open the doors and dragged me out by the throat. Because I'd evaded her, she wanted to make an example of me. She took me to the living room where all her vampire friends were and humiliated me, stripped me naked. Beat me. Made me crawl on all fours through my friends' blood. Made me drink their blood until I threw up."

Nausea swims in my gut, I go to wipe my face again and my hand comes away wet. I'm crying?

Amelia kneels at the foot of the armchair I'm in and takes my hand. "Octavia turned up. There was an enormous fight. She ripped the heads off all of three of Dahlia's vampire friends. That, of course, made Dahlia worse, but she was more furious that the rest of her friends deserted her."

"I regret my actions, if I'd left her friends alone..." Octavia trails off.

"NO. If you'd left them alone, I'd have been forever dead," Amelia says and turns to me. "It was a standoff; Octavia was holding Dahlia's best friend. So in a fit of rage, Dahlia picked me up and held her teeth next to my neck.

She said she'd trade. Octavia let Dahlia's friend go, but Dahlia drained me anyway. And then she left me for dead, racing out of the house after her friends."

Octavia kneads her temples. "I was too late. There was nothing I could do to save her other than turn her."

"She gave me the choice, Red. She asked me if I'd rather die or be turned. It was consensual. And I wouldn't be here without her. That's when you turned up."

I rub my face, trying to claw through my memories, but every time I do, they slip away like sand through my fingers.

"I... I don't..." I say.

"It's okay." Amelia squeezes my hand. "I know you don't remember." She glances at Octavia and nods for her to continue.

Octavia leans forward, "You arrived too late. Amelia was already mid-transition. You were hysterical blaming yourself. I tried to stop you, but you were desperate to be near her. Amelia attacked you. It was a frenzy of chaos. I got Amelia off you before she drained you. I didn't have a choice, I fed you just enough blood to save you, heal your wounds."

"No," I say. "No. I was taken to the Hunter Academy. They used herbs on my wounds."

"No, Red. I saved you," Octavia says.

"Then why don't I remember?"

Octavia glances at Amelia, the two of them sharing knowledge I don't have. I've never felt more alone.

It's Octavia who continues. "When Amelia finally snapped out of the transition haze and then realised what she'd done, she was distraught. You, though, were hysterical. We couldn't calm you down."

"You snapped, Red," Amelia says, clutching my hand. "You completely lost it, we couldn't get through to you. It was like you weren't even in your own body anymore. Over and over you screamed, blaming yourself for everything. No matter what I said, you'd convinced yourself it was your fault I'd been turned. That you weren't good enough, you'd failed as a sister."

I close my eyes not wanting to see and rub my hand on my chest trying to erase the shadow of an ache I can feel now.

"What did you do?" I say to Octavia, my teeth gritted.

"The only thing I could. I compelled you to forget. Wove stories of hatred into your mind leading back years, I played your villain. Let your mind focus on hating me so your heart could learn to love your sister again."

Everything shatters. I have no idea how I'm supposed to feel about this.

"Would you really have chosen to die?" Amelia says, rubbing her thumb over the back of my hand.

"I...They took everything from us... you, Mum, Dad... How could you so willingly become one of them?"

"Because it was that or leave you. And I didn't want to leave you with no one. Fuck, I love you. But do you think you could please forgive us? I've really, really missed you."

I throw my arms around her shoulders and lean into her neck. "I want to. I really do. But it's a lot to process. I am still furious about the whole thing. And I swear to the Mother of Blood, if you ever compel me again, Octavia, I will stake you myself."

"We did it to save you," Amelia says.

I shake my head and glare at Octavia. "I don't give a shit. I swear, you ever do it again and that will be it. You don't get to fuck with my head like that. You don't get to determine my fate or control my mind like that, understand?"

Octavia pales, swallows hard and then nods.

I relax a bit. "But maybe we can move on, what with

354

this whole cure... there's a chance, Amelia... a chance you could be human again, you know?"

She pulls back, her brows cinched together. She glances at Octavia, both of their expressions shift as if a thousand things pass between them.

"Amelia?"

"Sure, I've heard of the cure."

"You're going to take it, right?"

She leans up and kisses my forehead, "If you can forgive me, you can forgive Octavia."

Then she pulls me into a hug, lifts me off the chair and swings me around.

"I love you, but I need to go. There's a killer party at the Whisper Club tonight." She winks at Octavia as she puts me down and then she's gone in a swoosh, the balcony curtains rippling in the wake of her speed. And I'm left there standing next to the vampire who took my sister's life and saved it all at the same time.

CHAPTER 35

I t doesn't matter that you stole the amulet before I could reach it.

It doesn't matter that you have five teams racing toward the artefacts.

What matters is that I work out who the dhampir is first, and when I do, it won't matter what you throw at the boundary. I will open that door and then I will destroy everything you love.

I will have my vengeance.

And you'll never see me coming.

CHAPTER 36

OCTAVIA

It's late afternoon, Red is still snoozing when Wendell arrives at my bedroom door holding an envelope.

"Your mother, ma'am. It was delivered by her personal messenger." He hands it to me, I open it and sigh.

"Can you ready the carriage?" I say.

"Certainly." He bows his head and leaves.

Three hours later, Red and I are exiting the underground tunnels and making our way up the mountain to Mother's castle. It's becoming déjà vu this process of carriage to castle.

Red has been quiet since she spoke with her sister. She left for Fenella's funeral and returned, but she moved back to my spare room rather than sleeping in mine. Still furious with me for having compelled her memories away.

Which is why I still haven't told her the rest of the truth. Fuck, I wanted to. But the fury that was laced into her features last night when we told her about the night Amelia turned. I've never seen her so angry.

If she knows what I did, why I did it, I don't know how

she'll react—especially if she's already distancing herself from me. I want to ask her, to pry her emotions from her so I can understand how she's feeling. But I don't know how. All I've ever done is push people away.

As we enter the ballroom, the atmosphere is thick, and we're hit by a wall of silence.

In the centre of the room there is a vampire noble. His hands are tied to a wooden pole. The type they used to use to burn witches millennia ago.

"Well, this doesn't look good," I mutter.

The ballroom has returned to the stage and tiered seating arrangement of the pairing ceremony. Though now, the segregation between vampire and hunter is even more stark than that first night. There's a physical gap between the two species. Shit.

My siblings are sat in the front row all together: Sadie, Dahlia, Gabriel and Xavier. On the other side of the gap in the front row are the hunters who paired with them. Keir, Lincoln, Talulla and two spaces left, one for Red and one that will remain empty where Fenella should have been.

"And I thought we were making progress with reintegrating our kinds," Red whispers.

"Clearly not."

I glance back at the pole. Around the base, blood pools, deepening to the colour of dried wine.

Cordelia and the Chief prowl around the vampire, circling like vipers ready to strike. The vampire whimpers.

"P-p-please," he says.

"Quiet," Cordelia shrieks. "Confess. Or forfeit your life."

"PLEASE," he whines.

"Mother?" I call just as she swings back her fist. She falters and turns to us. "Ahh, Octavia. I have unearthed the traitor in our midst."

"Traitor?" I ask.

Beside me, Red shifts on the spot, her body tenses like she's preparing for an assault and I'm not sure she's wrong. I scan the crowd of vampires and hunters in the stands. There are as many hunter guards as there are vampires. Security though, doesn't seem to be easing the unrest. There are people physically growling at each other.

"What's going on?" I say.

She swings around and grabs the vampire by the throat. "This vampire is responsible for the attack on the carriages as you were making your way to the amulet."

"He's responsible for the death of Fenella," the Chief says.

And here we have the real reason everyone is tense. He broke the accords.

"It... it wasn't me, I didn't lay my hand on them."

"But you did pay someone to do it," the Chief snaps.

The vampire nods.

"Confess to the first attack. On the night of the partnering."

The vampire's eyes go wide, "I—I swear it wasn't me. I'll admit to paying vampires for the attack during the trial. But that first night wasn't me."

"CONFESS!" Cordelia shrieks and smashes her fist into his face.

The vampire's nose shatters, blood pisses down his chin but it dries just as quickly as his body repairs itself.

"I said, confess." The way Cordelia's voice snarls out the words it makes a shiver slide down my back. The malice, the level of malevolent control in her tone sounds like death himself.

Mother paces in front of him. "I'm tired of this. Given your hunter died, you have my support to end him."

Support? What the hell is this? Why isn't she persisting?

Why is she giving up torturing him so quickly? That is not the Mother I know.

Unless... the first attack really wasn't him and she knows that...

"What's wrong?" Red whispers, grabbing my hand.

But I can't breathe a word of my theory with everyone around us. "Not in here, too many ears. I'll tell you later."

The Chief doesn't hesitate. There's no time for me to suggest we try alternative interrogation methods. I don't even see the stake she pulls from her trousers, it's whipped out and in his heart before I can blink. It was so fast it was practically vampire speed.

There's an explosion of cheering from the hunters and muffled jeers from the vampires. Cordelia faces her crowd and says, "Who dares question me?"

The vampires fall silent. This is dangerous territory we're treading on. We're going to end up with a mutiny. I see now why ruling with fear is not necessarily the best way to lead. The harder Cordelia squeezes, the more dissent she sows.

The vampire's skin turns a sickly shade of grey, veins track purple across his skin and he hangs limp. Parts of his head flake away. In a few hours there will be nothing left but the clothes he wore.

"And now that nasty business has been dealt with, it's time for the second trial," Cordelia says, gesturing for the Chief to follow her back to the stage. They climb up and she hands the mic to the Chief.

Something shifts uneasy in my gut, the way the two of them are tolerating each other. I've never seen anything like it in all the years they've known each other. Something else is going on and I need to uncover what it is.

The Chief steps up to the lectern "This is the trial of beauty. While Sadie St Clair is now on her own, the rest of the teams will remain paired. You will only have forty-eight hours for this trial. If you do not make a decision or bring an artefact to us, you will forfeit your place in the competition. The risk of death in this challenge is low, but you only have one opportunity to compete."

One? I glance at Xavier, whose eyes have narrowed at the stage, his lips curled into a smile.

The Chief passes the mic back to Cordelia. "Your task is to find the most beautiful item in the city and bring it back to us. Each team will get exactly one chance to present their item. And you will attempt to store this item inside the amulet. If the amulet accepts your offering, you'll be declared the winner."

"What about the size of it?" Dahlia says. "The amulet is tiny."

Cordelia nods. "This is true, but the amulet still holds magic from the witch-gods. So do not misinterpret the size of the object for an indicator of beauty. If the amulet decrees it to be the most beautiful, it will accept the object regardless of the size."

"How are we supposed to figure it out? At least with the maps we had books and the library to research in," Gabriel whines.

"That, boy, is your problem," the Chief says.

Gabriel huffs, but it makes me smile. The spoilt brat won't be able to win this one so easily. Though I suspect Xavier will. He is the most beautiful man in the city, he fills his mansions with every ounce of beauty possible from antiques to jewellery to women, men and everything in between. There's no doubt in my mind, he'll be the first to work this out.

"Fuck," I hiss.

"What's wrong?" Red says.

"These trials are rigged, I swear. They're playing to everyone else's strengths. I have no idea where to start."

"We'll work it out." Red steps closer. I glance down at where our hands are laced together and suppress a smile. If she can forgive me for turning her sister, maybe she'll forgive me for stealing her memories too.

Cordelia opens her arms and a mirage of an hourglass appears above the stage. The purple sand inside it glistens.

"You have forty-eight hours to find and test your object. And you only get one chance, choose wrong and you lose the round. Only the team whose offer is accepted will earn points this round," she says.

The Chief pulls the amulet out of her pocket. It shivers and then rises up to dangle from the hourglass.

"Your trial begins..." the Chief spins her hand around and the hourglass tips. "Now."

CHAPTER 37

CORDELIA

One Thousand Years Ago

I should have known not to come here. Known, that after what the Randalls did to me, they wouldn't stop. Known that our love was cursed.

But love is a magnet, and I was doomed the moment I met her.

I snuck out of the manor long after the butlers had retired from their duties and gone to bed. It's close to midnight by the time I arrive at Eleanor's cottage.

She opens the wooden door and falls to her knees, her hand clasped to her mouth.

"Who did this to you?" she breathes through her hand. "I was so worried. A week, Cordelia. An entire week and I don't hear from you. I'd no idea what had happened."

I try to smile, but the movement cracks my healing wounds open and a bead of blood billows up onto my lip. My face is a mosaic of purples and greens.

She reaches up, clasps my hands to hers and kisses my knuckles. "Who?" she demands. "I'll brew a curse."

But I shake my head. "It doesn't matter. I'm alive and I'm here. May I come in?"

She hurries me into her cottage, warmth envelopes me like a healing hug. She flutters around me, putting me in an armchair by the fire, the kiss of heat from the open flames a comfort.

"I don't have all my supplies, but I have enough," she says from the kitchen. There's a clattering of jars and glass. Her footsteps clacking against her cobbled stone floor. I close my eyes, relief that I'm finally here washing over me. I listen to the rhythm of her body sweeping around the cottage.

I must fall asleep because I wake to her placing an array of items at my feet. She kneels next to the armchair and begins applying the most potent-smelling herb mix I've ever smelt.

"What in the name of the gods is that?" I whine.

"Hush, it's powerful and it will remove most of the bruising by tomorrow. Now. Tell me who did this to you?"

"Why?" I say, leaning my head back against the chair.

"Cordelia," she snaps. "What the hell do you mean why? I should think that patently obvious."

"Is it?"

"I swear on the witch-gods, I will slaughter them all. Was it at the behest of your mother? Did your father beat you? I will kill them. I'll spell them or torture them, but they won't get away with this."

I turn away from her, watch the flames dance, remembering the summer nights we lit fires by the river and danced till the embers flitted into the sky and turned into the dawn sun.

"You're a healer, you'll do no such thing. I came here

because... because..." But I can't get the words out. They're clogged in my throat refusing to be spoken, because in my heart, I know I don't want to say them. I don't want to have to do this.

I turn to face her, tears streak her cheeks. I reach up, wipe the tears away with my thumb.

"I'll do it," she says.

But I shake my head. "You have to leave it... we... we need to end things. It's too dangerous. Our families won't allow this to continue, and I think that deep down, you know that too."

She chokes out a sob. Her whole body trembles now. She wipes her arm over her eyes and attends my face again.

"Is this because I'm a woman?" she asks.

That, at least, makes me smile. "If only it were so simple. Mother is livid about that too. But no. It's because you're a Randall. Because our families know only hate for each other. We were never going to be able to live this life."

She drops the parcel of herbs she was holding, her eyes going wide.

"Oh my gods, it was my family, wasn't it? My family did this to you?" she barks and stands, pacing the living room.

"I'm sorry," I whisper, tears welling in my eyes.

She kneels beside me again, clasping my hands. "I don't want you to leave. I can't bear the thought of not being with you," she says and clutches her chest like her heart may give out. She takes a shuddered breath and then she looks me in the eye.

"Stay with me tonight, Cordelia. One more night together and then run with me."

"Run?" I say, frowning.

She nods, already packing up her herbs. "We can take what we need, I'll give you some of my clothes and we can leave this city. Find a new one that will accept us. One that knows nothing of our familial history."

I grab her hand, stop her from flustering.

There's a thick pause.

We stare at each other, unspoken words flitting between us. The air potent with emotion.

And then I pull my eyes away, staring at the fire.

"No," she shrieks at me suddenly, wrenching her hand out of mine. "Don't you dare give up. We. Are. Not. Giving up. What do I need to do to convince you to stay with me? To run at dawn?"

She shuffles around to sit beneath me on floor. Her fingers find the hem of my skirts and the skin of my ankles.

I close my eyes as her palms brush against my calves, the sensation sending a shiver of tingles up my legs and straight to my core. She wraps her hands around my legs and tugs gently until I plop onto the floor. She reaches up and gathers the pillow and slides it under my head.

"Eleanor," I plead, knowing what she's going to do, knowing how she's about to make me feel. Knowing that none of that will change the fact we have to end this before it takes one of our lives. I'd rather she live without me, than die because she loves me.

Her hands brush my ankles again, sliding the skirts higher, higher until they rest on my tummy. Her fingers skim my belly, my hips, everywhere she touches an explosion of delight as if she's pouring waves of pleasure through her hands.

She's careful to avoid the bruises on my legs, the boot prints, the fist marks. "Look at what they did to you."

"They tried to break me, to make me stop loving you."

"Hush now, let me make you feel better," she says and places a tender kiss on my knee. She scatters them down my legs, her lips soft and warm against the bruised flesh of my thighs.

Eleanor's lips find my core, kissing my apex until I breathe a deep moan of pleasure. Her mouth parts, her tongue tenderly gliding down my core. Long, slow swipes drawing out waves of bliss and soft whimpers from me. One of her hands finds mine, her fingers lacing through, knotting us together.

The way we were always meant to be.

She draws her tongue between my folds and lavishes me with the sweetest pleasure. I moan and arch my back off the floor. She moans into me, praising me, worshipping me like I'm her witch-god and not the very real being she loves.

"Eleanor," I pant as she swipes her tongue down my core, sucking and licking every inch of my skin. She releases my hand and instead pushes her way into me, one thick finger. She slides in and out and in and out until I'm panting and crying out her name and any thought of my aching face and bruised body vanishes in the swelling tide of orgasm.

She slips another finger inside me; I gasp at the pressure. The way her strong fingers fill me fuller than I've ever experienced.

"Eleanor," I gasp.

"Tell me, Cordelia," she says. "Tell me everything. I will give you the world."

"Harder, I need you harder. I need more of you."

She switches into a different position leaning on her knees and I cry out as it shifts her fingers inside me. Making them curl into the most exquisite position. I moan and my nipples harden. Her mouth worships my apex, sending rivers of tingles and electric bolts from my core around my body until my eyes are squeezed shut so tightly that I swear I'll never see again.

"More," I pant. "More."

I want to cuss, to swear and cry and tear us from this world so that we're never parted. But I can't. And as she focuses her tongue on my swollen nub, I tip over into the explosive bliss that only she can deliver.

When the pulses spread through my entire body, I find myself weeping.

Tears pour down my cheeks and then I'm in her arms and Eleanor is cradling me, kissing my bruised cheeks and promising me things she has no right to.

"I swear we'll be together, I swear it, Cordelia. Nothing can come between us."

"You d—don't kn—know that," I sob into her shoulder. "You can't make that promise."

"I can and I will. Nothing will tear us apart, let me spell it so."

I lean back. "You can do that?"

She nods. "There are darker magics, blood magic used differently not just for healing. There are many things we can do, many that we shouldn't. But our love is fated, I feel it in my bones."

"What would we need to do?"

"I can consult my grimoires. I suspect share blood, swear oaths and a small spell. But I'll need to read up to be certain. It's not something I can do hurriedly. A mistake when working with that magic would cost us dearly."

I nod, the sobs dissipating.

"In that case," I say, grinning and nudging her down toward the ground, "I owe you something rather delicious."

"But your face..." she says, touching my lips.

"My face will feel considerably better between your legs. Besides, your rotten herbs have all but fallen off my cheeks now and I am feeling decidedly better. Now, quit protesting."

I push her the rest of the way to the carpet and tug at her trousers until she's bared before me.

I smile, looking at her thighs and belly and all the inches of skin I want to lick and kiss. "You are my favourite thing, Eleanor Randall."

"And you are mine, Cordelia St Clair."

And so I spent the night between her legs making her moan my name just as loud as I moaned hers, and when the fire had burnt itself to embers and ash, she took me by the hand and led me to bed where she slept the rest of the night away.

I, though, couldn't rest.

Something in the air made sleep fitful, and eventually, I gave up, choosing instead to nestle against her hair and drift to the rhythmic lull of her heavy breathing. Knowing that everything would be fine as long as we stayed together.

CHAPTER 38

RED

It's been twelve hours, and we still have absolutely no idea what the most beautiful object in the city could be.

"This is a waste of fucking time, we're never going to win this damn trial," Octavia says and slams her fist into the side of the carriage.

"Do you feel better now?" I say, folding my arms and raising an eyebrow at her.

"What? I can pay to fix it." She pouts at me.

"Don't behave like a child."

She sticks her middle finger up at me, which is bleeding, cut on a splinter from the wall.

My nose flares, her eyes widen. "Sorry," she says, all the tension dissipating.

We've agreed that we should try and ween me off her blood as soon as possible. While the trials aren't the best time, we can at least lower the amount I take when I take it.

It's not working exactly, but I am happy about it. I'm feeling clearer too and more like my old self even if I spend half the day wracked with shivers and sweats while my body is trying to get used to the smaller doses. This is the right thing. For both of us.

She wipes her finger on her leg and sucks the wound into her mouth until it clots enough the smell isn't so strong.

The carriage pulls to a stop in the heart of the Midnight Market. We step out by the library and Gabriel and Keir walk out.

"Too bad for you, we've already found the most beautiful item," Gabriel says.

"Oh, really?" Octavia sneers.

The pair of them hold four ancient books, one in each of their hands.

"Looks like you've really decided what that object is," Octavia says, glancing between their hands. "Of course, you think it's a book."

"Not a book, the knowledge within it. There's no greater power than knowledge. Nothing more beautiful than the preservation of history, what else could it be?"

Keir nods as if that's the most obvious thing in the world. But I remain unconvinced. The pair of them step into a carriage and we stand side by side, staring after them long after the carriage disappears out of sight.

"He's wrong, isn't he?" I say.

"So completely wrong he'll probably pitch a fit and burn the book when the amulet rejects it."

I laugh.

Octavia slips her hand in mine, "I can just imagine the tantrum he will throw when he realises the trials aren't going to be as easy as the first. He's running on the arrogance of a win. Taking things for granted. That's his loss. I made the same mistake underestimating him in the first trial."

"Is this okay?" she asks, tugging my hand.

I hesitate, we're in public, but it really does feel okay. It feels like I don't want to hide anymore.

We stroll through the market area, circling stalls, the Church of Blood, the square, the Whisper Club. We walk miles. We pass the Church of Blood for a second time, its ancient spires towering into the sky like spears.

Sadie appears in the entrance. She's holding a small red vial. She secretes it in her pocket and then speeds away before Octavia can question her.

"Interesting," Octavia says.

"What?"

"Sadie thinks the most beautiful thing is something religious."

"It looked like blood. It was definitely red."

"There's no way she'd have stolen a drop of the Mother of Blood's actual blood. We have vials of it that the monks use to go through their Trial of Spirit to become ordained. But there's no way. She respects the church too much."

"I'm telling you it was blood," I say.

"Shit. She must really want to win." Octavia pauses, takes a band off her hand and ties her hair up into a messy bun. "It's not a bad line of thinking. But even if we could get a drop, she'll have already tested it and won by the time we get back to the castle."

"Do you want to go into the church anyway?" I ask.

"It can't hurt."

So we do, I follow her in. We end up staying in the church for a couple of hours. Walking the long aisles, staring at the incredible structure. The roof inside the church is covered in ancient art. The sweeping paint strokes older than many of the vampires in the city. The seat cushions are all red, the tall pillars and wooden beams stained a reddish mahogany. We pass the pulpit and the basin filled with blessed blood where the monks pray for residents and bless them. The stench of iron-rich blood is overwhelming. I haven't dosed yet today, and it almost makes my legs buckle.

Octavia grabs me under the arm to support me and we veer to the other side of the church, examining the stained-glass windows instead. All of the scenes in them are depicted in varying shades of red glass. The images are savage, depicting the death of the witch-gods, the birth of Octavia, the turning of Cordelia, the curse, the death of the dhampirs a thousand years ago, the loss of almost all of our magic.

The blood monks walk around the church lighting candles and taking donations of blood to the pulpit.

"I'm not coming up with any ideas in here," I say.

"Neither am I, shall we try somewhere else?" Octavia asks.

We leave, both of us feeling sullen. We pass Dahlia and Lincoln in the market. Dahlia snips a lock of hair off the most attractive woman I've ever seen while Lincoln stands there keeping her distracted with his charm and, dare I say, muscles.

I glance at Octavia, she shakes her head. "They're wrong too. But there's something about Sadie's choice I can't let go of. I just wish I knew *what*."

"Just Xavier to go..." I say.

"I wonder where he even is. Let's head back to the club. I think better in my office."

"Fine by me, I'm starving, and it won't be long before the dawn rises and then we lose twelve hours anyway, or at least I'll lose eight to sleep and then what? Twelve hours to figure it out."

"It's going to be okay. Let's get a drink and try and think through the options we have."

It takes us half an hour, and the dawn is beginning to

kiss the horizon, making its long lips blur orange by the time we arrive.

"We're stuck here now till evening," I say.

"Then let's make the most of it." Octavia grins and I'm convinced she's thinking about the last time we were here.

The way she fucked me in front of every patron in the club. Made me bare my pussy to everyone as she claimed me, claimed my body, my pleasure.

"You okay?" she says, pushing a stray strand of hair behind my ear. "You're looking pale. Do you need a drink?"

"I definitely need a drink."

"No. I mean, do you need a drink?" she runs her hand over her neck, and I realise she means blood.

"No. At least, not yet, tonight I will. I can feel the tremors beginning and if we're not sleeping tonight, then I will need something to keep me going."

We head towards the heart of the club and as soon as we step out into the main club room, I'm relieved it's not as busy as I was expecting.

"It's late," she says. "The club closes shortly. Though I think there's a lock-in planned for today. Oh—" she says and stops dead.

I peer over the balcony to the dance floor below. Xavier is balls deep in Talulla's cunt. Three other vampires and a couple of hunters are also stark bollock naked with various appendages in various holes. Talulla is sucking another vampire's cock while Xavier fucks her, and his fingers are inside another vampire's pussy.

"Well. That's... Um..."

"Mother of Blood," Octavia says and kneads her temples.

"I'm not sure if this is awkward or arousing. Xavier is rather handsome. And gods, he's well endowed."

"Do you mind? He is my brother."

"Brother in vampire blood, not genetics."

"Still. Brother enough. Gods. I'd love to tell you that this is the first time I've seen him fucking an array of people, but truly, it's not even the hundredth time. It's a part of who he is, I'm just surprised he's sharing Talulla. He can be..."

"Possessive?" I ask.

"Yes, how did you—"

"Oh, I don't know, Octavia. Never met a possessive vampire before. Nooo. You're nothing like him."

Her eyes narrow. "How dare you."

But she's smirking. She steps up to me, making me step back until my back is against the wall. She places her forearm above my head, so she's leaning down over me. "I'm not possessive, I just refuse to let anyone else touch you, feed you or fuck you. I just make it clear that you're mine, you always have been, always will be and Mother of Blood save anyone that tries to behave otherwise. What's possessive about that?"

I laugh, "Ohh, nothing. Nothing at all."

We grin at each other. She shrugs and steps back. "Seriously though. If anyone touches you or tries to give you their blood. I will kill them."

"Octavia... Behave."

We make our way down to the main club floor where the... err... antics are happening, and Octavia goes to the bar and grabs both of us drinks. Thankfully an array of shots are poured too, I'm not sure who needs them more.

Xavier seems to be coming as he thrusts into Talulla once, twice more and then he groans, his whole body goes taut. His shoulders ripple, his muscles bulge, his ass squeezes tight as he drives into her, and she all but screeches his name.

"Damn, that must have been one helluva orgasm," I say, downing a shot.

As his group dresses, the club fills a little more.

Then Erin appears. "Club's locked for the day, this is it. No one in or out till sundown."

"Thanks, Erin," Octavia says, and Erin takes her leave.

Xavier finally notices us and draws his group to the bar, handing out the shots Octavia ordered.

"Favourite sibling," he says and bends to kiss Octavia's cheek. She moves back out of his way.

"While I'd love you to kiss me hello, I'm unclear where that mouth has just been. So, I'll take the words instead and we'll leave it there."

"At least three pussies, his arse hole and two cocks. But who's counting?" Xavier says.

I choke on the sip of wine I just gulped.

"So glad I deferred the kiss to later," Octavia says.

He laughs, and then grows serious as he tugs his shirt back on. "We need to talk."

"Sure," Octavia shrugs and waits for him to explain.

"No... I mean... can I have a word in private?"

I frown, but Octavia nods and they disappear up to her office. I stand and watch the crowd writhing and dancing and wishing I was high on blood but recognising that is probably the last thing I should do now. The alcohol is fending off the worst of the tremors for the moment, but it's going to be a long day and I should probably try and sleep some of it away before the tremors are so bad I can't.

I check my watch, twenty-four hours left and counting.

We have nothing.

And with less than a day to go before the end of the trial, the only thing I have on my mind is the fear that I'll never get the cure. I think back to the balcony and the conversation we had. The way Amelia glanced at Octavia.

A frown creeps across my forehead as I realise she never actually agreed to take it.

CHAPTER 39

OCTAVIA

"What's wrong?" I say as Xavier takes a seat in my office guest chair. He gestures at Frank.

"Frank, would you mind giving us a few minutes, please?"

Frank startles but then smiles at me. I think he's warming up to me. He bows and leaves us, closing the door behind him.

Xavier leans across my coffee table and grabs a whiskey bottle, pouring both of us half a glass into the discarded tumblers. I'm not even sure they were clean, but he doesn't seem to give any shits.

I notice then that there's a scar on his throat where Dahlia stabbed him. "She scarred you?"

"Yes, and I haven't forgiven her for that. You know how I feel about my appearance."

He would be pissed with her, beyond pissed. This is the kind of thing that could cause an outright sibling war.

"What the hell was the blade made of?"

"She claims she doesn't know, it was left for her. She found it and pocketed it."

"And you believe her?" I ask, picking up the tumbler and taking a sip. It burns as it slides down my throat. Good vintage.

"If I didn't, I'd have torn her throat out and placed the blade in *her* neck so she couldn't recover."

"Still pissed then."

"Deeply. Listen. Have you figured it out?" he says and takes another gulp of his whiskey.

"No. I've seen what the others are thinking."

"Tell me..."

"Gabriel had books from the library. Sadie took something from the church, possibly blood, and Dahlia snipped a lock of hair from the most beautiful women I'd seen in town."

Xavier shakes his head. "They're all wrong."

"I know. But I just can't work out what is right."

He presses his lips together, staring into his tumbler as he swills it.

"Fuck. You already know?"

He nods. "I do."

"But you're going to tell me?"

He glances up at me, holding my gaze.

"Tave..."

"Why are you telling me? You could take it and win the round."

He lowers his eyes. "First, I care more about Dahlia not winning, than I do about winning myself. What am I going to do with a whole city to look after? It sounds deeply tiresome. Therefore, I am willing to sacrifice this round in order to see her lose."

"You could still take the object and win this round, that

would still stop her winning. Why are you giving me the win?"

"Because I owe you a debt. You and Red saved me, it's the least I can do. And unfortunately, while I know what the most beautiful thing is, I can't get to it. I believe you're the only one that can do that."

My eyes narrow at him. He runs a hand through his long raven locks, the wave bouncing up and settling in exactly the same position and then he takes another gulp, finishing the whiskey.

"Just tell me already," I say and pick up an ashtray from my desk and lob it at his head. He smiles and catches it. He twirls the crystal around his hand, examining the way the stone is cut as if it's going to give him a different answer than the one he's holding.

"I'll tell you, but you can't blame me..."

"Xavier," I snap.

"Fine. But you're really not going to like it."

CHAPTER 40

RED

Octavia is livid.

She storms out of her office and grabs my hand, spilling my drink, and drags me from the club.

"What are you doing? It's fucking daylight," I say.

"We're going to the underground station. I need to get out of here. We'll get a carriage straight to Mother's castle. By the time we're there, we'll have a half a day or so before the end of the trial."

"What about the object. We can't leave without securing whatever we're going to give the amulet."

"We already have it," she says and tugs me down towards the Whisper Club station.

"What the hell do you mean we already have it? We have nothing! Octavia, for blood's sake?"

She pulls to a stop as she pulls open a carriage door and gestures for me to get in. "To Castle St Clair," she says and then hustles me inside.

The driver whips his reins and the carriage jerks forward. She pulls the window blinds down to make sure no sunlight filters through and then sits back. I've never seen her so cross. Her hair is a mess. Her cheeks are flushed.

"What the fuck did Xavier tell you?"

"Nothing I wanted to hear. He's bowing out of this round."

"What, why? Does he know what the right answer is?"

"Yes. But he's not willing to do what it takes to get it."

"And you are?"

"It's different."

"Octavia, for fuck's sake, I thought we were a team. What's with the smoke and mirrors? Do you not trust me?"

"I trust you. I just... can you give me a minute? I will tell you. And we can decide together whether we're willing to do what's needed. Okay?"

I nod. But I huff at the same time, fold my arms and sink back into the carriage seat. I must fall asleep because I'm shaken gently awake.

"We're at the castle. It's almost sunset," Octavia says.

"Shit, how long did I sleep?"

"A few hours. But it's dark enough I should be okay. I wanted to take you somewhere. If you're okay with that?"

"Is there time?"

She glances at her watch. "We still have about fourteen hours, so I'd say so."

"Okay."

She holds out her hand and I take it as we step out of the carriage and into the castle's carriage station.

It's still a bit of a walk up to the main building of Cordelia's castle through the underground tunnels, which include far too many steps. Especially given the tremors now wracking my body. But eventually we emerge into the main foyer.

"We're going up," she says, pointing to the castle roof.

"More stairs?"

"There's a lift this time."

"Thank fuck, because my stake was starting to look real appetising," I say.

She laughs, but everything about her tonight is tense, including the way she smiles. It reaches her eyes, but they don't close and crinkle the way they normally do when she laughs.

We get into the lift, and she presses the roof button.

"Is it dark enough for that? I swear I saw some tinges of orange still."

"I should be okay, the sun sets in about three minutes."

We step through the doors out onto the roof and I gasp. "Oh, wow. It's stunning."

"That's the other reason I should be okay."

She points at the woven greenery that has been shaped into an arched living tunnel we can walk through. The broad leaves and smooth vines are peppered with the sweetest smelling flowers. The archway bends and twists as we walk along the rooftop. Finally, it breaks out into a large open area, the vines combining with tall shrubs to form a roof overhead. The waning sunlight speckles the castle roof in freckled patches. But she's right. For a vampire of her age, there's little enough light to cause more than a bit of itching.

And by the time we walk to the jacuzzi on the other side of the space, the sun has fully set.

"Beautiful, isn't it?" I say, staring out at the horizon and the molten sky. It's like a thousand fires smoulder in the distance.

"It is, but don't you feel like sometimes the sunset is a goodbye?"

I stare at her, wondering where that came from but before I can question it, she rounds on me. "Strip."

"Pardon?"

"You heard me. I'll be right back." She speeds away and I huff as I was about to protest. But the jacuzzi does look absolutely divine and I'd rather like a dip. So I do strip. I drop my clothes on a seat behind me and dip my toe in the water. It's warm and very fucking appealing.

I glance at my watch before taking it off, acutely aware that this is probably a big waste of time. But Octavia seems convinced she knows the answer. I decide to trust her and slip into the water.

As I sink my shoulders under the glistening surface, she reappears, holding a strap-on. It's one of those double ended ones that will vibrate inside me and her at the same time. Like the one we used in her castle.

"Oh," I say.

"I want you to use it on me," she says.

"Ohhh," I say and immediately grin. "I mean, I'd love to, but like... don't we have a trial to finish?"

"Do you trust me?"

I nod.

"Give me this. One last bit of fun together and then we will discuss the trial."

"Okay," I say, and she flings the strap at me. I climb out of the water and slip one end inside my pussy. It's more difficult with my skin already wet, but she helps me in and then I'm peeling her clothes off and she's slipping into the water too.

"No," I say. "Not yet, you sit here." I pat the ledge of the jacuzzi.

She sits obediently, legs shut, dangling in the water. I grin at her, knowing exactly what I want. I push her knees apart and edge my way between her legs.

I kick up and use the ledge under the water to stand high enough to kiss her. I slide my hand around her neck and push my lips over hers. She meets my mouth and kisses me tenderly, her fingers tracing circles around my shoulders. She pulls me in and holds me so tight and so safe.

"I'm sorry for how I treated you. For assuming the worst about you and Amelia."

She shrugs. "In your defence, I did turn her. You just turned up to the mansion at the wrong time."

"I know that now. I needed someone to blame and that became you. I couldn't cope with the fact she was now the very thing I'd been trained to hate."

"That's understandable."

"I'm a hypocrite, standing here knowing I've spent a week fucking you, despite being pissed with her for making the choice she did."

"Being messy is part of being alive," Octavia says. "Would you have made a different choice?"

"That's the thing, the more I've thought about it, the more I realise I don't think I would have. I like living. I would have had Amelia at the front of my mind, worrying about who would look after her if I was gone."

Octavia brushes a wet strand of hair away from my cheek.

My stomach churns as I pluck up the courage to say what I need to say next. "And the thing is, how can I hate her when I've fallen in love?"

She tenses under my grasp. "In... In love?" she whispers.

I nod. "With you. That is. I have fallen for you. The very thing that I'm meant to hate."

"You've fallen for the villain in your story."

"That's the thing, Octavia. I don't think you were ever really my villain. I just couldn't see it."

She leans in and kisses me but her cheeks are wet. And I'm such an idiot for taking so long to realise. But I know exactly how I can make it up to her. I know what I can give her to make her see I mean it. That I don't hate her or her kind anymore...

I kiss her again and then I slide lower, cupping her breast and sucking her nipple into my mouth until it hardens, and I scrape my teeth against it. She flinches and then moans, pushing her torso into me harder.

I lick down her chest, kissing and biting bits of her skin. And then I slip between her thighs and find the thing I covet. I push her and she leans back on her hands making more space for me.

I draw my tongue down her pussy, slipping it between her folds. She moans, her hands slip further back and then she's lying down, giving me full access. I suck her clit into my mouth and lap at the hardening nub until she's bucking and rocking her hips into my face. I pull my tongue down to her entrance and slide it as far in as it can reach. She moans as I tease her.

"Fuck," she says.

And then I'm slipping that finger inside her and her swearing descends into moans and carnal noises.

I slide a second finger inside her and pump in and out until she's soaking. I lap at her clit, giving her long, luxurious swipes until her pussy clenches and twitches around my fingers.

Then I pull out and grab her hips. "In the water. Now."

She obliges, slipping in. I sit my ass on the ledge, my shoulders are out of the water, but it will give me a base to fuck her on.

"Sit on my lap," I say and then I pick up the remote she left on the side of the jacuzzi and hit the buttons for both ends of the strap-on. It flares to life inside me and it takes my breath away.

"Good, huh?" she says.

I nod. "I think it's my new fave. Now sit on my lap."

The grin that peels across her face is exquisite. I position the cock at her entrance. She leans down and kisses me as I pull her hips down onto my lap, sliding the shaft inside her.

"Fuck," she says.

"I need your blood," I say as I rock my hips slowly. She bounces up and down, her breasts moving with the motion of us and making me want to salivate.

"Take it," she says and flicks her hair to the side exposing her neck.

"Really?"

"Just bite," she orders and arches back, moans slipping out of her as I continue to bounce her up and down on my lap.

I lean in and the scents of oud and spice and fresh winter winds fill my nose. It's exquisite. I inhale her skin, kiss her neck, my tongue sliding up her throat, seeking a vein closest to the surface. I worry my teeth are too blunt for this, but even as I think it and they graze across her skin, they seem sharper. Almost as if... It has to be the withdrawal.

There.

I feel the vein beneath my tongue and I bite down. Sinking my teeth into her flesh. I am certain I won't be able to feed from her, but my teeth cut her flesh as if I were a vampire just like her.

My mouth fills with her blood, the sweet iron taste flooding my throat. With the vibrations inside my pussy, I can hardly contain myself. I moan against her neck swallowing mouthful after mouthful.

When I finally pull myself off her neck, I grab her chin and turn her to face me.

"Fuck, that is the most beautiful thing I've ever seen," she says.

"What do you mean?"

"You, covered in my blood. It's enough to steal my heart forever."

I glance down, it's spilled down my jaw, dripping between my breasts and over my nipples.

I meet her gaze, the crimson irises swollen with desire and so much more beneath. And that's when I'm sure I want to do this.

"Feed from me," I say.

"What?" she says, alarmed.

"Feed. From. Me. Bind us."

"But... what you're saying..."

I brush her long locks over her shoulder as she slows her rocking against me.

"There's no coming back from this. If I bite and feed, while you have my blood in your system..."

"I know. Do it," I say.

Despite her piercings, her nipples harden and just saying the words is worth it for the view.

"Are you sure?" she says, even though her fangs are already dropping.

"I've never been more sure of anything in my life. In a strange way, I feel like I've been here a thousand times before. I feel like I was always meant to love you. Like maybe I've loved you before."

Doubt seeps into her expression. She opens her mouth as if she's going to say something, but the blood lust is soaking into my system, and I need to make her come. I need to come. So I lean up and kiss her forehead.

"Feed from me. I want you to do it. Own me the way you really want to. Take me. Fuck me. Drink from me and make me yours. While my heart beats, it will only beat for you."

I hold my hands up, and she laces hers into mine, interlocking us the way I know our hearts have been for so, so long.

She opens her mouth, and I tilt my neck exposing the long carotid artery for her. She growls and then lowers her head to my neck.

"Last chance t—" she says.

But I lurch up and make her fangs sink into my neck.

There's a blazing white pain that flashes across my vision and then a pulse of the most intense electric pleasure I've ever experienced.

"Fuck," I cry out as my vision hazes, and I drive the cock up and into her. My own pussy tightens against the vibrations of my end and the intoxication of her venom flowing into my system.

Her fingers dig into my back where she pulls me to her, her tongue laps at my neck. My blood threads through my veins and out of my neck. It's hot and stings but underneath it is a pulse, like the rhythm of her heartbeat, and with every thud electricity spills into my body. I lean my head back, gasping as wave after wave of pleasure tears through my body. She pulls off me only to angle her neck.

"Feed from me," she says.

So I do. And as I sink my teeth into her neck again while she drinks from me, the entire world shifts. My vision becomes a blur of colours, my senses ignite, everything rushes to my core. My cunt tightens as she rides my lap, both of us feeding like the savages we've become. My cells swell, my soul shifts, fraying at the edges as it mats together with hers. My life drifts through my mind, memories, black spots, heartache, loss and her.

Always her.

My constant.

My villain.

My hero.

She rips her mouth off my neck and roars into the night as both of us tip over into the most intense orgasm I've ever had. My whole body shivers against hers.

We hold each other, the night wrapping it's dark cloak around us, knowing everything is different and it can never go back to the way it was.

CHAPTER 41

CORDELIA

One Thousand Years Ago

There are some loves that transcend time, space and law. Eleanor was that for me.

I'd spent a year hiding, making excuses, leaving the manor in the depths of midnight, finding ailments and issues that would mean I could justify a visit to the apothecary. Mother was strict you see, the longer I remained unmarried, the more she would fluster and book events and balls. It became tiring rather quick and unfortunately, harder to see Eleanor. But I stole what moments I could.

I should have realised Mother would figure out something was up. But Eleanor swept me away, made me forget reality. She captured me in her arms and filled me with love and joy that bent the shape of my world and convinced me that fate would help us last. That we could have this love that our families thought shouldn't be.

But dreams like that never last. Love like that isn't meant to be. And I should have known better.

We're curled in her bed above the apothecary, my arms wrapped tight around her round belly, the softness of her skin keeping me dozing.

We forgot to draw the curtains last night, so I stare out of the window, as Eleanor sleeps in my arms. Morning hasn't broken, but soft violets and sparks of orange streak the sky. I'm not sure why I'm awake, perhaps the aching that still plagues my jaw and my eye socket. But I'm comforted by having her with me.

I sigh as I lean into the tendrils of her waves draped across the pillow and inhale the scent of her hair. Vanilla and lavender and hints of woody forest.

She smells like home.

As the sun's orb rises, cresting the horizon, something shifts in the air. An energy. It's wrong. All sharp around the edges like broken turrets and carriage spokes.

That's the last thought I have before an explosion rips through the cottage. The screams of men shred the air and heavy footfall echoes around us.

More screams.

Then an unnatural heat.

Four men burst through the door. I shriek. Eleanor wakes, her eyes meet mine and then she's dragged from my arms.

The men I barely recognise, but the emblems on their shirt breasts tell me they're St Clair men.

Mother.

Oh no, no, no.

I've been so careful. I ensured I had reasons to be out of

the house. I know I wasn't followed last night. I knew if she discovered I'd escaped, if she found out who hurt me, she would seek revenge. Someone must have ratted me out. But it doesn't matter, I need to protect Eleanor.

"You filthy, disgusting whore," the first man says. His nasty sneered features harsh against the smoothness of his bald head. He raises his fist and slams it into Eleanor's jaw.

I scream. Blood splatters against the wooden floor. He raises his fist again and I am leaping out of bed, but someone wraps thick arms around my middle and yanks me back. I kick and scream and wriggle, but it's useless.

The bald man's fist comes down.

Again.

Again.

Again.

Blood sprays everywhere. Bones crack and snap. Eleanor's beautiful face melts into a puddle of macerated flesh. Her eyes disappearing beneath swollen purple lids.

I wrench myself around and sink my teeth into the man holding me. Biting so hard blood wells in my mouth. I spit it out and throw my head back connecting with his face.

He roars as the almighty crack of his nose shatters against the force of my skull. The hit reverberates through me. But still, he holds tighter. What the fuck is this man made of?

Eleanor's body hangs limp in the bald man's hands. He drops her to the wooden floor and kicks her in the gut once. Twice. Three times.

It hurts, I cry out with each savage boot he drives into her. I'm sobbing now, fat tears rolling down my cheeks.

It's now that I notice what the other men were doing. They stand holding empty buckets.

A strange bitter stench like alcohol but purer, more vicious, more deadly fills the room. My eyes widen. "What are you doing?" My voice is high and screechy. "What the fuck are you doing?"

"Get her the fuck out of here," the man holding the bucket says as he strikes a match. A surge of energy rips through my body. I flail and kick out, lurching forward and swinging my arms. Driving my elbow back into the man's gut and slamming my foot down onto his boot. Then I drive my heel back and up into his balls. That, finally, makes him release me.

I leap out of his grasp and run straight to Eleanor, picking her up as tenderly as I can. "Eleanor?" I shriek, I hold my fingers to her neck, searching for the pulse like she taught me.

"For fuck's sake, get her out of here," the man holding the match barks again, then he turns to Eleanor's bookshelf filled with grimoires and journals and he drops the match. The wooden case explodes in a flurry of flames that crawl up the case, engulfing the grimoires and licking at the ceiling.

The man who lit the case staggers back. "Fuck, yeah!" he bellows.

I lean down to Eleanor and press my fingers harder against her neck, desperately searching for a sign of life. But before I can establish whether her heart beats, I'm being picked up and carried from the room.

How I fight. Spitting and scratching and biting any flesh I can reach. But it's futile.

It doesn't matter how I scream or protest, I'm carried further and further from my love. And with every step we take, the house swarms higher with flames.

The heat, a furnace of roaring power, consumes the cottage, the straw roof catching faster than I can cough and splutter the smoke away.

The men have to carry me several yards from the

cottage because the heat from the flames is singeing our skin, filling the atmosphere with the stench of burnt hair, smoke and rotten hate.

They stand watching until the house is consumed and when they're satisfied, they carry me off and bundle me into Mother's carriage.

I beat my fists against the walls until my knuckles crack and blood smears over the walls. I scream until my throat is dry. I cry until my body is parched of liquid. But still I'm taken further and further from Eleanor.

And when, at last, the carriage draws into the manor, and Mother is stood on the porch of the house, I'm dropped at her feet and the men vanish.

She picks me up by the collar of my nightdress.

"Disgusting," she snarls. "I hope you realise the gravity of what you've done?"

I wrench myself free from her grip, pull my arm back, and I slap her so hard she stumbles and falls onto her bottom.

"Do. Not. Speak. To. Me," I snarl the words and march into the manor.

All the while, Mother is hollering behind me about the damage I've caused and the problems I've created in trying to secure a suitor.

But I stop listening and instead, I plot my escape. I will find my way back to the cottage and I will take my love's body and give her the burial she deserves.

I curl myself into the corner of my room, barricading the door so Mother can't enter, and I plead with the witch-gods. Beg them to listen to me, even though they're not my gods, and plead with them to save her.

I trace my fingers over my palm, trying desperately to remember whether there was a heartbeat. Trying to call back the imprint of her neck, the shadows of my memories already fading.

But there's nothing.

Nothing other than the violent rage spilling out of my heart and the need to run. I turn to my window and glance down at the cobbled-roof porch at the back of the manor. There's no one outside. But there is a horse already saddled in the corner of the paddock. Someone must be about to leave. I don't think. I don't question it. I move.

I pull a small bag together. Clothes, the mini grimoire I was reading of Eleanor's, the bag of silver I've been saving. Then I wrench open the window, dropping the bag onto the roof. I leverage myself out and hang on the windowsill by my fingers.

I take a deep breath and let go. I bite down on my tongue, suppressing the urge to scream as I fall several feet to the porch roof.

My body rolls right off the porch roof, and I drop to the ground. I pick up the bag and run as fast as I can to the paddock. The horse shies from the unexpected motion, but I untether him, climb on and dig my heels into his sides. He rears up, and then we're galloping through the morning, following the trail of smoke rising into the sky like a beacon.

"I'm coming, Eleanor."

CHAPTER 42

OCTAVIA

I leave Red sleeping under the stars on the roof of the castle. She was so high from my blood and me taking hers that after we came, she fell into the deepest sleep I've ever known. Her breathing was heavy and slow, and she looked so peaceful that what I had to do next broke me.

After I tasted her, I knew that Xavier was right. I knew that if I wanted to protect her, protect her the way I've done for the last three years, then I had no choice.

I wanted to tell her. Fuck, I've been desperate to remove the compulsion and explain the mistakes I made. Explain that I really fucked up. I was selfish wanting her to choose me over everyone else.

Twice she has loved me.

Twice I have taken her memories.

Twice I have lost.

But now she has chosen me, it makes what I must do hurt even more. What a joke. The gods finally gave her to me, and I have to let her go.

I have what I need, I stole it the same way I stole her memories, and then I left her sleeping with the moon.

I slip away down the castle stairs, my heart thudding against my ribs in a way that vampire hearts never do.

But I've tasted her now.

I know what she is.

I know who she is.

What I do now will confirm it.

When I find my way to the ballroom, Xavier is already there, leaning against the door cloaked in shadows waiting for me. He tucks his hair behind his ear.

"Did you feed from her?" he says, his voice deep and husky.

I can barely bring my eyes to meet his.

He sighs, deep and breathy. "And?" he says.

"And I fear you're right."

His lips press together in a thin white line. "I hoped I was mistaken. I could see you falling and I prayed to the witch-gods that I was wrong."

"Falling? Xave, I have loved her for three years."

His brows knit. "Oh gods, what did you do?"

"It was the only way..."

"You bonded with her?" he says, his eyes suddenly wide.

"What choice did I have? You realise that who she is... what she is, that's why she's been addicted to blood. I'm the fucking reason she's activated. I won't allow her to take from another vampire. Not while her heart belongs to me."

"How the hell are you going to manage this," he says, but it's not a question, it's a statement. He understands the choice I made, though neither of us know how I'm going to handle the consequences.

I grasp Xavier by the neck and pull his forehead down to kiss.

"I'm sorry, this is the only way I can protect her."

"What are you—"

"I don't think I've said this before, but... I love you, brother..."

"Tave," he says and his voice breaks. "You don't need to do this. I will protect her with my life. I can help you protect her, you'll need a friend."

"It's your memories or your life, Xavier. And I am too fond of you to take that. Will you submit?"

"After all these years you still don't trust me?"

"I do. Of course, I do. It's the rest of the world I don't. If anyone were to find out, they could take you from me. Use you to get to her. I promise I'll give them back when I can."

His refined features harden, and then his expression softens. "Only because it's you. And you absolutely owe me a favour of the highest order."

"Consider it banked."

He nods. "I'm ready."

I rise onto tiptoes and kiss his cheek and then I pull his head to face mine and I stare into his eyes.

"Forget what you know about Red. Forget who she is. Forget how you found out. Forget what she did for you. You never drank her blood. You only know that I am in love with her and will do anything to protect her."

I kiss his forehead again and then I leave him there in his daze and step into the ballroom.

The amulet hangs beneath the timepiece, floating in mid-air; it sways in a moonbeam, dust motes drifting past it. There aren't many grains left in the hourglass. I need to hurry.

I pad across the floor. The room seems so empty and so full all at the same time. Like ghosts and secrets fill the seats instead of air and shadows. I scan the room, my back crawling like there are eyes on me. But there's no one here. I shut my eyes and listen, pushing my hearing to its limits, but it's silent.

I'm just paranoid.

I pull the vial of Verity's blood out of my pocket and tug the amulet down so I can reach it better.

The glass stone in the centre opens, it knows what I have. My hands tremble where I hold the vial.

This is it.

If I pour it in and it reacts the way I think it will, then it seals both our fates.

"Please be wrong. Please?"

I tip the vial and her blood runs into the crystal. It flares bright as it swallows her blood, the whole amulet trembles and vibrates in my hand. It shoots up, expanding and glowing and when it falls back to my hand, the crystal has resealed itself. Inside floats a single drop of the most beautiful blood in the city.

The blood of the first dhampir in a thousand years.

"No," I breathe.

My hands ball, a single tear falls to the plinth as I realise what I have to do. I must protect her no matter what. I'd die for her, and if it means I have to give her up in order to save her, then I choose her life over my happiness.

It's too dangerous for her to know who she is.

My back crawls. I glance around the room again, but I'm definitely on my own. I can't wait any longer.

I race out of the ballroom, using vampire speed to power up the castle stairs and all the way to the roof. My heart thuds so fast I swear it's in my throat. I have to get to her before anyone else does.

I pause before I enter the rooftop, knowing that I need to calm down.

She's safe.

I'm safe.

Xavier doesn't remember and that means I'm the only one who knows.

Everything is fine.

Except when I step onto the rooftop, she's awake. Her eyes are vivid green, they burn like fires are buried beneath them.

She holds out her hands, turning them this way and that. Dark veins track across her skin.

"It's me, isn't it?" she says.

I don't want to answer. But we both know it's true. This is where I tell her. This is my déjà vu, my curse I carry.

"Verity, listen to me. I need tell you something. You said earlier you felt like you'd loved me before..."

"I have, haven't I?" she says, her voice soft in the night air.

I nod. "Yes..." I stop, my heart breaking.

I take a shuddering breath. "I took your memories, compelled you to forget me."

"Why would you do that?" she steps forward, holds her hand to my cheek.

"So many reasons. You chose work, Amelia. You hated yourself for loving me because of who I was. What I was."

"My addiction?" she whispers.

"It was always me. Everything is my fault. I was attacked, a mob of villagers. You jumped in to protect me and they stabbed you in the gut. I gave you my blood to heal you. But you ended up addicted. It was my blood. The first time. Every time. Gods. I compelled all the dealers in the city. It was always me. And you couldn't stand it. You had to choose between being the head of security or me, and it was all too much..."

She pulls her hand away and that cold impression hurts more than watching the tears fall down her face.

"So I played your villain, I let you hate me rather than

hate yourself."

She's shaking. I reach out to pull her into my arms when she slaps my hand away and I realise the mistake.

"Fuck you, Octavia. Fuck you for taking my memories. For fucking compelling me. How dare you."

"Don't you get it? I did it to save you. To protect you and let you live happy."

"And what? Now we're bonded and you've activated my dhampir genes? Was that your plan all along? You used me so you could win this fucking game. Find the dhampir, take the city? Did I mean nothing to you?"

"You think I'm happy it's you? The whole fucking city is going to hunt you down, Red. Everyone is going to want a piece of you... I can't let the city tear you apart like it's torn me apart."

"There's nothing you can do to stop them."

"There is..."

Her eyes widen. "No." She steps back, one pace, two.

But it's too late, there is no other option.

I rush forward, grab her by the shoulders before she falls into the water, "I hoped and prayed this evening wasn't goodbye. Tell me you didn't feel it?"

Her eyes well.

"I'm sorry, Red. But you are mine. And I can't put you in harm's way. I would give you up a thousand times before I let anyone hurt you."

"You don't have to do this... We're bonded now..."

"It's because we're bonded that your genes activated. I understand the prophecy on the door now: '*A dhampir born, a dhampir turned. In shadows they walk, with pulse of sun and moon. The first of their kind, with fangs that hunger and a heart that beats.*' It's you, it was always you."

She lowers her eyes because she knows it's true.

"If I erase me, the bond, who you really are from your

memories, then you're safe. No one can use you. That way, I'm the only one who knows anything. And I would slaughter every vampire and burn the city to the ground before I let anything happen to you." I kiss her forehead.

"Octavia. Please. Don't do this."

Red's face is streaked with tears. I wipe a thumb over her cheek, smearing them away and then I kiss her one last time.

I kiss her like it's forever.

Like I'll never stop.

Like she'll never forget me.

I kiss her with my whole heart, with every cell in my body. Our tongues move against each other, our hands gripping and clawing at each other's clothes, but I know this has to end. This has to stop, and I have to lose her all over again.

I pull back, lean my forehead against hers.

"One day, our souls will meet, and we will get to keep each other."

"Octavia—" she pleads. Her words come out as choked sobs. My heart shatters into a thousand pieces because this time, she loved me back with all her heart. She loved me for who I am. She loved me despite the fact I'm a vampire.

As I find her gaze, tears falling, my heart shredding, I whisper tales of compulsion.

"Forget me, Verity Fairbanks. Forget me in your heart and mind. Forget that you ever loved me. Forget that we're bonded. Forget that you're the chosen dhampir..."

She goes slack in my arms, her gaze is distant, vacant, and I know the compulsion has taken hold.

"Goodbye," I breathe.

I know that when she next speaks, she won't remember that she loves me, and I'll become her villain all over again.

Red shakes her head, her vision clearing. "Hello?"

CHAPTER 43

*I*f *Cordelia thinks she can use these trials to get to the dhampir before me, she's wrong.*

Because the dhampir has awakened.

I know who it is...

And now, I'm coming for you both.

W ant to find out what happens next? Preorder book 2, *House of Crimson Kisses* today: **books2read.com/crimsonkiss**

If you'd like to read a free prequel to my *Girl Games* series, full of just as many lesbians and just as much spice, you can do that by signing up here: <u>rubyroe.co.uk/signup</u>.

Last, reviews are super important for authors, they help provide needed social proof that helps to sell more books. If you have a moment and you're able to leave a review on the store you bought the book from, I'd be really grateful.

About the Author

Ruby Roe is the pen name of Sacha Black. Ruby is the author of lesbian fantasy romance. She loves a bit of magic with her smut, but she'll read anything as long as the characters get down and dirty. When Ruby isn't writing romance, she can usually be found beasting herself in the gym, snuggling with her two pussy... cats, or spanking all her money on her next travel adventure. She lives in England with her wife, son and two devious rag doll cats.

The Girl Games Series

A Game of Hearts and Heists
A Game of Romance and Ruin
A Game of Deceit and Desire

instagram.com/sachablackauthor

tiktok.com/@rubyroeauthor

Printed in the USA
CPSIA information can be obtained
at www.ICGtesting.com
CBHW031842010324
4847CB00012B/449